IN THE NAME OF THE FATHER

In the Vatican three senior clerics meet in the highest secrecy to discuss a new formidable threat to the Pope's life. They know that a plot has been organised by the KGB on the direct orders of Yuri Andropov, who has sworn not to rest until the Polish Primate is destroyed.

These men decide that the only option they have is to eliminate the Soviet leader. The agent they select for the apparently impossible task of travelling through central Europe to penetrate the very heart of the Soviet empire is a renegade member of the Polish secret police, Mirek Scibor, a man driven by a dark and violent hatred. He is horrified to discover his companion is the beautiful, reserved Ania, who is deeply religious. As well she might be, since she is a nun!

The suspense of their mission is matched only by the tension that develops between them. From terrorist training camp to high-tech hospital, Vatican intrigue to Kremlin powerplays, IN THE NAME OF THE FATHER is a novel of relentless drama and excitement.

Praise for A. J. Quinnell

SIEGE OF SILENCE

'Technically and psychologically A. J. Quinnell climbs a few more rungs with this breathless thriller'

Observer

'As spare, tense and dovetailed, if hawk-winged, a thriller as crafty Mr Quinnell has yet concocted'
Sunday Times

'An exceptional thriller . . . Here is a writer who can make characters come alive and build tension so you cannot wait to turn the page . . . He uses a triple first-person technique which works brilliantly . . . a memorable novel'

Daily Telegraph

'Every once in a rare while, an unheralded book comes along that is so well written, so intelligent in its characterisation, that it demands immediate attention, SIEGE OF SILENCE is such a book . . . Every sentence in SIEGE OF SILENCE is believable. Quinnell has written a book you can't put down until its very satisfying conclusion'
Los Angeles Herald Examiner

BLOOD TIES

'Romantic, exotic, endearing – try it'
Sunday Telegraph

'A splendidly woven tale'
Yorkshire Evening Post

'Thoroughly absorbing and very satisfying'
Bolton Evening News

'The bare bones of the plot have been equipped with muscle, blood and a soul by an imaginative story-teller'
Financial Times

'A highly original storyline and finely drawn characters'
Daily Telegraph

Also by the same author,
and available from Coronet:

BLOOD TIES
SIEGE OF SILENCE

About the Author

A. J. Quinnell is the author of MAN ON FIRE
(nominated for the 'Best Novel' Edgar in 1981 by
the Mystery Writers of America), THE MAHDI,
SNAP SHOT, BLOOD TIES and SIEGE OF
SILENCE. A. J. Quinnell is a pseudonym

In the Name of the Father

A. J. Quinnell

CORONET BOOKS
Hodder and Stoughton

Author's Note

*With thanks to Maurie for his advice on this and other
books, and to my Polish friends, particularly Maciej,
Mirek and Andrzej; and to Matthew Berry.*

AJQ

Copyright © 1987 by
Sandal A. G.

First published in Great Britain
in 1987 by Hodder and
Stoughton Limited

Coronet edition 1988
Third impression 1988

Printed and bound in Great Britain
for Hodder and Stoughton
Paperbacks, a division of Hodder
and Stoughton Limited, Mill
Road, Dunton Green, Sevenoaks,
Kent TN13 2YA (Editorial Office:
47 Bedford Square, London
WC1B 3DP) by Richard Clay
Limited, Bungay, Suffolk.
Photoset by Rowland
Phototypesetting Limited, Bury St
Edmunds, Suffolk.

British Library C.I.P.

Quinnell, A. J.
    In the name of the Father,
    I. Title
    823'.914[F]   PR6067.U56
    ISBN 0-340-42465-6

For Chris

'You can't run the Church on Hail Marys.'

Archbishop Paul Marcinkus

Prologue

First he cleaned the gun; then himself. He did both meticulously. The gun was a Russian Makarov pistol. He cleaned it at the table in the tiny kitchen. He worked automatically. His fingers were practised. He used very fine engine oil soaked into a soft cloth; then he wiped the oil off with a chamois leather. It was an hour after dawn but the kitchen light was still on. Occasionally he raised his head to look out through the small window. The sky over Cracow was overcast. It was yet another grey, winter day. He emptied the magazine of its bullets and tested the spring. Satisfied, he reloaded it and snapped it back.

His fingers curled around the butt. The weight felt balanced and comfortable. But when he screwed on the fat silencer it became front-heavy. No matter. The range would be close.

Carefully he laid the gun on to the scarred wooden surface and stood up, stretching leg and arm muscles.

He washed himself in the cramped shower cubicle. The size of the bathroom did not stretch to a bath. Even so, he remembered his pleasure on being assigned the apartment on his promotion to Major. It was the first time in his life that he had been able to live alone. The solitude had been welcome.

Using a French shampoo that he had bought in one of the restricted shops, he lathered his hair and his whole body. After rinsing himself he repeated the process twice more. It was as though he attempted to clean even beneath the skin. He shaved carefully without seeing the face in the mirror. His uniform lay neatly on the bed. He remembered his pleasure, almost sexual, on first putting it on. He dressed slowly, all his movements measured, as though going through a ritual. Then, from under the bed he pulled out a canvas bag. Into it he packed a pair of black shoes, two pairs of black socks, two pairs of dark blue underpants, two woollen plain shirts, a thick navy-blue woollen sweater, a black woollen scarf, a khaki anorak and two pairs of blue corduroy trousers. On top he placed his toilet bag.

His black leather briefcase was in the narrow hallway by the front door. He carried it into the kitchen and laid it on the table beside the gun. The twin locks had the joint combination number 1951 – the year of his birth. The briefcase was empty except for two leather straps attached to the bottom. He placed the gun between them and strapped it down tight.

Two minutes later, carrying the briefcase and canvas bag, he let himself out of the door without a backward glance.

The rush-hour traffic had eased and it took him only twelve minutes to reach SB Headquarters near the centre of the city. He could hear the rattle from the engine of the little Skoda. It was supposed to go in for a major service on the coming Monday. Automatically he glanced at the dashboard. The car had done just over ninety thousand kilometres since it had been assigned to him, brand new, on his promotion.

Normally he would have parked it in the compound behind the building. On this morning he left it in a side street just around the corner from the main entrance. He climbed out with the briefcase. Normally he would have locked the door. This time he left it open but he did check again that the boot which contained the canvas bag was securely locked. Passers-by, on seeing his uniform, averted their eyes.

He had not brought his overcoat and the wind chilled

him as he walked briskly around the corner and up the steps into the building.

With his increased workload, they had recently assigned him a full-time secretary from the pool. The building was overcrowded and he had found a place for her in an alcove opposite his office. She was middle-aged, prematurely grey, and a worrier. She looked up as he strode down the corridor and said anxiously, 'Good morning, Major Scibor . . . I tried to phone you at home but you must have just left. Brigadier Meiszkowski's secretary phoned. The meeting has been brought forward.' She looked at her watch. 'It's to start in twenty minutes.'

'Good. You have finished typing the report?'

'Of course, Major.'

'Please bring it in.'

He went into his office, put the briefcase on his bare desk and opened the blinds. Grey light filtered in.

She followed him, carrying a laced-up brown file and put it beside the briefcase saying, 'You'll have time to check it. May I say that it represents a brilliant piece of work, Major . . . I'll bring your coffee now.'

'Thank you. I won't take coffee this morning.'

Her face reflected surprise. She already knew him as a man of routine.

'Thank you,' he said again. 'I don't want to be disturbed before the meeting.'

She nodded and turned away.

He worked the combination locks of the briefcase and opened it and for a moment stood looking down at the gun. Then he unstrapped it. The brown file had the words 'SLUBA BEZPIECZENSTWA' printed in black on its cover. He unlaced it. Inside were about a dozen closely typed pages. He did not bother to read them.

He laid the gun with its silencer on the top page, then sat down. He turned the file so that the flap opened away from him. He put his right hand on the butt and slipped his finger through the trigger guard. Twice he lifted the

11

gun, then laid it down again, and laced up the file. It was now bulky. He put it into the briefcase and locked it up.

For the next fifteen minutes he sat perfectly still, gazing through the window at the side of a grey building across the street. A light rain had begun to fall.

Eventually he glanced at his watch, pushed himself erect and picked up the briefcase. On the wall to his left was a large-scale map of the city. He gazed at it for a few seconds and then strode to the door.

Brigadier Meiszkowski's office was on the top floor. His secretary sat in an outside office. She was an attractive woman with long auburn hair. It was rumoured that she and the Brigadier had a relationship that went deeper than work. She gestured at a leather settee across the room and said, 'Colonel Konopka is already inside. The Brigadier will call for you shortly . . . Coffee?'

He sat down and shook his head, laying the briefcase on his knees.

She smiled at him and went back to typing. Occasionally she glanced up. Each time his gaze was fixed at a spot about four feet above her head.

She decided that he looked tense on this morning and wondered why. The coming meeting held no difficulties for him. On the contrary, he was due for a commendation.

She glanced up again. His gaze had not shifted. She estimated that he was in his early thirties. Very young to be a Major. He was an attractive man in a saturnine, sardonic way, with black hair longer than normal in the service, and dark brown eyes. A lean, almost thin face, but a full lower lip and a cleft chin below that.

Brown eyes should be warm, but his were as cold as a Siberian wind.

She was wondering why she had never noticed that before when her phone console buzzed. She picked up the phone, cocking her head to one side. The bell of her hair swayed away and she placed the phone to her ear.

12

'Yes, sir . . . Yes, he is . . . Yes, sir.'

She put the phone down and nodded to him and watched as he stood up, automatically straightening his tie.

The Brigadier's office was befittingly large, with a good thick carpet and red curtains. He was sitting behind a walnut desk. There were two chairs in front of it. One of them was occupied by Colonel Konopka. The Colonel was thin and angular, the Brigadier florid and overweight. He smiled and gestured at the empty chair, saying, 'Mirek! Good to see you. Did my girl give you coffee?'

Scibor shook his head. 'Thanks, I didn't want any.'

He nodded to the Colonel and sat down, laying the briefcase on the desk.

Konopka said, 'Your work on the Tarnow Group has been outstanding. The question is, will your report be strong enough for us to recommend prosecution?'

Scibor nodded. 'I'm sure it is. But you – and the Brigadier – must be the judge of that. It's brief and very much to the point.' He leaned forward and flicked the dials of the combination locks.

There was a silence. The Brigadier had an expectant look on his face. He smiled when he saw the bulkiness of the file and said, 'I thought you said it was brief?'

Scibor put the file in front of him and lowered the briefcase to the floor beside his chair.

'It is. I brought along something else to show you.'

Slowly he began to unlace the file. He had begun to breathe more deeply. It went unnoticed. The other two had their eyes on the file. As he pulled the lace through the final few eyelets Scibor said, 'Brigadier Meiszkowski, Colonel Konopka, you will remember when I was initiated into the brotherhood – the *Szyszki*. You knew all about that initiation. I only found out the full details yesterday . . . This is my answer . . .'

He lifted the flap. As his hand closed on the butt of the gun he looked up.

The Brigadier's mouth had opened in shock. His torso

rose in the chair. With his left hand Scibor closed the flap. He raised the gun and squeezed the trigger.

The sound was a sharp thud. The Brigadier's head snapped back as the bullet smashed through his open mouth, up through his brains and out through the back of his cranium.

Scibor turned the gun. Konopka was rising, terror on his face.

Three sharp thuds. Three bullets into the heart. As he fell he grabbed at the chair, pulling it with him on to the carpet. His voice was a gurgle as he tried to speak. Scibor stood up, took careful aim and fired a bullet into his head just above and in front of his left ear.

The Colonel lay still. Blood had spattered the carpet.

Scibor walked around the desk. The Brigadier had toppled backwards in his chair. His head lay twisted against the angle of the floor and the wall. The wall was smeared with blood.

Scibor stood still, looking and listening. The door to the office was thick. He doubted if the secretary would have heard anything. He breathed very deeply several times and then unscrewed the silencer. He put the briefcase back on the desk. His hands were shaking a little and he fumbled for a few seconds with the locks before getting them open. He dropped the silencer in and closed the briefcase, then he opened the holster at his waist and took out the wadded newspaper he had used to give it normal bulk. He slid the Makarov into the holster, snapped it shut, picked up the briefcase and turned to the door.

The secretary was surprised at his quick reappearance. Over his shoulder he said, 'Thank you, Brigadier. I'll be in my office.' He closed the door and smiled at her. 'Brigadier Meiszkowski and Colonel Konopka wish to discuss my report privately. They'll call when they need me. Meanwhile he said that he's not to be disturbed . . . under any circumstances.'

She nodded. He smiled at her again and walked out. Unconsciously she patted her hair into shape.

*

14

He ignored the lifts, which were notoriously slow, and walked down the five flights of steps. As he walked out of the building the duty desk officer threw him a laconic salute. He acknowledged it with a wave of his hand.

It was twenty minutes later when the doorbell of Father Josef Lason's modest house on the outskirts of Cracow rang.

He sighed in exasperation. For two hours he had been trying to compose his homily for Sunday's service. The Bishop was doing him the rare honour of attending the mass and was notoriously critical of slapdash homilies. During those two hours the phone had rung constantly, mostly on matters concerning trivia. He had considered taking it off the hook but sometimes a call to his phone could be vital.

He shuffled to the door in his favourite old carpet slippers and opened it while assuming an expression of impatience. A man stood there in the light drizzle holding a canvas bag. He was wearing blue corduroy trousers and a khaki anorak. A black scarf was wound around his neck and the lower part of his face. His black hair was wet.

In a slightly muffled voice he said, 'Good morning, Father Lason. May I come in?'

The priest hesitated for a moment, then, realising the man was getting wetter, stood aside.

In the hall the man unwound the scarf and asked, 'Are you alone?'

'Yes. My housekeeper is shopping.' As he said the words the priest felt a stab of fear. The man's face had a menacing set.

The man said, 'I am Major Mirek Scibor of the SB.'

On hearing those words the priest's fear increased a thousandfold. The SB – Sluba Bezpieczenstwa – was the notorious arm of the Polish Secret Police that was directed against the Catholic Church. Major Mirek Scibor was known and feared as one of its most deadly agents.

The priest's fear showed on his face. Scibor said softly, 'I am not here to arrest you or harm you in any way.'

The priest regained some of his composure. 'Then why are you here?'

'As a refugee . . . I seek sanctuary.'

Now the expression on the priest's face changed from fear to suspicion. Scibor noted the change. He said, 'Father Lason, less than half an hour ago I shot to death a Brigadier and a Colonel of the SB. You will hear about it on the news.'

The priest looked into Scibor's eyes and believed him. He crossed himself and murmured, 'May God forgive you.'

Scibor's lips twisted into a sardonic smile. 'Your God should thank me.' He emphasized the word 'your'.

The priest shook his head as though in sorrow and asked, 'Why did you do it? . . . And why did you come to me?'

Scibor ignored the first question. He said, 'I came because you are a link in an escape route to the West. I have known about you for the past four months. I suspect that the dissident Kamien was smuggled out through your route. I would have arrested you but had hoped to uncover more links.'

The priest was silent for several seconds. Then he said, 'Come into the kitchen.'

They drank coffee, sitting opposite each other across the kitchen table. The priest again asked, 'Why did you do it?'

Scibor sipped from his mug. His eyes were fixed on the table. In a cold voice he said, 'Your religion preaches that vengeance belongs to God. Well, I borrowed a little from Him . . . That's all I will say.'

He raised his eyes and looked at the priest and the priest knew the subject was closed. He said, 'I admit nothing. But if you get to the West what will you do?'

Scibor shrugged. 'First we will have much to talk about; but when I get to the West I will talk to the Bacon Priest. Tell him that . . . Tell the Bacon Priest I'm coming.'

1

They chose Carabiniere General Mario Rossi to convey the news. It was a good choice. Rossi was not the kind of man to be overawed by a Pope or any other earthly being. Also it was a rational choice. He was the chairman of the committee which the Government had set up to oversee the safety and security of the Pope on Italian soil. His driver turned the black Lancia into the Damaso Courtyard. Rossi straightened his tie and climbed out.

He was an urbane and elegant figure, dressed in a three-piece suit of dark blue worsted with just a suggestion of a darker pinstripe. A pearl grey cashmere coat fell from his shoulders. In a city of fastidiously dressed men, he was a master tailor's pride. A cream silk handkerchief gave a discreet contrast of colour at the top of his breast pocket. Above that another contrast of maroon from a small but perfect carnation in his lapel buttonhole. The whole assemblage could have looked effeminate on another man, but whatever anyone said about Mario Rossi, and they said plenty, no one ever questioned his masculinity.

His face was well known to the Swiss Guards. They saluted him respectfully.

At the Apostolic Palace he was met by Cabrini, the Maestro di Camera. With barely a word they walked to the lift and were sped to the top floor. Rossi could practically feel the vibrations of curiosity emanating from Cabrini. A totally private Papal audience was a rarity. Especially one organised at such short notice; the Italian

17

Secretary of State requesting it only that morning – a matter of State importance.

They reached the dark, heavy door of the Pope's study. Cabrini rapped on it sharply with bony knuckles, opened it, announced Rossi in his nasal voice and ushered him in.

As the door closed behind him Rossi watched the Pope rise from behind the small paper-strewn table that looked like the work station of a middling business executive. By contrast the Pope resembled exactly what he was. He wore a pristine white silk cassock, a small white skull cap, a dark gold chain and cross, and a patrician but warm smile of welcome.

He moved round the table. Deferentially Rossi knelt on one knee and kissed the proffered ring.

The Pope leaned forward, put a hand under his arm and gently raised him to his feet.

'It gives us pleasure to see you, General. You are looking well.'

Rossi nodded his appreciation. 'I am, Your Holiness. A week at Madonna di Campiglio works wonders.'

The Pope raised his eyebrows.

'Ah, how was the skiing?'

'Excellent, Your Holiness.'

With a twinkle in his eye, the Pope asked, 'And the *après ski*?'

'Also excellent, Your Holiness.'

The Pope smiled wanly. 'How we miss the slopes.'

He took Rossi's elbow and steered him to a grouping of low leather chairs around a walnut table. As they seated themselves, a nun appeared through a side door bearing a tray. She poured coffees together with a Sambucca for Rossi, and for the Pope a small glass of amber liquid from an old unlabelled bottle. As she withdrew Rossi drained his coffee, took a sip of Sambucca and said, 'I wish to thank Your Holiness for agreeing to see me at such short notice.'

The Pope nodded, and Rossi, knowing that he was a man impatient with small talk, plunged straight in.

'Your Holiness, you will have heard about the defector Yevchenko.'

Again a nod.

'We have questioned him for the past ten days. Now he moves on to the Americans. The first thing of note is that although his Embassy ranking here was rather low, he was far more senior in the KGB than we ever suspected. In fact he was a General, and one of the most significant defectors in decades. He has been co-operative . . . most co-operative.'

Rossi finished his Sambucca and laid the glass carefully on the table. 'In our final debriefing session with him last night he talked about the lamented attempt on your life of May 19th, '81.'

He glanced up. Until now the Pope had been listening with polite interest. Now the expression in his eyes had changed to intense interest.

Rossi said, 'He confirmed what is virtually self-evident: that the assassination attempt originated and was directed from Moscow through their Bulgarian puppets. Yevchenko also confirmed beyond doubt that the mastermind, the driving force behind it, was the then head of the KGB, Yuri P. Andropov.'

The Pope nodded and murmured sombrely, 'And since elected Secretary General of the Communist Party of the USSR . . . and subsequently that country's President.' He shrugged. 'But General, this was assumed from all the analysis.'

'Yes, Your Holiness,' Rossi agreed. 'But what was not assumed was that because Andropov failed once, he would try again.'

A silence while the Pope digested that; then he asked quietly, 'And Yevchenko indicated that he will try again?'

Rossi nodded. 'Positively. He does not know details, but he was consulted. It appears that Andropov is obsessed with this matter. He is convinced that Poland is the linchpin of Soviet control of Eastern Europe. Its position has always

19

been vital and, in their eyes, always will be. He is also convinced that Your Holiness represents a dire threat to that linchpin . . .' He paused for effect and then said, almost sternly, 'And frankly, Your Holiness, your actions and your policy towards Poland and Communism in general, these past eighteen months, will have done nothing to dispel those fears.'

The Pope waved a hand dismissively. 'We have done everything with caution and in the light of Our Lord's teachings and guidance.'

Rossi couldn't help thinking: 'And a dash of patriotism for good measure,' but he didn't voice the thought. The Pope gestured at him.

'Would he really consider such a risk? After all, if the Polish people knew positively that we had been murdered on the direct orders of the leader of the Soviet Union, that could cause an uprising to shake the foundations of the Soviet Empire.'

'True,' Rossi conceded. 'Indeed, Yevchenko indicated that there is much opposition to this in the Soviet hierarchy, but Andropov's position appears to be totally secure. Also we must assume that the KGB learned something from the last attempt . . . You must face the reality, Your Holiness. One of the most powerful, amoral and ruthless men in the world, with vast resources at his disposal, is determined to see you dead.'

Another thoughtful silence while the Pope took a sip from his glass. Then he asked, 'Are there more details, General?'

Rossi grimaced. 'Very little. Only that the attempt will take place outside of the Vatican City, and outside Italy. Your Holiness is committed to a series of pastoral visits overseas. The details of your itineraries are well known. They have to be. You are to leave for the Far East in about two months. The attempt could be there or on a future trip. I believe that it will be sooner rather than later. Andropov is known to be an impatient man and is also not in good health . . . Your Holiness, an ailing man with an obsession is likely to wish to have that obsession satisfied quickly.'

The Pope sighed and slowly shook his head in sorrow. Rossi had the feeling that he would utter some words about God's will and the forgiving of our enemies. It was not to be. There was a very long silence. The Pope's eyes were half closed in thought. Rossi let his gaze wander round the room, taking in the blond wood panelling, the priceless paintings, the tall windows draped in gold damask. Windows up at which billions of pairs of eyes had stared in awe and reverence. His eyes came back to the Pope. He thought he saw a decision being taken. The Pope's eyes opened. Thought was over. Those blue eyes that smiled so easily were now frosted.

With a wince of pain the Pope stood up. With uncertainty Rossi did the same. The two men faced each other. Quite curtly the Pope said, 'General, this news is not welcome, but thank you for giving it to me personally and so promptly.'

Purposefully he moved towards the door. Rossi followed, saying with some bewilderment, 'You will take every precaution, Your Holiness? You do realise the seriousness . . . perhaps you should cancel . . .'

He got no further. The Pope had turned at the door and was shaking his head emphatically.

'We shall cancel nothing, General. Our life, and the way we lead it, will not be governed by any other power than that of the will of God. That atheist criminal in Moscow will not be allowed to affect or impair our pastoral mission on earth.' He opened the door. 'Again, thank you, General. Cardinal Casaroli will impart our thanks to the Minister.'

Slightly dazed, Rossi kissed the proffered ring, muttered a few words and was led away by Cabrini, who was looking even more curious. As they reached the lift, Rossi noticed the Pope's personal secretary, Father Dziwisz, slip into the study.

*

Stanislaw Dziwisz had followed his beloved Wojtyla from Cracow. It was always thus when a new Pope was elected. Luciani had brought his entourage and household from Venice and Paul had surrounded himself with Milanese.

Father Dziwisz had been the Pope's personal private secretary for fifteen years, and looked on him as a father. He also believed that he understood him as a father. Now he wasn't sure. The Pope's voice contained a tone he had never heard before. His stance and bearing, as he stood in the centre of the room, was rigid and cold.

'Ask Archbishop Versano to come here immediately . . . and cancel all our other appointments this afternoon.'

Stunned, Dziwisz asked, 'All of them, Your Holiness . . . ?' He saw the impatience in the Pope's eyes and said diffidently, 'There's the delegation from Lublin, Your Holiness.'

The Pope sighed. 'We know. They will be disappointed. Explain to them that something unexpected and urgent has arisen. Something that requires our time . . . and our duty.' He thought for a moment, then said, 'Ask Cardinal Casaroli if he has a few minutes to spare for them. He will know the right words to soften their disappointment.'

'Yes, Your Holiness . . .' Dziwisz waited. He waited to hear what such an important development could be. The Pope always took him into his confidence.

Not this time. He found himself staring into those cold blue eyes. They contained an expression: impatience. He turned away to summon Archbishop Versano.

The Archbishop took his seat and gratefully accepted the coffee. He had been made Archbishop by this Pope; a promotion that had stunned most Vatican observers, particularly since the embarrassing difficulties of another American in the Vatican hierarchy, Archbishop Paul Marcinkus of Chicago. The name of Marcinkus had become linked in one way or another with the financial scandal of the Banco Ambrosiano. He was, to all intents and purposes, confined to the tiny state-within-a-state of the

Vatican. If he stepped outside, he risked arrest. Many thought this would have the effect of hindering the progress and aspirations of other Americans in the Papal entourage. Yet the new Polish Pope had quickly come to rely on Versano, an American of Italian parentage who had rapidly worked his way up through the Vatican bureaucracy. Now, he supervised much of the Pope's security arrangements and was also deeply involved in the urgent restructuring of the Vatican Bank, to get it fully functioning again in the world markets.

Versano was not without his enemies. One of the youngest men ever to be made Archbishop, he was also tall and good-looking and – so some people said – appeared to enjoy to the full the high profile that his position brought him. He was charming and affable. Also, manipulative and ruthless. Still, he was getting the job done – both in terms of protecting the Pope and reviving the futures of the bank – and his star was very much in the ascendant. Since being elevated to Archbishop he had become part of the Pope's inner circle. He knew just about everything that went on in the Vatican. He knew, for example, that only half an hour earlier His Holiness had given a private audience at short notice to Carabiniere General, Mario Rossi. He was mightily intrigued.

His curiosity was fast satisfied. Even before he had finished his coffee the Pope had succinctly briefed him.

His reaction was practised and immediate. With his resonant, controlled, logical voice, he soothed. He reminded the Pope that since his election there had been half a dozen documented attempts on his life. Only one had come close to succeeding. There may have been a dozen others unknown. There would be scores more in the future. But security now was honed almost to perfection. Even on overseas trips. He did acknowledge that this threat was particularly dangerous in view of the power of its source, but everything possible would be done to mitigate it. The Pope was prone to discuss details of the enhanced security on the forthcoming trip to the Far East, but again Versano soothed. Relax, was his message, there was still a long time to go. Much could happen in that time. Perhaps Andropov would succumb to his illness. In that case, in view of opposition in the Kremlin, the whole project might well be dropped.

At the mention of Andropov the Pope rose and walked over to the windows and stood silently gazing down at St Peter's Square. Then he turned and said quietly, 'Mario, if it is the will of God then that evil man will die before he can perpetrate that atrocity. If not, then it is we who may die.'

Versano also rose and walked slowly across the room. They stood facing each other. The Pope was a big man, but the American was a head taller, if not as thick-set. Versano drawled huskily, 'It will be the will of God. Your Holiness is a beacon to mankind. A unique force for good. Such evil cannot and will not overcome that.'

He went down on one knee, pulled the Pope's hand towards him and fervently kissed the ring.

Back in his office, Archbishop Mario Versano gave instructions that he was not to be interrupted. Then he sat behind his desk and for the next hour smoked a series of Marlboros and exercised his considerable intellect. In spite of his happy-go-lucky appearance, the desk was remarkably neat. A telephone console close to his right hand; filing trays on the left; neat stacks of paper to the front; a solid silver Dunhill table lighter exactly centred. On the walls were framed and signed photographs of leading personalities from the banking, diplomatic, ecclesiastical and even showbusiness worlds. Some – in the banking section – had been taken down in the light of continuing investigation by authorities outside the Vatican, but Versano did not feel touched by that. He had tilted his chair on to two legs and was resting his broad back against the wall. After an hour he tipped his chair forward, reached for the lighter, lit another cigarette and punched a button on his telephone console.

There came the tinny voice of his very private personal secretary. The one who knew almost all the secrets.

'Yes, Your Grace?'

'Is the Bacon Priest still in town?'

'Yes, Your Grace, he is at the Collegio Russico. He leaves for Amsterdam in the morning.'

'Good. Get him on the line for me.'

A short pause, then Versano said heartily, 'Pieter, Mario Versano. When did you last eat at L'Eau Vive?'

'Too long ago, my young friend. I'm just a poor priest, you know.'

Versano's answering laugh was conspiratorial.

'Nine o'clock tonight then, in the back room.'

He hung up and summoned his secretary, a pale thin priest with spectacles thick enough for a telescope. Brusquely Versano ordered, 'Book the back room at L'Eau Vive for tonight. And tell Ciban that I would deem it a favour if he would have the entire restaurant carefully "swept" this afternoon.'

The secretary made a note and then said diffidently, 'It's very short notice, Your Grace. What if the room is already booked . . . by a Cardinal, say?'

Versano smiled broadly. 'Speak to Sister Maria personally. Tell her that no one, apart from His Holiness himself, will be more important than my guests.'

The secretary nodded and left. Versano reached for a fresh Marlboro, lit it, dragged appreciatively and then made one more phone call and issued one more invitation. Then he tilted his chair, rested his back against the wall and sighed contentedly.

2

It was raining lightly but Father Pieter Van Burgh left his taxi near the Pantheon and walked the last few hundred yards. Habits die hard, especially when they protect a life. He pulled his cloak around him and hurried down the narrow Via Monterone. It was a cold night and there were few people on the street. With a quick backward look he ducked into the recessed doorway.

It was brightly lit; not at all plush. At first an ordinary looking restaurant. But his cloak was taken by a tall black girl dressed in a long batik gown; she wore a gold crucifix at her neck. The priest knew that she was a nun, as were all the serving girls. They came from a French missionary order that worked in West Africa.

Another woman bustled up. She also wore a long dress but in a soft white cloth. She was older and white. Her face held a look of studied piety. The priest remembered her from a previous visit years before as Sister Maria, who ran the restaurant with fierce discipline. She did not remember him.

'Do you have a reservation, Father?'

'I am expected, Sister Maria. Father Van Burgh.'

'Ah yes.' She was immediately deferential. 'Follow me, Father.'

He followed her through an extraordinary restaurant. Although open to the public, lay customers were rare. Almost one hundred per cent of the clientèle were from the clergy or from people close to the clergy. Van Burgh noticed that it was practically full. He recognised several

26

diners: a Bishop from Nigeria, his ebony face glistening in the warm atmosphere, dining with the editor of *L'Osservatore Romano*. A Curia Bishop deep in conversation with an official of Vatican Radio. In one corner stood a large plaster statue of the Virgin Mary.

Sister Maria drew aside a red velvet curtain, opened a varnished door and ushered him in. The contrast was immediate.

The walls of the room were hung with rich tapestry. The deep carpet was ruby red. The single table covered by a cream damask tablecloth. Candlelight glistened on silver and crystal and the faces of the two seated men. Versano wore the simple cassock of a parish priest. The other guest was resplendent in purple Cardinal's robes of a quality that Van Burgh knew could only come from the House of Gammarelli – Papal tailors for two centuries. He recognised the pinched ascetic face: the newly elected Cardinal Angelo Mennini. The Cardinal was known as one of the shrewdest and most intelligent men in Rome. His Order, which had missionaries and influence all over the world, made him one of the most powerful and well-informed as well. Van Burgh had only met him once briefly many years before, but he well knew his reputation.

Both men rose. Van Burgh deferentially kissed the Cardinal's proffered ring and then heartily shook Versano's hand. He had heard all the rumours and believed some of them, but he instinctively liked the giant American.

Versano pulled out a chair for him and they all sat. Close to the Archbishop's right hand was a drinks trolley.

'Apéritif?' he asked.

Van Burgh chose a single malt whisky. Versano topped up Mennini's dry vermouth and his own Negroni. The plopping of ice cubes seemed to amplify the pregnant silence. They raised their glasses in a wordless toast, then in a businesslike voice Versano said, 'I've taken the liberty of ordering the meal beforehand. I don't think you'll be disappointed. Also it means we'll have fewer interruptions.' The youngest man present seemed to have no difficulty in establishing his authority over the meeting.

He paused for effect, and then said sombrely, 'For what I have to tell you tonight has the gravest implications for our beloved Father and for the entire Church.'

Van Burgh coughed and looked dubiously around the plush room. Versano smiled and raised a placating hand. 'Don't worry, Pieter, this room – the entire restaurant – has been "swept" this afternoon. There are no bugs, and I can tell you that the entire Vatican itself is now secure.'

He was referring to the incident in 1977 when Camilio Ciban, head of Vatican Security, had persuaded Secretary of State Cardinal Villot to have the Secretariat checked for listening devices. Eleven sophisticated 'bugs' had been found of both American and Russian origin. One of the most secret institutions on earth had been shocked to its core.

Cardinal Mennini was studying the Dutch priest opposite him. With his round, ruddy cheeks and wide girth he could have been Friar Tuck straight out of a medieval Sherwood Forest. He had a habit of rubbing the pads of his fingers against his palms and of looking around with a slightly surprised air; a bit like a child finding himself suddenly alone in a chocolate factory. But at sixty-two he was no child and Mennini well knew that his simple manner hid a razor mind and a vast repertoire of talents.

Father Pieter Van Burgh headed the Vatican's Iron Curtain Church Relief Fund. Since the early '60s he had made numerous clandestine visits to Eastern Europe in a variety of disguises. The Vatican allows no publicity to surround him. He is loathed by anti-Church officials in Eastern Europe but although they know of his activities they have never been able to trap him. He is a 'Pimpernel' called the 'Bacon Priest' because, on his frequent incursions behind the Iron Curtain, he always carries slabs of bacon to hand out to those in his secret flock who are particularly deprived or lonely in their clandestine work.

He had been a close friend of the Pope since his early days as Archbishop of Cracow.

A door silently opened and a beautiful black girl wheeled in a trolley. They watched in appreciation as she modestly served the *fettuccine con cacio e pepe*. She then poured the Falerno and silently retired. The food served in the main restaurant was French, moderately good and inexpensive. In the back room the food was Italian, superb and vastly expensive. In dining there a parish priest would wipe out a month's stipend.

Versano picked up his fork with anticipation but was stopped by Van Burgh's discreet cough. He was looking at the Cardinal expectantly. Mennini had a puzzled expression, then he understood. He nodded, lowered his head and muttered rapidly, '*Benedictus benedicat per Jesum Christum Dominum nostrum. Amen.*'

They raised their heads and with an unrepentant grin Versano tucked into the pasta. He ate rapidly, impatiently, as did Mennini, as though food was nothing more than a necessary fuel.

Van Burgh took his time, savouring the delicate flavouring. There had been many times in his life when a meal consisted of nothing more than a heel of bread and with luck a lump of cheese; and several times when there had been no meal at all.

Versano sat back and said, 'I told them to leave a little time between courses.' He held up a cigarette. 'Do you mind? I like eating here,' he said, 'even if no one can see us in this room!' Van Burgh allowed himself a smile at the younger cleric's self-deprecating comment, but he knew they were not here for small-talk.

'I wonder why we find ourselves thus separated from the other guests?' he mused, pointedly.

'Ah, Pieter,' said the American. 'Like you, I have to resort to disguises and subterfuge. I find it stimulating.'

Van Burgh grunted through a mouthful of *fettuccine*, and wondered whether the Archbishop would find it so stimulating if arrest meant subsequent torture and death.

Mennini, fingering the heavy gold crucifix at his waist, showed signs of impatience. He said, 'The company and surroundings are congenial, Mario, but apparently the matter at hand is less so. Perhaps you had better explain.'

Versano nodded, his face turning serious. He laid his cigarette carefully on to an ashtray. Looking first at Mennini and then Van Burgh, he said, 'I gave much thought as to whom I should consult on this matter.' He paused and his voice dropped to a deeper note. 'I can say that there are no two people in our entire Church who are better equipped to advise and take part in this fateful matter . . . However, before discussing it, I need your assurances of total confidentiality . . . total.'

Van Burgh had finished his pasta. He pushed the plate away, picked up his glass and took a gulp of wine. Versano was watching Mennini. The thin-faced, grey-haired Cardinal sucked on his teeth in thought. Van Burgh could see the curiosity in his eyes. He knew what the answer would be. Finally Mennini nodded.

'You have it, Mario. Within the grounds of the Faith, of course.'

'Of course. Thank you, Angelo.'

He turned an enquiring look on the Dutchman. Van Burgh didn't hesitate. A lifetime of conspiracy could not allow that. He said firmly, 'Naturally I follow the Cardinal's example.'

Versano leaned forward and lowered his voice and said, 'The sacred life of our beloved Pope John Paul is in imminent danger.'

To his rapt and pained audience of two, he spelled out precisely what he had learned that afternoon.

The second course was *abbacchio alla cacciatora* and during it they discussed the general picture. Versano and Mennini deferred to the Bacon Priest. He was the most junior in rank but his knowledge and insight into the Russian mind was legendary. He propounded the theory that the Russians were quite satisfied that the last attempt

30

on the Pope's life by Ali Agca was generally thought to have originated in Moscow. In his view it was a barely veiled warning that this Pope, or any other, had better not meddle in their affairs. If it had succeeded, so much the better. They had done their sums. It was unlikely that another East European prelate would be elected Pope for generations. If it narrowly failed, as it did, then the warning would be perceived.

At first it looked as though it had been. Papal anti-Communist rhetoric diminished. The American Bishops' stand against Reagan's nuclear policies went unanswered by the Vatican. Solidarity was crushed, witnessed by Papal anguish but without action. But, explained Van Burgh, this was not a change in Papal policy, but a shift in emphasis, and a new pragmatism. The Pope had been busy redefining the role of the Church; heading off an internal liberalism that he believed threatened the Church in a more subtle but dangerous way. In recent months the Kremlin would have perceived that the *Papa*'s anti-Communism was in no way diluted and, as he fashioned the Church more firmly to his own image, it would endanger them even more.

From what he knew of Andropov, and he knew a very great deal, Van Burgh was not at all surprised that he was planning another attempt. He summed up solemnly by stating that a betting man, knowing all the facts, would not give the Pope even a ten per cent chance of survival. It would be one thing to assassinate someone like Reagan whose country could retaliate, but ironically, to quote Stalin: 'How many Divisions does the Pope have?'

Versano then turned to the Cardinal. 'Angelo, we are all pragmatists here and need no false modesty as to our sources and no inhibitions as to our opinions. You head the most pragmatic of all sections of the Church. We know that the *Papa* was pleased and relieved at your election as the head of the Society. We need betray no confidences in discussing how we were all pained by your predecessor's

31

policies. There is relief throughout the Curia, you know that. Now, I invited you tonight for your wisdom and for your help in what I propose . . . but first, your opinion on Father Van Burgh's prognosis?'

Cardinal Mennini, who had risen from a peasant background in Tuscany, wiped his plate clean with a hunk of bread – fuel should not be wasted – chewed on it contemplatively and then nodded.

'I agree with the Father here. In both cases. It is logical that Andropov will try again. It is also logical that with the machinery at his disposal, and with the determination of the *Papa* to continue his pastoral work abroad, the attempt will succeed.' He wiped his mouth with a napkin, slid a look at Versano and said, 'Incidentally, my sources in South Korea indicate that Kim Il Sung in the North would be delighted if the Pope came to harm on his visit.'

Versano's eyes met those of Van Burgh. They knew that the members of his Order were thick on the ground in the Far East. The Dutchman asked, 'You have advised him of this? Advised him not to go?'

Mennini shrugged. 'Of course. But the *Papa* is determined. His comment was that fishermen must sometimes face stormy waters.' He turned to Versano. 'Now, Mario, what is your proposal?'

But they were interrupted by the arrival of the last course, a *tartuffo*. They were truly oblivious to the beauty of the serving nun.

Versano felt a rare nervousness. The nun departed. He waited a few moments. The only sounds in the room were the chinks of silver against bone china. Then he said very quietly, 'I propose that a secret Papal envoy be sent to Andropov.'

They both looked up sharply. The Dutchman had a piece of ice cream on his chin.

'What would he say to Andropov?' Mennini asked. 'What would be the message?'

Versano again waited a few moments, the actor in him savouring the moment. He looked from one to the other, into their curious eyes, and then stated flatly, 'He would say nothing. He would kill Andropov.'

He expected surprise, astonishment, outrage, laughter, the clatter of a spoon on a plate, a snort of derision, a look of incomprehension.

Nothing. Nothing but total silence and stillness. They could have been two figures woven for ever into the tapestry hanging on the wall.

The first things that moved were Mennini's eyes. They swivelled to look at the Dutchman. He was gazing down at his plate as though seeing ice cream for the first time. Very slowly he moved his hand and spooned up a little, and carried it to his mouth. He swallowed and sadly shook his head.

'The Pope . . . this Pope would never consider such a thing . . . never.'

Mennini nodded his gaunt head in agreement. Versano was inwardly elated. He congratulated himself. He had chosen his men well. Like a wolf in an Arctic winter, he had chosen only the strongest to run with him. He took a cigarette, lit it, blew smoke at the chandelier and said, 'Of course, but he would never know; must never know . . .'

Another silence while again Versano mentally preened himself on his intuition.

Then the Dutchman asked, 'How could a Papal envoy be sent without the Pope's knowledge and consent?'

Versano chided him gently, 'Pieter, you of all people have to ask that?'

Van Burgh surveyed him across the table and then gave a nod and a grim little smile. The American smiled back.

Mennini mused: 'It would be a great sin.' It was said matter-of-factly, as though he had said, 'It would be a great pity.'

Versano had been waiting for this. He was not about to pit his intellect against this renowned debater. Few men would be foolish enough to try that. He remembered Mennini's remark to the renegade Hans Kung. 'Your religion is practised within the confines of your brain, and your brain does not acknowledge the existence of your heart.'

Versano had decided to debate with extreme simplicity and rock solid logic.

'Angelo, if one of your missionaries in Africa awoke in a mud hut and found himself cornered by a poisonous snake, what would he do? What would you expect him to do?'

The corners of the Cardinal's thin lips twitched as he answered immediately.

'Of course he would take a stick and kill it . . . but that is a reptile. You are talking of a human being.'

Versano had his next line ready but was surprised when the Dutchman said it for him. Van Burgh, emphasising every word by tapping his fingers on the table, said to Mennini, 'In acknowledging the devil and his works and his ways we recognise that man can become animal. There are precedents in our teachings and in our reactions.'

Versano knew that the Bacon Priest was running beside him. From the sides of his eyes he watched and waited for Mennini's reaction.

The Cardinal ran a hand across his forehead, shrugged and said, 'Sin apart, what about the mechanics of such a thing?'

Slowly Versano let his breath out. They were all running together. Quickly he pointed a finger at Van Burgh.

'Pieter. Think of this. Through your network which spirits thousands of people in and out of the Soviet bloc, is it not possible to put one man secretly into the heart of Moscow? Even into the Kremlin?'

'I don't have to think.' The Dutchman leaned back and stretched his bulk, his vast belly protruding. The fragile chair squeaked ominously. 'In such matters we are the equal of the KGB, if not their masters. Yes, I could send a man across Europe and into Moscow . . . indeed into the Kremlin. But there are then three questions. How to get him close to the snake? What kind of stick does he carry? And, after he kills the snake, how to get him out again?'

While Versano was formulating an answer Mennini interjected.

'And another one. Where to find such a man? We are not Islam. We cannot guarantee such a man automatic entry to paradise. We cannot give absolution for suicide.'

Versano said confidently, 'Somewhere there is a man and somehow we shall find him. Our contacts are extensive – worldwide. Moscow found Agca . . . there are other such men.'

Mennini, although seemingly committed, was now playing the devil's advocate. 'But what about motive? Agca had a mental illness fuelled by hatred for the Pope and others. Would you try to find a man who is motivated by faith . . . or insanity?'

Again Van Burgh interjected, seemingly able to read Versano's thoughts.

'In Eastern Europe it would not be impossible to find a man with a motive . . . and it should certainly not be religious –' Versano started to say something but the Dutchman held up a hand. 'Wait . . . let me think . . .' He was quite still for two minutes, his eyes narrowed, then slowly he nodded. 'Even now I know of such a man. It would appear that he has the motive –'

'And what is that?' Mennini asked.

'Hatred, pure and simple. He hates the Russians. He abhors the KGB . . . and in particular he loathes Andropov, apparently with an intensity that defies description.'

Fascinated, Versano asked, 'Why?'

The Dutchman shrugged. 'I don't know – yet. I had a report about four weeks ago that a renegade SB man was on the run.' He waved a hand apologetically and explained. 'The SB is short for Sluba Bezpieczenstwa, the department of the Secret Police in Poland which is directed against the Church. This man, his name is Mirek Scibor, was a Major

35

in the SB. A very well-known Major; and at thirty years old very young to be a Major. He owed his position not to family or party influence, but to intelligence, dedication and ruthlessness.' He smiled ruefully. 'I can attest to that. Four years ago when he was still a Captain he almost caught me – in Poznan. He laid a very sophisticated trap which I avoided only by luck.' He raised his eyes. 'Or, I should say, heavenly intervention.'

'But why the hatred?' asked the Cardinal.

Van Burgh spread his hands. 'I don't yet know, Your Eminence. I do know that on the seventh of last month Mirek Scibor walked into the SB headquarters in Cracow and gunned down his immediate superior – a Colonel Konopka – and a Brigadier. It was almost a miracle that he escaped from the building but he did. He contacted one of our priests, obviously one whom he had under surveillance, and begged help to escape from Poland. Naturally the priest was suspicious. Mirek Scibor is a name to strike terror into such people. But fortunately the priest was also intelligent and intuitive. He hid Scibor for several days during which time we learned of his killing of the SB Brigadier and the Colonel. He questioned him at length. Scibor offered a vast amount of information about the State's policy and tactics against our Church. Much of it we were able to corroborate. He expressed a desire to meet me and to tell me more. He refused to talk about the reason for his turnabout or for his hatred. The priest reported that he had never seen a man so consumed with that passion . . . and the centre of its target is Andropov. I gave orders for him to be brought out through one of our pipelines.'

'Where is he now?' Versano asked.

'The last news I had was four days ago. He was in a Friary in Esztergom. By now he should be in Budapest, looked after by the same brotherhood. In a week he'll be in Vienna.'

This information brought a sober silence to the room. They had been speculating and theorising and now, abruptly, they were faced with the reality of having at hand the possible tool.

Mennini broke the silence.

'What about the other questions? How to get him into the Kremlin? How does he perform his task? How does he get out?'

The Dutchman spoke firmly.

'Your Eminence, you must, for the time being, leave those questions to me. It is possible that we shall need the help of your Society but that will come later. First, if this man Mirek Scibor proves suitable, he must be trained. My organisation obviously does not have the facilities to train an assassin . . .' He drank the last of his wine and, with a glance at both of them, said quietly, 'But we are in touch with organisations that do have such facilities. During his journey to Moscow we cannot use any of our existing pipelines. For such a mission it is too dangerous. If caught he will talk. Either physical torture or drugs, or a combination. We shall have to create a new and very temporary pipeline.' He gazed down at the empty wine glass in his hand and mused. 'Of course, he cannot travel alone. He must have a companion – a "wife".'

'A wife!' Versano's face expressed his astonishment. 'On such a mission he takes a wife?'

Van Burgh smiled and nodded. 'Certainly, Mario. Usually when I travel in the East I am accompanied by my "wife". Sometimes she is a middle-aged nun from Delft. A woman of great courage and fortitude. At other times a member of the lay religious from Nuremberg. In all I have four such "wives". All virtually saints. They risk much for their faith. You see, a man and wife travelling together excite little suspicion. An assassin would hardly take his wife along.'

Mennini was intrigued.

'And where would you find such a woman?'

Van Burgh smiled. 'Well, I cannot lend him one of mine. They are old enough to be his mother and no one travels with his mother if it can be avoided.' He gestured confidently. 'It is not a problem. I know where to look for such a woman and exactly what qualities she will need. Perhaps you can help, Your Eminence.'

Mennini asked, 'And her motive? Will that too be hatred?'

The Dutchman shook his head.

'On the contrary. Her motive will be love. Her love for the Holy Father . . . and also obedience to his will.' He looked into their eyes and saw the disquiet. 'Don't worry. Her mission will be to travel with him as far as Moscow. The real danger comes when the "envoy" enters the Kremlin. Long before that she will be whisked away to safety.'

There was a moment of cogitation, then Mennini expressed the thoughts that were in all their minds. In a voice as though talking to his conscience he mused, 'We involve others. Inevitably there will be many.' He raised his head and looked at the priest and the Archbishop. 'We are three clerics . . . men of God . . . How quickly and easily we decide on murder.'

The Archbishop straightened in his seat. His face showed the earnest expression of a mind bent on persuasion, but before he could speak the Bacon Priest said laconically, 'Your Eminence, if you want semantics, change the word "murder" to "defence". Change the word "decided" to "impelled"; change the word "clerics" to "instruments" . . . We are three instruments impelled to the defence of our Holy Father and through him our faith.'

The Cardinal nodded thoughtfully. Then he smiled and said, 'Unlike the Holy Father, we do not have the balm of infallibility. We are left with the palliative of action; with the knowledge that if what we do is a sin, it is a sin shared . . . and a sin condoned by the excuse of unselfishness.'

The door opened and coffee was brought in, carried by Sister Maria herself. She fussed about, enquiring if everything had been satisfactory. Assured so in triplicate, she then said to Mennini, 'Your Eminence. It is to be "Ave Maria" tonight. A little untraditional but Cardinal Bertole is dining in the main room and it's his favourite.'

She went out leaving the door open. Versano grimaced.

'I think I'd better stay here. You two frequently have reason enough to be talking, but for the three of us to be seen together – that might look too suspicious.'

The other two nodded in understanding, picked up their cups of coffee and moved to the door.

The serving sisters had all gathered in front of the plaster statue of the Virgin Mary. There was a silence in the full room. Mennini nodded at a few familiar faces. At a signal from Sister Maria the girls raised their heads and began to sing. It is a tradition in the L'Eau Vive that they always sing over coffee; usually a hymn. The patrons are urged to join in. Most of them did so this night and the room was filled with rich sounds. Van Burgh added his deep baritone and, after a verse, Mennini chimed in with a cracked tenor. The chorus of serving sisters sang in perfect harmony as they gazed rapturously at the statue.

The last angelic tones died away. There was no applause but everyone in the room felt somehow uplifted and satisfied.

Mennini and Van Burgh turned back into the private room and closed the door behind them. Versano was pouring, from a very old bottle, three tots of brandy of an age lost in antiquity. As they settled themselves he said, 'We must decide on a *modus operandi*.'

Mennini immediately agreed. 'We are sworn to secrecy. This thing must be accomplished by us alone and those whom we recruit. In their tasks they must never know the objective except of course for the envoy.' He turned to the Dutchman. 'Father Pieter, how long will it take you to evaluate this man Scibor?'

'No more than a few days, Your Eminence.'

'Then I suggest we meet again here in two weeks' time.'

Versano nodded in agreement and pulled his chair closer. In a low voice he said, 'We may have to communicate by phone. I suggest a simple code is in order.'

The others leaned closer, drawn by the lure of conspiracy. Versano said, 'The envoy shall be known as just that. It's an innocuous word. The woman who travels with him will be known as *la cantante* – the singer.' He gestured towards the outside room, presumably indicating that the inspiration for this had come from the singing sisters. 'And Andropov, the target, will be known simply as *l'uomo* – the man.'

'And we?' Van Burgh asked. 'What will we be known as?'

There was a silence for thought, then Mennini, with a thin smile, supplied the answer.

'*Nostra Trinita*. Our trinity.'

They all liked it. Versano raised his glass.

'*Nostra Trinita*.'

The other two echoed the toast, then the Bacon Priest proposed another and they raised their glasses and toasted: 'The *Papa*'s envoy!'

Then Mennini, as if determined not to allow his co-conspirators to forget the full implications of what they were doing, gravely proposed a toast of his own.

'In the name of the Father.'

3

Mirek Scibor sat on the third bench on the second path after the clock tower in Vienna's Schönbrunn Palace Park. It was exactly the spot that he had been told to sit and wait. Sitting further down the bench was a fat old woman dressed in black. She wore a grey lace scarf over grey hair and she irritated Mirek. His contact was to arrive in five minutes and she showed no signs of moving. She had been there twenty minutes, frequently coughing into a grubby handkerchief. He looked down at her black stockinged feet. They bulged arthritically out of scuffed pinch-buckle shoes. She also emitted a rancid, unwashed odour. Distastefully he looked away and around him at the city, and his irritation faded. This was only his second day in the West and he was elated by his escape and by the wonders of what he had seen, an elation that sometimes almost dampened the hatred that was an oven inside his belly. It was not the grand buildings that impressed him. They had such buildings in Poland and Russia, equally steeped in grandeur and history. It was the people and the luxuries. The people of Vienna were carefree and the luxuries abundant. He was intelligent and informed enough to know that this was not universal in the West. In places there had to be poverty and unhappiness, but that was not apparent here. He had arrived in the city in the back of a closed van. Ironically, or deliberately, the van had been packed with crates of smoked bacon. In the hour it had taken to drive from the border to the city the smell had permeated his clothes and his skin and he had become heartily sick of it.

The doors of the van had opened on to the dark of a high walled courtyard. By this time Mirek had been nauseous from motion sickness. A friar had been waiting for him. He gave a curt nod and said, 'Follow me.'

Clutching a small bundle of clothes, Mirek followed him down a low vaulted corridor. It was three in the morning. There was no one about. The friar indicated a door and Mirek went through. It was a cell-like room containing a metal bedstead and a thin mattress with three grey threadbare blankets folded at the foot. There was nothing else in the room. It was as hospitable as a prison cell. He turned. The friar's face was just as hospitable. He gestured: 'There is a toilet and showers down the corridor. Apart from going there you must stay in this room. Food will be sent to you at seven o'clock . . . that's in four hours. The Father Vicar will see you at eight.'

He turned away. Mirek said with a trace of sarcasm, 'Thank you, good night.'

There was no reply and Mirek was not surprised. He guessed that even here he was known for what he was and what he had done. His reception had been the same all the way. Bare, cheerless rooms and hostile faces. To these people he was worse than a leper. To a leper they would show compassion. To him they showed the face of duty, carried out with distaste.

But in the morning the Father Vicar had been slightly less forbidding. Mirek, of course, was an expert on the Catholic Church, its structures and its hierarchy. He knew that as Father Vicar the old man opposite him was, under the Father Provincial, number two in the province. He was the most important Franciscan he had met during his clandestine journey. Presumably he would have news for him. He had.

'You will stay here for one more night. Tomorrow you will take your clothes and at one p.m. be sitting on a certain bench at a city park. A "contact" will approach you and ask for a light. You will say, using these exact words, "I never carry matches." You will then follow that person.'

'Where will he lead me?'

The Father Vicar shrugged.

'Where?' Mirek pressed. 'When will I meet the Bacon Priest?'

The old man raised his eyebrows in puzzlement. 'The Bacon Priest?'

Mirek sighed in frustration. He'd had the same reaction whenever he'd mentioned the man. His journey had been long, lonely, uncomfortable and dangerous but he had been sustained by a screaming curiosity to be face to face with the man he had hunted for years. That curiosity was the only emotion he had felt alongside the ever-present hatred. The Father Vicar may have seen something of it. He had said in a softer tone, 'Scibor, this is your first day in the West. But even in the West our facilities are spartan. Vienna is a beautiful city. Why not go out and see something of it? I think you will not be here long. Go and try some of the delicious Viennese pastry. Walk in streets that are free. Breathe air that is free.' His lips twitched into a small ironic smile. 'Go into churches and see people worship. People whose only fear is the fear of their Lord.'

Dubiously Mirek said, 'But is it safe?'

The old man's smile widened. 'Don't worry. They will not attack you. Such people will not know who you are.'

'I didn't mean that.'

'I know. Forgive a little sarcasm. Two of our brothers from this Friary have been in gaol in Czechoslovakia these past ten years.' He gestured at a cloistered window from which a shaft of sunlight brightened the room. 'It's a cold but fine morning for December. Mingle with the crowds. Vienna is safe for you; no one knows you are here. Have a meal. Drink some of our good wine.'

'I have no money.'

'Ah, of course.' The Father Vicar opened a drawer in his desk, pulled out a bundle of notes, counted off several and placed them in front of the Pole. 'I think that should be adequate.'

So Mirek had gone out into the streets of Vienna and been stunned.

The Friary was in an eastern suburb, close to a huge market. He spent his first hour there slowly walking and watching. In his life he had never seen such mountains of food. Not even in his native countryside at harvest time. And the variety. Within ten minutes he knew that at least half the produce had come here from far away. Bananas, pineapple, avocados and fruits that he had never seen or heard of. He watched in amazement as one rosy-cheeked woman vendor carelessly threw away apples that were only slightly rotten. He bought a small bunch of grapes from her and was warmed by her cheerful smile. Slowly he walked towards the city centre, eating the grapes. He paused often; once at the window of a butcher's, shaking his head in awe at the array of hanging carcasses and the row upon row of trimmed steaks and chops and fowl. He had eaten only a little bread and cheese for breakfast but he felt no hunger. Only shock. All his thinking life he had been a true and dedicated Communist. He had read his party's newspapers, listened to the speeches and taken part in the debates. He knew, of course, that some of the propaganda had been just that. But he was secure in that knowledge because he knew too that the propaganda from the West had to contain even more lies.

He next paused at a newsstand and ran his eyes over the array of newspapers and magazines in a dozen European languages. Shock and confusion filled his brain. He had retraced his steps to the butcher's shop, walked in and almost aggressively asked an attendant if all the meat was available to anyone without rank or ration coupons. The attendant had smiled. He had heard this question many times before. From Poles, Czechs, Hungarians, Rumanians. Vienna is a conduit for East European refugees.

'Money,' he had said. 'All you need is money.'

Instinctively Mirek almost reached into his pocket to

buy a whole red beef fillet lying on the slab next to him. In his entire life he had eaten beef fillet only once. The time that bastard Konopka had taken him to dinner at Wierzynek's in Cracow. But he stopped himself. He had nowhere to cook it. No matter, on this day he would find a restaurant and have fillet steak for lunch.

Back on the street his attention turned to the people. In the streets of Warsaw or Moscow or Prague people walk with a grim purpose. These people walked quickly and mostly were intent on going somewhere. They carried shopping bags and briefcases and parcels under their arms but no one was grim. Not even the policeman directing traffic. He stopped at a tobacconist's and bought a packet of Gitanes cigarettes. A colleague had once been given a carton by the leader of a visiting French Communist delegation. He had grudgingly given Mirek a single cigarette and the aroma had lingered in his nostrils for days. He was surprised to find the brand in Austria but then he saw brands from all over Europe and even America. He was about to buy a box of matches but noticed a rack of brightly coloured lighters under a sign saying 'disposable'. He bought one – a blue one. He walked on puffing contentedly and flicking away at the lighter like a child with his first toy. In Alexanderplatz he found a café with chairs and tables on the street behind glass screens. He sat down and a young blonde waitress dressed in a checked red and white dress with a frilly white apron gave him the menu and, with a smile, waited patiently while he studied it. Being still early he decided not to spoil his appetite for the promised steak. His eye caught the word *Apfelstrudel* and he ordered that together with a cold lager. He watched appreciatively as the waitress swung her hips away between the tables. And when he turned his gaze back to the square it was the women and girls his eyes sought. There were many of them in different shapes and sizes. At first he considered that the prettier ones were more so than those in Poland. But then he reconsidered. There were equally beautiful women in Poland. Maybe it was because during

45

the past weeks he had seen no beautiful women. He feasted his eyes. Long fair legs scissored beneath short but elegant skirts and dresses. It made him realise that it had also been months since he had been with a woman. He felt the urge, abruptly and forcibly. So forcibly that his mind turned to practicalities. He reasoned that there must be prostitutes in this city. After all there were prostitutes in Warsaw and Cracow and in many, even most, cities of Poland . . . and this was the decadent West. He wondered whether the money that the Father Vicar had given him would cover such an eventuality. Perhaps not both that and a fillet steak. Then he discarded the idea. He had never been with a prostitute and found the idea repugnant. Besides he had never had to. He well knew that he was attractive to women. Had been since puberty. Even now he noticed that several of the women who passed by cast interested looks in his direction. So did the blonde waitress when she put the plate and glass beside him. His nostrils caught the musky aroma of her perfume and again came the powerful urge. He noticed the fine blonde hairs on her forearm and the slim fingers bereft of rings. Then his nostrils and his eyes were diverted to the plate and the massive slice of *Strudel* topped with a mound of fresh cream.

He finished it all and three hours later savoured every mouthful of steak and every sip of wine while again his thoughts dwelled on finding a woman. Such thoughts were instantly dispelled when he was presented with the bill. After paying it he was left with a few coins. He estimated it cost him what would have been a week's wages. There was nothing left for a disco or café or bar where he might pick up a girl. Instead he had walked for several hours in the city and then made his way back to the Friary. In his cell that night he thought first of the Bacon Priest, and then later again about women. Had he been a less disciplined man he might have masturbated, but walking the streets that afternoon he had promised himself that the next time he ejaculated it would be into a real woman whose passion would be genuine.

Now he found himself sitting next to what must be the smelliest old hag in Vienna. He wrinkled his nose in distaste and impatience and glanced at his watch yet again. It was three minutes before one. He supposed that his contact had him under observation. He felt irritation at the whole set-up. It was unprofessional. He had been told only to be at this place at this time. There was no fallback if the 'meet' failed. No alternative place or time. Stupid! What if the old hag had been a policeman instead? Silently cursing the Bacon Priest, he cast his gaze around trying to spot his possible contact. There was no one who remotely resembled such a person. A young couple were strolling arm-in-arm down a path, oblivious to anyone but each other. On the grass fifty yards in front of him two young boys were kicking a striped rubber ball around, watched over by a matronly woman in a starched blue uniform whom Mirek took to be a nanny. There was no one else nearby. He cursed again under his breath and glanced again at the old woman. She was fumbling about in a tattered cloth handbag. Then he heard sharp piping voices. He looked back to see the striped rubber ball heading towards him and the two tots gesturing behind it. He reached out a foot, gave it a sharp tap and watched with satisfaction as it headed straight back towards them. The nanny called '*Danke*' and then a voice beside him said, 'Do you have a light, please?'

He turned. The old hag was holding a cigarette. She had screwed her features into what she expected to be a coquettish look. It made his stomach turn. With yet another inward curse he reached into his pocket for his new bright blue lighter. He decided he'd give the damn thing to the hag in exchange for her going away. But even as his hand encountered it the years of mental training took over and his muscles froze. Surely it couldn't be. Hesitantly he said, 'I don't carry matches.'

She tut-tutted, shook an admonishing finger at him and said, 'You were supposed to say "never", not "don't".'

Hell, this really was the contact.

'That's . . . that's right,' he stammered. 'I never carry matches.'

She glanced around her and lowered her voice.

'So you are the Pole?' She giggled. 'Such a handsome young man!'

Impatiently he replied, 'Yes. Are you going to pass me on . . . to the Bacon Priest?'

'No.'

'No!'

'No, Mirek Scibor. You are talking to him.'

The words took several seconds to penetrate, then his mouth literally opened in surprise.

'You? The Bacon Priest? Pieter Van Burgh?'

She nodded. He recovered and studied the face carefully. He reviewed what little he knew of the Bacon Priest. The man was known to be between sixty and sixty-five years old. Just under six feet tall, well built with a big paunch. Round faced. This apparition looked like nothing more than the scabrous hag he took her to be. He was about to express his scepticism when he remembered the Bacon Priest's legendary reputation for disguise. He studied her some more. She sat slumped on the bench making it difficult to judge her height. The voluminous black dress could be hiding a girth. Her face was round but covered with pancake make-up and rouge; also partly obscured by straggles of limp grey hair and the grey lace scarf. But still her posture and gestures were that of a woman of at least seventy. He did know one way to tell. The dress had sleeves that came down almost to her knuckles. He leaned forward and said sternly, 'Show me your wrists.'

She smiled without trying to be coquettish and slowly raised her arms. The sleeves dropped to reveal the thick sturdy wrists of a man.

Mirek shook his head in admiration. 'I would never have known.'

The Bacon Priest chuckled. 'Three years ago I stood this far away from you on the railway station in Wroclaw.'

48

'Maybe,' Mirek conceded. 'But you weren't dressed like that.'

'No. I was dressed in the uniform of a Colonel in the Polish Tank Corps. We travelled on the same train to Warsaw . . . but I went first class!'

Again Mirek shook his head in wonderment.

The Bacon Priest's voice dropped several decibels to its normal tone.

'Come closer.'

Mirek edged down the bench and said, 'Hell, but you stink!'

The priest's teeth showed in a smile.

'Mirek Scibor, you should know that it's a major element in a good disguise. I mix the solution myself. People stay away from body odour and don't look at the source too closely. You will have to suffer while we talk.'

Mirek nodded. 'I will suffer. I suffered during a long journey to get here.'

'You did. I know why you needed to escape but why did you insist on seeing me?'

Mirek was looking at him curiously. He asked, 'Weren't you . . . aren't you worried that I might be a "black" planted into your organisation to compromise it? Even on this journey I have discovered a great deal.'

The priest smiled and shook his head. 'Neither the SB, nor even the KGB would sacrifice two of its top officers to effect a plant. Meanwhile you have come down only one of half a dozen pipelines and the least important. Besides I trust the judgment of Father Lason. He talked to you for several days. He reported that you have a great hatred and in particular for Yuri Andropov. Why do you hate him so?'

At the mention of Andropov's name Mirek's features hardened like concrete. The priest had to lean towards him to catch the quiet words. They were washed along on a tide of loathing.

'I discovered that he had done something to me so foul as to be beyond comparison.'

49

'He personally?'

'He gave the order.'

'And the people you killed carried it out?'

'Yes.'

'What was it?'

Mirek had been looking down at the gravel path. Now he lifted his head and looked at the playing children. He opened his mouth and closed it. Then he said, 'First I have something for you. Call it a present from me . . . in part payment for getting me out.' He turned and looked at the priest and again had to force himself to realise that he was not an old woman. 'Father, it's a list of renegade priests in Poland. Priests in your organisation who have been turned by the SB. It's in my head but it's a long list. You had better write it down.'

The priest's voice was sad. 'I too have a good memory . . . tell me.'

Looking into the priest's eyes, Mirek intoned, 'Starting from the north down. Gdynia: Fathers Letwok and Kowalski. Gdansk: Nowak and Jozwicki. Olsztyn: Panrowski, Mniszek and Bukowski . . .' He droned on while the priest sat mute with half-closed eyes. One hundred and twelve names later Mirek came to the end. There was a silence, then the priest sighed shudderingly and murmured, 'God have mercy on their souls.'

Curious, Mirek asked, 'Did you know about any of them?'

He nodded. 'Quite a few and we suspected others, but . . .' He murmured two names and shook his head in sorrow, then took a breath and said briskly, 'That information is invaluable, and it will save lives. Now, Mirek Scibor, I have something to offer you.' He stood up. 'Let's walk a little. That bench has become hard.'

They walked slowly down the path towards the lake, the priest adopting exactly the gait of an old woman.

He asked, 'What are your plans now?'

Mirek spread his hands. 'I don't know. My objective

was to meet and talk to you.' He smiled grimly. 'Do you have any ideas?'

The priest stopped and looked at the lake. It was mirror smooth. At one end white lilies were pancaked across the water. Three swans drifted close to the shore, vying for grace.

'I have no ideas,' the priest said. 'But I have a plan. You may be interested.'

'What plan?'

'To kill Yuri Andropov.'

Mirek laughed loudly. The swans took fright and the water rippled as they surged away. The priest said sharply, 'You laugh. I thought you hated the man.'

Mirek's laughter stopped and he looked at him curiously.

'I do. I would literally give an arm and a leg to kill Andropov. But I assumed you were joking . . . I mean you stand there and simply state that you have a plan to kill Andropov as though you were talking about a plan to go to the theatre.'

The priest turned and resumed hobbling along in his ridiculous shoes. He said, 'You may not have heard. A senior General of the KGB, Yevchenko, defected in Rome.'

Mirek nodded. 'I read some newspapers this morning. I know of Yevchenko. It must have made the KGB wet themselves.'

'Yes, well, he advised Italian Intelligence that Andropov and the KGB were planning another attempt on the life of our beloved Holy Father.'

'Ah.' Mirek nodded thoughtfully. The path was skirting the lake and to their right the swans kept pace with them.

Briefly the priest sketched out the plan and the reasons for it. In a dazed voice Mirek asked, 'And the Pope approves? It's hardly Christian.'

'The Pope knows nothing of it. The plan derives from . . . well, from a group within the Church.'

At this Mirek slightly smiled. 'Yes, I can imagine that such a group could be formed. Of course you are telling me this because you want me to be the envoy. The assassin.'

'Yes.'

A long silence broken only by the crunch of their feet on the gravel and the distant, muted roar of traffic. The priest spoke at length. Not in a tone of persuasion but conversationally. Mirek above all knew of the capabilities of his organisation. So a hundred or so of his people had defected. Sad, but a drop in the bucket. There were tens of thousands more. Specialists in every field. Secret priests in factories who had been given special dispensation to marry and have children to tighten their cover. Secret priests in Governments, in agriculture, universities, hospitals. Even within Secret Services. When a Soviet grain shortage loomed the Vatican knew about it before the CIA. When a power struggle shaped up within the Polish Politburo the Vatican knew even before the KGB. At this point Mirek stopped walking and held up a hand.

'I know. As you said: I know. I've spent eight years tracking and studying your organisation. I believe that you can put a man into the Kremlin. Especially as he won't be expected. But can you get him out . . . alive? Or is that not in your plan?'

'Indeed it is. Our best minds are working on it at this minute.'

Mirek's lips moved in an ironic smile. 'Jesuit minds, no doubt.'

'Some of them.'

'There were Jesuits on that list.'

'Two of them.'

They continued walking. Mirek asked, 'And what if I do it? What then? What happens to me afterwards?'

Without hesitation the Bacon Priest answered, 'A new life. A new name. Even a new continent. North or South America, or Australia. The Church would resettle you . . . and protect you.' He paused and then said, 'And, of course, pay you. Substantially.'

The Pole's lips twitched into an ironic smile. 'Imagine. The Catholic Church paying Mirek Scibor! Money is not important. The resettlement would be . . . that, and plastic surgery.' He took a breath, held out his hands palms upwards and said, 'I'll do it. You have your Papal atheist envoy. I'll take your message.' It was said simply, without a trace of drama.

The priest nodded. 'Good.'

Another silence while both men collected their thoughts. Mirek mused, 'I had a lot of training in the SB but not for this type of thing.'

Without stopping, Van Burgh pointed to the bench they had recently vacated. A man was sitting on it reading a newspaper.

'That man there, he's called Jan Heisl. When we've finished talking you will follow him. You will never see me again. He will give you papers, a passport . . . genuine . . . a whole identity. He will arrange for you to go to another country south of here . . . to a terrorist training camp in a desert. You will have strange bedfellows. Right wing, Left wing. Sometimes even from the same country.'

Astonished, Mirek asked, 'You can arrange that?'

'Certainly. Of course, they will think somebody else sent you. Heisl will arrange everything. They will teach you twenty ways to kill and to survive. Heisl will arrange money for you, and any equipment you might need.'

'Does he know what my mission is?'

The priest nodded solemnly. 'Yes. He is my right hand. He, and now you, are the only ones to know, the only ones who must ever know outside of *Nostra Trinita*.'

Mirek glanced at him.

'So you are only three?'

'It is enough . . . and safer.' He took Mirek's arm and they walked along like a down-at-heel mother and her son who has made good.

'Now tell me why you hate Andropov.'

4

Cardinal Angelo Mennini offered his hand and the nun knelt and kissed the ring. He made a sign with his eyes to his secretary. The secretary nodded and withdrew. As the nun rose the Cardinal graciously indicated a chair in front of his desk. Then with a rustle of his robes he moved around the desk and sat in a high-backed chair. For several moments he studied the face in front of him. The only sound in the room was the ticking of an ormolu clock on the wall. The nun was sitting erect with her hands folded in her lap. Her white habit and black headpiece were starched and immaculate. The Crucifix at her breast was highly polished and reflecting the light from the chandelier. Her head was held high but her eyes were modestly cast down.

'Sister Anna, look at me.'

She raised her eyes and stared straight at him. He wanted to see her eyes. The eyes are important in evaluating a person. He had been assured that this nun was extraordinary, but of course he wanted to see for himself. It had been a week since he had sent out the instruction to the very senior members of his Order in Europe. He was looking for a nun with certain characteristics and talents. She must be aged between twenty-eight and thirty-five. Be physically strong and not unattractive. She must be fluent in Czech, Polish and Russian. She must be practical and have a disciplined character. Above all she must be truly devout.

There had been a rapid feedback with several suggestions but the report on this one had been conclusive. It had come from Bishop Severin of Szeged in Hungary, a man whose judgment the Cardinal much respected. He reported that Sister Anna fitted the description exactly, except that she was only twenty-six years old. However he was sure that in all other aspects she more than compensated for that.

Indeed Mennini could see the strength in her face. It was an attractive face – very attractive. She was Polish and he guessed that there was Tartar blood there, for her cheekbones were very high, her eyes slightly slanted and her skin olive. She had a high forehead balanced by a wide, full mouth and the sweep of a symmetrical jaw. He looked at her arms and hands. The fingers were long and slender and he guessed that her figure would be similar. She was not at all embarrassed by his silent inspection. She gazed back at him, modest but composed. He questioned her for a few minutes and learned that she was an orphan who had been brought up by nuns in Zamose. She had been much influenced by her Mother Superior and from her earliest years had wanted to be nothing else but a nun. Recognising her intellect early, they had sent her to a school run by the Order in Austria. There she developed her linguistic talents, becoming fluent in Russian, English, Italian, German, Czech and Hungarian, as well as her native Polish. She also discovered a second vocation: teaching. After taking her final vows she had been sent to teach in a school run by the Order in Hungary. She was happy there, getting much joy from her work and also continuing her own studies and beginning to show a particular interest in Oriental languages. She hoped one day to be able to teach with the Order in Japan when she was fluent in that language.

She had a husky rasp to her voice. Not unattractive but curious, and a way of emphasising her words by lifting her chin slightly after completing a sentence. Within a few minutes the Cardinal was convinced that Bishop Severin's judgment had been correct and should be endorsed.

He marshalled his thoughts and then said slowly, 'Sister Anna, you have been selected for a mission which is of vital concern to our Church and the well-being of our beloved Holy Father.' He watched her face for a reaction but she stared back intent but impassive. 'Your life as a devout sister will have prepared you for some aspects of this mission . . . but not for others. You will need training. However, before going into further details there is something that you must see.'

He reached to his left and pulled a gold embossed leather folder in front of him. Slowly he opened it and looked at the single sheet of heavy cloth paper and the firm thick handwriting.

'I assume you read Latin.'

'Yes, Your Eminence.'

He turned the folder and pushed it towards her. She leaned forward. This time there was a reaction. Her eyes widened slightly as she saw, at the bottom of the paper, the red circle of wax and embossed into it the Papal seal. Her eyes moved up and her lips moved silently as she translated the Latin in her mind. 'To our beloved Sister Anna.'

By the time she was half way down the page her lips had stopped moving. They moved again as she read the signature: John Paul II.

She crossed herself and then looked up at the Cardinal. He thought her eyes were slightly glazed.

'Have you ever seen one of those before, Sister Anna?'

'No, Your Eminence.'

'But you understand it?'

'I think so, Your Eminence.'

He reached out and pulled the folder back to him, looked down at the paper for a moment and then firmly closed the folder. Musingly, as if to himself, he said, 'No, not many people ever get to see a Papal dispensation of that nature.' He pushed the folder to one side and looked up. 'In essence, Sister Anna, it gives you special dispensation to set aside your sacred vows during this mission.

You will of course be a nun always in your heart. Now I am going to tell you the very brief details of that mission. You may after that refuse it, if you wish.'

She glanced at the folder and in her husky voice said, 'I cannot refuse the wish of the Holy Father.'

He nodded in approval. 'Good. Now, what I have to say is, of course, a sacred secret. You understand that? A sacred secret now and for ever.'

He watched her nod solemnly and then in measured tones said, 'Sister Anna, your mission will be to travel and live with a man for several weeks . . . to travel and live with him as his wife.' He saw the shock in her eyes and her lips open to ask the immediate question. He held up a hand. 'No, Sister. As his wife only in appearance, although you will of course have to share accommodation with him and in public act towards him with wifely affection.' He could detect a measure of relief in her eyes. 'I must tell you that he is not a good man. In fact in some ways he is very evil. He is an atheist and in the past has been a terrible enemy of the Church. This now has changed. Although he remains an atheist this mission is to the good of the Church and to the good of our beloved Holy Father.' He paused and took a white lace handkerchief from the sash at his waist and dabbed at his thin lips. Then, with a sigh he went on. 'I must also tell you that this journey will take you through Eastern Europe to Moscow. Therefore it will be dangerous. Your mission ends in Moscow and you will then return to us here and to our eternal thanks . . . Now, are you willing to go?'

She replied immediately. 'Yes, Your Eminence . . . But what exactly is the mission?'

'Just that, my dear. Of course, you must help this man as much as possible. You are travelling with him so that the authorities will think you are man and wife. You will have papers proving it. In essence you are there to make his journey appear innocent.'

'And it is not?'

He inserted a slightly stern note into his voice. 'All you

need to know, Sister, is that it is to the good of our Church. You know that very often we have to act with great caution in the Soviet bloc.'

He watched her nod dutifully. Satisfied, he opened a drawer, took out an envelope and handed it to her. 'Tomorrow you report at eight a.m. to the Collegio Russico on Via Carlino Cattaneo, here in Rome. There you will meet a Father Van Burgh and place yourself under his obedience. He will tell you more. He is in charge of this mission. He will supervise your training over the coming days.'

He looked up at the clock and then rose. She did the same. He came around the desk and took her hands in his and said gently, 'It will be difficult, Sister Anna, sometimes embarrassing. But remember what I told you. In your heart you will always be a nun.'

She murmured, 'I will always remember it, Your Eminence. Please give me your blessing.'

He did so and she kissed his ring. As he led her to the door he smiled and said, 'Of course during this time you will have to revert to your birth name. It's Ania, isn't it?'

'Yes, Your Eminence. Ania Krol.'

He patted her on the shoulder. 'Ania; it's a nice name.'

No sooner had he closed the door than his phone rang. With a tired sigh he crossed the room and picked it up. His secretary informed him that the *soffrigenti* were here. He sighed again and told his secretary to wait ten minutes, then show them in. He settled himself in his chair and struggled to compose some words in his mind. His election as head of the one hundred thousand strong Order had taken place six months before and with it more work and problems than he could ever have imagined. Occasionally over the months he had received small delegations of what the Order called *soffrigenti*. These were priests who, in the course of their work around the globe, had suffered greatly. Some had been imprisoned for decades, others tortured, some maimed. There were also those who had spent lifetimes in solitary, obsessive study. It was the Order's policy that, when possible, such priests should come to Rome to receive the thanks of their leader and his blessing and inspiration. This was one such delegation, assembled from priests who worked and who had suffered in the Soviet bloc.

Mennini was very conscious that the words he spoke to them would always be remembered. Every single word must have profound significance. He must be for them a father and a mother and a rock on which to cement their own faith. Their final allegiance, of course, was to the Holy Father, but it was definitely channelled through him. He hated to repeat himself on such occasions and struggled to find words which would sound fresh and inspiring. It was difficult. His eyes were constantly drawn to the leather folder on his desk and its single content. He opened it and read again the sheet of paper. Marvelled at the perfection of the signature and seal. He had seen both many times. These contained not a trace of deviation. The Bacon Priest was truly a genius. That reflection was replaced by another. By its use and what lay beyond, he, Cardinal Angelo Mennini, was committing a cardinal sin. Was it a sign to test his real faith?

Much troubled, he opened a drawer and slid in the file. He turned the lock and slipped the key into a hidden pocket of his gown, hoping, in a way, to lock away the thoughts. He turned his mind again to formulating words but it was hopeless. He would have to rely on his visitors to give him inspiration.

They did. Seven old men filed into the room. The youngest was in his early sixties. The oldest over eighty. Mennini greeted them all by name as they kissed his ring. The oldest, Father Samostan from Yugoslavia, tried to kneel. Very gently Mennini lifted him up and enfolded him in his arms and then led him slowly to a comfortable chair. The others sat on two angled settees. They had already been given refreshments in the anteroom. The audience would last no more than ten or fifteen minutes.

Mennini studied them. Seven tips of the Order's tentacles. They were in the forefront of the Order's battle, but they did not look like warriors. Just seven bent, black-clad old men. There was Botyan from Hungary. Over forty years a secret priest, hunted and haunted by a solitary life; bald head, cadaverous face, eyes deep in their sockets. But what eyes! They were luminous in faith, honesty and determination.

Next to him sat Klasztor from Poland. Eighteen years in the Gulags. The Bacon Priest had somehow got him out five years before. He had refused to retire comfortably to the West but insisted on doing pastoral work in his native land. Dangerous pastoral work. Mennini knew the histories of all these men. Inevitably his attention was drawn to the bony figure sitting at the end of one of the settees. This man was Father Jan Panrowski, the youngest of the group. He did not appear the youngest. His frail body was twisted as if by terrible arthritis. His hair was stark white and down his right cheek ran four parallel pink scars half an inch apart. Mennini had met several of the others but not this priest. He knew that of all of them he had suffered perhaps the most. Also a Pole, he had been put into a concentration camp by the Nazis in 1941 because he gave food to the Resistance. He miraculously escaped and made his way East and again worked with the Resistance, but in the Russians' eyes he had been in the wrong group. When they rolled through towards Warsaw they shot most of his group. He again was spared, after a fashion. They sent him further East into Russia itself where, for seven years, he was made to work virtually as a slave. He combined this labour with a huge effort to give spiritual love and solace to his fellow slaves. With the death of Stalin he was one of the lucky few to be released and the Order managed to bring him out to Rome. However, like Klasztor, he had refused the comforts of a quiet secure life and in 1958 had gone as a secret priest to work in Czechoslovakia – the most virulent anti-Church state in the Soviet bloc. For two years he worked in an agricultural machinery factory in

Liberec and then he was caught one afternoon saying the Angelus. He had spent the next eighteen years in solitary confinement in the notorious Bakoy Prison in Kladno. Solitary confinement, except for the times when they had taken him to the torture rooms. They let him out in 1980. After six months in a Rome hospital and a further six months in a monastery near the Pope's summer residence in Castel Gandolfo, he had sought an audience with the then head of the Order and begged to be allowed to return to his birthplace in Poland, the city of Olsztyn. His mother and an aunt, both in their nineties, were still alive and he wished to care for them. The city also had an ancient seminary and he would like to teach. He was reluctantly allowed to go. That city was also on one of Van Burgh's pipelines out of Russia and occasionally he proved helpful. Several times travellers going the other way dropped off a slab of bacon.

He sat now like a bent sparrow, his eyes on his leader. Eyes that sent out a miasma of remembered pain.

Mennini looked at all their faces and into all their eyes. The phrases he had composed vanished into the sea of his compassion. He started to say, 'I am made humble before . . .'

Then he broke down. He did not lower his head. He sat there erect while the tears filled his eyes and rolled down his cheeks.

The tears had more eloquence than words. His visitors knew him to be an austere unemotional man. They looked at the tears and the humility in his wet eyes and they too wept in response. All except Father Panrowski. He put his arms around his bony shoulders and sank back deeper into the corner of the settee. He lowered his chin to his chest as though once more experiencing physical pain. All his tears had long since been shed.

The Cardinal recovered. Father Botyan offered him a handkerchief which he accepted with a wan smile. He dried his eyes and face and when he tried to hand it back the old priest merely smiled and shook his head. Mennini tucked it into his sash with a grateful gesture of acceptance. Then he completed his sentence.

'I am made humble before your suffering and your faith.'

He heard their murmurs of deprecation. Now the words came easily to him. In a strong voice he talked about the martyrs and saints of the Order and how their faith and devotion had changed history and the face and mind of the world. He talked to them as equals about his hopes for the future, both for the Order and for the Church as a whole. He invoked their prayers for the beloved Holy Father.

They said a short prayer together and then he gave them all his blessing. The audience over, they moved towards the door. He could tell by their faces that he had given what they had travelled far to receive. It struck him that he too had received from them the gifts of love and inspiration.

He watched as Father Panrowski shuffled his broken body across the thick carpet and suddenly he realised that there was yet another priceless gift he could give this old man, and in giving receive comfort himself. Quietly he asked him to remain behind for a few minutes.

When the door closed behind the others he took the priest by the arm and helped him to a well-cushioned, high-backed chair. As Panrowski settled into it, his face puzzled, the Cardinal said, 'Father, we have all been uplifted by your suffering and your faith. I would be deeply moved and honoured if you would hear my confession.'

At first the old priest did not seem to understand. He raised his head and asked, 'Confession?'

'Yes, Father, my confession.'

Father Panrowski was dazed. He had heard that such things occasionally happened. Even that the Holy Father sometimes asked this of a humble parish priest. He stammered, 'But Eminence . . . I am not . . . not worthy.'

'Father, there are none more worthy in our beloved Church.'

The Cardinal pulled up a low velvet-topped stool. He

sat on it next to, and below, the priest. He took his hands in his and bowed his head.

'Please, Father.'

Father Panrowski heard his own voice. A hoarse whisper.

'What do you remember?'

The Cardinal spoke, his voice low, humble but resonant.

'Father, forgive me, for I have sinned. I have let my temperament and my impatience dominate my pastoral mission. On occasions I have failed to understand the frailties and humanity of some who are around me and who would help me.'

The priest breathed more easily. This would be the confession of the natural infringements of a powerful personality whose intellect occasionally overshadowed his compassion.

So it took its course. He listened sympathetically and admonished gently. He assumed it was over but the Cardinal remained sitting, his head bent. Perhaps a minute or two passed. The Cardinal raised his head slightly. He was looking at his desk. The priest felt his hand squeezed; clasped tight by his leader. Mennini was breathing deeply. He lowered his head again and spoke in a whisper. Spoke of a thing far beyond any infringement. Queried painfully whether he was perpetrating an act of God or an act of survival and could the two be compatible? It was a plea from one who suffered a little to one who had suffered a lot.

The priest was rigid in mind and body. Many seconds passed, spaced out by the soft ticking of the ormolu clock. It was too much for this priest but he was the confessor and he had to find words. Words of comfort. Words of understanding. They were expected. Yearned for. He was as old as this man at his feet, but infinitely older in relating faith and truth to pain and reality. He lowered his head and said softly, 'My son, yes, my son, it is wrong to do wrong for what you think is right. But it is wrong to do nothing against evil. We sin because we are human and

Our Lord understands and judges . . . and you will be forgiven.'

He felt the pressure on his hands lighten. Slowly the Cardinal raised his head and crossed himself. Then he lifted the gold Crucifix from his waist and kissed the tiny, spreadeagled image.

They rose and he helped the priest across the room. Silently the priest lowered his head and kissed the Cardinal's ring. Then he straightened his bent body and looked him in the eyes. A look of understanding. He said, 'Eminence, I shall pray for you.'

'Thank you, Father. Have a safe journey. God be with you.'

As the heavy door closed Mennini raised a hand to his side and felt the outline of the key in its little secret pocket. He also felt comforted.

5

'You are too beautiful, much too beautiful!'

'I'm sorry, Father.'

The Bacon Priest laughed.

'Ah, I wonder if a woman ever said that before in all history.'

He pushed his bulk to his feet, moved out from behind his desk and slowly walked around her. Ania Krol stood very still, a troubled look on her face.

A middle-aged nun stood in a corner with a smile on her lips. She said, 'Sister Anna looks wonderful!'

Van Burgh rounded on her. 'Ania,' he said sternly. 'From this moment she is Ania! Her name will change at times but you and she must remember. Sister Anna is temporarily a non-person.'

'Yes, Father,' the nun said dutifully, but in no way abashed. 'But why is she too beautiful?'

He sighed. 'Because great beauty attracts attention. That's the last thing we want.'

He stood in front of Ania and studied her. She was dressed in a plain white blouse and dark blue pleated skirt and black polished high-heeled shoes. He shook his head.

'I sent to the East for authentic clothes and cosmetics designed by good party designers and made by the proletariat for the proletariat and you look like you stepped off the cover of a fashion magazine. Imagine what couturiers in Rome or Paris would do to you?'

'But what can I do, Father?' she asked.

He ignored the question and did one more circuit around her.

'It's the hair,' he said finally. 'It really is your crowning glory.'

Her hair was thick and long and so black it seemed to glow with ebony blue streaks. It swung like a dark bell to her shoulders.

'We shall have to dye it,' he stated emphatically.

'Oh no!' cried the nun in the corner. 'It would be a crime.'

'Silence,' he admonished. 'But first we shall cut it. I think a sort of page-boy style. We must not make you too plain. The man whose wife you are supposed to be is handsome . . . and I dare say appealing enough to women to have an attractive wife. But you cannot be as beautiful as you are.'

He was looking at her legs. They were neither slim nor sturdy, but they curved gracefully to slim ankles. The high heels accentuated the curve of her calves.

'The high heels have to go,' he announced. 'Flat, sensible shoes and a lower hemline.'

Ania hardly heard him. She was in mourning for her hair. Mentally it was her only feminine vanity. As a child the nuns had trimmed it, combed it, admired it and taught her to take care of it. At night before she slept and in the mornings before prayers she would always stroke her brush through it a hundred times, taking pleasure from its caress on her neck and shoulders; moving her head from side to side, letting it swing like a dark flower in a breeze. Then in the mornings she would tuck it up into her starched, austere headpiece, like a glittering piece of onyx wrapped and hidden in a pristine handkerchief.

'We shall make you a little garish,' Van Burgh said. 'It's the fashion now in the East.' He pointed to her fingers. 'Not colourless nail varnish but a slightly loud red and more rouge on your cheeks . . . and a darker lipstick more thickly applied. Also some bright metal bangles for your wrists and a cheap silver-plated chain round your neck, holding the letter "A".'

Yet again he circled her, obviously now seeing, in his inner eye, a different woman. He stopped again in front of her. 'And a few patent leather belts with shiny buckles just too big to be in good taste.' He looked again at her hair. 'We shall need two or three wigs of different style and colour . . . obviously with your skin colouring not blonde. Auburn, dark mousy, and so on. Ania, take your shoes off and walk across the room.'

She slipped off the shoes and walked back and forth in front of him. He sighed again.

'You walk like a nun.'

'I am a . . . How does a nun walk?'

'Like this.'

He held his head up, pulled back his shoulders, put his hands by his sides and, with short steps, walked across the room with an expression of great piety on his face. The two women laughed in surprise. In their eyes his brown cassock was suddenly a white habit. Van Burgh was a perfect mimic and could have made his fortune on the stage. He walked exactly like a modest, demure nun.

'So how should I walk?'

'Like this.'

His entire posture changed. Even before he took one step he was a young woman, aware of her looks and sensuality. His hands and arms moved differently. He patted an imaginary lock of hair into place and walked again. Now there was a swing to his stride. He glanced to left and right. His left elbow was cocked against his side as though carrying a handbag.

Again the two women laughed, but then Ania was thoughtful. She had seen the complete difference.

'But Father, I don't have your talent. How can I learn to walk like that?'

'I will teach you, Ania. Also you will spend time in the streets of Rome. Watch how other women walk, and talk to each other . . . and to men. Watch how they shop and use the telephone and carry bags. You must watch with a different eye than you have been used to. You will do that in the mornings. Every morning for the next week. You will go into coffee shops and ride on buses. You will walk the lobbies of big hotels and visit tourist attractions. Do you have any lay friends in Rome?'

Her hair swung as she shook her head. 'No, Father.'

He frowned. For all her common sense and intellect she must get used to the close proximity and the conversation of people outside the clergy.

'I will arrange some acquaintances for you: men and women. You will take coffee with them and lunches and, yes, sometimes drinks and dinner in the evening.'

'I don't drink, Father.'

'Of course not, Ania. Just soft drinks – and you will tell these people that you were a nun who has just renounced her vows.'

Her lips tightened. 'I certainly will not.'

He sighed. 'Ania, listen to me. In the coming days we will build up a convincing cover for you. But it will take time. You will have much to learn and remember. You will be doing that in the afternoons and evenings along with other things that will be necessary and useful. In the meantime you must get used to the world outside of a convent. So it is important that your temporary cover is that you renounced your vows.'

She said stubbornly, 'To say such a thing will make me physically sick!'

A glitter came into Van Burgh's eyes. He looked at the nun in the corner. 'Please wait outside, Sister.'

With a sympathetic glance at Ania she rustled away.

The priest moved behind the desk and sat down heavily. He pointed to a chair opposite him. She sat and arranged her skirt self-consciously over her knees.

He spoke rapidly. Short, blunt words. 'You have Papal dispensation to suspend your vows temporarily. But the Pope did not intend that you suspend obedience to your superiors.'

A silence. Then she lowered her eyes and said, 'I'm sorry, Father.'

His voice cracked at her. 'Don't be so demure! You are not a nun, Ania.'

Her head snapped up and he saw the steel in her. She looked him in the eye and said firmly, 'I'm sorry.'

'All right. So until you're rehearsed in your permanent cover you will tell anyone who asks that you were a nun who renounced her vows. Very recently.'

'Yes, Father.'

His tone softened just a little. 'The people I will have you introduced to will not ask. They will have been told that you are sensitive to the matter.'

'Thank you, Father.'

Again he studied her face for several minutes, assessing. Then he made up his mind. 'Ania, I know you have strength of character and a fine mind. But naturally your years of seclusion and piety have made you sensitive in certain areas. That sensitivity, unless concealed and controlled, could be dangerous to you and the man who is travelling with you and his entire mission. Now, if I feel that you cannot conceal or control that aspect then I will not send you. I will have to find someone else.'

She considered that and then nodded. Again he could see her inner strength. She said firmly, 'I understand that very well, Father. I will control it and conceal it.'

'I hope so.' He picked up an ivory paper knife and turned it in his fingers. 'Ania, you will have seen modern films in the convent but they will have been carefully selected by the Mother Superior. You will have read books – but again selected. Even what you listened to on the radio and saw on television.' He made a broad sweep with his arm. 'Out there it is different. Censorship is almost non-existent in the West. You will see and hear things which will make you wonder what has happened to civilisation.'

She said, 'Father, I have been cloistered all my life but I'm not unaware of trends in the Western world. You asked me if I had lay friends and my answer was no. My friends are, and always have been, women like myself. Sometimes, Father, I have regretted that because I am curious about the other world . . . but I have been studying continuously. I believed that my curiosity would be satisfied in the future. So I am grateful now for this opportunity.'

'Good.' He opened a file, studied it for a moment then, all business, said, 'Ania, you're a very accomplished linguist. Now tell me, what is the Russian word for "fuck"?'

He saw her recoil in her chair, her eyes wide in shock. Then the shock turned to anger at herself as she realised she had failed this first test. He stayed silent, letting the lesson sink in. She leaned forward and said, 'Father, I was schooled by the Order. They didn't teach us such things . . . but . . . I know the word for copulate.'

'Brilliant.' With a clatter he tossed the paper knife back on to the desk and gestured again with his arm. 'You tell someone out there to "copulate off" and they're going to get suspicious.' He leaned forward, made a note on the file and said, 'We are going to have to extend your vocabulary. That will be embarrassing for one of our linguists here . . . but then he doesn't have to control or conceal it.' He tapped the pen and looked at his watch. 'Do you have any questions, Ania?'

She nodded. 'Just one, Father. His Eminence, Cardinal Mennini, told me that this man I am to travel with . . . impersonating his wife . . . is an evil man. Will there be much danger for me on this journey?'

He spread his huge hands. 'Ania, any clandestine journey through Eastern Europe involves danger.'

'I meant from the man, Father.'

'Oh.' He hesitated. 'You mean physical?'

'I mean rape, Father.'

His brow furrowed. 'I think not . . . He will possibly – no, probably – try to seduce you. He is without morals as we know them . . . but rape, I think not.'

Diffidently she said, 'I'm not afraid. But would it not

be possible for me to take some sort of short course in self-defence . . . judo or something?'

Ruefully he shook his head. 'Ania, that man is already physically very powerful and well trained. About now he's starting a crash course that will make him totally lethal. In such an eventuality you will have to rely on your wit and intellect.'

She nodded soberly.

He said, 'Now you must go to the hairdresser.'

She rose and, as she turned to the door, he asked, 'What is the Russian word for shit?'

She answered immediately over her shoulder, '*Guwno*.' Then she strode across the room, hair and hips swinging. As her hand closed on the door knob he called, 'Ania.'

She turned. His expression was stern and a little sad. He nodded.

'Very good.'

6

The *SS Lydia* docked at Tripoli at dusk. Cypriot owned and crewed, she plied regularly in a triangle between Limassol, Trieste and Tripoli, carrying general cargo. Mirek had boarded her surreptitiously in Trieste in the middle of the night three days earlier. A short journey but he would be glad to get off. He had virtually been locked into a dirty cabin in the fo'c'sle and been left to his thoughts. The food had been foul and the air fetid. The only contact he had with the crew was when food was delivered.

His thoughts on the journey often encompassed the Bacon Priest. It was nothing short of astonishing that he should be able to arrange for Mirek, the would-be assassin of the head of Russia, to be trained in a terrorist camp in the Libyan desert. The same camp, Father Heisl had informed him with an ironic smile, where Ali Agca had been trained for his attempt on the life of the Pope. Heisl assured him that no one in authority at the camp would question him about his background. They had simply been told that he was a foreign recruit for a cell of the Red Brigade. His credentials were in order. This camp trained terrorists without discrimination. In the four days that passed between his meeting with Van Burgh in the Vienna park and his boarding the *SS Lydia* much had happened.

He had travelled from Vienna to Trieste by car with Father Heisl. The cleric drove like a heretic. When Mirek at one stage pointedly remarked that they had just touched 160 kph the priest grinned, pointed to the St Christopher medal stuck to the dashboard, and said: 'Have faith.' It was small solace to an atheist.

He snorted and said, 'Don't you know that Christopher has been desanctified?'

Heisl had grinned and shrugged and said, 'No matter. He's looked after me for many years.'

The priest had talked during the whole journey. First explaining what he would learn in the training camp. The kind of people who would instruct him. Mirek must pay attention and learn well. It was an expensive business. With transportation, plus instruction charges the Church would see little change from US$15,000. Mirek had been impressed and remarked that terror didn't come cheap. Heisl agreed and explained that it was only one of a dozen such camps spread through the Middle East. At any given time between twenty and thirty 'students' would be at each camp. Such camps had been and would be the nursery for European and Arab terror. Both Left and Right wing. The man who would arrange it all was the leader of a Red Brigade cell in Trieste. His cell specialised in transportation and training. Other cells handled weapons; fund-raising by bank robberies; kidnappings and killings for political purposes. This man believed that Father Heisl was the head of a cell of the German Red Army Faction. They had worked together once before and Father Heisl had paid well. When Mirek asked him for what he had paid well, he got a shrug and a look that told him to mind his own business.

Just before the Italian border the priest showed him his new passport. His name was Piotr Poniatowski. He had escaped to the West twelve years earlier and received French nationality seven years later. His birthplace was listed as Warsaw. The birth date was two years earlier than his own. As he leafed through the pages looking at the old stamps and visas Heisl had remarked, 'It's perfect. There was such a man. He was born in Warsaw on that date. He was killed in a car crash near Paris last year.'

'Were you driving?' Mirek asked.

The priest smiled. 'No. I never have accidents.'

They passed through the border post without incident and half an hour later were carrying their suitcases into a small house in a poor district near the docks. It was looked after by an old woman dressed all in black. Mirek assumed that she belonged to a lay religious order. She hardly said a word but cooked them an excellent lunch. Afterwards Mirek had a siesta while the priest went out on business.

They stayed in the house for three days. Mirek had wanted to go out and see something of the city. Maybe find a woman. He didn't tell Heisl that but even so the priest was adamantly opposed. This was a transit point for Mirek, both in and out. It was a good rule never to hang around in public in a transit point, especially one like Trieste which is a very international city and used by Intelligence Services both from the East and West. So while Heisl came and went Mirek kicked his heels watching television, reading magazines and eating too much pasta. During their conversations Heisl outlined some of the possible routes they would use to get him into Moscow. He was vague, saying that a choice would be made nearer the time. Mirek had tapped his French passport and asked, 'Why don't I just fly in on Air France, as a tourist or businessman?'

Heisl had shaken his head firmly.

'You may have to be in Moscow for quite a long time both before and after the event. A tourist or businessman is always monitored. There must be no record of your being in the city or in the country. But don't worry, it's our job to get you there and out again – and we will. Our best minds are working on it.'

On the third night Heisl brought back a small black canvas bag. He gave it to Mirek and told him to pack his toilet articles, underwear, handkerchiefs and a change of trousers and shirt. He should be ready to leave at midnight. At ten minutes to that hour he went to Mirek's room and collected the rest of Mirek's clothes.

'Where's your passport?'

74

Mirek pointed at the canvas bag.

'Give it to me. You won't be needing it.'

Mirek opened the bag and passed it over. The priest tucked it into an inside pocket, brushed past Mirek and rifled through the bag.

'There's nothing in here except clothes and your toilet bag?'

'Nothing.'

Satisfied, the priest zipped it up and said, 'There's a flask of hot coffee in the kitchen. Take it with you. It's going to be a long night.'

They left just after midnight. This time Heisl drove his Renault slowly, constantly checking the rearview mirror.

'It's the greatest time of danger,' he had remarked, 'when you are making contact with another group whose security may have been penetrated. The Italian counter-terrorist people have become very expert. Sometimes they penetrate these cells and just lie low hoping they'll lead them on to something else.'

Mirek knew the technique well, having used it himself many times.

'And what,' he asked, 'happens if we're caught making contact?'

'It would be very embarrassing,' the priest conceded. 'By the way, from now on until I see you again in a month your name is Werner. Just that. You are to answer to no other.'

'And my nationality?'

'You have none. You are simply a member of the terrorist international.'

They had made a wide circle through the city and finally came back into the dock area. The priest checked his watch and pulled into a narrow street between huge warehouses. Most of the street lights were not working and long dark shadows made patterns on the high walls. Heisl eased the Renault to a stop and turned off the lights. He left the engine running. It was the only sound for five minutes then, up ahead, there was a rattle as a warehouse door slid open a few feet. A shadowy figure appeared. After a moment two pinpoints of light came from it. The priest leaned forward and flicked the car's lights on and off twice in reply. Then he reached into the glove compartment and handed Mirek a thick brown envelope.

'Give him this. I'll see you right here on your return. Good luck.'

They shook hands. Mirek reached for his bag and opened the door. Without looking back he walked quickly to the warehouse. As he reached it he heard the priest's car accelerating away. The man waiting for him was young, in his early twenties. He had the earnest look of a keen student. He asked, 'Werner?'

Mirek nodded and was ushered inside. The warehouse was stacked with wooden cases. Three large ones were loaded on to the low trailer of a truck. Two older men in overalls were standing by it.

'You have something for me?'

The young man had an educated voice; even cultured. Mirek handed him the envelope. He immediately slit it open with a thumbnail and extracted a wad of notes. Mirek noticed they were hundred dollar bills. They were quickly counted. Then the young man nodded in satisfaction, walked over to the two men and gave them several each. He turned to Mirek.

'Come and I'll explain.'

They walked to the trailer. One of the wooden cases had one side lowered. On the outside arrows were stencilled pointing upwards, together with the shape of a wine glass and the word 'fragile'. Mirek peered inside. It had been lined with foam rubber padding. A plastic chair had been fixed to the bottom. Next to it a deep enamel bowl had been nailed down. The young man gestured.

'You make the first part of the journey in there. You leave in ten minutes. It will be fifteen minutes to the Customs check. Anything up to an hour there. Then it could be two or three hours before the crate is loaded by a derrick. If it swings a lot you can brace your arms and legs against the sides. The ship should sail at six this morning but there are often delays.' He pointed. 'There are plenty of air holes and the ventilation is adequate. They will let you out as soon as the ship clears the coast.' He pointed at the enamel bowl. 'You can piss or be sick in there. Did you bring something to drink?'

Mirek nodded. 'Has anyone been caught going this way?'

'So far no. Some very brave men have been in that crate. Are you ready?'

'Sure.' Mirek tossed his bag in, then pulled himself up. The chair was quite comfortable. He could almost sit upright. He put his palms against each side. He could support himself well.

The young man said, 'The worst thing is the darkness. Don't try to light a match or anything; the padding is very inflammable. You don't suffer from claustrophobia?'

He shook his head. He had been tested for that when he joined the SB.

'OK then.' The young man gestured at the other two and they moved forward with hammers and nails. To Mirek he said, 'Have a useful journey, Comrade.'

Mirek had nodded and then it was dark and the hammer blows were echoing around his head.

The ship was delayed and it was twelve hours before he felt the vibrations of the engines and another three before they prised open the crate and let daylight and fresh air into it. Up until then his mind had roamed over the obvious possibilities. Had there been a mix-up and they didn't know he was in the crate? Had they got the crate number wrong? Total darkness gives a great boost to the imagination. Mirek had used the technique himself for interrogation. Only now did he appreciate its true effectiveness.

There were two of them. Cheerful, tow-headed Cypriots. He was so cramped that they had to help him out and on to the deck. Straightening his legs was agony. The crate had been deck cargo. He looked around him in the watery

77

sunlight. The ship was rolling slowly on an oily swell. In the distance he could see the smudge of a coastline. One of the Cypriots pointed. 'Yugoslavia.'

He walked a few painful steps. He would have liked to walk around the deck a few times to loosen up but the crewmen wouldn't hear of it. One of them collected his bag and they helped him to the fo'c'sle: first to a toilet and then to the cabin.

Now he peered through the single small porthole at the docks of Tripoli. They looked drab. For something to do, he repacked his bag. An hour passed while he fought against the impatience every sea traveller has while waiting to disembark. Finally there was a tap on the door. It opened to reveal a middle-aged Arab in army fatigues. There were no rank badges or insignia. 'Werner?'

Mirek nodded.

The Arab pointed and asked in English: 'That is your bag?'

'Yes.'

'Take everything out of it.'

Mirek unpacked and laid everything on the bunk. The Arab conducted a search as thorough as Mirek had ever seen. He felt the seams of all the clothing, checked buttons and collars, carefully examined the soles of the shoes and every item in the toilet bag. Then he went over the bag itself. Then he checked the clothes and shoes that Mirek was wearing and gave him a thorough body search. Finally satisfied, the Arab told him to pack his bag and follow him. There were members of the crew working on deck but they studiously ignored Mirek and the Arab.

An army truck was waiting at the foot of the gangway. There was a driver in the cab, also wearing unmarked fatigues. The Arab led Mirek to the back of the truck, opened the canvas flap and gestured. Mirek dumped his bag in and climbed after it. As he sat down the canvas flaps were laced tightly shut from the outside.

The journey lasted two hours. The first hour was on a

smooth road, then the truck made a left turn on to what was obviously a dirt road. It slowed down by about half and lurched and bumped along so that Mirek had to hold on tightly. His backside was getting sore when they finally came to a stop. He heard voices in Arabic and then the flap was opened and he jumped down.

His first impression was that he was in a concentration camp. The truck had pulled into a compound surrounded by high wire fences topped by floodlights. Their glare lit the place like the noonday sun. To his right was a long, modern concrete building. To the left, three rows of wooden prefab huts that looked as if they had been there a very long time.

The Arab motioned and led him to a door in the concrete building. He opened it, put his head through, said something in Arabic and then ushered Mirek in and closed the door behind him.

It was a Spartan office. There was one desk, a chair behind it and a chair in front. A tall, wide man was sitting in the chair behind. He had blond, crewcut hair above a face that had travelled long and sometimes painfully. He was in his late forties. Next to him on a small low table was a radio set. He was dressed in faded army fatigues, again without insignia. He was reading a slip of paper. Without looking up he said in American-accented German:

'This says you are fluent in German. You're to get the Grade "A" course and Grade "A" accommodation.' He looked up with a grin. It didn't reach the slate-blue eyes. 'That means you get a room to yourself and a lot of personal instruction.'

He pushed himself to his feet and held out his hand. 'Werner, I'm Frank. I should say that I hope you'll enjoy yourself here, but I know you won't.'

They shook hands. Mirek winced from the pressure and tried to apply it back. It was like gripping a piece of mahogany.

'Have you had dinner?'

Mirek shook his head. Frank looked at his watch and gestured at the vacant chair.

'OK, sit down. We'll just go through a couple of formalities and then go over to the canteen. Have you had a long journey?'

'Very long,' Mirek answered, sitting down. 'You might say months, and none of it comfortable, especially the last few days.'

Frank arranged his features into an expression that sought to convey sympathy. He chuckled and said, 'Well, this isn't the Hilton but like I said you're on the Grade "A" course. Your people must be loaded. The food is good. I saw to that myself when I arrived last year. You just can't train people on lousy food. Now to business.' A hard tone crept into his voice. 'This is not a political or ideological camp so there are no lectures of that nature. Nor is there any discussion. None, you understand? Discussion is taboo.' He was looking hard at Mirek, who nodded firmly.

'Second: no personal questions. Right now there are twenty-five trainees here. From all over. Like you, they've been given a single name. That's all to be known about them. In a set-up like this we have to guard against infiltration. Our lives depend on that. It's been tried twice since I've been here. So anyone asking personal questions gets punished . . . and Werner, the only punishment here is death . . . understand?'

'Is that what happened to them?'

Frank's lips grinned again. 'Yes, eventually. One was French – SDECE. The other German – BND. We did you people a favour . . . You're gonna be here thirty days. It's not long though it will seem at times like thirty years. There'll be no days off. When you enter here you enter our discipline. You do what the instructors tell you. Every tiny thing they tell you. You will leave here a highly trained assassin or you won't leave at all. Got it?'

'Got it!'

*

Mirek was fit from a lifetime of habit and discipline. The SB had trained him to shoot accurately with a rifle and hand gun. They had trained him in unarmed combat.

After two days in what was called camp 'Ibn Awad' he felt nothing but a novice.

The fitness instructor was a woman. An Arab terrorist called Leila; named, he assumed, after her illustrious predecessor. She had a severe, attractive face and a lithe body. At their first meeting she asked him how fit he was and he replied with masculine pride, 'Very.' An hour later his pride was shattered. She did every exercise with him. At the end, while he lay with his cheek against the hot sand gasping for breath, she had only a faint sheen of sweat on her upper lip.

'You will be fit,' she said. 'In thirty days you will.'

The firearms instructor was a small saturnine Portuguese in his fifties. His first question was: 'Can you shoot straight?'

'Yes, I've been trained.'

'At still targets?'

'Yes.'

'Then forget every single thing you've learned.'

The camp boasted a very sophisticated animated range. Painted metal figures rose and sank, moved left and right and sped forward and back. They were painted to resemble Israeli soldiers, male and female, their faces hideous caricatures of Jewish features. The Portuguese gave Mirek a Heckler & Koch VP70. 'There are twelve rounds in the magazine. You get a point for every hit.'

Mirek got one point. He couldn't believe it. The instructor was sanguine. He picked up half a dozen stones, walked away a few paces, turned and said sharply, 'Catch.' One by one he rapidly tossed the stones towards Mirek. To his left, to his right, high and low. Mirek caught them all. The Portuguese walked back, stood squarely in front of him and held out his hands, palms up.

'Put your hands on my hands.'

Mirek did so. The instructor's hands were small, the fingers dry. The tip of one little finger was missing.

'You may have played this game as a boy. I try to slap the top of one or both of your hands. The moment I move, you pull your hands away.'

Mirek had played it as a boy – and been good. They took turns at it. After ten minutes the tops of Mirek's hands were red and stinging. He had only laid half a finger on the Portuguese.

Without a word the little instructor picked up a stick and drew the letter 'S' about forty feet long on the sand. He pointed.

'I want you to walk down that line rapidly. Try to keep both feet on it.'

Mirek asked, 'What's this got to do with shooting?'

'Everything. Do it.'

He did quite well.

'Now back. This time at a trot.'

Again he did well. The instructor drew a very straight line about fifty feet long.

'Stand at the end.'

Mirek stood at the end.

'Look at that line closely. Then close your eyes and walk down it slowly.'

Mirek did so. He walked until the instructor called, 'OK.' He turned and looked back. He had strayed very slightly to the left. He looked at the instructor. He was nodding in satisfaction.

'Werner, you have co-ordination, timing and balance. I will teach you how to combine that so you are able to shoot a man at ten yards, a hundred yards or a thousand yards. Shoot him and kill him.'

Frank was the instructor for unarmed combat and knife fighting. The camp had a well-equipped gym. They stood facing each other across a broad mat.

'What do you know about this sort of thing?'

'I've done a little judo and some karate.'

Frank grinned. 'Forget all that crap. That stuff is for ego and exhibitions. I'm going to teach you how to kill or maim a man in half a second. To maim is easy: eyes, throat or testicles. To kill is a bit more complicated but Cavalho tells me you're fast and well balanced so you'll learn. Hold out your hands.'

Mirek raised his arms.

'Spread your fingers.'

Mirek spread his fingers.

Slowly Frank touched each of them in turn and counted to ten.

'Those are your ten primary weapons.' He pointed at Mirek's feet. 'Those are your two secondary weapons.'

'What about the outer edges of my hands?' asked Mirek.

Frank shook his head in disgust. 'I told you to forget that karate crap. Look.' He moved closer and grasped Mirek's right wrist and extended his arm. He ran a finger down the arm to a point opposite the palm and bent the elbow slightly. 'The karate chop. In your case the point of impact is about two feet from your shoulder.' He pulled the arm straight and stiff. 'Now the tips of your fingers are about nine inches further forward. It's like boxing. The longer you reach, the better. I'll tell you a fact, Werner. No black belt karate would have ever laid a finger on Mohammed Ali.'

He took Mirek over to a long table. On it was a row of small buckets filled with coarse sand. Next to them was a row of springed finger exercisers. Frank pulled a bucket towards him, stiffened the fingers of both hands and plunged them one after the other deep into the sand. He did it rhythmically for about a minute and said, 'Take one to your room. Do this for half an hour in the mornings and at night.'

He shook the sand from his hands and pointed at the exercisers. 'They're different strengths. Choose one that you can just squeeze closed. Do the same thing with that. Every few days move up to a more powerful spring.'

He took both of Mirek's hands in his and studied them.

Then he raised his head, looked him in the eyes and said with emphasis, 'They're good fingers. Do what I tell you and in a month you'll have ten good weapons.'

He dropped the hands and pointed to Mirek's shoes. 'On a mission, in fact all the time, wear hard shoes. Preferably with steel inside the toe caps. Buy ordinary shoes a size too large and give them to a cobbler. He'll put the steel in.'

They moved on to knives. There was a selection on the table. Hunting knives, flick knives, spring knives, a Bowie knife, ordinary kitchen knives and, next to them, a stubby felt-tipped marker pen. Frank gestured at them with a disdainful sweep of a hand. 'If you're in a situation where it's dangerous to carry a concealed hand gun then it's equally dangerous to carry an obvious weapon, including these. This, though, is different.'

He picked up the marker pen, uncapped it and drew a broad blue line on the table top. 'Innocuous, no?' Suddenly he turned. Mirek heard a click and jumped back at the sharp pinpoint of pain on his chest. He looked down. There was a splodge of blue ink on his fatigues. Frank laughed and held up the pen. It still had its felt tip but now it was at the end of a thin tube of tapering metal. He up-ended it on the table and pressed. The metal slid back into the casing. He drew another blue line. Once again the marker pen was just that.

Frank gave Mirek that smile again. 'Light-weight alloy with a titanium tip. Sharper than a needle.' He hefted it in his hand. 'Weighs only a few grammes more than a normal pen.' He showed Mirek the brand name: 'Denbi'. 'You press the "D" . . . so.' The blade slid out like a snake's tongue. 'If I'd wished it you'd be dead now.' He took his arm and led him over to a plastic dummy of a well-built man. The plastic was transparent. Mirek could see all the organs inside brightly coloured. The dummy was on a stand. Frank turned it slowly, saying, 'There is not one vital spot in a human body that is more than four inches from the skin. That blade is four inches long. You will learn where to put it and how. With that in your hand you carry death within three seconds.'

The explosives instructor was a Japanese called Kato. Mirek had been led to believe that Japanese were polite people. Kato was not. He confronted Mirek outside a thick concrete bunker. A short, stocky man of indeterminate age. His face was square and his lips downturned in a permanent sneer. One arm was stiff with a black glove on the hand. Kato held it up.

'I lost this because somebody fucked up. Not me. A fucking fool.' He gestured with it at the bunker and then at a thick high wall fifty yards away. 'Here it is not only theory. Here we make things to blow things up. Buildings, cars . . . and people. It is fucking dangerous, Werner. If you make a mistake here you are dead. I don't give a fuck about you dead or alive, but your mistake can also blow me up . . .'

Mirek nodded soberly. Kato snorted. 'You think you understand but you don't. When you're holding a rocker bomb in your hands, trying to place it . . . then you'll understand. You'll understand with the sweat in your eyes and your balls cringing into your fucking belly.' He smiled evilly and pointed to the thick high wall. 'But you'll be doing that on your own behind there and I'll be here waiting with a bucket and spade in case the explosion is premature.'

Coldly Mirek said, 'I'm sure with such a good instructor such an event won't happen.'

Kato's sneer deepened and he turned to the bunker saying, 'I've lost two in this camp. Such things usually go in threes.'

The bunker was air conditioned and dehumidified. One part of it was sealed off with steel doors. To one side were half a dozen wooden chairs facing a blackboard. The other side, screened off by a glass partition, was a fully equipped laboratory. Kato gestured at the blackboard.

'Here you learn the theory. Here you learn how to make the bombs; rocker bombs, radio-controlled bombs, body bombs, land mines, sea mines, door mines, limpet mines . . .' The evil grin again. 'I could even teach you how to make nuclear bombs . . . but I won't. I'm Japanese. The Emperor would not like it.'

Mirek could not tell whether he was being serious or ironic.

Kato gestured at the lab. 'There you do the practical. You learn how to make a bomb with ingredients you can buy in any chemist shop. You learn to make a bomb as small as your finger or big enough to blow up a city block.' He tapped Mirek gently on the arm. 'You will also learn to make a bomb which you can swallow and carry in your body into any place and destroy anyone.' He sighed sadly. 'But I assume you are not a Muslim anxious for instant and eternal paradise.'

Mirek shook his head.

'Not even by accident.'

He did not settle into a routine. He was hammered into it. The camp arose an hour before dawn. Everyone without exception. For half an hour Mirek did his finger exercises, then washed and shaved. Frank was strangely insistent on that. Either you had a beard or you shaved every day. Clean fatigues were worn every day. There was no precision drill as such, but Frank liked things done in an orderly way. Just before dawn the trainees gathered in the canteen and drank tea or coffee or tinned fruit juice. At dawn they were in the compound doing exercises. Everyone did them, trainees and instructors alike, led by Leila. These varied, but after about forty-five minutes always ended with press-ups. Each trainee had to go on until he could not do a single one more. When the last trainee was flat on his stomach, body heaving and face twisted in agony, the instructors would continue and do a brisk ten more. Mirek vowed on the third morning that by the time he left he'd outlast them all. Even Leila.

After exercises came the 'run'. Again, everybody in the camp did it. On alternate days it was either four miles carrying a twenty-kilo pack, or eight miles carrying nothing. Leila always brought up the rear, driving the slower runners, but inevitably, as they approached the camp, she would lengthen her stride and cruise past everyone to be first through the gates.

After that, half an hour was allowed for breakfast. This was buffet-style and good. Mounds of fresh baked bread, plates of cheeses and cold meats, eggs and even steaks. There was no bacon or ham.

After breakfast the trainees split up into groups. Obviously some were specialising in certain aspects of terror and spent more time on that aspect. Mirek was getting a general training. About half of his instruction was in groups and the other half individual. The lunch break was two hours to avoid the full heat of the sun. Lunch was a light affair. Usually a soup followed by cold meats and salad. After lunch some of the trainees slept. Others sat around in the mess chatting or reading from the selection of books available – mostly thrillers, westerns or science fiction. There were no political books on the shelves. There was also a television and video. This was only used in the evening. The selection of videos paralleled the books. On his first night in the camp Mirek had been fascinated by the contrast of two dozen diverse terrorists engrossed by *Gone With the Wind*.

After lunch, four more hours of instruction. Then a shower, a change of fatigues and dinner. This was a lavish spread. Soup, a selection of pastas, Arab dishes, joints of beef and mutton and goat and fruit. Only water or fruit juices were drunk.

After dinner many of the trainees went straight to bed. The schedule was punishing. Others watched the video or read or chatted. Inevitably, in spite of the dire warnings against asking personal questions, they learned something about each other. No one actually asked questions but information was gleaned. Any group of young people

87

living, learning and exercising together communicates. Within a week Mirek knew where the others had come from. There were two small groups of Spaniards: one Left-wing Basque Separatist; the other Francoite Fascists. There were two Italians from the Red Brigade and three from the Blacks. The group of five Germans which included two girls were more cohesive; all from a modern off-shoot of the Baader Meinhof vine. Two Filipino women, one very pretty, and one man, presumably from the Muslim Rebels. There was a solitary Irishman, a mournful man who sat by himself humming strange tunes. The rest were Arabs, mainly from the Lebanon. Four were Shi'ites of the Islamic Jihad group. They were the only ones who regularly unrolled their prayer mats and prayed to Mecca. They kept apart and had strange, set expressions on their faces. Mirek guessed that they would be the ones to swallow the body bombs and blast themselves and others to paradise and elsewhere.

On the tenth morning he did a hundred and fifty press-ups. The other trainees had given up long before. As he lay panting he sneaked a look at the instructors. Only two were still going. Frank and Leila. Frank was struggling. Leila was pumping her slim body up and down easily. Her dark eyes were watching him.

That night after dinner he was sitting naked on the bed in his room squeezing the hand exercisers. The door opened. It had no lock or bolt. Leila stood there. She silently looked at his body, then closed the door. He started to put aside the exercisers. She said, 'Finish.'

He continued squeezing. She slowly undressed. She did it without obvious provocation but the combination of the masculine army fatigues being slowly discarded to reveal the lithe, dark, shapely body was intensely erotic. She dropped the shirt. High, pointed breasts with large aureoles and small nipples, a deeply recessed navel and narrow waist. He pumped the exercisers and felt his erection rising. She unzipped the mottled trousers, dropped them and stepped out. Her panties were brief and black. She slid them down sleek muscled legs. The triangle of pubic hair was as black as the panties. Now his erection was almost a pain. She slowly moved forward, raised her hands and cupped her breasts.

'Squeeze these – hard.'

He dropped the exercisers and made to stand but she put a hand on his shoulder. He lifted his arms, moulded her breasts with his hands and squeezed. They were soft but firm. Her expression never changed. He squeezed harder, very hard. Her lips opened slightly, a pink tongue slid along between them. He pulled her forward by her breasts. She pushed him flat. That was the end of the foreplay. She slid a leg over him, grasped his erection and forced it into her. He held on to her breasts as she rode him, then pulled her down and tried to kiss her. She turned her face and he nuzzled her ear instead. It could not last long. He felt it building and tried to contain it but failed. His back arched involuntarily and he gasped with relief as he spurted into her.

Her face showed her disappointment. She sat back on him panting slightly. He could feel the muscles inside her still moving, trying to squeeze pleasure from his shrinking penis.

He muttered, 'It's been a long time for me . . . months.'

She shrugged and pushed herself up and off him. By the bed was a metal washbasin on a stand and a towel. She took the towel and wiped herself between the legs, then bent to pick up her clothes.

'Wait.'

She turned. He was sitting upright on the bed.

'Wait a few minutes. It will be all right.'

Sceptically she looked at his flaccid penis. He patted the bed beside him. With a shrug she dropped her clothes and sat down. They sat in silence for several minutes. He put an arm round her shoulder. Her flesh was unresponsive. It was as though she was waiting for a dental appointment.

With his other hand he reached for hers and placed it on his penis. She moved her fingers and it stirred.

He muttered, 'Kiss it. Take it in your mouth.'

Emphatically she shook her head. But her fingers moved faster and gradually it grew. She tried to push him back on to the bed but he resisted. Instead he twisted her by the shoulders, forcing her on to her back. This time he would be on top.

This time it was fine. He fitted himself into her and slid in and out rhythmically, coming down hard each time. For the first few minutes she was still; but then she started to arch up to meet him. Minutes later she locked her ankles behind his legs and began making short, urgent grunts as they slapped together. Her mouth opened and he lowered his head. Her arms came round him tight as their mouths met. She sucked at him and then thrust her tongue at his throat, gnawed with her teeth at his lips, tried to crush his ribs into hers. They rose towards it in a long, steady climb. He increased the pace. Her grunts got louder, her hot breath gusting into his mouth, then she pulled her face away, moaned loudly, clamped her mouth on to his shoulder and shuddered into her orgasm.

He climaxed in a mixture of pain and passion. When he pulled away from her blood dripped from his shoulder on to her breasts. She raised her finger and touched the teeth marks gently. For a moment he thought he saw compassion in her eyes, then it was gone.

Minutes later she, too, was gone. Again she wiped herself with the towel and rapidly dressed without looking at him. At the door his voice had stopped her.

'Next time you will kiss it . . . and take it in your mouth.'

She had given him a long, level stare, then opened the door and left.

A half hour before dawn his door opened again. He was standing in his shorts exercising his fingers in the bucket of sand. He thought it must be her, but it was Frank. He was holding a piece of paper and he watched with approval as Mirek plunged his hands deep into the sand, then he noticed the bite mark on his shoulder.

'Aha! I see Leila's been giving you a little extra PT,' he leered. 'She's OK that one, but a little too straightforward for my taste. You ought to try that little Filipino girl; now she knows all the tricks.'

Mirek ignored him and kept on with his exercise. Frank held out the piece of paper.

'Signal for you.'

'Who from?'

'Obviously your people.'

Mirek shook the sand off his hands and took the paper. On it was written in longhand: 'Werner, do not cut your hair. Grow a moustache.'

Frank saw his look of puzzlement. He said, 'It must be in code. You don't know what it means?'

Mirek shook his head. 'I was given no code; expected no messages.'

Frank grinned. 'They must think this is a bloody barber's shop.'

That morning Mirek did two hundred press-ups. Only Leila was still going when he finished.

For the next two nights he waited for her. She did not come. On the third night at dinner he noticed the pretty Filipino girl watching him. He indulged in a little eye contact and body language.

She came to his room an hour after dinner. She was, he supposed, a nymphomaniac and Frank was right, she did know all the tricks. At one stage he sat on the bed while she knelt and fellated him. Looking down at her bobbing head and lustrous black hair he wondered how she could ever kill anyone. Just then the door quietly opened. He looked up to see Leila standing there. The Filipino girl tried to pull away but he held her head firmly, gazing steadily at Leila. She turned and went out, closing the door behind her.

*

The next morning he passed two hundred and fifty press-ups. He looked up. Leila was spreadeagled on the sand, her arms stretched out on either side as though crucified.

7

Archbishop Versano popped another piece of *osso buco* into his mouth and murmured with approval. After swallowing he said, 'The chef here is touched by God. No one makes it better.'

The Bacon Priest and Cardinal Mennini agreed. It was the second meeting of *Nostra Trinita* in the L'Eau Vive, and Van Burgh had much progress to report. Mennini was very gratified when he announced, 'Eminence, your choice of the nun Anna was perfect. She is intelligent, composed and devout.'

Mennini inclined his head graciously.

'And how is she doing in her training?'

'Excellently. She has a natural acting talent. Having been in cloisters since infancy she is obviously sensitive about certain aspects of modern life. However I am exposing her to some such aspects and she is adapting well.' He glanced at his watch and smiled. 'Right now she's doing aerobics.'

The other two looked at him blankly.

'It's a new sort of dance exercise. I want her to be fit. One of the lay girls she was introduced to is a dancer. Afterwards they'll have dinner. Then on to Jackie "O".'

Again he got blank looks and laughed.

'That's Rome's most sophisticated disco.'

The Cardinal looked a little troubled. 'Is that really necessary, Father?'

Van Burgh nodded emphatically. 'Yes, Your Eminence. It is very necessary to broaden her horizons . . . after all they have discos in the East and are conversant with the latest Western pop music . . . so must she be. *La Cantante* must know the songs.' He injected a placating tone into his voice. 'Don't worry, Your Eminence. Her faith is strong enough to protect her mind from such influences. Also the people she is with are sensible and respectful.'

'What about the man?' Versano asked. 'Tell us about him.'

The Bacon Priest thought for a few moments, then said, 'Had we searched for years for our envoy we would never have found one better. His background gives him expertise in certain vital areas. In other areas he is being trained now. He will have the skills, the equipment, the back-up and, of course, he has the motive.'

'Which is?' Versano asked. 'He told you?'

Both he and the Cardinal were watching Van Burgh with curiosity. The Bacon Priest was looking down at the fine damask tablecloth. He nodded sombrely.

'Yes, the motive is pure hatred centred on the person of Yuri Andropov. The reason for that hatred was an act perpetrated by Andropov some years ago. An act so base and vile that I should have never believed it possible . . . but I do believe.' He looked up. They were watching him expectantly. He sighed. 'But before he told me I had to swear on the Blessed Virgin that I would never, ever, tell anyone.'

They could not keep the disappointment from their eyes. On seeing it he said softly, 'He told me only to convince me of his total determination . . . I can tell you this: after hearing the story any qualms I had about our causing the death of Andropov were completely dispelled.'

They were somewhat mollified by his words. He quickly changed the subject. To Versano he said, 'Mario, I have done a costing on the operation. It is going to be expensive; certainly far too much for the resources of my Iron Curtain Church Relief Fund.'

'How much?' Versano asked cheerfully, happy to be back on familiar, fiscal ground.

'In American dollars, about three hundred thousand.'

Mennini gasped in shock.

'But how . . . ?'

Van Burgh held up a hand.

'Your Eminence. That is cheap compared with what the CIA or KGB would spend on such an operation . . . Just a fraction of what they would spend.' Mennini was looking sceptical. He was in no way naive about Vatican finances but his natural asceticism gave him qualms.

Feeling a little irritated the Bacon Priest explained. 'First we have to train the "envoy". That training, for example, will cost fifteen thousand. Then we have to set up a completely new pipeline through to Moscow. I cannot – will not – use any of our existing routes.'

He broke off as the door opened and two serving girls came in. One was pushing a trolley which was laden with fruit and a cheese board. The other quickly cleared the dirty plates, laid clean ones, put the fruit and cheese in the centre of the table and asked, 'Three *espressos*?'

'Later,' Versano said, smiling at her. 'In about half an hour.'

As soon as the door closed Van Burgh turned to the Cardinal and went on, almost aggressively, 'Your Eminence, I want you to understand what that entails. Several dozen people have to be positioned or repositioned. Certain properties have to be rented or even purchased. Transport certainly has to be purchased – and in the East that's difficult and expensive. A safe house must be established in Moscow itself. Couriers must come and go. Some bribes may have to be paid . . . I assure you not a cent will be overspent.'

Immediately Mennini interjected.

'Of course not, Father. I meant no such inference. It's just that I was shocked by the amount. Of course I know such things cost money . . .' Another thought struck him and he turned in concern to Versano. 'But how can we account for such an amount . . . this is supposed to be a secret?'

The genial Archbishop took charge. Van Burgh might be the expert on subterfuge but now they were on his territory.

'Please don't let that concern you, Your Eminence. That money will show in no accounts of the Vatican, or indeed the Church anywhere.' He smiled. 'In fact I assure you that the money will not even come from the Church.'

Puzzled, Mennini asked, 'Then from where?'

The American Archbishop made a very Italian gesture with his hands. A gesture which indicated that all things were possible. He said simply, 'From friends.'

There was a silence while the other two digested that. The Bacon Priest, who knew more of such things than the Cardinal, guessed that the 'friends' would be either certain shadowy bankers, business tycoons who could always use a future favour from 'God's Financier', or the Mafia. Or a combination of all three.

From inside his robes Versano had taken out a little black leather notebook and a thin gold pencil. He asked Van Burgh, 'Where do you want it and how?'

Mennini felt out of it now as they settled the details. The Bacon Priest wanted two-thirds of it in dollars paid into a numbered bank account in Strasbourg, and one-third in gold. If possible in 'Vietnam' style sheets. The Cardinal was mystified by this, but Versano nodded in understanding. The Vietnamese boat people, the lucky ones who got through, brought gold with them. Tons of it. So much that in the early stages gold dealers were allowed to set up shop in some of the refugee camps. Such gold was fashioned into small, paper-thin strips, easy to bend and mould into places of concealment. Versano assumed that if bribery was necessary the gold would be the medium. Van Burgh wanted it delivered to a priest in Amsterdam. Versano jotted down the name and address, then tucked away the notebook and pencil.

'How soon?' the priest asked.

Versano reached forward, picked up a plump orange and started to peel it, his squat boxer's fingers surprising adept. He said, 'The dollars will be in Strasbourg within seventy-two hours . . . The gold in Amsterdam within a week.'

'Good, and I account for it direct to you?'

Versano laughed. 'No.' He glanced at Mennini. 'I suggest that no accounting is done – ever. That's always how people get found out. That's how Al Capone got caught by the tax people.' With another glance at the Cardinal he said quietly, 'Pieter, use the money for our purpose. If there's a surplus divert it to your relief fund . . . If you need more, let me know. If you do so by phone use this code: a dollar will be a single tulip. If you tell me, for example, that you saw a field filled with tulips – "there must have been fifty thousand" – then I'll send fifty thousand dollars to Strasbourg. An ounce of gold will be an Edam cheese. Tell me that a monastery in Zeeland makes a hundred Edams a day and I'll send a hundred ounces of gold to your priest in Amsterdam . . . but no more mention of accounts.'

Van Burgh was looking at Mennini expecting some dissension from this fastidious man who liked everything to be recorded and in its proper place. But the Cardinal nodded.

'I agree, and after it's over *Nostra Trinita* disappears and never was.' He cut himself a small piece of Fontina, broke some bread and nodded again before eating. The Bacon Priest could see that both the Cardinal and the Archbishop were getting a vicarious enjoyment from the brotherhood of conspiracy. Versano had finished peeling the orange. He dissected it into segments, popped a piece into his mouth and asked, 'What about your game plan? Is it worked out yet?' He liked to talk in sporting metaphors.

Van Burgh decided he might as well massage their pleasure in clandestine activities.

'Nothing is finite in this business. The most important word we use is "contingency". We assume that things will go wrong – and we plan for that. Now this operation is in five phases.' He held up his hand, spread his fingers and tapped one of them. 'Phase one is the preparation. That will soon be complete. Phase two is the journey. The "*Papa*'s envoy" will journey from Vienna through Czechoslovakia to Poland, then across Poland via Cracow and Warsaw to the Russian border. Then on to Moscow.' He tapped the next finger. 'Phase three is entry into Moscow, establishing a secure base and making the necessary dispositions for,' he tapped the next finger, 'phase four – the assassination of Andropov. Phase five, of course, is the escape of the envoy.'

Versano leaned forward to ask a question but Van Burgh held up a hand.

'Currently all plans for phase two have been worked out and our people are moving into position. The pipeline will be ready by the time the envoy has finished his training in two weeks. There will be a back-up pipeline in case of problems.' He glanced at Mennini as if to emphasise that 'back-ups' were costly things. The Cardinal was now eating grapes and listening intently. 'Planning for phase three is also complete. I already have two people in Moscow and three more will be there within a week. A "safe house" and transport is arranged. Also the method for bringing Ania – Sister Anna – safely out at that stage.'

Versano was determined to ask a question.

'Back down the same route?'

Van Burgh shook his head. 'No. That's bad strategy. That pipeline is temporary and the longer it's in place the more chance of detection. We'll bring her out through Helsinki. We have a tried and tested method. As to phase four . . .' he shrugged non-committally. 'Planning is still under way. We have identified three possibilities. They are all promising. But so far only one seems to offer a real chance for the envoy to escape.'

Versano was intrigued. Eagerly he asked, 'And that is?'

Van Burgh shook his head. 'That's premature. Besides,' he looked around the opulent room, 'I prefer not to talk about that here. I know you've taken every precaution,

Mario, but that phase is too delicate to discuss in any room. Even in the Vatican itself.'

They both nodded in understanding. The Bacon Priest sighed and said, 'That brings me on to some unpleasant news.' He looked sadly at the Cardinal. 'As you know, we always have defections behind the Iron Curtain. It's inevitable, no matter what precautions we take. Some of our people are weaker than others. You could say more human. Sometimes they cannot take the terrible pressure. I cannot find it in my heart to blame them.' His listeners were watching him intently. With another sigh he said, 'Mirek Scibor was in a unique position to know of these defectors. He gave me a list of over one hundred names.'

Versano drew in breath sharply. 'Oh God! That's terrible.'

'No, Mario, that's to be expected. We have thousands. It's a tiny percentage. Most of them are unimportant. We are now quietly isolating them.' He turned sadly to Mennini. 'Your Eminence, it pains me greatly to have to tell you that two members of your own Order were on the list. Fortunately one was never used and the other not for a long time.'

Gloomily Mennini asked, 'Who are they?'

Van Burgh chose the easy one first. 'Father Jurek Choszozno of Poznan.' He could see that the name meant nothing to Mennini, who was sipping at the remains of his wine. With over one hundred thousand priests within his Order that was not surprising. But Van Burgh guessed that the second name would get a reaction. 'And, Your Eminence . . . this so pains me . . . Father Jan Panrowski of Olsztyn . . .'

Mennini's reaction was far greater than he could ever have expected. The Cardinal's head jerked back. There was a sharp tinkle as the stem of his wine glass snapped and then the white tablecloth was stained red. Both Versano and Van Burgh started to rise. The Cardinal was looking at the priest as though he were a sudden and ghastly apparition. His mouth twisted as he tried to speak.

'Jan Pan . . . No . . . God, no!'

Then his lips pulled back from his teeth in agony and he was clutching at his chest and moaning and falling sideways.

Versano caught him. Shouting at Van Burgh, 'Quick! Get someone! A doctor!'

The priest ran for the door, cursing himself. He knew that Panrowski must have been revered by his leader. He should have broken the news more gently.

Thankfully Sister Maria was standing near a table close by. She saw the priest's face and moved quickly towards him.

'It's the Cardinal,' he whispered urgently. 'Taken ill. I think it's serious. Maybe a heart attack.'

She was instantly in command of the situation. Most of her clientèle were senior, elderly clerics and such things had happened before. She swung into action. First her gaze swept the room; occasionally a doctor or two dined in the restaurant but not tonight. Quietly and firmly she said to Van Burgh, 'Go back inside. An ambulance will be here within minutes with a doctor and special equipment. Then I'll phone the Cardinal's own doctor. Loosen his clothes.'

She moved away quickly but not in a way to excite curiosity. He turned and went back into the private room.

The Cardinal was on the floor. Versano was cradling his head with one hand and with the other holding a glass of water to his lips. Van Burgh quickly knelt on the other side and started loosening the clothes. He pulled at the tight sash and got it free and then reached behind Mennini's neck and loosened his collar. A glance at his face made him sure that this was a heart attack. The Cardinal was gasping for air and his skin was ashen and clammy. He clutched at Van Burgh's arm trying to say something.

Just then one of the older serving girls came running in. She had two pillows and a blanket.

'The doctor and ambulance are coming,' she said and then quickly put the pillows under the Cardinal's head and they lowered him down. He was still clutching at Van Burgh, who tried to comfort him.

Versano stood up, saying gravely, 'I must phone the Vatican. His Holiness must be informed immediately.'

He backed away and walked quickly through the door into the restaurant. By now the patrons knew that something was amiss in the back room. He saw several familiar faces and saw their surprise as they recognised him. He ignored them. Sister Maria was in the foyer talking into a phone. She hung up at his approach and said calmly, 'An ambulance will be here shortly from Policlinico Gemilli. The Cardinal's own doctor is also on his way.'

She hurried to the back room and Versano picked up the phone. He quickly dialled a number. It rang three times and then he heard the voice of the Pope's secretary.

'Dziwisz here.'

Succinctly Versano told him the news. He heard Dziwisz sigh over the phone and then there was a silence while the Pole considered the implication. Versano could imagine what was going through his mind. The Cardinal's Order was arguably the most radical section of the Church and one of the most powerful. It had often been a thorn in the side of past Popes. There had been a general sigh of relief in the Vatican when Mennini had been elected its leader. This time the man filling this most influential position had been on the same wavelength as the Pope and the Curia Cardinals. If he should die a new leader, perhaps a radical, would be elected. Dziwisz asked which hospital the Cardinal was being sent to. Versano told him the Policlinico Gemilli. Another silence, then Dziwisz made up his mind.

'I shall inform His Holiness now. Even if he's asleep. I'll phone you back. What is your number there?'

Versano gave him the number and hung up. As he walked back through the restaurant he heard the distant wailing of a siren.

In the back room Father Van Burgh was kneeling beside the Cardinal. His head was lowered close to Mennini's mouth. The lips were moving painfully and sporadically, then the head jerked back and the body arched. Van Burgh put one hand on his chest and the other under his neck. Versano heard him mutter something like, 'Did you tell . . . ?'

Then Sister Maria was pushing forward. She carried a tray. On it was a tiny vial of water. She really is prepared, Versano thought. She put the tray on the carpet next to the Cardinal, then turned to look at Versano, her eyebrows raised in a query. Van Burgh straightened. His face was a mask of shock.

Sister Maria said firmly, 'Archbishop, I think you must give him Absolution.'

Versano nodded numbly and started to move forward. Then he stopped with a frown. It had been so long since he had been a pastoral priest that the Latin words were lost to him.

He gave an appealing look to Van Burgh, who seemed to understand. He was still kneeling. He leaned across the recumbent figure, picked up the vial of holy water and uncorked it. The wailing of the siren was much louder, homing in. As Van Burgh spoke the words, memory came back to Versano and his lips moved silently as he repeated them to himself.

'*Se sapax, ego te absolvo a peccatis tuis, in nomine Patris et Filii et Spiritu Sancti. Amen.*'

'If it is possible I absolve you from your sins, in the name of the Father, and of the Son, and of the Holy Ghost. Amen.'

Van Burgh made the sign of the cross on Mennini's forehead, then moved his thumb, touching Mennini at all points of the cross.

There was movement at the door but the priest ignored it. He sprinkled the holy water.

'*Per istam sanctum Unctionem*

'Through this holy Anointing . . .'

Then the doctor was literally elbowing him aside. The priest pushed himself to his feet, still muttering the Absolution. Two attendants laid a stretcher and various bags and boxes alongside the Cardinal. They and the young doctor worked with practised skill. The top half of the Cardinal's robes were scissored away. Versano leaned forward and was astonished to see beneath them a coarse hair shirt. This too was cut away. The bony chest beneath had been rubbed red by the hair shirt. It must have been agony. Versano felt a new and uncomfortable respect for Mennini. The doctor was asking short, sharp questions. Versano answered them equally shortly. The doctor listened to the chest and then issued a series of orders to the attendants. Wires snaked out from one of the boxes. Pads were pressed on to the Cardinal's chest. A nod from the doctor, a flick of a switch. Then Mennini's body arched as the electricity went through him. Versano had seen such things on American television. Three times the doctor tried, listening after each attempt. Then wordlessly he pointed at the stretcher. The attendants lifted the Cardinal, placed him on it and covered him with a blanket.

They headed for the door with the doctor behind.

'Is he dead?' Versano asked him.

Without turning the doctor said, 'We'll try again at the hospital.'

'Is he dead?' Versano demanded.

The doctor was at the door. Again, he said over his shoulder, 'At the hospital.'

Versano started after him, but Van Burgh called sharply, 'Mario! Wait!'

He was still standing with the vial of holy water in his hand. He had a strange expression on his face. Slowly he recorked the vial and placed it on the table. Impatiently Versano said, 'I must phone the Vatican again.'

Determinedly the priest shook his head.

'No, Mario. There are more important things. I must make a phone call and then we must talk – urgently.'

Sister Maria had returned to the room. There were tears in her eyes and she fingered her Crucifix muttering a prayer. Firmly the priest said, 'Sister, please bring us two coffees – *espresso*. And brandy. After I return we must not be disturbed.'

She looked at him in surprise. Versano himself was about to object but now this priest was showing his character and his strength. He turned to Versano.

'Wait here, Mario. I will explain in a minute.' He fixed his eyes on Sister Maria. 'Do it, Sister. Now, please.'

She turned away and Van Burgh followed her out of the door. He was gone ten minutes. As the minutes passed Versano's irritation grew. A serving girl brought the coffee and brandy and made to serve it. He waved her away. Sadly she picked up the tray from the floor and the vial. After she had left Versano put three sugars into his cup, stirred and swallowed the lot in two gulps. He was just pouring the brandy when Van Burgh returned. Versano let his irritation show.

'Father Van Burgh, will you explain yourself?'

'Yes, Archbishop. I'm angry with myself. First for killing Cardinal Mennini and secondly for ever getting involved with amateurs such as he and yourself.'

This silenced Versano totally.

The priest poured himself a good measure of brandy and sat down on the opposite side of the table. He spoke harshly and Versano sat silently.

'Mario, the Cardinal had a history of heart trouble. My revelation that Father Panrowski was a turncoat was a great shock. But not such a shock as to give him a heart attack. It appears that Panrowski was part of a delegation to Rome last week. The delegation had an audience with the Cardinal. At the end apparently Mennini must have had a feeling of great humility. He asked Panrowski to remain behind and . . . and he confessed to him. Confessed to him about *Nostra Trinita* and "*Papa*'s envoy".'

'Damn it to hell!' The expletive came out as Versano lowered his head and tiredly massaged his brow. Then he asked. 'How do you know?'

'While you were out telephoning. In the last words he

told me – struggled to tell me. I think he died in torment.'

Versano sat back and blew out his breath. His mind began working again.

'Just what did he confess?'

The priest shrugged. 'I don't know exactly. He mentioned just three things. *Nostra Trinita* and its purpose. The "*Papa*'s envoy – the instrument; and his deception of His Holiness.'

Versano leaned forward. 'And where is this Panrowski now?'

Van Burgh's thick lips twisted in a grimace. 'That's what I went to phone about. He left Rome the day after the audience and returned home. He must have arrived in Olsztyn at least four days ago.'

Versano stared gloomily into his glass. 'And presumably informed his masters.'

Van Burgh nodded. 'It's possible that he didn't, but we must assume he did. We must assume that even by now Andropov knows that there is a plot in the Vatican to kill him.'

'What will he do?'

The priest reached for the brandy bottle, poured some into both glasses and said, 'Andropov will take the threat very, very seriously. He will know of Yevchenko's revelations. He knows well our capabilities. I doubt if Mennini mentioned our names but the KGB will certainly work out that I must be involved. Apart from putting my life even more in danger it makes the operation infinitely harder and more risky.'

Versano was fully in control of himself again: decisive and incisive.

'You want to call it off?'

He watched Van Burgh keenly as he pondered the question. Finally the priest shook his head.

'No, but Mirek Scibor might want to. He knows the implications.'

'You'll tell him?'

'Certainly.'

A silence. This time the priest studied the Archbishop, waiting for a reaction.

Versano sighed and nodded. 'It's the only thing to do . . . Will he go on?'

'He might, but in the meantime, Mario, we have to change our own strategy. Let me explain. In Rome alone the KGB will have at least ten agents and scores of informers. Dozens more agents will swarm in. Assume they're on their way already. They will backtrack on all of Mennini's movements. They will know he died here. Will know he also ate here on the occasion of our first meeting. They will try to find out who his dining companions were. They will probably succeed. They will try again – harder than ever – much harder, to plant listening devices in the Vatican – even in your bedroom. Also at the Russico. We cannot meet here again or anywhere outside the Vatican. You must never leave the Vatican while the operation is on – if it is on. The KGB are more formidable than the Italian fiscal police. If they want to talk to you and you step out of Vatican City – then they will talk to you. And not politely.'

Belligerently Versano said, 'They don't scare me!'

Van Burgh leaned forward. 'Then you're a fool, Mario. They scare me. All the time. Maybe that's why I've survived. So far. Now, thanks to Mennini's humility, they scare me even more. They will know that I'm directing the "*Papa*'s envoy". They will leave no stone unturned to find me. Andropov will see to that. In your case you must talk to Camilio Ciban and arrange extra security. In your office, your apartments. Everywhere you go inside the Vatican.'

Versano thought about that and then nodded.

'Pieter, I know you think I'm an amateur but I take your warnings seriously. But how will I explain this to Ciban or, for that matter, to His Holiness?'

'Very simply,' Van Burgh replied. 'Within the next few days you will receive several death threats . . . by mail and telephone. One will be addressed to L'Osservatore

Romano. They will purport to come from the Red Brigade. That will justify the security.'

Versano managed a smile and said, 'But they will come from you, of course.'

'Of course.' Van Burgh did not smile. 'But you must balance it out. The KGB will learn of it. They will understand it and receive confirmation that you are a member of *Nostra Trinita*.'

Versano's hand gestured between them. 'I guess now we ought to call ourselves *Nostra Due*.'

Sadly the priest shook his head. 'Let us assume that the Cardinal, rest his soul, is still with us in spirit.'

8

'He told me that I wouldn't be seeing him again.'

'You won't.'

Mirek turned to look at Father Heisl. They were in the same car, retracing the same route through Trieste's dockland that had started Mirek's journey to Libya a month before. It was two o'clock on a moonless morning and Father Heisl was driving with care and keeping a close watch on his rearview mirror.

Mirek stretched again, easing his cramped limbs. He had just climbed out of the same packing case but this time after only a five-hour sojourn.

'But you said he's waiting at the house.'

The dim shape of Heisl's head nodded. 'He wants to talk to you but you won't see him.'

Mirek took a swig from the cold bottle of beer that Heisl had thoughtfully brought along. His small canvas bag was at his feet. It contained exactly what he had taken with him with the addition of a 'Denbi' marker pen, a parting gift from Frank. He had given it to him as they stood by the truck waiting to take him to Tripoli.

Mirek had thanked him, and said, 'I know questions are taboo, but I've finished the course and I want to ask you one.'

Frank had not said anything but his eyes had narrowed.

Mirek asked, 'So, Chief Instructor, how did I do on the course?'

The engine of the truck started up. An Arab dropped the back flap. Frank gestured at it. Mirek climbed in assuming that he would get no answer. Silently Frank laced up the cover. Then Mirek heard his voice through the canvas.

'Werner, this camp specialises in training assassins. I don't know or care who your target is . . . but I'm damned glad it's not me.'

The truck had pulled away with Mirek feeling somehow complete.

Now as they passed through the dark streets Mirek knew that he was different. He was less a human being than a deadly weapon. He knew a score of efficient ways to kill. He was in the prime of his physical life and at the apex of fitness. He was also sexually sated. That had been seen to by Leila and the pretty Filipino girl. He felt totally masculine. Like a lion leaving his pride of lionesses and stalking off to make a kill. He raised a hand to his upper lip and stroked the two weeks' growth of hair.

Father Heisl sensed something in him. He glanced sideways occasionally. Apart from stretching once in a while and raising the bottle to his lips, his passenger sat quiet and composed. He had a stillness and an emanation. A blend of confidence and calmness.

They reached the house and went in through to the dining room. Mirek looked around. There was no one there. He was vaguely disappointed. He was looking forward to meeting the Bacon Priest again. He asked Heisl, 'Where is he?'

The priest pointed upwards with a thumb. 'Sleeping. I'll wake him while you eat.'

He went out and a few minutes later the old woman came in with a plate of *spaghetti carbonara* and a bottle of wine. He greeted her but she ignored him. She put the pasta and the wine on the table and went out. He was ravenous. Between the thirty days of his journey out and back the food on the *SS Lydia* had not improved.

He was sucking in the last strands when Heisl opened

the door. He silently watched him mop up the plate with a hunk of bread and then beckoned.

Mirek followed him up the stairs chewing the last mouthful. The room was split by a sheet hanging over a cord stretched from one wall to the other. There were two chairs placed in front of the sheet. Dim light came from a shaded lamp in a corner. Heisl took one chair and gestured at the other. As Mirek sat down the Bacon Priest's voice came from behind the sheet. Mirek realised that the lamp was so placed that his own outline was visible but the other side of the sheet was in darkness.

'Welcome back, Mirek. Was the training satisfactory?'

'Very. Why the charade with the sheet?'

'It saves me the trouble of putting on a disguise. Did you have any problems?'

'None at all.'

'Good. Now listen carefully. Father Heisl is a very accomplished artist. During the next two days while you rest from your journey I want you to describe to him everybody in that camp. Trainers and trainees. He will make sketches. You will tell him how to correct them. You well know the procedure. Also tell him about their personal characteristics, habits, anything you can remember.'

'Why?'

Behind the curtain Van Burgh sighed. He was used to unquestioning obedience from his operatives, but he acknowledged to himself that this one was different. So he explained.

'Mirek, in our work we co-operate sometimes with certain Western intelligence agencies. It's very much a two-way street. In certain areas we are strong on the ground. We give them information; generally background stuff. For example, the state of agriculture in the Ukraine, harvest forecasts, and so on. The state of morale among certain occupied peoples. Obviously our priests, covert and overt, learn a lot in their work. That sort of thing. In return they help us with information, sometimes financial donations

110

and occasionally with items of equipment we find difficult to come by. You understand?'

Mirek did. Once he had raided a vestry of a church in Cracow. His men had gone over it from top to bottom and found nothing. The priest under suspicion had been full of righteous indignation. Instinctively Mirek had known that he was hiding something. He renewed the search. Four hours later he found, concealed in a container of consecrated bread, a tiny but powerful radio transmitter, so sophisticated that neither he nor his superiors had seen anything similar. It had been sent to Moscow and a week later the KGB had advised that it was of West German manufacture and only recently in use by the BND.

Van Burgh saw the shape of his head dip in acknowledgment.

'Well, right now, Mirek, our friends' main concern is terrorism so any help we can give them in that department will be greatly appreciated.'

Mirek now knew where the Bacon Priest got much of his funds for his relief operations behind the Iron Curtain.

He said, 'You should have told me before I went. I would have been more observant.'

'True,' Van Burgh replied. 'But they get suspicious of people who are too observant. I wanted you to be natural. A couple of people have been killed in that camp.'

'I know,' Mirek answered drily. 'You might have told me that beforehand.'

The Bacon Priest merely chuckled.

Mirek asked, 'How are your preparations going?'

'Well. But I'm afraid we have a problem.'

'What problem?'

Without mincing words Van Burgh told him. At one point he was silenced as Mirek stood up and stormed about the room venting his rage in curses. The two priests waited patiently, unperturbed by the language. They had witnessed such things before. The frustration of meticulous planning and training. The building of fear and the coping with it. Then the sudden numbing set-back.

Finally Mirek sat down and asked, 'What now?'

Van Burgh answered flatly, 'That's up to you.'

Mirek's voice changed. 'Why did you tell me? It was bad procedure. I could never have known.'

The Bacon Priest sighed. 'Mirek, I recruited you on the basis of one set of circumstances. That has now changed. It was decided that you should be told. It was the only moral way.'

Mirek snorted. 'Morality! You plan such an operation and then you talk of morality?' A thought struck him. 'Who else is in on this? Who knows apart from we three in this room?'

'One other.'

'Who is he?'

Without hesitation Van Burgh said, 'Archbishop Versano.'

He waited, curious, for a reaction. With Mirek's knowledge of the Catholic Church he would know about Versano.

Mirek simply said, 'It fits.'

Now for the first time Heisl joined the conversation. He said to Mirek, 'The risk is greatly increased. You know that as well or better than we do.'

With the thumb and forefinger of one hand Mirek was thoughtfully stroking his embryonic moustache. It reminded him of something. He said at the sheet, 'Did you send me a signal?'

'Yes.'

'What did it mean?'

'What it said.'

'Why?'

'Father, show him the photograph.'

Heisl rose and went to a table in the corner near the light. He said, 'Come here.'

Mirek went over and watched as the priest slid a thick file out of an envelope. He opened it. Pinned to the front cover was an eight-by-ten black-and-white photograph of the face of a man. Heisl tilted it under the lamp. It was a youngish man. Perhaps in his middle thirties. Handsome and quite rugged. Dark hair cut stylishly long and a black moustache curling on each side to the corners of his lips. Mirek noted a reasonable similarity to his own features. He asked, 'Who is he?'

The answer came from behind the sheet.

'Dr Stefan Szafer of the University of Cracow. His parents defected with him to the West when he was fourteen. Brilliant mind. Studied medicine at Edinburgh University and then at Guy's Hospital, London. Later did postgraduate work at the John Hopkins in the United States. Was always an idealist. Two years ago at the age of thirty-four he returned to Poland.'

Mirek was studying the photo. He said, 'And if I go he is part of the plan?'

'He is part of one of the three plans we have under consideration. I must say the most promising one at this stage.'

'Tell me more.'

'No.'

Mirek turned and walked back to his chair. The Bacon Priest's voice went on.

'If you decide not to go, and in such a case I'll completely understand, we may be able to find somebody else. It's better then that you know no more.'

There was a pause, then Mirek said firmly, 'I'm going.'

He could detect relief in the Bacon Priest's voice.

'Good. Dr Stefan Szafer, even at his young age, is one of the world's top specialists in renal medicine.'

'So?'

'So Yuri Andropov is suffering from, among other things, chronic kidney deficiency.'

'Ah!' Mirek quickly worked it through his mind. 'And he's been attending Andropov?'

'Not yet. But it's not entirely impossible that he will be some time soon. It would be quite natural. We shall try to see that it's inevitable.'

Mirek glanced sideways at Heisl who was smiling

113

slightly. He marvelled at the audacity of their thinking.

'How will you make the switch?'

In a throw-away voice, Van Burgh answered. 'That's being worked out . . . by our best brains. Meanwhile two other plans are being designed as contingency. There is no need for you to know about them until you reach Moscow. The pipeline to get you there is almost in place. So is the safe house and back-up team in Moscow. As yet they have no knowledge of the actual operation.'

Mirek felt the tingle of fear and excitement.

'When do I leave?'

'That day has not been fixed. After you leave here I had wanted to send you to Rome to spend a week in a hospital funded by the Order learning something about kidney diseases and how to comport yourself as a specialist. That's not possible now. The KGB will soon be swarming all over Rome. Instead you will go to Florence. They will not be interested in that city. A specialist there will instruct you on kidneys. Also during that week you will make the acquaintance of your wife.'

'My what?'

Van Burgh chuckled.

'Your wife . . . or your supposed wife. A nice Polish girl. She will travel with you to Moscow.'

Mirek leaned forward and hissed at the sheet.

'You're crazy! When I go in there I go alone!'

Van Burgh's voice hardened.

'You are very experienced at hunting down people and sometimes catching them. You have no experience of the other side of the coin. I've had forty years of it – and never been caught. That day I stood near you on the platform at Wroclaw . . . well, my "wife" was next to me. That one was a rather dowdy woman, I admit. Mirek, a man travelling in those parts with his wife rarely excites suspicion. Think on it.'

Mirek did not. Instead, he said bitterly, 'You told me that Versano was the only other person in the know. Bacon Priest, you lied to me.'

'I did not. The woman's mission is to travel with you to Moscow. Then we bring her out. She knows nothing of your purpose. And, of course, you will tell her nothing.'

Mirek remained totally sceptical. He remarked, 'A woman will be a weak link on such a mission. I don't like it.'

The voice came back through the sheet. 'She goes with you or, Mirek Scibor, you do not go. It is time that you clearly understand. I run the operation. I plan and you execute. You must be under my discipline. From this moment you understand that – or I discard you.'

Father Heisl slowly turned his head and watched Mirek. Van Burgh had told him of the Pole's words, 'I would literally give an arm and a leg to kill Andropov.' A minute passed, then another. Mirek was looking at the floor in front of him. Gradually he raised his head and stared at the sheet with such intensity that Heisl had the crazy thought that his gaze could penetrate it. The Pole stated flatly, 'Bacon Priest, I understand. You command. I will obey for the sake of my purpose. Now who is this woman?'

'Her name is Ania Krol. And if anything she will be the strongest link in your chain.'

'Her background?'

Heisl noted the pause before Van Burgh answered.

'In fact she is a nun.'

Mirek's laughter echoed around the room. He threw his head back and laughed. Then he stood and laughed. He walked to a wall, placed his forearms against it and his head against them – and laughed. When finally he stopped he pulled out a handkerchief and wiped the tears from his cheeks and eyes, then said in an incredulous voice, 'On that journey you're sending with me a nun? As my wife? Will she be wearing a habit and Crucifix? Will she be saying her rosary under the noses of the SB?'

In a tired voice the Bacon Priest said, 'Sit down, Mirek. For the last month you have been in training. So has she. No one will ever guess she is a nun.'

Mirek sat down. Heisl saw his grin.

'So she travels as my wife. In all things? Is she attractive?'

Before the Bacon Priest could answer Father Heisl did it for him. As he spoke he had an impression of Ania Krol's face in his mind. His voice was as cold as an icicle.

'She happens to be beautiful in her body and in her love of Our Lord. You will travel together. She has been taught to behave towards you as a devoted wife – in public. Only in public. There will be times, many times, when you will be alone with her. Even sleeping in the same room. Understand this, Mirek Scibor: if you harm her mentally or physically, I will hunt you down myself.'

Mirek opened his mouth to speak, then even in the half light saw the expression on the priest's face. He closed his mouth.

Van Burgh's voice came through the sheet.

'You must be tired, Mirek. Sleep now. I will be gone when you awake. I may talk to you again after Florence, depending on developments. Father Heisl will travel with you and make all arrangements. Listen to everything he has to say – everything.'

Mirek followed Father Heisl down the staircase. Half way down he stopped abruptly. Heisl turned.

Mirek said, 'He did lie to me. He said "our best brains are working on it". So others do know details of the operation.'

Heisl smiled. He turned and proceeded down the stairs. Over his shoulder he said, 'Relax, Mirek. Our Bacon Priest is a man of many parts. He is our best brains!'

116

9

Victor Chebrikov carried an elephant-hide briefcase – a gift from his station chief in Zimbabwe. As he strode down the corridor it lightly brushed the seam of his trousers. Colonel Oleg Zamiatin strode three paces behind him. There were guards spaced at intervals down the corridor. All of them recognised the tall erect figure as the head of the KGB. As they drew close each one would click his heels and snap off a salute. Chebrikov ignored them all. He had much on his mind.

They came to doors that stretched from floor to ceiling. Two KGB guards with sub-machine guns stood at ease in front of them. They did not come to attention at Chebrikov's approach and did not salute. The sub-machine guns were firmly held and ready for instant use.

Both Chebrikov and Zamiatin produced small flat yellow plastic cards. Each was embossed with a series of black stripes. They held them up to one of the guards. He studied them carefully and then said, 'Proceed, Comrade Chebrikov and Comrade Colonel.'

They went through into a large room lit by two fine chandeliers. There were three desks ranged down one side. On the other side was a settee and chairs grouped around a low table. Across the room was another set of floor-to-ceiling doors.

An elderly woman sat behind one desk. She was reading a sheet of paper and making notes in the margin. She merely lifted her head briefly at the entrance of the two officers and then went back to work. At the next desk was a middle-aged man. He too was working over a paper. He looked up, smiled and nodded a greeting. At the third desk was a young KGB captain. He jerked to his feet and saluted stiffly. This was Andropov's ADC. Unlike most of his predecessors Andropov liked to follow a military formality. The captain glanced at a wall clock. It showed five to three. He said:

'Please have a seat, Comrade Chebrikov; Comrade Colonel. Will you take tea?'

Chebrikov said, 'Not for me, Captain.'

Zamiatin shook his head. They sat down and Chebrikov worked the combination lock of his briefcase, opened it and extracted a thin folder. He closed the briefcase and passed it to the Colonel, who put it at his feet. Chebrikov opened the folder and studied the single sheet it contained.

At precisely three o'clock the Captain picked up one of the three phones on his desk, punched a button and after a pause spoke softly into it. He hung up, stood stiffly and said, 'The Comrade First Secretary will see you now, Comrade Chebrikov.' He moved out from behind the desk and walked towards the doors. Chebrikov followed, leaving Zamiatin behind. The Captain opened the doors and Chebrikov strode through.

He had been in this room many times but it never failed to please him. A soft Bokhara carpet, silk tapestries, gilt chandeliers. The room was perfectly proportioned from floor to ceiling and wall to wall. There was a desk in the middle. A man was reclining on a large chaise-longue in a corner. He looked to be asleep, his head resting on a big black pillow; his eyes were closed. They opened with the sound of the door closing. The supreme leader of the Soviet Empire sighed, swung his feet to the floor and slowly stood up.

Victor Chebrikov studied his mentor closely. This was the man who had risen to the top of the KGB and then manoeuvred himself from there to be supreme leader of the entire country.

He hardly looked the part. He was wearing dark blue

trousers with turn-ups, felt slippers, a cream shirt and an old grey cardigan buttoned half way up. His thin grey hair was tousled and the skin of his face pale and waxy. He looked avuncular until one noted the depth of coldness and calculation in his eyes.

They greeted each other warmly. Andropov was obviously fond of his subject. After enquiring about each other's families Chebrikov apologised for disturbing him. He knew that on Wednesday afternoons, apart from a few absolutely necessary duties, his leader liked to rest and meditate.

Andropov waved to a chair in front of the desk and then shuffled round behind it and sat down. Chebrikov wanted to ask about his health but did not. He was aware that of late Andropov had become irritated at such questions. There was no formality between the two men when they were alone.

Andropov pushed a silver cigarette box across the desk. Gratefully Chebrikov took one. They were Camel filters. He lit it with a matching lighter. As he exhaled the smoke Andropov said, 'So, my dear Victor, what is so important that you cannot discuss on the phone, that brings you hurrying here?'

Chebrikov had laid the file on the desk. He leaned forward and tapped it.

'Yuri, we have uncovered a plot to kill you.'

Andropov's response was immediate. 'Internal or external?'

'External. The plot is centred in the Vatican.'

Andropov was renowned for his imperturbability and his poker face, but he could not hide his astonishment.

'The Vatican! . . . The Pope is trying to kill me?'

Chebrikov shook his head and opened the file.

'Not the Pope. Our information is that he is personally unaware of it. Apparently it's some kind of cabal in the Curia. We have few details at the moment but that will change. Obviously the traitor Yevchenko talked to the Italians about our operation "Ermine". He knew no details, but it is equally obvious that the Italians passed on the bare information to the Vatican. This is their reaction.'

Andropov's own reaction was succinct.

'Impertinent bastards!' He sat back in his chair, anger showing in his eyes. 'What exactly do we know?'

Chebrikov turned the file and pushed it across the desk. 'Only this.'

Andropov read the words on the sheet of paper. Then he sat back again and said maliciously, 'So the damned Cardinal died a few days after his confession. May he rot in hell . . . ! Where is this priest Panrowski now?'

'Being brought to Moscow. He will arrive tonight. We will squeeze every drop from him but I fear he has told us all he knows.'

Thoughtfully Andropov said, 'It's just as well he did. We were lucky. Forewarned is forearmed. This is a serious threat.'

There was a silence as they both considered the implications. Andropov had previously been the head of the KGB for fifteen years. For the last five of them Chebrikov had been his deputy before taking over the top job. They knew very well what the Vatican was capable of.

'We should have been tougher in Poland,' Andropov said bitterly. 'Tougher a long time ago. Back in the Fifties we should have smashed the Church. Just like in Czechoslovakia. Stalin made a bad mistake, and Khrushchev compounded it . . . bloody fools!'

Chebrikov kept silent. He knew from past experience that Andropov would vent his spleen for a while about a problem and then turn his formidable mind to solving it. He was looking down at the paper.

'*Nostra Trinita*,' he snorted. 'Sounds like an offshoot of the Mafia. Well, it indicates there were three in the cabal. Now Mennini is dead – two left. They will follow him . . . the "*Papa*'s envoy" . . . what an obscenity! They are impudent!' He took a deep breath and looked up at Chebrikov. 'So Victor, what are your counter-measures?'

Chebrikov was prepared.

'Of course, my first reaction was to drop everything and devote my personal attention entirely to smashing this plot. However I know what your reaction to that would have been. You would have reminded me of my duties in other areas.' He was pleased to see that Andropov was nodding in agreement. 'Nevertheless, it is important that our counter-measures are handled by the most competent officer under my command . . . Yuri, that does not mean to say a General.'

Andropov smiled and interjected. 'Certainly not. Half your Generals got there by kissing Brezhnev's arse . . . when they could find it. So who will you appoint?'

'Colonel Oleg Zamiatin.'

'Ah yes, Zamiatin.' Andropov nodded in approval. 'A good brain and very dogged. He thinks like a detective.'

Chebrikov knew he had chosen well. Zamiatin had been personally promoted to Colonel by Andropov after a very successful operation in West Berlin. He said, 'This information only came in late this morning. Since then we have analysed our response. Zamiatin is waiting outside . . .'

'Good.' Andropov leaned forward and picked up a phone. 'Send in Colonel Zamiatin.'

As the door closed behind the Colonel he placed the briefcase on the carpet, came to attention and saluted smartly.

Affably Andropov waved at a chair. 'Sit down, Colonel. I'm pleased that you are directing this.'

Zamiatin sat down, keeping his back straight and his head erect. He was in his late thirties. A narrow face, sallow skin and a slight tic in his left eye. He said stiffly, 'Comrade Secretary, this filthy plot against your person is an outrage and will be crushed. We will show no mercy. I pledge my duty to yourself and our Motherland.'

Andropov inclined his head in acknowledgment. 'Colonel, the threat must be taken very seriously. Now what is your strategy?'

The stiffness left both Zamiatin's voice and his back.

He relaxed as he moved into the familiar territory of Intelligence planning. He had no need to refer to notes. Everything was contained in his head. He explained that the strategy of response would be four-pronged. The first prong would be directed at the Vatican itself. It was necessary to learn the identity of the other perpetrators. The assumption was that there were two. He considered it very possible that one of them would be the Bacon Priest. Certainly they would have to use his network. In any event a major operation would be immediately mounted in Rome. Resident agents would concentrate on identifying the individuals and extra agents would be sent in. He himself would go to Rome shortly to co-ordinate the operation. Once identification had been achieved a massive surveillance would follow. Extra efforts would be made to eavesdrop electronically on the Vatican. The extra risk of detection would have to be accepted. A decision would have to be taken once identification had been made whether an abduction and interrogation should be carried out.

At this Chebrikov gave Andropov a meaningful look and got one back. Zamiatin noticed the interchange and he went on confidently.

The second prong would be to identify the 'envoy' himself. For such a mission the cabal in the Vatican would have to recruit a top assassin. With the vast funds at their disposal this would not be difficult. And so every arm of the KGB and the satellite agencies would be put on the alert. Computer profiles would be run on all possibilities. Every station inside and outside of the Soviet bloc would be alerted. Every known assassin and terrorist would be investigated.

The third prong was physical protection on the outer perimeters. The screening of people at every border crossing would be intensified to the maximum. Not just Soviet borders, but those of the satellites, particularly Poland. There would be protests from the various tourism ministers but in the coming weeks they must be ignored. Again a look passed between Andropov and Chebrikov who gave a slight nod of understanding.

Zamiatin explained that counter-measures against the Bacon Priest's network would be intensified. Suspects, many of whom had been under surveillance, would be interrogated with the utmost severity.

He paused briefly and there was a silence. All three men knew what utmost severity meant.

The fourth prong would be the personal protection of the First Secretary himself. Security of the Soviet leader was already the tightest in the world. It would be made tighter still: even if, against all odds, the '*Papa*'s envoy' managed to reach Moscow, the chances of him getting within a mile of the First Secretary would be so remote as to be negligible.

Having made his report Zamiatin once again resumed his stiff and erect position. There was a reflective silence. Andropov scratched his left arm. Chebrikov reached forward and mashed his cigarette into an ashtray. He brushed a little ash from his uniform jacket and said, 'Of course, Comrade Secretary, a team of our best brains is being assembled to work under Colonel Zamiatin. For the duration of this alert they will operate under a separate directorate. Their requirements will supersede any other. In order to stop speculation it would assist us if you issued personal instructions accordingly.'

Andropov nodded. His mind seemed to be elsewhere, but Chebrikov knew that he could listen and think at the same time. He knew that as soon as the interview was over instructions would be sent to the top dozen or so people in the Soviet hierarchy. He and Colonel Zamiatin were to be given total and unquestioned assistance. Andropov ran a hand through his grey hair and ceased his cogitation. He pointed a finger at Zamiatin.

'Colonel, I approve of your strategy. I want a short report from you every forty-eight hours. The original to me and a copy to Comrade Chebrikov. No other copies. I agree that the Bacon Priest is sure to be involved. Find him. If you can, eliminate him. That will be difficult. During all my years at the KGB I tried to do just that. You must try even harder than I did. Put a team solely on that. With him out of the way his organisation will be a headless chicken. In the case of Poland, concentrate your attention on the Order. It is no accident that the Cardinal Mennini was part of this "*Nostra Trinita*". They are the most disciplined arm of the Catholics, and the most dedicated.'

Zamiatin jerked his head forward in a short bow.

'Yes, Comrade Secretary. Thank you for your advice. I will not fail you.'

'I know, Colonel. You have my confidence. Now wait outside for a moment.'

Zamiatin stood up, saluted, turned and marched to the door. As he reached it Andropov called sharply.

'Colonel Zamiatin!'

He turned, his sallow face showing attentive devotion. He listened to Andropov's words, dripping like syrup.

'On the day that you catch or kill that man I will promote you to General. You will be given a dacha in Usovo.'

Zamiatin could not disguise his pleasure. He actually gasped and muttered, 'Thank you, Comrade.'

Usovo was the area where the elite had their dachas. It was not until he had left the room that he realised there had been no mention of the consequences of his failure. But then that had not been necessary. If an assassin's bullet killed Yuri P. Andropov the same bullet would, in effect, kill Colonel Oleg Zamiatin.

Andropov pushed the cigarette case towards Chebrikov again. He shrugged.

'Victor, there is always the stick and always the carrot. It is necessary to know when and how to use them. Zamiatin is a brilliant officer . . . and ambitious. I judge that he responds to the carrot more than the stick. Just as you always did.'

Chebrikov lit another Camel nodding his head in agreement.

'He will think of only two things now. Catching this man, and his reward.'

Andropov smiled. 'I agree. Tell me how preparations for operation "Ermine" are going.'

'Very well, Yuri. The team finish their training in Libya in a few days. They will take a circuitous route and be in the Far East two weeks before the Pope's visit. Their cover is perfect and at arm's length. Don't be at all concerned. This time we will succeed. They will destruct themselves at the same moment. The plan is perfect. Even Karpov could not extricate himself.'

Andropov smiled and pushed himself to his feet, shuffled to one of the tall windows and gazed out towards the massive edifice of the Arsenal. Chebrikov puffed away into the silence, waiting patiently.

After a few minutes Andropov turned and said musingly, 'The Bacon Priest . . . Imagine that he has survived so long. It's ironic, Victor. In '75, an operation I mounted tracked the Bacon Priest to a house in Rome. We could not identify him but we knew he would be one of two dozen clerics meeting there on a certain day and at a certain hour. I proposed to eliminate him using the Red Brigades. They were very willing. Their price was a billion lire – peanuts! Brezhnev turned it down. It would have meant blowing up the whole building. The death of everyone inside. Brezhnev was squeamish about killing a couple of dozen priests . . . there were also two or three nuns . . . But then he never really understood our work. By that time he was interested only in his fancy cars and his nepotism.' He smiled without mirth. 'And now for the sake of a few priests and nuns the Bacon Priest threatens me.' He massaged his face, looking very tired.

Victor Chebrikov stood up. He could not keep the concern from his voice.

'Yuri, I'll leave you now. Please try and get some rest.'

Immediately he regretted the words. He saw Andropov's lips tighten, then speak.

'Don't worry about my health. I promise you one thing . . . I will outlive that bastard Pope!'

10

'Go over it again,' Father Lucio Gamelli demanded.

Mirek sighed and repeated, 'The kidney is a four-inch-long organ supplied by the renal artery and drained by the renal vein. Urine passes from the kidney down the urethra to the bladder.'

The priest sharply tapped the chart. 'Ureter, not urethra. Concentrate. Fix your attention! You only have five more days. In total, twenty-five hours of instruction, and much more to learn.'

Aggressively Mirek asked, 'How long have you been studying medicine?'

'General medicine six years, and ten years renal medicine.'

Mirek grunted. 'And you expect me to learn about it in two weeks?'

Father Gamelli gave one of his very rare smiles. In the past nine days he had driven this young man very hard. Father Heisl had impressed upon him that a reasonable or superficial knowledge of the kidney could mean the difference between his life and death. In fact he had been impressed by Mirek's intelligence, dedication and learning ability but Gamelli would not let up. As a teacher that was not his nature. He said, 'You will have to absorb a little of what I have learned. In five days from now you will be tested by somebody independent. Someone who is unaware that you are not a doctor. If you can fool him you will pass the test. If you fail, Father Heisl will be unhappy with me and I do not want that.' He looked at his watch.

'Come, we must be in the operating theatre in ten minutes. Time to scrub up.'

Mirek stood. 'OK, Doctor.'

It would be his fourth operation. They were in the St Peter's Institute of Medicine. Father Gamelli was chief surgeon specialising in the kidney. He had a worldwide reputation. Over the past few days Mirek had formed an immense respect for the man, if not affection. For five hours a day he had given Mirek personal instruction. Mirek knew that he did not allow those five hours to detract from his time away from his other students and his patients. Consequently for the past nine days Father Gamelli had been working an eighteen or nineteen hour day. Mirek also knew that for this he would be drawing a pittance. He found it difficult to understand. True, he had sometimes worked such hours in the SB but then there had been the rewards of promotion and special privileges.

They scrubbed up while Gamelli explained the case, both to Mirek and his assistant, a shy young intern. The patient was a woman in her early forties.

She had irreparably damaged kidneys as a result of multiple infections over the years. Her heart was now defective and her only hope lay in a kidney transplant.

In the theatre Mirek stood between Gamelli and the anaesthetist. He watched the surgeon's capable fingers make the huge incision, then quickly and competently cope with the flow of blood. In ten minutes he had exposed the kidney.

The assistant was on the other side of the table. Both he and Mirek peered forward as Gamelli explained, 'Now the patient's blood is being adequately dialysed by the machine. We can safely remove the kidney and replace it with the donor part.'

The operation lasted two hours. Afterwards as they washed and dressed outside the theatre Mirek guessed that Father Gamelli was satisfied.

'What are her chances?' he asked.

Gamelli shrugged but then gave one of those rare smiles.

128

'Certainly better than fifty per cent. Maybe even eighty per cent.'

That smile gave Mirek an insight as to why this man worked such hours for a pittance. Perhaps he had just extended a life by thirty or forty years.

He was still reflecting on that as he walked across the Ponte Vecchio back to the safe house. It was twilight and the bridge was crowded. Noisy vendors selling trinkets and souvenirs to passing residents and tourists. There were beggars here and there. That had surprised him at first – beggars among such wealth – but Father Heisl had shaken his head and told him that here even the beggars were wealthy.

He was half way across the bridge when he felt someone jostle him from behind. He turned and saw a black-haired youth darting away. With a curse he slapped at his back pocket. His wallet was gone. He started to give chase but a scooter pulled up and the youth jumped on to the pillion. He made an obscene gesture at Mirek as the scooter weaved away.

Mirek was next to the stall of a fruit vendor. Enraged, he grabbed a bright yellow lemon the size of a tennis ball but much heavier. He raced down the bridge dodging through the crowd. At the end of the bridge the scooter had been slowed down by traffic. Mirek saw the driver skilfully swing in between a small truck and the kerb and slip down the narrow gap. The scooter turned left off the bridge. Mirek was forty metres away broadside to it. He hurled the lemon.

It connected just behind the scooter-driver's ear. The dull thud was clearly audible and the result immediate. He went off the scooter sideways. The handlebars twisted, the front wheel hit the high kerb and it reared up on to the pavement narrowly missing a woman and a young girl who screamed piercingly. The pickpocket was thrown against a plate glass window and bounced off on to his back.

When Mirek arrived on the scene the scooter driver was

on all fours trying to push himself to his feet. Moving fast, Mirek swung his right leg and slammed his boot into the youth's face. He heard and felt the crack of bone. As the youth rolled away unconscious Mirek turned to the other one. He was coming to his feet fast, his pretty-boy face showing fury, his right hand scrabbling in the pocket of his denim jacket. Mirek saw the glint of steel and then he was mindless as his recent training took over. He feinted with his left hand, saw the youth turn his eyes towards it, then pivoted and stabbed out with his right hand, two fingers extended like a cobra's tongue. He felt the ends pulp into the youth's eyes, heard the scream of agony. This time he swung with his left foot fast and high into the youth's crotch, felt the contact; first soft, then hard. The youth went over backwards and down, his hands covering his eyes, his body curling into a ball of agony. In all it had taken less than five seconds. Mirek swept his gaze in a circle. People were standing like petrified rocks, shock on their faces. There was a crash and a tinkle of glass as a taxi bashed into a bus whose driver had stopped abruptly to see what was happening. A police whistle sounded from down the street.

The scooter was lying on its side with the front wheel spinning. Mirek's wallet was on the pavement next to it. He scooped it up and walked rapidly away past the stunned faces, remembering the words of his instructor.

'Don't run unless you're actually being chased. Walk quietly with head lowered, looking neither to left nor right. Use your ears rather than your eyes. You will always hear pursuit.'

He heard no pursuit.

There were three places set for dinner. Mirek wondered who would be joining them. Father Heisl was in the other room talking on the telephone. An appetising aroma drifted in from the kitchen. Heisl seemed to have a legion of little old ladies dressed in black who looked after these safe houses and happened to be culinary geniuses. He supposed they were nuns or members of a lay religious order.

He helped himself to an Amaretto from the bottle on the sideboard and sipped at it, liking the sweet almond taste. He heard the tinkle as the phone was hung up and turned as Father Heisl came in. His face was sombre. Mirek held up the bottle. Heisl shook his head and said:

'One of them has his jaw broken in three places. It will have to be wired up. The other will certainly lose the sight of one eye. They are trying to save the other – that, and his reproductive organ.' He looked down at the shiny tips of Mirek's new shoes. 'Don't you think you over-reacted somewhat?'

Mirek drained his glass and poured himself another shot.

'They were criminals. What should I have done? Stroked their cheeks and said, "Sorry, please return my wallet"?'

Heisl sighed and murmured, 'Both only eighteen . . . you're sure no one saw you come here?'

'Positive. After about a kilometre I caught a taxi to Santa Croce. Then I walked again for ten minutes and caught a taxi to the railway station. From there a taxi to half a kilometre from here. I went around the block twice. I was not followed.'

Heisl nodded in satisfaction.

'Well, the police will be looking for you . . . but I imagine not too diligently. Anyway you cannot take that route on foot any more. Some of the vendors might recognise you and they often supplement their income by being informers for the police. I would prefer to move elsewhere but there isn't time. So for the next five days I will arrange for a car to pick you up and return you.'

He looked glum. Mirek drank and then said lightly, 'Anyway, you know now that your fifteen thousand dollar investment wasn't wasted.'

The comment did nothing to cheer Heisl up. Mirek gestured at the table.

'Who's the dinner guest?'

Heisl glanced at his watch. 'Ania Krol. She should be here in a few minutes. Her training in Rome is complete. I'll be working with her the last few days until you finish at the Institute.'

Mirek nodded but said nothing, although his anticipation was keen. Since his argument with the Bacon Priest over the woman, and his subsequent submission, his curiosity had been quickening. He wondered what sort of a nun would suspend her holy vows and take off across Eastern Europe with a strange man.

Heisl must have been reading his thoughts. He said sternly, 'Mirek, you are to remember: she knows nothing of your ultimate purpose. She has been told only that you are a secret Church envoy travelling to Moscow. That is all.'

'Does she know I'm an unbeliever?'

'Yes, she knows that you're an atheist . . . she was also informed by Cardinal Mennini that you are, by our lights, an evil man.'

He walked to an easy chair and sat down, his ears filled with Mirek's laughter. Mirek drained the glass again but Heisl noted with satisfaction that he did not refill it. All too often men on the edge of danger turn to alcohol for comfort. Over the past days there had always been good wine on the table but Mirek had drunk in moderation. He said with a mocking smile: 'So she must really be looking forward to the trip.'

Heisl spoke bluntly. 'She is prepared to do her duty out of her love and devotion to Our Lord. She did express concern about her physical well-being . . . at your hands.'

Anger washed over Mirek's face. 'I'm not a bloody rapist! Does an atheist have to be a rapist? That bloody Mennini . . . what hypocrisy! Well, I've caught your priests shacked up with women! Last year I arrested one for molesting a ten-year-old girl!'

His dark eyes were bright with anger. Heisl held up a hand.

'Mirek, calm down. We are hundreds of thousands around the world. Of course some are weak and some falter . . . very few, but it's inevitable. We are human and sometimes we are lonely and we have human frailties. No one is accusing you of being a rapist. You are a dangerous man but I think you have your own code.'

Mirek was mollified. He turned to look out of the window through the lace curtains at the street below. A taxi pulled up on the corner. A woman got out with a small blue suitcase. She put it on the pavement and leaned towards the driver's window counting out the fare. She was wearing a beige raincoat belted tightly at the waist. Instinctively Mirek noted the curve of her calves. The taxi pulled away and she picked up her suitcase and walked down the street towards the house. From his foreshortened view Mirek could not properly see her face. He could see the ebony black hair cut in a page-boy style, and the lithe swing of her confident stride. She paused, checking the house numbers. Mirek turned and said to Father Heisl, 'You are right, Father . . . but that code will not stop me from accepting a woman who wants me . . . even a nun.'

Heisl opened his mouth to answer but was interrupted by the doorbell.

Dinner was *cannelloni* followed by *trippa alla fiorentina*. Father Heisl sat facing Mirek with Ania on his left. As usual the old lady served the food in silence, barely acknowledging the compliments to her skills.

By the time the first course was finished Heisl was a worried man. The atmosphere around the table was frigid. Every word of small talk was hung with icicles. Half an hour before he had been concerned that Mirek would be playing the suave seducer, not worried at the likelihood of success but not wishing to be made uncomfortable by the situation. The opposite had happened. Since being introduced to Ania Krol and shaking her hand Mirek had been morose and uncommunicative. He had picked at his food and had taken only a couple of sips of the excellent

Chianti. His mood had communicated itself to her. She kept glancing at Father Heisl as if for assurance. She noted that the priest was perturbed and asked, 'Is everything all right, Father?'

Before Heisl could reply Mirek said bluntly, 'No, the Father is upset because this evening I badly hurt a couple of petty criminals.'

Heisl said irritably, 'I don't think it's necessary for Ania to hear about that.'

'Oh yes it is,' Mirek responded, equally irritated. He turned to Ania. 'They tried to pickpocket my wallet. I broke one's jaw, very badly. The other one has lost an eye and maybe his manhood. Father Heisl thinks I over-reacted. I don't.' He leaned slightly towards her and waved a hand to his left. 'If such an incident occurs over there during our travels I would kill them. Kill them so they could not give a description of us. Do you understand that?'

She nodded gravely. 'I understand that our journey is dangerous. I hope you won't have to kill anyone.'

'And another thing,' Mirek went on. 'You ought to know that I was against you travelling with me. Very much against. I was overruled.'

'Thank you for telling me. I will try to be a help to you.' She spoke calmly looking him straight in the eye. 'I believe that a couple travelling together will be less conspicuous. I am fluent in the languages of the countries we shall be travelling through. I am fit and I am not unintelligent. Before we reach Moscow you will be glad that I am travelling with you.'

Mirek grunted sceptically but before he could answer the old lady came in with the *trippa alla fiorentina*. After she had served them and left he said, looking at Heisl, 'Everyone should understand, including you and the Bacon Priest, that my mission comes first.' He gestured at the woman. 'If she gets in my way I dump her. If we are chased and she cannot keep up I leave her. If she is wounded I abandon her . . .'

It was said abruptly. Heisl stirred uncomfortably in his seat. As he nodded he heard Ania's husky voice.

'That is understood, Mirek Scibor. Now, a wife should know something of her husband's habits and tastes . . . do you like music?'

Heisl could see that Mirek was thrown by the sudden change of subject. He stroked his now well-grown moustache and then shrugged and said, 'Some.'

'Like what?'

He said almost defensively, 'Our music. Good Polish music. Chopin; his sonatas and . . . yes, particularly his mazurkas.'

She smiled with pleasure. 'Me too. I love his études. My favourite is "The Butterfly". Do you know it?'

Mirek nodded. Father Heisl noted that for the first time there was some animation in his eyes. For the next twenty minutes until the meal was finished they chatted about Chopin and Polish music in general. Father Heisl, being tone deaf, had little interest in music and so was more or less left out of the conversation.

At the end of the meal, though, Mirek curtly refused coffee, announced that he would be having an early night and left the room.

Gently Father Heisl said to Ania, 'Your task will be difficult, my child. He is not an easy man. However, although you may be in danger with him I am confident you will not be in danger from him.'

'I think you are right, Father, but if he is prepared to kill so casually the mission must be of total importance to him . . . not just the Church. Do our interests completely coincide?'

She was pouring coffee into two cups. She remembered that he took two sugars and a little milk. As she stirred he collected his thoughts.

'They do, Ania. For certain reasons which are operationally logical you cannot know the mission.'

'In case I get caught?' she interjected, pushing the cup towards him.

'Well, yes.'

'And not for my peace of mind?'

Father Heisl lifted his cup, thinking rapidly. This young woman was too intelligent for platitudes. He sipped and said firmly, 'I am not permitted even to answer that. The Bacon Priest has already told you all that you are allowed to know. You must deal with your peace of mind with the power of prayer.'

'Yes, Father,' she said obediently, but Heisl knew that her intelligence would continue to stimulate her curiosity. He said, 'You handled him well tonight, Ania. It will be easier when he has fully accepted you and realised that you can make a contribution.'

She smiled. 'Don't worry, Father. I can handle him. I'll take care of my peace of mind and you take care of yours.'

In his room upstairs Mirek was troubled. The woman had unsettled him and he found that hard to understand. He usually unsettled women. He analysed his reaction and realised what had happened. Many men, perhaps most, have fantasies about nuns. Young, pretty, virginal nuns. He recalled having occasion once to question two nuns in Cracow. They were suspected of being in touch with dissidents. One had been middle-aged and plain, the other had been young, with an attractive face. He had questioned them separately and at length. With the young one he had felt that his looks and masculinity had affected her somehow. She had worn a long loose habit and he mentally undressed her, trying to visualise her hidden body. All he could see was her face from forehead to neck but he visualised a plump naked body attached to that face and had been sexually stimulated.

Now with Ania Krol a strange reversal had taken place. She did not wear a habit. Indeed her soft brown woollen dress had been quite revealing. He had immediately noted the full breasts, the narrow waist and curved flow of her legs. Her face too was very beautiful with its high cheekbones and olive skin and crowning ebony hair; but perversely in his mind's eye he could only see her in a nun's habit with its constricting and concealing headdress.

His room was Spartan. A single bed down one wall, a cupboard for clothes and a small table with a single chair. He walked to the window and stood looking down at the street. A light drizzle had started and the road and pavements glittered from the street lights. A couple walked along arm-in-arm but they were arguing, gesturing angrily with their free hands. He supposed they must be married. He had almost been married himself once. The daughter of a Colonel in his department. She had been pretty and vivacious and an energetic lover. He supposed that she had a temper which she controlled well, but that did not concern him. He liked women with spirit. He knew that an attractive, intelligent wife would be an asset to an ambitious officer. After a few weeks he decided to propose. He had been brought up in the traditional way and before making his proposal he asked for an appointment with her father on a personal basis. This was granted in the Colonel's office, after office hours. Mirek had tapped on the door with some trepidation for the Colonel was a forbidding man and a stern disciplinarian. The Colonel must have noticed his nervousness. He waved him to a chair, opened a desk drawer and took out a bottle of vodka and two glasses. He had also taken off his cap and tossed it on to the desk between them to indicate that Mirek could talk freely and off the record.

The fiery liquid had warmed and calmed him. Formally and confidently he said, 'Comrade Colonel, I have come humbly to petition you for the hand of your daughter Jadwiga, in marriage.'

The words had an astonishing effect on the Colonel. He sat bolt upright and gave Mirek a piercing look to be sure he was serious. Satisfied that he was, he tipped the vodka down his throat, shook his head vigorously and said, 'No chance! No chance at all.'

At first Mirek had felt humiliation. But anger quickly followed.

'Colonel, sir. I come from a good family. I was the youngest officer promoted Captain in our section and have every hope . . .'

The Colonel held up a hand. 'How long have you known my daughter?'

'Well, only five weeks . . . but I would be in no hurry . . .'

'Shut up, Scibor, and listen to me.'

The Colonel leaned forward. He had a drinker's red-veined nose, and small round eyes. He pointed a finger at Mirek's chest.

'I like you, Scibor. You're intelligent and you work hard. You'll soon be promoted Major . . . you could go right to the top –'

'Then why?'

'Shut up and listen. I said I like you. My daughter Jadwiga is the second biggest bitch in the world. The biggest is my wife – her mother. Oh no! I'm saving Jadwiga up for some bastard I don't like. She can make his life as miserable as her mother's made mine . . . I like you. Get out.'

Mirek had stumbled out of the room flabbergasted. Her own father! But then reason had prevailed. Who would know her better than her father?

He took Jadwiga out for dinner one more time and watched her with a more critical eye. Noticed that the pretty mouth had a petulant lower lip, the wide blue eyes often slid away to watch the entrance of a man alone, followed him if he was attractive. He noticed how she ordered expensive items on the menu while knowing that his funds were limited. Silently he thanked the Colonel and decided that marriage could wait.

After that there had been a succession of girls. He almost always had one in tow, but they only lasted a few weeks at the most.

He turned and walked to the table and sat down. There were several medical textbooks in a pile. He selected one and opened it at a marker. For the next hour he read, pausing occasionally to make a note in an exercise book. He heard a door close downstairs and a stair creak. The soft footfall of her walking past his room. He knew it was her. Heisl was an insomniac and never went to bed before the early hours. He heard the bathroom door open and close. A pause, then the sound of the bath water running. He imagined her unbuttoning the brown woollen dress. What sort of underwear would she be wearing? Something flimsy? No, probably great big bloomers.

He tried to concentrate again on his book. Forced his attention on to it. He decided that the kidney was mankind's most boring organ. How the hell could Father Gamelli spend his life in such intimate contact with it?

He heard the bathroom door close, the creak of a floorboard and then the door of the room next to his open and close. The walls were thin. He faintly heard the squeak of the bedsprings. He imagined her sitting there drying her hair, that thick black lustrous hair which until recently had been hidden away. Was she naked? He closed his eyes and tried to conjure up a picture. It was ridiculous. All he could see was her face from hairline to chin. The rest was a blur of white and black. She was wearing her nun's habit.

He closed the book and went to bed and slept fitfully.

'What is it?'

The visiting professor pushed a large jar across the table. Mirek picked it up and studied its contents.

'It's part of a kidney.'

'Are you trying to be funny?'

'No, sir.'

The professor sighed. 'What's wrong with it?'

They were in a room at the Institute. Just the professor, Mirek facing him and Father Gamelli sitting at the back near the door. Mirek had completed his crash course. This was the test. He drew a deep breath and turned the jar in his hand. The section of misshapen kidney slopped about in the formaldehyde. He noticed a mass of grape-like clusters of cysts containing a dark fluid.

'It shows advanced polycystic kidney disease.'

The professor nodded and made a note. 'Anything else?'

Mirek decided to be bold.

'The patient did not die of old age.'

He noticed the professor looking over his shoulder at Father Gamelli. He wondered if he had made a fool of himself.

The professor asked, 'What treatment would you have used?'

Mirek remembered what he had been reading the night before. He said, 'The fatal nature of the disease cannot be altered except by a transplant depending on the other variables.'

The professor nodded and made another note.

The questions went on for half an hour. Mirek knew that he had messed up on some of them, but later, back in Father Gamelli's cramped office, the priest was pleased with him.

He smiled. 'The professor is completely puzzled. On some questions you were brilliant – on others a complete blank. Never mind, you did well enough.' He held out his hand. 'Good luck in whatever you're about to do.'

Mirek shook the hand warmly and thanked him. 'Father, if I ever get a kidney disease I'll know where to come.'

The priest shook his head. 'People like you don't get diseases like that.'

Driving back to the safe house Mirek wondered what he had meant. He sat next to the driver, a young red-headed priest. In the five days that he had driven Mirek to and fro he had not addressed one word to him. Mirek assumed that this was on Heisl's orders. It was just after noon when they reached the safe house. Mirek climbed out and pointedly thanked the driver, who merely nodded and drove away. Mirek did not care. He was feeling relaxed, the hard studying over. He rang the doorbell and waited. It was opened by Ania. She was wearing her beige raincoat. She took his arm and turned him around and announced,

'You are taking me for lunch. Father Heisl left for Rome urgently two hours ago. He won't be back until this evening. Signora Benelli is taking the day off.'

He let himself be led down the street and asked, 'What was so urgent?'

'I don't know. He got a phone call and left immediately. He seemed worried. He said we should be ready to leave first thing in the morning. We are finished here now.'

'Where are we going?'

'He didn't say. Do you have plenty of money?'

'For what?'

She smiled up at him. 'For an expensive lunch. I feel like shellfish. The Signora recommended a good place. It's not far. Does my husband like shellfish?'

He looked down at her. The top of her head came level with his shoulder. In spite of his anxiety about Heisl's sudden departure he began to catch something of her mood.

'I don't really know. I've only ever had tinned prawns and mussels. You will have to order for me.'

She had released his arm. He reached out and took her hand. She turned and looked at him quickly. He held up her hand and said lightly, 'It's natural for a young married couple to hold hands. You must remember the part we are playing.'

She nodded dutifully. The skin of her hand was a little damp. He squeezed it but got no response.

They chose a table in a quiet corner. A waiter moved to pull out a chair for Ania but Mirek beat him to it. As she sat and began unbuckling her coat Mirek bent down and brushed the nape of her neck with his lips. He felt her stiffen. The waiter was looking on approvingly. As Mirek moved to his own chair he said, 'Darling, this reminds me of that lovely bistro in Taormina.'

She looked blank. He smiled at her. 'Don't you remember, darling? On our honeymoon. I think it was the third night. I can remember being quite exhausted.'

He thought she would blush but he was disappointed.

141

'Ah yes, of course. We had lobster. You were exhausted from all that swimming and too much sun. You really overdid it, dear.' She turned to the waiter. 'Do you have lobster?'

He shook his head sadly and handed her the menu. 'But we have lovely giant prawns fresh this morning.'

She didn't consult Mirek. She ordered mussels cooked in white wine and garlic, followed by the prawns – grilled, with a mayonnaise sauce and a salad. She asked the waiter to recommend a wine and he suggested a Soave. Mirek sat watching her, marvelling at her poise. He knew she had been in a convent practically from birth. Heisl had told him that she had been out in the world for only a few weeks, yet she had the poise and confidence of an experienced woman. She handed the waiter back the menu with a smile and then shrugged off the raincoat. Underneath she was wearing a dark blue plain blouse and a cream skirt. The whole image was exquisite. A thought struck him. He said, 'Your beauty will attract attention over there.'

'Don't worry,' she answered. 'That has been thought of. I have been taught how to make myself look plain. But it's only a short time before we leave . . . and afterwards . . . after the journey I shall go straight back into the convent . . . so today I thought I would look the way I would like to . . . if I had not become a nun.' She smiled. 'Do you mind?'

He shook his head. She was wearing just a trace of lipstick and perhaps a little eye shadow; he couldn't be sure. When he had kissed her neck he had smelled no artificial perfume: just the yeasty muskiness of her skin. For a moment she reminded Mirek of his sister. Of the times they had played together as youngsters. Such thoughts had long been subdued. Now it was a bitter-sweet memory.

The mussels arrived. Mirek immediately leaned forward to eat but paused as she lowered her head and murmured a prayer. He smiled and waited. She raised her head and smiled back. The waiter opened the wine and poured a little into Mirek's glass. He shook his head.

'My wife will try it. She's the expert.'

The waiter smiled condescendingly and put the glass in front of Ania.

She picked up the glass and held it high, twirling the wine slowly. Then she brought it to her nose and inhaled the bouquet. Finally she took a sip, frowned in concentration and swallowed. She nodded with dignity to the waiter, who filled both glasses. As he went away she started to giggle. Mirek asked, 'Did they teach you that as well?'

'No, I saw someone do it on television.' She picked up the glass and held it to the light again. 'It's a beautiful colour. It's the first time I have drunk wine which was not sanctified . . . I belong to a strict order.'

'Do you like it?'

She sipped again and nodded. 'Yes, Mirek, I suppose because it's dry. Our holy wine is sweet.' She smiled. 'Also perhaps because it's like eating forbidden fruit.'

He quickly took up that point. 'Naturally in your life there must have been many forbidden fruits.' He noted the wary look come into her eyes. 'Are you going to try all of them?'

'No. A glass or two of wine is not sinful.' She sipped again and said thoughtfully, 'I hope you are not going to make it difficult for me.' She was looking into his eyes. He stared back and then merely smiled. The waiter brought the prawns, breaking the silence.

During the rest of the meal he touched her just once, when they were dipping their fingers in the finger bowl. As they touched he resolved to himself that before they reached Moscow he would know her body. She was the first woman he had met whom he knew was, beyond all doubt, a virgin. The knowledge made his breath quicken.

She seemed unaware of his thoughts. She wanted ice cream. The waiter, who by now was practically her slave, suggested *tartufo*. Mirek declined.

On the plate it looked quite unappetising. A round

143

chocolate covered lump. But when she dug her spoon into it and tried the first mouthful she exclaimed in delight. She insisted that Mirek try it and held a spoonful to his lips. He too found the taste fascinating and they finished it together with alternate spoonfuls.

Over coffee she announced that she wanted to go to the Uffizi.

'What's that?' Mirek asked.

'One of the most famous art galleries in Italy. I'm told there are some wonderful works of art there . . . I may never have the chance again.'

So they went to the Uffizi. Mirek had no knowledge of art and not much appreciation, but her enthusiasm was infectious. They latched on to a group of German tourists and listened as the guide pointed out and explained the Leonardos and Caravaggios.

They walked back to the safe house. Again Mirek took her hand. She was unresponsive but did not pull away.

In the evening she found some ham and salami in the fridge and served it at the kitchen table with a salad. Mirek opened a bottle of wine but she refused a glass. Her mood was introspective.

He asked her, 'Ania, have you been realising that there's a different life to lead? That the walls of a convent can be much the same as the walls of a prison?'

She stood up and stacked the dishes and took them to the sink. As she began to wash up he thought he would get no answer but then she said quietly, 'I was never locked up. I chose that path knowingly. I have been happy. Of course I knew life outside would be very different – and it is – but I would not want it. Yes, it's interesting seeing it, like going to another planet. But I tell you, I will be happy when this is over and I can return to my vocation . . . and to my vows.'

He tried to think of another avenue to explore but she turned, drying her hands, and said, 'I shall go to bed now. I enjoyed it today, Mirek . . . thank you.'

He pushed back his chair and stood up. 'So did I. And I learned a few things.'

As she moved towards the door he said, with a trace of sarcasm, 'Won't you give your husband a goodnight kiss?'

She turned at the door and in her husky voice answered him.

'Indeed I will. I am wedded to my Lord. I have my Crucifix in my room. I will kiss it before I sleep.'

He went to the sitting room and found a bottle of cheap brandy in a cupboard. It burned his throat but he drank half a glass before he heard the sound of a car and then the latch of the door.

Father Heisl looked tired. This time when Mirek held up the bottle he nodded acceptance.

'It's lousy stuff,' Mirek warned.

'No matter. It will clear the dust from my throat.'

As he passed the glass Mirek asked, 'What happened?'

Heisl coughed on the brandy. 'How did your test go?'

'Apparently I passed.'

Heisl drank more brandy and grimaced. 'Good. Tomorrow you and Ania leave for Vienna. The next day you cross into Czechoslovakia. Your journey begins.'

'Good. What happened to send you rushing to Rome?'

Father Heisl sighed. 'Only confirmation of bad news. Obviously Mennini's confessor did pass on the information. Now the KGB know you are coming. Last night they started cracking down on all border crossings. They are being meticulous. Long queues are piling up.'

He held out his glass and Mirek poured two more fingers and said, 'But you expected that.'

'Yes. But they are reacting with unprecedented severity. We have learned that many of our people in the East have been picked up in Poland, Hungary, Czechoslovakia and Russia itself . . . scores of them.'

He drank and massaged his forehead. Mirek said, 'That too must have been expected.'

Heisl grunted in exasperation.

'Yes, Mirek, but not to that extent. Several were beaten in their homes before being dragged away . . . even in Poland. I pray for them.'

'In that case,' Mirek said thoughtfully, 'the KGB, indeed Andropov, are close to panicking . . . they are taking me seriously. Is my route likely to be compromised?'

'No.' Heisl finished his brandy and set the empty glass firmly on the table. 'But we think one of our other pipelines has been smashed and another is threatened.'

'That can help,' Mirek answered. 'It could divert attention.'

'Yes,' Heisl agreed with a sigh. 'At the cost of a lot of suffering. You know what the KGB can do when they are desperate.'

'Be sure that I know,' Mirek said grimly. 'And that reminds me. I want a gun – a pistol.'

Heisl's response was firm. 'Forget it, Mirek. The Bacon Priest would never agree. He's totally against that.'

Mirek poured himself a little more brandy. He looked at the priest over the top of the glass.

'Father, you tell him that I am not one of his usual operatives – and neither is Ania. OK, they've picked up some of your people over there. They will be roughed up, some will probably go to the Gulag, but if they ever catch me I would prefer to die early – and by my own hand. I'd rather go straight to hell than have a few months' initiation to it . . . And the girl. I don't know how good your imagination is, but just try to think what will happen to her. She may well end up in heaven, but she will pass through hell to get there. If they catch us, the first bullet will be for her, the second for me.'

Heisl looked very unhappy. He picked up his glass. Mirek drained the last of the brandy into it. The priest sipped and said, 'The Bacon Priest will not countenance it. Anyway it's too late. I shall be unable to see him or talk to him before you leave.'

Mirek chuckled sarcastically. 'You take me for a fool.

You know your Bacon Priest better than I do, but I know he will be in Vienna tomorrow. It is not possible that he would stay away from the beginning of this operation. He will certainly be in Vienna, in one of his disguises. You tell him that without a pistol I don't go.'

'That's blackmail.'

'No. That's insurance. Mine and the girl's.'

In exasperation Heisl said, 'Where would I find a pistol?'

Mirek burst into scornful laughter.

'You can put me into the most notorious terrorist camp but can't find one little pistol in a city like Vienna?' He prodded the priest in the chest. 'Heisl, if you wanted to you could lay on a battery of field artillery complete with laser range finders. All I want is one pistol.'

Heisl shrugged. 'I'll think about it.'

Mirek was satisfied. He tapped Heisl's almost full glass with his empty one. The sharp ping echoed in the room.

'One pistol with a spare magazine. Good night, Father.'

After he left the room Father Heisl walked to the window and stared out gloomily. He wondered why his beloved Bacon Priest had ever got involved in this. He had a feeling of great disquiet about the morality of the whole operation, apart from his own part in it – and apart from the awful danger that they were sending the young nun into. He felt no disquiet about Mirek's fate.

11

Colonel Oleg Zamiatin considered himself primarily a solver of complicated puzzles. He had a good mind for it. He was a master of crossword puzzles and a formidable and imaginative chess player. He approached this puzzle with the relish of an addict and with the added weaponry of three assistant addicts and the most sophisticated computer centre in the Soviet Union.

The three assistants sat at three desks in a line facing him at the far side of the spacious room. Zamiatin believed in the open-plan office theory. He could monitor his assistants' work rate and also bounce questions off them.

The Ryad R400 computer and its satellites were housed in the basement. Zamiatin was pleased with his new organisation and its location. Although it was on Dzerzhinsky Street it was not exactly in the KGB headquarters' building but next to it in an annex of the department store Detsky Mir – 'Children's World' – which sold everything from baby clothes to sports gear. The irony of its proximity was lost on him.

The priority given him by the First Secretary had wrought immediate co-operation in all corridors of Soviet power. He had been able to requisition whatever people or equipment he had wanted without question. On one wall of the vast office was a giant electronic map of the European USSR and its immediate neighbours. Different coloured lights showed all border crossings according to their status and usage. An information room next door, staffed by a dozen experts, monitored all incoming and

148

outgoing communications and operated the computer. All this had been achieved in four days. Zamiatin had spent one of those days in Rome closeted with the senior KGB officers of that city's station. He had perused and examined their plans for infiltrating the Vatican, being both critical and encouraging. He approved the risks of detection they were going to take. It might mean a few expulsions but the prize was worth it. Before catching his evening plane he had himself driven to the Vatican.

It had been a cool evening but nothing to compare with Moscow. He did not bother to take off his coat. He had strolled around just like any other tourist. In St Peter's Square he had stood looking up at the lighted windows of the Papal apartments. He wondered if the Pope was behind one of them.

An elderly American couple stood next to him. Reverently the woman said to her husband, 'Do you think he's eating, honey?'

The man wore a brightly checked coat and a German-style hat with a green feather in the band. 'Naw,' he replied, 'too early. He's probably prayin' or somethin'.'

He'd better be, Zamiatin had thought, turned on his heel and walked briskly back to his car.

The three men sitting at the desks opposite him were all Majors and in their early or mid thirties. They were the best young analysts in the KGB. Academics rather than Intelligence agents. To Zamiatin's satisfaction all had been abruptly pulled off other high-priority work. For three days now they had been sifting through the flood of information that flowed in, twenty-four hours a day. They worked mainly in silence, occasionally conferring in low voices. They only addressed Zamiatin when they thought they had something significant.

So far the dramatic clamp-down at the borders had netted a variety of criminals. Scores of smugglers of drugs, religious tracts and pornography on the way in, and illegal exports of icons and other works of art on the way out. A suspected courier of Britain's MI6 had been picked up. They had also intercepted four dissidents with false papers trying to cross the Finnish border. All in all a good haul, but nothing relating to the '*Papa*'s envoy'. Of course, the Minister of Tourism had protested vehemently at the chaos and ill-feeling caused, but a phone call from Andropov had silenced him.

Zamiatin had already submitted his first forty-eight-hourly report to the First Secretary. It had succinctly detailed all the initiatives taken by Zamiatin. He was now working on the second report. He would dearly have liked to include something significant but it was early days yet and surely Andropov would understand that, impatient for concrete news though he might be.

In the background he heard the quiet voices of two of the Majors consulting, then one of them called, 'Comrade Colonel Zamiatin.'

Zamiatin looked up. It was the youngest and perhaps the brightest, Boris Gudov. He always looked a bit scruffy and had a distinct body odour but he had a brain like a needle. Now his normally sleepy eyes were animated.

'What is it?'

Gudov glanced at Major Jwanow on his right, then said confidently, 'Four days ago an order was given activating certain of our long-term dormants in Western Intelligence Services.'

'Yes,' Zamiatin said, remembering the brouhaha that had caused among certain senior KGB officers.

'You remember the agent in the German BND code-named "Mistral"?'

'Of course.' Zamiatin remembered very well. 'Mistral' had been planted in the BND as early as '63, long before the big shake-up that followed the Guillame scandal. He had survived the shake-up and risen steadily until he had reached the top level, becoming, in effect, Director of Strategy. Even in that position he was kept dormant in the hope that he might one day become Director of the entire agency. Only Andropov's fear of his own life had prompted his activation.

'Well,' Gudov said, 'he and the others were ordered to report only on matters of vital State interest . . . and matters relating to the Vatican and the Catholic Church and its Intelligence network.'

'So?'

Gudov tapped a file on his desk.

'"Mistral" made contact with his case man in Bonn yesterday. He passed on this file which contains an Intelligence "gift" from a third party. It gives portraits of twenty-four trainees and seven instructors in the terrorist camp of Ibn Awad in the Libyan desert as of the twenty-second of last month.'

'Go on,' Zamiatin prompted. He was not impatient but he felt a tingle of anticipation. Gudov spoke with a precise inflection. The other two Majors were watching him.

'Well, Colonel, normally that would not be significant. All Western Intelligence agencies, especially the CIA and Mossad, spend a lot of time trying to crack the security in these camps. But this gift came from none of them . . .' He paused.

Now Zamiatin was impatient. Sharply he said, 'Who gave it to them?'

Gudov smiled. 'The Iron Curtain Church Relief!'

Zamiatin frowned and then as the implication sank in, he, too, smiled.

'Ah. Our friend the Bacon Priest . . . bring it here.'

The Major picked up the file and carried it over. The other two Majors were watching Zamiatin. He beckoned and they joined him, crowding round the desk.

Zamiatin slowly turned the pages of the file. Each page contained two ink drawings of a man's or woman's head. One full face, the other in profile.

Beneath the drawings were written descriptions. With his assistants peering over his shoulder he came to the drawings of a young, pretty Oriental girl. Major Gudov pointed to a sentence at the end of the written description.

It read: 'Sexually promiscuous to the point of nympho-mania.'

'So,' Zamiatin murmured. 'The compiler of this did a little more than mere training in that camp.'

Gudov nodded. 'He sure did. There's more later.'

Five pages further on they were looking at the severely attractive face of Leila. Again Gudov pointed at the last sentence. It read: 'Sexually active. Sado-masochistic tendencies.'

One of the Majors grinned and said, 'How do I get into that place?'

They all laughed, including Zamiatin who was feeling elation and relief.

'You don't,' he said. He jerked a thumb at Gudov. 'But Boris here does, and very soon. Sit down all of you.'

They went back to their desks and sat and waited patiently. Zamiatin turned over the last pages of the file, then sat silently in thought for a few minutes. Finally he raised his head and spoke with brisk authority.

'Major Gudov, you will go home now and change into civilian clothes and pack an overnight bag and proceed to Lublin Air Force Base. A military jet will be standing by waiting to fly you to Libya. You will be met there by a senior officer of Libyan Intelligence who will accompany you by helicopter to Ibn Awad camp. They are not sup-posed to photograph the trainees but you can be sure they do, surreptitiously. You will obtain those photographs and compare them with the drawings in this file. Obviously there will be one extra. That is our man . . . or woman. Presumably a man, unless the "*Papa*'s envoy" is a lesbian.' No one smiled; his expression and tone of voice precluded that. 'You will then interrogate all the instructors and any trainees in the camp who were there up to the twenty-second of last month. Particularly the Filipino woman and the instructress Leila. You will do all this in twelve hours. I want your report on my desk by ten o'clock tomorrow night. Try to sleep on the way out and back. Do not fail me. Go now.'

Major Gudov stood up, saluted smartly and headed for the door. Zamiatin's voice stopped him. He was holding out the file.

'You'll need this.'

Gudov walked over, looking sheepish. Zamiatin was not angry. He knew that great brains are often absent-minded. He ignored Gudov's retreating figure and said to one of the other Majors, 'Comrade Major Worintzev, you will arrange the transport and liaison with Libyan Intelligence through our resident in Tripoli. Utilise the special orders.'

'Yes, Comrade Colonel.' Worintzev reached for one of the phones on his desk.

Zamiatin was looking at the last Major who waited expectantly. Finally Zamiatin said, 'Major Jwanow, you will order tea for all of us!'

Jwanow grinned and reached for the phone. After placing the order he hung up and said, 'How on earth did the Bacon Priest get a man into that place?'

Zamiatin sighed. 'We shall try to find out, but I fear we will come to a dead end. That damned cleric is never to be underestimated . . .' He took a deep breath and picked up his felt-tipped pen. 'But we are on his tail now.'

On the bottom of his draft report to the First Secretary he wrote: 'There is a possibility of a breakthrough in establishing the identity of the assassin and obtaining a detailed description. I expect this to be to hand in time for my next report.'

Archbishop Mario Versano was uncomfortable. The chair itself was soft but the situation was not.

Gently the Pope repeated, 'What is going on, Mario?'

The Archbishop shook his head in puzzlement. 'I really don't know, Your Holiness. Except that it all seems a bit strange.'

'Very strange,' the Pope said. He stood up, walked to his desk and picked up a piece of paper. 'We have a report from Cardinal Glemp in Warsaw. The SB are cracking down all over on direct orders from Moscow. We have already protested but it goes unheeded. It is happening all over the Eastern bloc. They don't seem to care about world opinion. Hundreds of our people have been arrested. It has not happened in recent times.' He dropped the piece of paper and picked up another. 'Ciban reports to our secretary that in the last two days three attempts have been made to bribe maintenance workers in the Vatican to install listening devices. Fortunately the good people immediately went to him. He advised Counter Intelligence and they have picked up an Italian with a criminal record who is believed to have connections with the KGB. At the same time they advise that there is much increased KGB activity in the city. Ciban is very anxious about our safety. There are the mysterious threats to your life, supposedly from the Red Brigades. He wishes us to cancel our visit to Milan tomorrow.'

'Will you?' Versano asked.

The Pope dropped the paper on to the desk, walked back to his chair and sat down heavily.

'We will cancel nothing. Do you think Andropov is behind it? Do you think he will try to kill us here . . . in the Vatican . . . in Italy?'

'No, Your Holiness.'

'Then what is going on?'

Versano crossed his long legs, edging forward in his seat. His mind was ranging ahead, feeling out a path. Deciding which way to go. He said hesitantly, 'Your Holiness, I hear things of course. I think there could be a measure of misinformation here. I think some people may be manoeuvring in subterfuge.'

'Explain.'

Versano nodded emphatically. 'Yes, that's probably it. Your Holiness, you know that the Italian Secret Service has always had connections with certain elements here in the Vatican. That was obvious after the exposure of P2.'

The Pope sighed. 'Yes, but we have tried to limit that.'

'Even so, Your Holiness, it's very likely that elements in the Vatican have learned about the renewed threat to

154

your life from the KGB . . . from Andropov . . . some of them are hot-heads. Perhaps they talked a little too much.'

The Pope remained puzzled.

'What do you mean?'

Versano warmed to his theme.

'Well, they may have talked of retaliation.' He let the incredulous silence build and then said, 'Only talked, you understand. They hold Your Holiness in the highest reverence and would be aghast at this new threat to your life. See it as a threat to our entire beloved Church. I confess, Your Holiness, my own reaction was one of great anger. Of course at such times we must control that anger but some of us are more able to do so than others.'

The Pope was getting the drift.

'Do you know any more than that, Mario? Who would be involved? From the reaction in Poland we suspect that Father Van Burgh may be up to something. Ciban tells us that the Russico was one of the places in which they were trying to place listening devices. We have tried to locate Van Burgh but they told us he is in the East on a mission of mercy.'

Versano shrugged. 'It's likely, Your Holiness. That is his work.'

The Pope nodded. 'Yes, bless his soul. But we also remember that he is a priest who likes to go his own way. When we were Archbishop of Cracow he often got up to things we never knew about until later.'

Placatingly Versano said, 'I will keep my ear to the ground, Your Holiness, and report if I uncover anything. I will also try to find out what Father Van Burgh is doing and when he will return from the East. I think it's better if you leave this in my hands . . . Your Holiness has so much to concern himself with.'

John Paul grunted in agreement, massaged his jaw and said sadly, 'It was a great blow losing Cardinal Mennini. We pray for his soul every day. He had just begun to re-organise and discipline the Order. He is such a loss to us . . .' He sighed. 'And now we're advised that Cardinal

Bascones is favourite to be elected.' He held both hands out in a gesture of despair. 'He will radicalise the Order again . . . We may have to intervene, but we're loath to do so. It will cause even more polarisation within the Order . . . within the whole Church.'

Again Versano was placating. He was glad to be off the other subject.

'Your Holiness, I think you should not worry at this stage. My own information is that Bascones only has an outside chance.'

'We hope you're right.' The gloom left the Pope's face and he smiled at the Archbishop. 'Mario, how we wished you could come to Milan with us. We miss you on these trips, when you are not by our side.'

Versano smiled wryly. 'I also, Your Holiness. I hope the matter will soon be cleared up . . . I am determined to be beside you in the Far East.'

The Pope stood up. 'Nothing would give us more pleasure. Meanwhile, Mario, we rely on you to let us know as soon as you have anything more on this other business. It is unsettling to us.' He sighed yet again. 'Did you know that on his death poor Cardinal Mennini was found to be wearing the coarsest of hair shirts? His penance must have caused him agony.'

Versano shook his head. 'But I am not surprised, Your Holiness. He was a man with a soul of infinite purity. I too pray for him.'

From his great height he looked on his Pontiff and smiled reassuringly. 'On the other matter you can rely on me.'

The Pope smiled and lifted his hand and the Archbishop bent and softly kissed the ring.

Frank spread all the passport-sized photographs out on the desk. Some were clear, others less so. None were posed. Major Gudov, wearing a pale blue short-sleeved shirt and badly cut unfaded jeans, opened his file and leaned over the desk. Behind him stood the KGB Tripoli station chief, wearing a safari suit and a worried look. Next to him was

'Hassan' in a burnous. He was the deputy head of the Libyan Security Service. He looked irritated. Gudov represented Big Brother. Therefore he must be respected, but the Libyan did not like his domineering manner.

Quickly Gudov matched photo to drawing. Frank helped. He obviously had a practised eye. It took ten minutes. Slowly Gudov pulled the single remaining photo towards him and looked down at the half profile face of Mirek Scibor. Behind him Frank smiled and said:

'If that's your plant he never faltered; never asked a question out of line. Never created the slightest suspicion.'

Gudov grunted impatiently, 'Get me his file.'

Frank went to a steel filing cabinet, opened a door, rifled through some files and pulled one out. A slight smile was still on his face as he handed it to the Russian. Gudov looked at the single name written on the cover with a marker pen: 'Werner'. 'He's German?' he asked.

Frank shook his head. 'He spoke excellent German but with an accent. Also English. I'd say he's East European; Czech or Polish . . . could even be Russian.'

With a snort of disbelief Gudov turned to Hassan and asked sharply, 'From where did he come?'

Hassan said firmly, 'To answer that I'll have to get clearance from my chief . . . or even the Colonel himself.'

Gudov exploded. For two minutes he screamed abuse at the Arab. When he finished spittle was running down his chin. Hassan had backed up against a wall, seemingly pushed by the tirade. His face was rigid with a combination of shock and fear. Gudov pulled a handkerchief from his pocket and wiped his chin, then, emphasising every word, said: 'Your chief told you to give me every co-operation. Now tell me what I want to know or I promise you that you'll be dead by sunset.'

Without moving, and speaking like a robot, Hassan said, 'He came through Trieste. By ship to Tripoli on the *SS Lydia* – Cypriot – registered in Limassol.'

'Who sent him?' Gudov barked.

Hassan managed a shrug. 'We were told the German Red Army.'

'Do you have proof of that?'

'No, sir. We never do. You know how the system works. No questions are asked. We train all types from every ideology. Their only common denominator is indiscriminate terror.' His voice hardened slightly and he repeated, 'You know how the system works. The KGB devised it . . . for this camp and the others.'

Gudov sighed and asked, 'Where is this ship now?'

Hassan thought for a moment, then replied, 'It plies regularly between Limassol, Trieste and Tripoli . . . it should be in Tripoli in a few days.'

Gudov turned to the KGB station head. 'Lagovsky, I want the crew interrogated. You do it personally. Every detail they gleaned of this man. I want that information in Moscow twenty-four hours after that ship docks.'

Lagovsky bobbed his head in understanding. 'Yes, Major.'

He was nominally senior to Gudov but the signal that had preceded the Major's urgent arrival had left no doubts as to who was in charge.

'And the despatcher in Trieste,' Gudov continued. 'He must be run to ground and interrogated. Get the information from Hassan and signal Rome. They are to report to me direct in Moscow.'

'Yes, Major.'

Now for the first time Gudov opened the file. It contained reports on 'Werner' from all the instructors. Gudov read them quickly, flicking the pages. As chief instructor, Frank's report was at the end. He watched with the same little smile as the Russian read his final summing up.

'This man was dedicated to absorbing all aspects of the training and excelled in them all. On leaving the camp he was at the peak of physical fitness. Mentally and physically he is the perfect assassin.'

Gudov looked up at him as if asking a question. Quietly

Frank said, 'He's the best I've ever trained. The best I've ever seen. He's lethal.'

Gudov turned to the table and pointed to the photographs.

'How many of these people are still in the camp?'

Quickly Frank separated the photos, piling some up to one side. Finally there were twelve left. Gudov scanned them.

'The Filipinos have left?'

'Four days ago.'

'Pity.' He turned to Lagovsky and pointed at Hassan. 'Try to locate them. Apparently our man had sexual relations with one of the women. I want her interrogated.' He looked at his watch and frowned. To Frank he said, 'I will use this room to question all concerned. First the trainees one by one, then the instructors. You will be at the end. Leila before you.'

He waved a hand dismissively and they headed for the door. Frank said over his shoulder, 'You want coffee, Major?'

'No.' Gudov hesitated. 'Do you have Coca-Cola?'

Frank grinned. 'Sure thing.'

'Send me three bottles, cold.'

Gudov did not hold high hopes for extracting much useful information from the trainees and instructors, with the possible exception of Leila.

So it proved. He learned that 'Werner' had been a good listener but not much of a talker. He was getting desperate by the time Leila was ushered in. Her attractive face was impassive. With the others he had been blunt, almost menacing. With Leila he took a softer approach. It was not that she was a woman, but one look at her face told him that she could be obstinate. He also knew her history. She was unlikely to be intimidated.

He stood up and held out his hand. She shook it with a firm grip. He gestured at a chair and they both sat down.

The top buttons of her shirt were open and he found his eyes drawn to smooth brown skin at the top of her breasts. She sat easily, waiting patiently. He said, 'Leila, as you will know, we are investigating the man "Werner". We believe that he may be an agent for the Imperialists . . . and for the Zionists.'

Her lips twitched and she said, 'Well he wasn't Jewish. I can tell you that he was uncircumcised.'

He forced a smile. 'Yes, but they wouldn't be so obvious . . . Now Leila, we need your help. You had relations with this man . . . on several occasions.'

She nodded.

'How many occasions?' he asked.

She thought for a moment.

'I didn't count, Major. I suppose between eight and ten times.'

'What did you talk about?'

'Nothing.'

'Nothing! Come, Leila.' Gudov leaned forward and said intently, 'You and he became lovers . . . on at least eight occasions . . . and he said nothing?'

She took a breath and looked him directly in the eye. 'Major, please understand me. I will tell you anything I can about the man. I will never see him again. He means nothing to me emotionally. It was only physical. I often pick out one of the trainees for such contact. Now believe me, we hardly spoke a word . . .' She paused, and then seemed to make up her mind. 'You see, Major, that's the way I wanted it. So did he. The silence made it better . . . no affection . . . no soft words . . . soft lies . . . just two bodies. Do you understand?'

He did and he believed her. He felt close to despair. He had been relying on her. He looked down at the piece of paper in front of him. It was her face looking back with 'Werner's' words of description. He read the words, 'sado-masochistic tendencies'. He was about to ask a question when she said firmly, 'Major, since I heard, two hours ago, that you are investigating this man I have been thinking of

160

every detail I can that may help you. If you pick up your pen I will list them for you.'

A bit taken aback, Gudov picked up his pen and centred his notebook in front of him.

She started reciting a litany. 'His skin was unnaturally pale, even for a European. As if he had been out of the sun for a long time. He got a slight tan while he was here but was very careful not to get burned. He had a narrow scar about ten centimetres long on his lower right buttock. Another, wider but only half as long, above his left knee. His feet are average length for his height but highly arched. His fingers are slim but very strong. He has a moderate amount of bodily hair, especially on the chest. His pubic hair is very black, quite dense and more curly than the average European. His penis is average to large, uncircumcised. His scrotum is large.'

She paused while Gudov caught up with his notes. He finished writing 'large' and looked up. She went on.

'Prior to entering this camp he had not had sex for a long period. I know that from sexual experience with men who have been deprived, and also he mentioned it. His virility is above average. He can have two full orgasms within twenty minutes and a third an hour later. But he is not selfish about it. He knows how to give a woman pleasure and enjoys doing it . . .' Again she let Gudov catch up and then said, 'Apart from that, it was noticeable that in his training he drove himself to a degree that was exceptional. We see that normally only from the Islamic fanatics and the Japanese. Being neither, I suspect his obsessive drive came from hatred . . . of what I don't know. That's all I can tell you.'

Gudov wrote 'hatred' and then quietly asked, 'Is he a sadist . . . I mean sexually.'

She smiled slightly. 'You mean am I a masochist? Well to some extent I am . . . But "Werner" was not a sadist. He liked to dominate sexually – most men do – and there is a cruel part to him . . . but then, Major, many women are attracted to that.'

Gudov nodded as if realising a new truth. Then the corners of his lips turned down in disappointment. What she had told him was only marginally useful. It helped flesh out the character but gave no indication as to his background or origins. He had hoped for more. Hoped to be able to return to Colonel Zamiatin with more than just a photograph and a physical description. At the moment, in his mind's eye, 'Werner' was represented by a hairy chest and a large scrotum.

She must have noticed his disappointment. Almost contritely she said, 'I'm sorry, Major. As I told you, we didn't talk. I doubt if he talked to anyone in the camp.'

Gudov capped his pen and said, 'Not even that Filipino girl?'

He saw the flicker of anger in her eyes. It was quickly gone but it told him that he had learned everything she knew. She was not so unemotional. She knew the feelings of jealousy. 'Werner' had dominated her and used her when he wanted to. She hated him. He pushed back his chair and said, 'Thank you, Leila. Would you ask Frank to come in here.'

They shook hands and she walked towards the door. Half way there she stopped and turned; her eyes were a little puzzled.

'Major, he did say something that I didn't understand. He said it twice, both times just after he'd climaxed . . . said it to himself – not to me – just three words.'

'What were they?'

'*Kurwa ale dupa* . . . something like that.'

Gudov let out his breath in relief and thanked his stars for the four years of duty he had done in Warsaw and the Polish mistress he had enjoyed for the last two of them. He smiled.

'*Kurwa ale dupa*,' he laughed. 'Leila, it's Polish. It means he appreciated you, or something very much to that effect.'

She nodded thoughtfully. 'So he's a Pole. Is that a help?'

'Oh yes,' he breathed. 'A big help. Thank you, Leila . . .'

Half an hour later Frank watched Major Gudov climb into the helicopter. He was buoyant in spite of his punishing schedule. Obviously his visit had been a success. Frank's own interview with him had been brief. He had told him more or less what he had observed. There were two things that he hadn't told him. One was the signal that Werner had received telling him to grow a moustache and not to cut his hair. The other was his own gift to Werner of the 'Denbi' marker pen. As he watched the swirl of dust thrown up by the departing helicopter he wondered why he hadn't told Gudov. He really did not know. It was obvious that Werner, whoever he might be, was taking on the KGB. In spite of himself Frank was rooting for the underdog.

Major Boris Gudov reached Moscow at six in the evening. He had not slept on the plane but had spent the entire time working on his report. It was a minor masterpiece, showing of course how the Major's brilliant deductions had cut straight through to the truth. He knew that Colonel Zamiatin would have been informed of the plane's time of arrival but he did not report to his office immediately. He went first to the basement annex and had an animated conversation with the small, middle-aged, bird-like woman who was in charge of the Ryad R400 computer. She studied the photographs and nodded reassuringly. Within minutes the computer had enlarged and printed the photographs. The definition was vastly improved. Then for ten minutes it scanned for comparison. In those ten minutes tens of thousands of likenesses were compared. She had told Gudov that it could take up to half an hour. He couldn't wait that long and was immensely relieved when in ten minutes it came to the name and background of the assassin. Gudov tore off the perforated strip and clipped it on to the file containing his report. At seven o'clock he was in Zamiatin's office being congratulated. At seven thirty Zamiatin was in Victor Chebrikov's office being congratulated. It seemed that all the KGB were working late. But Chebrikov's face turned very sombre when he read the name in the report. Zamiatin started to explain his background but was cut off. Chebrikov obviously knew all about him.

At eight thirty Chebrikov was drinking vodka in Andropov's Kremlin apartment. Andropov was clad in a flowery silk dressing gown. 'A gift from my wife,' he had explained as though in apology.

He finished reading the report, closed the file firmly and looked up at Chebrikov.

'Victor,' he said. 'We do things sometimes which are remarkably clever at the time and then . . .' He left the sentence unfinished.

Diplomatically Chebrikov said, 'Yuri, it was never to be expected.'

Andropov tapped the file and said musingly, 'Mirek Scibor . . . they chose well those priests; they matched a man to a motive . . . You must catch him, Victor, and when you do he is to be killed, immediately. Not questioned. Not by anyone. Just killed.'

'We'll catch him,' Chebrikov said, injecting a note of enthusiasm into his voice. 'Now that we know his identity, the "*Papa*'s envoy" is as good as dead.'

'That's not good enough, Victor.' Andropov leaned forward. 'I want to see his body – and soon!'

In Cracow Professor Stefan Szafer worked quickly. Not hurriedly but faster than his normal steady pace. This surprised his assistant doctor, Wit Bereda, and theatre sister, Danuta Pesko. Not that his speed endangered the patient at all. His fingers were as deft as always. Then he truly surprised them. Having slowly unclamped the renal artery and checked the fine line of micro-sutures which closed the wound in the kidney, he turned to Bereda and said from behind his mask, 'Doctor, close up for me. I have an important lunch appointment and I'm running late.'

He stepped away from the table and walked briskly through to the dressing room. Bereda looked at Danuta

Pesko's eyes across the inert body. They were as surprised as his own. Many, even most, busy top surgeons leave the sewing up to their assistants, but not Professor Stefan Szafer – not ever. He took immense pride in that aspect of his work. Incisions for kidney operations are inevitably long and disfiguring. He sewed with the expertise of a Los Angeles plastic surgeon to limit the scarring.

'Must be someone damned important,' Bereda muttered as he moved around the table.

The 'someone' was important, but not in the way Bereda imagined. She was a struggling young actress called Halena Maresa and Stefan Szafer was totally, obsessively in love with her.

He arrived fifteen minutes early at the Wierzynek Restaurant. The head waiter recognised him as an important person and customer and ushered him to his usual alcove table. What was unusual was that he was lunching rather than dining. He usually took a quick lunch in the hospital canteen.

He ordered a vodka with lots of soda. While waiting for it he looked around the elegant room. It was an expensive place and so mainly frequented by high officials in the Government or armed forces and top academicians or people like himself who were in the top echelon of salary earners. Unlike his contemporaries he was not particularly impressed with the luxury of the restaurant or its prices. His time in the West had made him *blasé* about such things. In fact, with his stern idealism, he faintly disapproved. He would have been quite content in a simple, less pretentious place, but he knew that Halena enjoyed it. He had suggested it the first time he asked her out, trying to impress her. During that dinner he wondered whether she had accepted only because he was able to afford the place. But she had quickly dispelled the idea. With her beauty she must have had many such invitations. Also during that dinner her gaiety and attention towards him convinced him of her genuine interest.

After their second date she had kissed him. At first demurely but then towards the end with passionate intensity. He had concluded that she was immune to his 'problem'.

His drink arrived and he glanced at his watch. Ten minutes to go and she was always punctual; a habit he appreciated. He reached into his jacket pocket and took out a small Amplex tablet and popped it into his mouth quickly. That tablet represented his problem. It was chronic bad breath. It had been the bane of his life. He was a good-looking man and had the personality and the position to attract women, but the attraction never lasted long; his halitosis saw to that. He had tried every prophylactic known to medical science. He had tried varying his diet. He could contain the problem to some extent but never alleviate it. His grandfather had it. He supposed it was hereditary, leaping every other generation. He realised that his love for Halena derived not only from her beauty and personality but from her utter lack of concern about his 'problem'. He had even tentatively mentioned it to her once and she had merely laughed and said, 'I must have bad olfactory glands. I hardly ever notice it. Put it out of your head, Stefan.'

He had always thought that actresses were, by definition, somewhat promiscuous. He discovered that although that may be true in general, Halena was an exception. He had taken her out eight times since he met her four weeks before. She let him kiss her and lately they had petted fairly heavily. He had even caressed her bare breast; she never wore a bra. But so far that was as far as she would go. The promise of more was always there though in her mischievous eyes. Once after they had been kissing in his car and he had tried to go further she had pushed his hand away and sensed his disappointment and frustration.

'Don't think I'm a tease, Stefan,' she had said gently. 'I want to as well but I make a rule. First I must know a man well. Know that I love him.'

'Do you think you could love me?'

166

She had smiled at him, her eyes soft with affection.

'Would I have wasted my time and yours if I thought I couldn't? Give me a little more time. I eat slowly, I take a bath slowly, I get dressed slowly . . . and I fall in love slowly.'

He had been encouraged, his frustration tempered. He knew it would be satisfied in the moderately near future. He thought of the evening he had met her at a boring reception at the University. A distant acquaintance had introduced them. They had spoken only briefly at first. Being undoubtedly the most beautiful woman in the room, she had been quickly monopolised by all the would-be Romeos. But he kept his eyes on her and several times he had seen hers on him. Finally quite late she had broken away and crossed the room to where he was standing. With a smile she had said, 'I'm told you're a brilliant doctor. You don't look it – that's a compliment. Now I'm going to break a social rule and ask a doctor a medical question at a party. What's the best cure for a hangover?'

'Are you going to have one?' he had asked, seriously.

'No, but my flatmate drinks a lot of vodka. She gets them all the time. She insists that the only cure is a "hair of the dog".'

He had smiled. 'It's quite true, Miss Maresa. It's been medically proven that a couple of tots of what caused the malady helps alleviate it . . . but only a couple! That and a few breaths of pure oxygen.'

'I shan't tell her that,' she had laughed. 'She'll clutter up the place with oxygen cylinders.' She had glanced at her watch and muttered, 'Damn, I have to go or I'll miss my last bus.'

'I'll be glad to run you home in my car.'

'Are you sure? It's quite a long way.'

'I'm sure,' he had replied firmly.

She came in only two minutes late, glancing at her watch. She was wearing a calf-length sheepskin coat and a little black pillbox hat, her ash-blonde hair falling from under it in careful disarray. She waved at him and threaded through the tables. Heads swivelled to watch her progress and Stefan felt again that thrill whenever she came to him through a crowd. He stood up and she kissed him lightly. Her nose was cold. She unbuttoned her coat and handed it to a hovering waiter. Underneath she was wearing a dark blue knitted cashmere dress. A present from Stefan that he had obtained from London and given to her on their last date. She pirouetted for him.

'How does it look?'

'On you it looks perfect.'

Another waiter was holding a chair for her. She sat down, her face alive with excitement.

'So what's your good news?' he asked.

She held up her hand. 'Let's order first.'

After the head waiter had taken their order and left she announced, 'I'm going to Moscow for two weeks.'

'Oh? I thought you didn't like Russia.'

'Russians,' she corrected him.

'Is it a part?'

'No, Stefan. In a way better. It's a theatre workshop run by Oleg Tabakov. He's the best, even if he is Russian. There will be actors and actresses from Hungary, Czecho-slovakia, Rumania – all over. It will be a great experience . . . and useful to my career.'

He was pleased for her but also felt a twinge of disappointment. It was only two weeks but he would miss her.

'That's splendid, Halena. How did you get it?'

She gave one of her mischievous smiles. 'I didn't at first. The Academy selected Barbara Plansky but then Szczepanski gave her a part in his new play, lucky bitch, and she had to drop out. So I got the chance.'

He smiled. 'That's lucky, but you deserve it. When do you go?'

'The fifth of next month.' She cocked her head to one side and surveyed him. She had a little smile on her lips. 'Will you miss me, Stefan?'

'You know I will,' he answered.

She reached over and put a hand on his.

'Then come with me.'

His head jerked up in surprise. Before he could answer she went on persuasively, 'You've told me that you haven't taken a holiday for ages. I'll have plenty of time off from the workshop. We could even go to Leningrad for a couple of days. It's supposed to be beautiful. Irmina went last month. She said it's fantastic. She went on the train overnight . . . do try to come. We'll be together . . . together, Stefan.'

The word 'together' and the way she said it took on great meaning in his mind. He felt himself stirring.

'I could never get away for two weeks, Halena. That would be impossible at the moment.'

She was undeterred. 'So come for a few days. Even a long weekend would be worthwhile. Please, Stefan. Please.' She squeezed his hand as if in supplication.

He smiled. 'I shall try, Halena. Just for a few days though. This afternoon I'll check through my operation and lecture schedules and then talk to Professor Skibinsky.'

She laughed with pleasure. He loved to see her laugh. From the seat beside him he picked up a gift-wrapped box and put it on the table in front of her.

'What is it?'

'A camera.'

'For me?'

'Of course. You told me how much you enjoyed photography but could not afford one of the new reflex cameras. That's a Leica. One of the best.'

She looked at him fondly, her eyes shining, and said, 'Thank you, darling. I'm going to take lots of photographs . . . especially of you.'

After lunch the struggling young actress returned to her small apartment. On the way she stopped at a telephone box and made one brief call.

*

Two days later Professor Roman Skibinsky, head of surgery, had lunch in the same restaurant with Feliks Kurowski, director general of the hospital. Roman Skibinsky's father had been a Colonel in the pre-war Polish cavalry. He had been one of the thousands of Polish officers murdered in the forest of Katyn. He had never believed the Russian propaganda that the atrocity had been carried out by the Nazis.

After lunch, which was mostly taken up by a conversation on administration problems, they ordered coffee and brandy, and Skibinsky said casually, 'Feliks, when is the new medical department budget coming out?'

'In August as usual. If those idiots in Warsaw haven't lost their abacus or whatever else they use to do their sums.'

'Do you think you'll get the allocation for the new forensic lab?'

Kurowski sighed deeply. Skibinsky had touched a raw spot. For five years he had been trying to squeeze funds out of the Ministry for just that project; so far without success. It was always the same story – maybe next year.

He said, 'You know how it is, Roman. I've been pushing for years. Frankly, I doubt it. There are rumours that the total budget for the Ministry is going to be cut.'

The coffee and brandy arrived. With the departure of the waiter Skibinsky asked, 'Do you mind if I speak frankly?'

Kurowski smiled. 'Roman, I've never heard you talk otherwise.'

Skibinsky smiled back. The two men had a good working understanding.

He said, 'Feliks, in spite of being a good Communist you are also an excellent administrator. You run the best teaching hospital in Poland. Perhaps in the entire bloc.' Kurowski shrugged but he was obviously pleased with the compliment. 'But,' Skibinsky went on, 'you're a God-awful politician.'

'So what? I don't want to be a politician.'

'Ah Feliks, the only way you're going to get that lab is by being one. Look at Ratajski in Warsaw. He spends half his time at the Ministry kissing bums. Last year's budget gave him two new operating theatres.'

'Maybe,' Kurowski conceded. 'But I'm not the bum-kissing type and you know it.'

'Right, but there might be another way. The good Minister is very prestige conscious and without being disrespectful one could say that he has a very good impression of himself.'

Kurowski grinned. 'In what way is your devious mind working?'

'Well, it's strongly rumoured that Yuri Andropov is suffering from severe kidney trouble, among other things. Now if a certain Polish specialist were to be called in for consultation, then great kudos would attach itself to our Minister and the hospital whence the specialist came.'

Kurowski caught his drift immediately. 'You wouldn't be thinking of our own Professor Szafer by any chance?'

Skibinsky nodded seriously. 'He is exceptional. He had two papers published last month in *Sovetskaya Meditsina* which were highly praised. His work on dialysis has been accepted worldwide as breaking new ground. My suggestion is logical, Roman, and there are precedents. After all, that Swiss specialist Brunner was called in to attend Brezhnev . . . also it's rumoured that Andropov will need surgery.'

Kurowski immediately said, 'They'd never let a non-Russian operate.'

'True,' Skibinsky concurred. 'But if it's that serious they'll accept all the advice they can get. And they know of Szafer's reputation . . . he really is the boy wonder.'

For a few moments Kurowski considered the suggestion. Skibinsky was a masterful persuader. He waited for just the right amount of time and then said, off-handedly, 'And by coincidence Szafer is going to be in Moscow soon.'

Kurowski looked up surprised. 'He is?'

Skibinsky smiled disarmingly. 'Of course, you must give

approval. He came to me yesterday afternoon. His girl-friend, an actress, is attending some function there. He wants to take a few days off to join her. I agreed to take his lectures and I can easily reschedule his operations.'

Kurowski considered again, and again Skibinsky waited just long enough before putting in the clincher.

'And again by coincidence the Minister is making an official visit to Moscow next week. The timing is perfect.'

Kurowski laughed. 'You make it sound like a God-given opportunity!'

Skibinsky looked startled for a moment, then recovered and nodded.

'It is, Roman, and one not to be missed. Now when you talk to the Minister I suggest you try to make it appear that it's all his own idea.'

He leaned forward and carefully explained the strategy.

12

Mirek held the uniform in his hands and looked at Father Heisl in astonishment. The priest first laughed and then said seriously, 'I'm assured it's a perfect fit. Does it give you nostalgia?'

Mirek shook his head. Ania was sitting at the table looking puzzled. They were in the Vienna safe house. In twenty-four hours their journey would begin.

'What is it?' she asked.

Mirek tossed it on to the table.

'It's the uniform of a Colonel in the SB.' He tapped the two medals on the breast of the jacket. 'Obviously an efficient one.' He turned to Heisl. 'But what's it all about?'

'It's the Bacon Priest's idea. After all, you know the organisation intimately. You know the procedures and structures. It could be useful in a crisis.'

Mirek nodded thoughtfully. 'That's true, but what about papers?'

'Those will be given to you after you cross the Czech-Polish border. It will be the same system all the way along. At each contact point your documents will be exchanged for the next stage of the journey.'

Mirek remembered something. 'No Colonel in the SB is properly dressed without his Makarov.'

The priest nodded grimly and reached a hand into the large canvas bag at his feet. It emerged holding a black belt and flapped holster. He passed it to Mirek who quickly opened the flap and drew out a pistol. Its black-matt surface gleamed dully under the light. He weighed it in his hand with obvious satisfaction, then flicked the catch and slid out the magazine. He counted out the bullets and checked them carefully. As he reloaded them and thrust the magazine back into the grip Father Heisl said, 'I've got a spare magazine for you.'

'Good. So the Bacon Priest agreed.'

Heisl sighed. 'Reluctantly. He said it will make him very unhappy if you have to use it.'

'Me too,' Mirek replied grimly. 'Is he in Vienna?'

'I don't know.'

Mirek grinned at him. 'Sure you do. I'll bet he's not a million miles from here.'

Heisl shrugged and started lifting more items out of his bag and placing them on the table. First several small plastic bottles.

'Hair dyes,' he said. 'Ania has been taught how to use them. I have wigs for her but a wig on a man always looks obvious.' He put three wigs on the table. Ania reached for the auburn one, pulled it on and arranged it. The change in her appearance was startling. She brushed a finger over an eyebrow.

'I would have to dye these.'

She pulled the wig off and tossed it back on to the table. Heisl held a brown paper bag in his hand. He shook out the contents: several small round and oval shaped flat plastic pads.

'You know what these are?'

They both nodded. They had practised using them. Those pads, correctly placed inside the mouth against the cheeks, could subtly alter the shape of the face. Heisl put them back in the bag and said, 'That's it then. Except for one last thing. Ania, would you wait outside for just a minute?'

Dutifully she rose and left the room. Mirek was expecting to listen to some confidential information. Instead the priest said, 'Tell me again, in sequence, the contacts, the passwords, the fallbacks and the numbers.'

Mirek's eyes narrowed in concentration. Yet again a

picture formed in his mind. The names, the places, the secret words and the telephone numbers. They were all stamped on his brain. Without hesitation he reeled them off.

Heisl smiled and called loudly, 'Ania.'

She came back into the room and he put her to the same test. She too ran through the sequence without hesitation.

The priest walked to the sideboard and poured two brandies and a Tia Maria. He gave one brandy to Mirek and the Tia Maria to Ania. He raised his own brandy and said benignly, 'You are ready. Let's drink to a successful journey and mission.'

They drank. In spite of the toast the mood was sombre.

Mirek said, 'I think it's time you told us how we cross that first border.'

Heisl considered for a moment and then nodded:

'We consider it one of the most dangerous stages of the journey. It's the only border you will cross clandestinely. From Czechoslovakia into Poland, and Poland into Russia, you will cross with false papers and a convincing cover story. Originally we had planned the same for this border but that is now dangerous. Instead you will cross as "sardines".' He smiled at their raised eyebrows. 'It's just an expression we use. Such crossings take place in small hidden compartments. There is not much room.' He walked to a wall on which was hung a large-scale map of Eastern Austria and Western Czechoslovakia. He pointed to a spot on the border. 'Hate – used by heavy commercial traffic. You will be in the secret compartment of a truck taking machine tools to the Skoda factory. It is a truck well known to the Czech border authorities. It makes the journey on a regular, routine basis. Its arrival at the border post will be carefully timed depending on the volume of traffic. It will be judged so that the inspection of the truck takes place between eight and nine in the morning. Border officials change shifts at nine. It is regulated so that one team will not leave a truck half inspected. Like all bureaucrats

175

they like to leave work on time, hence inspections during that hour tend to be cursory.'

Mirek was looking sceptical. He had experience in the SB of searching freight trucks. He well knew that to conceal such a large compartment was difficult. Border guards had much experience. They also had equipment to help locate such places. The old days of running refugees through the Iron Curtain, hidden under a pile of potatoes in the back of a truck, were long gone. He expressed his scepticism. Heisl remained confident.

'Mirek, you must trust our judgment. We have considered very carefully. The truck is owned and will be driven by a true professional. To our knowledge he has spirited dozens of people safely through the Iron Curtain. We have used him ourselves several times.'

'Who is he?'

'An Australian.'

Mirek's face showed his astonishment. Heisl smiled. 'It is not uncommon. The trucking fraternity in and out of Eastern Europe has become quite international. Strangely there are lots of Irish involved . . . naturally, we wouldn't use one of them. There is a lot of money to be made – legitimately. Of course, very much more in the human traffic.'

'That's what he does it for?' Ania asked. 'Money?'

'Yes,' Heisl replied firmly. 'His motives are totally mercenary. He charges a great deal, but then he is the best. He's been doing it for over five years now – and has a perfect record.'

Mirek glanced at Ania. She shrugged non-committally.

The priest said soothingly, 'Even with the increased level of border security there should be no problem. The flow of trade across this border is very considerable. The Australian's load is vitally important for the Skoda factory. He has papers proving that. He is very experienced.'

Mirek was looking more confident. He asked, 'How long will we be sardines?'

Carefully Heisl replied, 'We think between eight and twelve hours.'

'Hell. In a compartment like the one in which I was loaded on to the boat?'

Slowly the priest shook his head.

'Much smaller, Mirek. It measures one metre by half a metre and is less than half a metre high.'

Incredulously Mirek said, 'For up to twelve hours . . . two of us?'

The priest nodded. 'And your bag. But you will not be conscious.'

'What do you mean?'

Heisl sighed. 'It's a sort of insurance that the Australian insists on. He was once transporting a man out of East Germany to the West. The man had a bad attack of claustrophobia and started screaming. They were very nearly caught. Since then the Australian insists on injecting his passengers with a drug that causes a deep sleep for about ten hours. It's a sensible precaution. You are both fit. It will do you no harm.'

Before Mirek or Ania could comment he pointedly glanced at his watch and said, 'Talking of sleep I think you should get some now; and in the morning take only a little food and no liquid. There are no ablution facilities in that compartment.'

He smiled and finished the last of his brandy.

The journey started from a warehouse on the outskirts of Linz. Heisl drove them there at five in the morning, with little conversation. There was not much to say that had not already been said. The warehouse was deserted except for a huge Scania truck, painted bright green, and a rugged, freckle-faced man with long red hair, long sideboards and a long, rough-cut beard. He was dressed in paint-streaked denim overalls. Deep blue eyes twinkled as he examined them. The eyes finally rested on Ania and he grinned. In workable but badly accented German he said, 'You'll be very cosy in my little cubby hole.'

He showed it to them. The concealment was simple but ingenious. He unscrewed the large fuel tank cap just behind the driver's door and put his hand inside. They heard a click and then a gap appeared at the lower edge of the panelling. He leaned down, got his fingers under it and pulled up. A flap opened, its hinge neatly concealed in the seam of the panelling which ran the length of the truck. The flap itself was very heavy and about six inches thick. The Australian propped it open with a stick.

'These Commies are bloody cunning,' he explained. 'They have plans of all common makes of trucks. If all the dimensions don't match they take everything apart.' He pointed under the flap. 'That was originally part of the fuel tank.' He squatted down and indicated the long bulge of the tank. 'It's cut my fuel capacity in half but that's no problem. I always keep a dozen big gerry cans of diesel in the back. The stupid buggers always suspect that I smuggle things in those.' He grinned through his beard. 'They always push sticks down them.'

Mirek bent down and looked into the compartment. It had padded sides and an old carpet on the floor. It hardly looked big enough for him, let alone the two of them. He said so. The Australian grinned again. His teeth were discoloured by nicotine. He said lightly, 'Don't worry, mate, you'll be snug as bugs in a rug.' He turned to Heisl. 'I had a call from Hate. There's quite a line building up. I want to get started earlier. In fact the sooner the better.'

'That's fine,' Heisl replied quietly.

The Australian walked over to a bench by the wall and came back with a small polished wooden box. He asked Heisl to hold it and then opened the clasp. Inside was a rubber-topped bottle and half a dozen disposable syringes. He took one out, and the bottle. With practised ease he slid the needle through the rubber top and measured up a quantity of the colourless liquid. Then he turned to Mirek with a grin.

'All right, mate. Roll up your left sleeve. Time to shoot up. How much do you weigh?'

178

As Mirek rolled up his sleeve he said cautiously, 'Eighty-six kilos. What is that stuff?'

'Trepalin, mate. It'll give you sweet dreams. When you wake up you'll have a mild headache and a bit of nausea. Something like a medium hangover. It'll clear up in a couple of hours. This will take effect in about fifteen minutes.'

He gripped Mirek's arm just below the elbow and pressed his thumb hard down on the inside. He watched the vein expand and then slid the needle in. Mirek watched his eyes as they watched the calibrated gauge on the syringe. It only took a moment then he pulled out the needle and tossed the syringe into a corner. He picked up another one and injected the rubber bottle top saying, 'Can't be too careful these days, hey?' He turned to Ania. 'What's your weight, lady?'

'Sixty kilos,' she replied in a confident voice. She had already rolled up her sleeve.

'And very nicely distributed too,' he said, gripping her arm.

She didn't flinch as the needle went in, just watched the Australian with an air of disdain. He tossed the syringe away and announced, 'Right, let's get you loaded up and on the way to the People's Democratic Paradise.'

The farewells were quick and, on the surface, unemotional, but as Mirek shook Father Heisl's hand and as Ania hugged and kissed his cheek they both felt sad and suddenly lonely. This priest, rapidly passing from middle to old age, had been a wise and caring mentor. He had, in his diffident way, been a teacher and friend. As they turned away with his words of good wishes in their ears they felt that their journey was truly about to start. Their few belongings were in a small canvas duffle bag. The Australian stowed that first, squashing it into the far end of the compartment and remarking that it would make a good pillow. The compartment was lit by a tiny torch bulb in one upper corner. He explained that it could be turned on and off from his cab and he would turn it off in twenty minutes when they were in lullaby land.

179

Mirek climbed in, sliding head first towards the duffle bag. He was beginning to feel drowsy. He rested his head on the bag. He could feel the holstered gun which he had packed close to the drawstring. It gave him comfort. Ania struggled in beside him. He could feel her soft body as it moved up against his. She had her back to him. He felt her buttocks against his knees and then his crotch. Her hair was in his face. He could feel her straining away from him.

'Are you all right? Try to relax.'

'I'm fine.' The tone of her voice belied the statement. She was acutely uncomfortable, not only physically but mentally. They heard Father Heisl's voice distantly.

'God go with you.'

Then they heard the flap being clamped shut and they were like twin chrysalises in a larva. Faintly they heard the slam of the cab door and after a moment the compartment vibrated as the engine started. A minute later and they felt the movement as the truck moved out of the warehouse. The brakes were applied and Ania was forced hard against Mirek. She edged away again, her body rigid. Impatiently he said, 'I didn't ask for you to be here. For God's sake relax . . . I'm not going to assault you. In a few minutes we'll be unconscious.'

She did relax a little. He felt the pressure of her back on his chest but she kept her bottom away from his crotch.

He was getting very drowsy now. In a crazy moment he wondered if she snored – or if he did. He moved his left arm, trying to get it comfortable. There was nowhere to put it except over her. He put it on her hip. She did not move. He could hear the deepening of her breathing. Her hair smelt like a pine forest. Almost of its own accord his arm moved and his hand felt up her rib cage and cupped her left breast. With a feeble effort she tried to push it away but she was already losing consciousness. He could feel the nipple rising against his hand. He followed her into sleep.

*

Father Heisl passed back the binoculars. The Bacon Priest put them against his eyes and readjusted the lenses. It was eight forty-five and they sat in the car on the crown of a hill four miles from the border town of Hate. Beyond it was the bridge over the March River. Trucks and cars crossed it at steady intervals. They were watching for the green truck. Neither of them displayed any anxiety but both were very tense inside. Weeks of planning were coming to fruition. When that green truck crossed that bridge the die would be cast. They had been the puppet masters, but from then on the puppets would be without strings.

The Bacon Priest lowered the binoculars and said, 'You gave him the gun?'

'Yes.'

He raised the binoculars again and said thoughtfully, 'It's better that way . . . I mean that he should ask for it . . . not that we pressed it on him.'

Heisl replied dolefully, 'I suppose so, Pieter, but I worry about the girl. Scibor is so determined, obsessed even, that he won't hesitate to get rid of her if he thinks she's a hindrance. He won't think twice.'

Without moving his gaze from the bridge and talking softly, almost to himself, the Bacon Priest said, 'We can't have it both ways. His obsession, his motive, gives the plan a greater chance of success. Having Ania travel with him also increases the chances. Yes, she is at great risk, even from him . . . but Jan, our Church was built on martyrdom and will always be sustained by it.' He took one hand from the binoculars and gestured in front of him. 'Even now over there some of our people are being tortured, mentally and physically. We must be compassionate for all and yet not fear for a single individual. In our task we –' He suddenly straightened and steadied the binoculars. 'There it is. They are through, crossing the bridge.'

With the naked eye Heisl could make out the bright green of the truck. He watched it reach the far side and

181

disappear behind some buildings. The Bacon Priest turned to him with a broad grin on his face.

'They are through. The "*Papa*'s envoy" is on his way.'

Heisl found that he could not share his boss's delight. He was touched by a sense of foreboding. The Bacon Priest punched him lightly on the shoulder.

'Come on, cheer up. You did a magnificent job preparing them. They will not fail.'

Father Heisl smiled back bleakly.

13

Ania woke before Mirek. Her head ached from the nape of her neck to her cranium. Her mouth felt gummy, her limbs were painfully stiff. Mirek's hand was on her left breast. Carefully she placed it on her thigh. She felt him move and then he settled again and his breathing resumed a deep rhythm. She flexed her muscles one by one. Her right arm beneath her was totally numb and without feeling. The truck was moving fast. She could feel the motion of it as it swayed around the long curves. She ran her tongue along dry lips and wondered how much longer. She hoped that Mirek would remain asleep until they arrived. She wished her watch was luminous. Mirek woke up. First she felt him stiffen and then his blurred curses as his brain registered his body's discomfort. She said thickly, 'Are you all right?'

'Yes,' he grunted. 'But if this is what he calls a mild hangover I'd hate to have a bad one. How do you feel?'

'I've never had a hangover but if this is like one I don't know why people ever drink. Can you see what time it is?'

He lifted his hand from her hip and twisted his head. 'Almost three. The Australian was right. It's just about ten hours.'

'So we should be there soon.' There was a note of anxiety in her voice.

He said brusquely, 'It all depends how long he took to clear through the border. It might have been ages. We could be in for several more hours. You'll just have to stick it out.'

She resented the implication and said angrily, 'I can stick it as long as you can.'

But it was only another half an hour. They felt the truck turn off to the right. From the rougher surface it had to be a secondary road.

'The Blovice diversion,' Mirek muttered. He had a clear plan of the route in his head.

Five minutes later the truck slowed and turned again to the right. This road was even rougher but in less than a minute the truck slowed further and then stopped. Nothing happened for ten minutes, then they heard and felt a slight thump which must be the driver closing his cab door. A minute later light and ice cold fresh air flooded in and they both breathed in with relief. Mirek twisted and peered down the length of his body. The light almost blinded him, then it was partially blocked by the Australian's hairy red face.

'You two all right . . . awake?'

They both muttered, 'Yes.'

'Good. We got here early. I was worried you'd still be asleep. Come on out quick; ladies first.' He grabbed Ania's ankles and pulled her swiftly out. At first she could hardly stand. With his hands under her armpits he half carried her across the road and helped her to sit on a fallen tree trunk. As he turned back Mirek was already out, leaning against the truck. Quickly the Australian reached in and pulled out the duffle bag. He dropped it at Mirek's feet and said:

'All right, mate, I'm off.'

'Hang on!' Mirek pushed himself away from the truck and staggered a few paces, then straightened up. 'Are you sure this is the right spot?'

The Australian was hurrying to the door of the cab.

'Sure,' he called out pointing off to his left. 'Blovice is four kilometres over that hill.'

Mirek looked. Below the hill was the small copse imprinted on his mind. He waved acknowledgment. The

Australian swung up into the cab and slammed the door. The engine was still running.

'Good luck,' he shouted out of the window. There was a hiss from the air brakes and the truck accelerated away, the rear wheels narrowly missing the duffle bag. The Australian expected no thanks. All the thanks he wanted were in another, much smaller, secret compartment in the truck. Ten pliable wafer-thin strips of pure gold.

Mirek retrieved the duffle bag and hobbled over to Ania.

'Come on,' he urged. 'We must get off the road quickly.'

He reached down to help her up but she shrugged off his hand, determined not to show any physical weakness.

It was a bright but cold afternoon. Far away to their left were neat fields. The earth in front of them was stony and obviously not arable. It was scattered with coarse clumps of grass and small bushes.

It took them half an hour to reach the copse. After half a kilometre they joined a rough cart track. By that time much of the stiffness had left their limbs and they were in better spirits. The grass here was greener and richer and as they approached they heard the sound of running water. A tiny stream tumbled down the hill and through the trees and then meandered off towards the fields. Ania expected that at weekends in the summer it would be a popular picnic place.

They sat down beside the stream. Mirek looked at his watch and announced, 'The first rendezvous time is in twenty minutes. I hope he makes it – I'm ravenous.'

He had put the duffle bag on the grass between them. Ania reached for it, untied the cord and rummaged about inside. When she pulled out her toilet bag Mirek grinned and asked, 'Going to repair your make-up?'

'No. I'm going to look after the health of my dear husband.'

She took out a bottle of aspirin, shook three pills into her palm and held them out. He took them with a grunt

185

of approval. Next she produced a plastic bottle of water. After he'd swallowed his three pills she took two and then stood brushing grass from her backside.

'I'm going to take a walk to try and warm up a little.'

She jumped over the stream and walked off through the trees, slipping a little on the frozen earth.

'Don't go far,' he called.

She waved in acknowledgment. He was a little amused by her attitude since they had started the journey. She was determined to show how tough and reliable she could be, woman or not.

Woman she certainly was. His eyes followed her as she stepped over a fallen log. Underneath her thick anorak she was wearing well-tailored slacks and they accentuated the curves of her waist and hips. He suddenly remembered how his hand had cupped her breast in the compartment. He could feel the warmth and softness and curve of it even now. Just as suddenly he recalled his reaction when he had first met her. How he could only visualise her in a nun's habit. In a way it was still true. When he tried to think of her sexually the tailored slacks and the limbs they moulded disappeared amid loose ankle-length white. But the feel of her breast in his hand was still warm.

She came back in fifteen minutes from down the hill, her face slightly flushed from the exertion. 'I climbed to the top,' she panted. 'I could see Blovice. It's a tiny and beautiful village, white houses and red roofs, and the steeple of an old church.'

He was about to tell her that the church would long since have ceased to serve a religious purpose when they heard the sound of a car.

He stood up and they watched an old grey box-shaped Skoda bump up the cart track. It stopped fifty metres away, close by the copse. A small man stepped out. He wore brown corduroy trousers, a large overcoat, and an old soft brown hat. He retrieved a knobbled walking stick from the back seat and then strolled towards them looking fondly around him. As he came closer they saw that he was in his middle or late sixties with a leathery, very lined face and small crinkled eyes.

Those eyes spotted them in the trees and he waved his stick cheerfully in greeting and called out, 'Hello there. What a lovely day for a walk.'

'Come on,' Mirek said and picked up the duffle bag. As they walked out of the copse he said to the man, 'Yes, but it's very cold among the trees.'

The man's face wrinkled even more as he smiled and held out his hand.

'Ah, my nephew Tadeusz and niece-in-law, Tatania. I'm so pleased you've arrived safely.'

He shook Mirek's hand warmly and embraced Ania and kissed her on both cheeks in a greeting befitting relatives who have been long parted.

'How well you look.' He chatted happily as he shepherded them to the car. 'Your mother is well, Tadeusz, and that old dragon Alicja?'

'Very well, Uncle Albin. They send their love – and how is Aunt Sylwia?'

'Ah, the same, always the same; never gives me a moment's peace. She has a little arthritis now but nothing too bad.'

In the car with Mirek in the front passenger seat and Ania in the back, the man's attitude changed from relaxed cheerfulness to brisk efficiency. He quickly unlocked the glove compartment and took out a large, well-used leather wallet. He handed it to Mirek saying, 'Your papers. Please check them carefully.'

Mirek flipped open the wallet and went through the papers thoroughly while going through a mental check list. It was complete. They were all there. Passports for Tadeusz and Tatania Bednarek, both properly stamped and signed with the signatures they had practised. Identity cards, return train tickets from Warsaw to Brno via Breslau with the outward section neatly clipped to denote use. Some old letters from a couple of friends. His pass for his place of work, the Pluch tyre factory. Her pass for the Kucharska clinic. Current ration coupons with the last dates stamped three days before. Everything was there exactly as Father Heisl had told them. Mirek knew that some of the papers would be genuine and others master forgeries. With all his experience in the SB he could not tell which was which. This gave him a surging feeling of relief and confidence.

'Perfect,' he said, closing the wallet and tucking it into his pocket.

'Good.' The man started the car and they bumped off. 'I'll drive slowly. Your train into Brno was half an hour late and in this old thing even a maniacal driver like me couldn't be expected to cover the distance in under two hours. By the way, your suitcases are in the boot. Leave that bag in the car and I'll fetch it out after nightfall . . . Our little cottage is on the outskirts but in a small village all eyes are curious. Especially when strangers are involved.'

Mirek was about to ask him when he had arrived in Blovice but then checked himself. Father Heisl had stressed that no one down the pipeline would ask them questions of that nature and neither should they. He knew that the cover for this old man and his wife, or surrogate wife, was that he was a retired electrician from Prague of Polish extraction who had rented a cottage in a small village in the countryside to see out their remaining years. As soon as Mirek and Ania had passed up the pipeline the man and his wife would decide that village life was, after all, too quiet for them. They would pack up, say their farewells and disappear.

The old man turned and glanced at Ania. 'Are you very tired?'

'No, Uncle Albin.' She chuckled. 'I slept all the way . . . I am hungry.'

'Don't worry, little one, your Aunt Sylwia will fill you up.'

Perversely Mirek felt an edge of irritation at the old man's choice of endearment. He was small and probably weighed less than Ania. Also it was hardly necessary to keep up their cover when they were alone. Brusquely he said, 'Is everything ready? When do we leave Blovice?'

They had come to the end of the cart truck. Albin waited until he had turned on to the tarred road and speeded up a little before answering. He glanced at Mirek and said tonelessly, 'Everything is prepared. Tomorrow you will rest up. In the afternoon take a stroll with us in the village and have a Slivovice in the café. It would be expected. The next morning we leave on our little tour. First the museum in Brno. It is worth seeing, I'm told. Then we shall drive to Ostrava and spend the night in a small hotel. The next day we shall have lunch in one of the tavernas and then drive through to Dieszyn, where you take the train.'

They were approaching the village now, passing a few small farmhouses. There were several people in the fields tending vegetables. One by one they looked up as the car passed. Traffic was a rarity here off the main road.

Ania could see the spire of the church ahead. She asked, 'Is the church still in operation?'

Albin answered angrily. 'You must be joking. It's been a transit warehouse for grain these past twenty years. These Communists are worse than animals!'

He spoke with such vehemence that Mirek guessed he was deeply religious. Perhaps even one of the secret priests who risked more in this country than any other.

'We are here,' the old man said and pulled up at a small cottage beside the road.

They climbed out of the car and Albin went round to the boot. The cottage was a simple two-up, two-down. It had a little patch of garden in front, a wicket gate and a concrete path leading to the front door. It opened and a smiling woman bustled out. She was the antithesis of her husband, tall, plump, smooth-skinned and looking about ten years younger. She was wearing a black dress and cardigan with a beige apron. She hurried down the path, opened the little gate and made a big fuss of greeting Mirek and Ania, hugging and kissing them. She took Ania with her up the path, while Mirek helped Albin unload the two

189

cheap suitcases. He looked down the street. Across the street an angular old man was walking a scruffy looking little dog. It lifted its leg against a tree. The old man waited patiently, his eyes on Mirek.

Inside, the little cottage looked exactly what it was. A temporary abode. The furniture was sparse and cheap, all second-hand; but the aroma coming out of the kitchen told tales of hearth fires, old copper pots and pans and earthenware pottery.

Sylwia took charge.

'Pour them a drink,' she commanded Albin, picked up the two suitcases and said to Ania, 'Follow me, Tatania.'

She led Ania up the steep wooden staircase and pointed with her chin to a door at the top. 'Toilet and shower. Sorry, no tub, but the water's hot and at least it'll warm you up.' She turned right, put down one of the suitcases and opened another door. Ania followed her into the room.

The room was small and overcrowded. There was a wardrobe, a chest of drawers, one white cane chair and the piece of furniture that took up most of the room: a double bed with a pink duvet; and a small electric fire with one bar glowing. As she looked at the bed Ania felt her heart sink. The older woman saw her expression and immediately understood. She said, 'Oh God . . . you are not really married . . . We were not told.'

'It doesn't . . . doesn't matter,' Ania stammered.

Sylwia put the suitcases onto the bed and said, 'Listen, I'll talk to Albin. He can sleep in here with Tadeusz. You share my room.' She gestured at the bed. 'The furniture was here when we arrived . . . They didn't tell us.'

At first Ania felt relief but then guilt followed. She would have to face this situation in the future. Better to get it over with at the start. Better that she and Mirek should understand each other now, at the beginning. Better that she got used to his nocturnal proximity. Firmly she shook her head and smiled.

'No, Aunt Sylwia. Stay with your husband. It will be all right.'

Sylwia gave her a dubious look. Something had told her that this girl was pure. She had seen it in others.

'Are you sure?'

'I'm sure. It's better this way.'

'All right. Now come down and have a drink and fill your stomach.'

Dinner was a rich vegetable soup followed by rabbit stew. Fat slices of home-baked bread accompanied it all. The conversation was pointedly not personal. It was political. Albin let it be known that he had recently visited Poland. Mirek was hungry for news, not of the broad issues but on the human level. They talked of Solidarity and the clamp-down; of shortages and bitterness; of the ever-rising hatred of the Russians; of the Church. The conversation about religion puzzled Albin immensely. Before dinner as they sat around the steaming platters he had glanced at his guest pointedly and then lowered his head. Immediately his wife and Ania had followed suit. He had said a simple prayer. At the periphery of his vision he had seen Tadeusz's head erect, a slight sneer on his face. Now as they discussed the situation of the Church in Poland and the Polish Pope in Rome, the old man was astonished at his young guest's insight and knowledge. He was disquieted. Mirek discussed the Church much as one would debate the workings of a party. He was intimately familiar with the structure and the personalities. With the state of Party-Church relations and the pressures that were building on both sides. He debated in a slightly arrogant manner, as though from superior and inside knowledge. Albin glanced occasionally at the girl. She ate silently; the cast of her face was sombre. Once in a while she raised her eyes as Mirek made a point. Finally she interjected to change the subject. She asked Sylwia, 'Where did you find such a plump rabbit?'

Sylwia smiled with pleasure. 'From a local farmer. There is much bartering in the village. Firewood for vegetables, tomatoes for cooking oil, and so on.' She pointed at the pot. 'For two rabbits I exchanged half a side of best bacon.'

'But where did you get the . . . ?'

Mirek coughed sharply, cutting off Ania's sentence. He glanced at Albin who was studying the end of his fork with great care.

Ania was bewildered but then understood. The Bacon Priest had visited these parts recently. She smiled at Sylwia and said simply, 'Rabbit stew is one of my favourite dishes. I have never tasted it so well cooked; but there is something in it I can't quite define. A little sharp on the tongue. It gives it a richness.'

Sylwia smiled at her husband and said, 'I learned to cook rabbit stew from Albin's mother. She came from the far north – Lebore. There they always put a little ginger in the stew.'

'That's it!' Ania exclaimed.

The two women started discussing recipes. Albin took out a packet of cigarettes and offered it to Mirek. On an impulse Mirek took one. It had been a month since he had smoked. The tobacco was coarse, the smoke acrid, but he inhaled hungrily. The old man surveyed him through the smoke. Mirek had the impression that he was disapproved of; for some reason that unsettled him. It should not have. This couple were merely a cog in the wheel. A pawn to help create an opening and move the queen on. The old man should have mattered nothing, but for reasons he couldn't define Mirek did not want his disapproval. He leaned towards him and under the voices of the two women said softly, 'I . . . we are very grateful for your help . . . for your hospitality.'

The old man waved his cigarette deprecatingly and said, 'We serve how we can.'

Mirek nodded and then, determined to reach through to the old man, found a little eloquence. He blew smoke through his nostrils, stubbed out the cigarette and said, 'Yes, serve is a word I thought I understood. I did not. In the past months I have learned something of its meaning.

192

I have learned that it demands not just obedience but unselfishness. Not just reward but true humility . . . I feel it in this house and in your company. We shall travel a little down a road, share that road and then part . . . We shall never meet again, but I will never forget you and your wife. You know nothing of our purpose . . . but you do know the awful risk you take. I will never know your real names – they don't matter. I will never forget the strength of the people I know as Albin and Sylwia Wozniak.'

The two women had stopped talking. They had heard the last part of his little speech and were watching him curiously. He felt intensely embarrassed. He had never spoken that way before. Anger at himself began to build. Then Albin rose and went to the sideboard and came back with a bottle and four small glasses. Wordlessly he poured the Slivovice and passed out the glasses. Then he raised his own and said, 'Let us drink to our mother . . . to Poland!'

'To Poland,' they echoed and simultaneously poured the liquid down their throats. It burned away Mirek's anger. He felt a glow that came not just from the alcohol. He could not understand what it was. Could not understand that for the first time in his life he was experiencing companionship.

The women got up and cleared the table. When the sounds of crockery being washed filtered through Albin winked at Mirek, got up and fetched the bottle to the table. With a practised hand he filled the small glasses exactly to the brim. There were no toasts this time. Just a relaxed silence. Mirek only sipped at his drink. He liked alcohol and its mellowing effects, but he knew its dangers. It was all right now. He could drink and go to sleep in safety; but out of a safe house it could be fatal. He knew its effect on him. It made him over-confident, sometimes arrogantly so. Over-confidence on this journey could be a disaster.

The woman came back and when she saw the bottle

Sylwia scolded her husband gently. Ania announced that she was going to take a shower and then go to bed. She kissed the older couple on the cheeks and climbed the stairs. Mirek watched her legs disappear up the steps. A few minutes later Sylwia bade them good night and followed her. Albin poured more Slivovice.

'Steady on,' Mirek murmured without great conviction. The old man smiled.

'Don't worry. This is the last one for the stairs. It will help you sleep well. Don't worry about getting up early . . . sleep late.'

'I'll try.' Mirek raised his glass to the old man but his thoughts were upstairs. The word sleep had made him think of the double bed and of Ania under the shower. He could picture her holding her head up to the water, her hair falling back, made even shinier by the water. Her body wet and glistening, water cascading between her breasts and buttocks and curved flanks. His pulse was quickened by the image. Suddenly he realised the old man was talking to him.

'The last communication I had was a week ago. It indicated you were the cause of the increased state police activities during the past days. It's not only at the borders, you know. There are snap road blocks and sudden searches all over. Do they know exactly who they're looking for?'

It was a question Mirek felt he could answer. He shook his head. 'They're looking for a man, presumably travelling alone. They don't know his age or nationality. All they know is that he's travelling clandestinely in Eastern Europe. They know his destination but not his starting point.'

Albin grunted in satisfaction and downed his Slivovice.

'Then the danger is not as great as I had feared. They are truly looking for a needle in a haystack.' He smiled. 'Two needles . . . It was clever of the Bacon Priest to send the girl with you.'

Mirek stared at him and then shrugged and said, 'Maybe.' He too drained his glass and then stood up. He had heard the bathroom door open and close. 'I'll get to bed. Thanks for everything, Albin.'

The bathroom was warm and moist and had a feminine aroma. Her toilet bag was by the washbasin. He unzipped it and went through the contents. Two lipsticks, a bottle of shampoo, a plastic bag of cotton wool, a comb, eye shadow, eye liner and mascara. And finally a packet of tampons. Unopened. He picked it up and turned it in his hand. Irrationally, he had difficulty associating tampons with a nun.

All the items were made in Poland. He put everything back except the shampoo. He knew there would be shampoo in his own bag but perversely wanted to use hers, although he knew it would be heavily scented.

Ania was sitting up in bed reading a book when he came into the bedroom; a towel was wrapped round her hair like a turban. A long-sleeved flannel nightdress came up to her neck. Mirek guessed that it reached down to her ankles. Father Heisl would have seen to that little detail.

She looked up as he came in. He was wearing a towel and carrying his clothes and shoes. Her eyes flicked back to her book. He folded his clothes neatly on the chair, then noticed she had laid out his pyjamas for him on the bed. He smiled and looked at her. She was rigidly watching the page. He gave a short laugh and tossed the pyjamas on to the chair. 'I never use them,' he said. 'Usually I sleep naked – it's healthier.'

She was watching him over the top of her book. He saw the glint of anger in her eyes. With a melodramatic sigh he bent over his suitcase, rifled through the clothes and found a pair of boxer-style underpants. He held them for her inspection.

'These will have to satisfy your sensibilities.' With his left hand he loosened the towel. It dropped to his ankles. He had one brief glimpse of her startled eyes before the quickly raised book cut off her view.

'Must you do that?' she hissed angrily.

He stepped into the shorts and remarked lightly, 'Ania, you'll have to get used to it.'

There was a silence and then from behind her book she said harshly, 'I will never get used to it. Obviously I will have to put up with loutish behaviour if you persist . . . but I tell you, Mirek Scibor, to me you are just like a smutty schoolboy. You happen to be in the house of a God-fearing couple. You should try to remember that!'

Her little speech angered him. Especially the bit about the smutty schoolboy. He said, 'I am in a safe house rented solely for my mission . . . *my* mission. You are just along for the ride, to admire the museums, enjoy the damned rabbit with ginger and the famous tavernas . . . And don't bore me with your bloody moralising . . . Dammit woman, in that museum in Florence you admired old masterpieces. Some even commissioned by your high and mighty Church. They depict nudity, women with bare breasts, naked men with everything showing . . . everything, dammit! But in real life that's sinful . . . I tell you, Ania Krol, that's hypocrisy. Not blind hypocrisy . . . open-eyed. How do you think those pictures got painted? Do you think Botticelli and the rest painted from imagination? They used live models; so in logic they sinned while they created masterpieces for your Church!'

She stared at her book as if oblivious to him, and he ran out of steam. 'Oh well,' he said with resignation. 'You can't argue somebody out of something they haven't been argued into. You can't argue with blind superstition.'

He pulled back his side of the duvet and climbed into the bed. The springs squeaked. The mattress was soft. She realised that with his heavier weight it would slope towards him. She sighed to herself, anticipating a sleepless night.

'What are you reading?'

Like everyone ever asked that question, she turned the book to look at the cover.

'*The Rainstorm* by Stefan Osowski. Sylwia lent it to me.'

He chuckled. 'I might have guessed. I had to read it

once. I was quite touched when he finally found solace in God.'

She glanced at him and saw the cynical curl to his lip. She went back to the book but it was hard to concentrate while her mind was waiting for the next comment that was bound to come. She said, 'Do you want to sleep? Shall I switch off the light?'

'No, carry on.'

She did not want to carry on. She did not want to talk but above all she did not want to switch off the light.

He said, 'I'll bet you've never read Kung. I'll bet they didn't give you his books in the convent.'

'No, they didn't.'

He plumped the pillows behind him and made himself more comfortable. She waited for the inevitable.

'Brilliant mind, Kung – and very radical. He puts forward a thesis that I would bet a lot of your priests would like to subscribe to.'

'Really.' She injected boredom into her voice but he wasn't deterred.

'Yes. It's really fascinating. You see Kung hypothesises that celibacy and chastity are two very different things. Now by the infallibility of a Papal bull, priests – and of course nuns – must be celibate . . . That's final, or until there's another Papal bull which says otherwise.' He warmed to his theme with obvious relish. 'Now Kung interprets celibacy in the meaning that was originally intended sixteen hundred years ago. That is, without marriage. It does not mean without sex. Chastity of course meant then, and means now, without sex. If a priest, or of course a nun, gets married they break their vow of celibacy and under Canon law cannot remain a priest or nun. However if a priest or a nun,' he laid emphasis on the word 'nun', 'has sexual relations, particularly casual sexual relations, they can obtain forgiveness from the Church by making a truthful declaration in the confessional . . .' He turned his head to look at her. 'Don't you find that interesting?'

'Not at all.' She closed the book with a snap and put it on the bedside table. The light switch was a cord suspended over the bed from the ceiling. She reached up and jerked it. Into the immediate darkness she said, 'I think we should try to sleep.'

As she slid down in the bed she heard him chuckling beside her.

She arranged her pillows and settled herself. He did the same. She inched over as far to the edge as she could. He sprawled comfortably. For about twenty minutes there was silence, then he yawned deeply and turned over. She heard his breath deepen, then she stiffened as his hand landed lightly on her thigh. It moved slowly to her buttock. She reached down and firmly pushed it away. He rolled over grunting in his throat as though asleep. Another twenty minutes and she had begun to relax and finally feel drowsy enough to sleep. Then again he rolled over. This time his hand alighted above her waist and began to move up. Again she pushed it away angrily.

'You don't fool me. I know you're awake. Stop it.'

He rolled over on his back, no longer feigning sleep. The curtains were thick and the room was pitch black. After about ten minutes he spoke conversationally.

'Ania, do you mind if I masturbate?'

She jerked upright in shock, her hand swinging about for the light cord. She found it and tugged. He put a hand up to shield his eyes from the sudden light. From under it he said, 'There are things you don't understand about men. That's hardly surprising. Now listen. I'm sexually aroused . . . very. That too is not surprising. When a man is aroused he either gets relief or he gets a pain in his testicles. We call it "lover's nuts". Now I've got it so I can't sleep . . .'

She looked down at him, breathing deeply in shock and anger, then she swung her feet to the ground and reached for her pillow.

'Do any filthy thing you want, you animal! I'm going downstairs. I'll sleep on a chair.'

He rolled over and grabbed her arm.

'No! It's all right . . . I won't do it.'

She tried to pull away but he held her firmly. Earnestly he said, 'Ania, relax. I promise I won't do that or touch you again. You'll never get to sleep on one of those chairs. If you insist I'll go down instead but I won't sleep either. Besides, it's cold.'

She tried to pull away again. He pleaded.

'Ania, please. I won't touch you. I promise on the memory of my mother.'

He no longer shielded his eyes. She looked into them and believed him.

Darkness again, and, for ten minutes, silence. Then his voice again. Low and husky.

'It's not such a bad thing, Ania. Old superstitions make a taboo about it but masturbation's not such a bad thing. Doctors, psychiatrists, will tell you that.'

She whispered bitterly, 'You promised on the memory of your mother.'

'I promised not to touch you and I won't. I won't touch you until you want me to.'

She put her hands over her ears but his head was near and his low voice penetrated.

'Did you never try it, Ania . . . lying on your cot in your cell in the convent . . . Did you never get warm feelings . . . in the night? Never slide a hand down there . . . rub yourself . . . feel yourself getting wet . . . open your legs . . . slide a finger in . . . maybe you used a candle?'

Something in her mind snapped. He heard her sudden movement. The light came on, momentarily blinding him. She was standing by the bed sobbing in rage and humiliation. Her breath gusting out in short spurts.

'All right! All right! You want to see a nun naked. All right!'

She reached down and pulled up the nightdress first to her waist, bunching it, then up over her shoulders and head. She flung it to the floor. She was wearing a stylish white bra and brief blue panties. She reached behind and unsnapped the bra, and flung that to the floor. Her voice

199

was twisted, hissing at him. 'You want to see a nun naked? Look . . . look!'

She pushed down the panties and stepped out, almost tripping, then stood straight. Her breasts were literally heaving. Her eyes had a madness in them.

'Look, Scibor. A nun's naked body. You want to feel it? Feel a nun's naked body?' She marched around the foot of the bed banging into it with her leg, then she was standing beside him.

'Feel a nun's body!' She waved a hand at his middle. 'Put that thing into a nun's body, if that's what you want.'

He was leaning up on one elbow, his mind in disarray. Inches from his eyes was her ebony curly triangle. He could sense, smell its muskiness. His eyes travelled higher. He could feel his penis rising in automatic anticipation. Without prompting from his brain his free hand followed his gaze: over the soft swell of her belly, higher to her moving breast. His hand stopped there, sending tactile messages of perfection. His gaze went higher to her face. It was wet with flowing tears. Her mouth was open, lips shuddering like her body. Her eyes were narrowed. All he could see in them was unbearable pain.

She sobbed. 'Do anything, but, please God, stop humiliating me!'

His hand dropped abruptly. So did his penis. He fell back on to the bed and covered his eyes, pressing his hands against them as if to blind himself for ever.

The dawn filtered in even through the thick curtains, casting a shadowy light over the bed. Mirek lay on his right side close to the edge. Ania lay in the middle, on her left side, an arm over his waist, her head resting among the hair on his chest between the opening of his pyjama jacket. They were both asleep as though drugged.

An hour after dawn she woke slowly, slipping in and out of consciousness. Her face was against the nape of his neck. Drowsily she realised that her body was alongside his, as close as two spoons. She stiffened and then reasoned

200

that the night had been cold. She must have rolled over in her sleep and instinctively, like any mammal, sought bodily heat. She was frightened to move. It might wake him.

For another ten minutes she dozed. One of a pair of warm spoons. Then she heard the faint clatter of pottery from the kitchen below. Slowly, and with infinite care, she withdrew her arm and inched across and out of the bed and turned on the fire.

He slept on as she dressed. At the door she looked down at his face. In sleep it was carefree and, even with the moustache, looking younger than his years. His nostrils flared slightly as he breathed. She stood looking down for several minutes, then she quietly opened the door and left.

14

George Laker whistled while he worked. The big Scania thundered down the highway towards Hate. George whistled a tune from *Joseph and his Technicolour Dreamcoat*. He liked rock opera. He'd seen that one back home in Melbourne. Australia seemed a million miles away but he didn't miss it. George whistled when he was happy and what made him happy was when he made money. The more the happier. This had been a particularly happy trip. Only two days in all, but he'd made a load of money. Twenty ounces of gold for taking the young couple in, two thousand sterling for bringing the old couple out. He changed tunes to 'I don't know how to love him' from *Jesus Christ Superstar* and thought about the old couple sardined into the compartment below. They were Russian Jews. He never asked questions but he'd guessed they had failed to emigrate from Russia and had managed to get to Czechoslovakia, probably on a short holiday visa. Anyway he didn't care. He did know that the two thousand pounds was already in his Swiss account. Probably paid in by relatives in Israel or one of the Jewish relief organisations. They were old but they seemed spritely enough. Nervous but in high spirits. They had readily accepted the Trepalin injections as though he was pumping pure gold into their veins.

He glanced at his watch, then at his kilometre gauges and did a quick mental calculation. He gunned the motor a little. He would risk the mandatory on-the-spot speeding fines. He grinned to himself. It represented the tiniest percentage of what he'd made this trip. And Elsa was waiting for him in Vienna. Elsa of the long legs. He began to whistle again.

Twenty kilometres out of Hate he stopped whistling. The big engine had begun to hiccup. He cursed. It was the fucking fuel pump again! He'd had trouble with it for the last month. Fortunately he'd bought a spare in Vienna and had it in his toolbox but he hadn't had time to change it before this trip. It was a time-consuming and messy job. He decided to try to nurse the Scania into Hate. He eased his foot on the accelerator and slowed right down. For the next half hour he covered fifteen kilometres and then, still five kilometres short, the engine groaned and spluttered and finally petered out as he pulled over to the verge. With another curse he glanced again at his watch. It would take him at least forty-five minutes to change the fuel pump and it was freezing outside. He had already cut it fine because travelling from the border to the West took much less time than going the other way. The old couple would start waking up in about two hours. Well, no matter. They'd keep quiet. Neither of them seemed to have a problem with claustrophobia; they had climbed into the compartment happily enough. He jumped down from the cab, hauled out the toolbox and set to work.

Two hours later he eased the Scania into line at the Customs post at Hate. There were eight trucks in front of him. Private cars and smaller vans were in another line. He switched off the engine, pulled on the handbrake, collected his satchel of documents from the glove compartment, climbed out and strolled into the Customs office. There was one driver at the counter explaining something to an officer. Six others were sitting patiently on a bench. Laker recognised one of them: a middle-aged Irishman from Dublin who specialised in trucking hanging garments East to West. He went over and shook hands and sat next to him.

'Only one on today?'

'No,' the Irishman replied in his soft burr. 'There's some fuss at the other office with a private car. The other two have gone over to add a little more bureaucracy.'

Laker looked at his watch again. It was going to take longer than he thought.

'Good trip?' the Irishman asked.

'It was until the fucking fuel pump packed up. Lucky I had a spare.'

The Irishman chuckled. 'I passed Ernst Kruger just outside Ostrava. Steam was coming from under his truck's bonnet – and from out of his ears. He'd picked up a nice little German girl – giving her a lift to Vienna. She was in a hurry so I did the decent thing and took her aboard.'

Laker laughed. 'Where is she now?'

The Irishman winked. 'Resting on the bunk in my cab . . . she looks the grateful type.'

The driver at the counter picked up his satchel with a muttered 'Thanks' and strolled out. The driver at the end of the bench stood up and walked to the counter. The others shuffled down the bench.

Laker said, 'Did I ever tell you about that bit I picked up in Prague a couple of months ago?'

The Irishman shook his head. Laker grinned at the memory.

'Christ, but she was a crazy Sheila. She hadn't been in the cab more than sixty seconds when . . .' His voice trailed off. A Captain of the STB had walked in. The STB were the secret police – and serious business. He wore polished black boots and a small quizzical smile on his lips. He surveyed the seated drivers as if looking for any signs of guilt, then asked pleasantly, 'Which of you is G. Laker?' Laker's stomach dropped as his heart beat speeded up. Slowly he raised a finger.

'And you are the driver of the Scania number AGH 5034D?'

Laker swallowed. His voice came out in a croak.

'Yes . . . What's the problem, Captain?'

The Captain smiled. 'The problem is that your vehicle is emitting strange noises from its innards – human noises, Laker – not unlike screams.'

The Australian sat paralysed. The Irishman had edged away from him and was surveying him with a look of pity, as were the other drivers.

The Captain said, 'I think you had better come with me and explain this phenomenon.' The softly spoken words sounded to Laker like a death knell.

Twenty minutes later he sat across a steel table from an STB Colonel. The Captain stood to one side with a contented look on his face. The Australian's hands were handcuffed together on his lap. From the barred window came the wailing sound of the departing ambulance.

The Colonel pulled a lined yellow note pad towards him, took an old-fashioned fountain pen from his breast pocket and wrote 'George Laker' across the top of the page in large letters. He had the kind of face that is used to writing reports. He also had ribbons on his chest that denoted not bravery but efficiency. He looked up. His eyes were hooded as though from avoiding too much cigarette smoke. As if on cue he took an old battered silver cigarette case from his jacket pocket and lit up. He did not offer one to the Captain. The Australian's system was screaming for nicotine. The Colonel blew smoke at the ceiling and said, 'You were not lucky, Laker. The old man probably had a bad heart. What you injected him with could have made it worse. You will tell us about that. His dear wife wakes up and finds him going stiff next to her and has hysterics. Very bad luck. In half an hour you would have been through.'

His voice was soft and relaxed. Now it turned hard.

'Of course an experienced man like you knows very well what the penalties are for smuggling criminal fugitives out of our country.'

Laker found his voice. 'Those two weren't criminals.'

The Colonel blew cigarette smoke at him. 'Their very act was a crime, Laker. Ten years' hard regime. Statutory minimum. It could be longer, much longer, depending on your level of co-operation.' He twirled the pen in his fingers expectantly. 'Now first: where did you pick them up and who put them on to you?'

Laker was thinking. His mind literally racing; considering all possibilities. He was a tough man physically and mentally; fully aware of what awaited him. All the truckers who ploughed the rich furrow of Communist trade knew the consequences of getting out of line. Laker had been out of line for over five years. He had nearly a quarter of a million dollars tucked away. He wanted time to spend it. He would do anything for that time. He was forty-seven years old. He would be sixty when they let him out – a broken old man.

'Well?' the Colonel demanded impatiently.

Laker held up a hand. 'Just wait,' he said harshly. 'Let me think a minute.'

He thought for two minutes, while the Colonel tapped the top of his pen against his nose. Then he said confidently, 'All right, Colonel, maybe we can do a deal.'

The Colonel laughed derisively.

'We don't do deals, you fool. You co-operate or else you spend your last living days in gaol. You know how it works. Now where did you pick them up?'

Laker leaned forward. 'Sure I know how it works. I've driven trucks in this country, in Rumania, Poland, East Germany, Yugoslavia, Bulgaria and Russia itself. We truckers talk among ourselves. Shit, we don't even need CB, we hear a hell of a lot. You bet I know how it works, Colonel, and after you hear what I have to say I'm going to do a fucking deal – but probably not with you or even your boss!'

He sat back and waited. He knew how these people thought. The Colonel glanced at the Captain and said, 'Go on.'

Laker decided to press his advantage. He knew that the

206

word 'boss' always triggered a Pavlovian response with these people.

'I remember better with a cigarette.'

The Colonel stared at him with distaste but then took out his cigarette case, opened it and pushed it across the table together with a lighter. Laker reached forward with his manacled hands and fumbled one out. Then he reached for the lighter. It was also battered – an old American Zippo. He used it to light the cigarette and then admired it and said, 'I bet you got this during the war.'

'I'm not that old,' the Colonel snapped. 'Now talk and you'd better not be wasting my time.'

Laker drew deeply on the cigarette, letting the smoke lie in his lungs. Savouring it. As he spoke it puffed out of his mouth and nostrils. 'What happened on the twenty-third of last month, Colonel?'

'I ask the questions . . .'

The Colonel's voice trailed off as the date and its implications registered in his mind. It was almost comical. Laker smiled at him.

'I'll tell you, Colonel. On that date you got orders. Orders to tighten up security to the maximum in your area and not just you, Colonel. Those same orders went out to every Customs post and Immigration point in the Soviet bloc. Air, land or sea. Or at least the Western end of it. From the Baltic to the Black Sea.' He puffed again. The Colonel was looking at him warily.

'It's not so strange, Colonel. Truckers criss-cross the entire bloc. We talk to each other. There's been a lot of speculation among truckers about the stepped-up security. It must cause problems. The movement of goods has been slowed right down. Even within the bloc. Tourism must be suffering. What with all the extra road blocks and identity checks, you chaps must be doing a hell of a lot of overtime. Must be costing the Governments a bomb. And it's not just an exercise . . . not for two bloody weeks.'

He stopped and let the silence build. Finally the Colonel said, 'So?'

'So there's a panic on. So you're looking for someone. The scope of it suggests that Moscow is looking for someone desperately . . . maybe a spy . . . probably even more than a mere spy. You don't know much yet. You don't even know if who you're looking for is in the bloc yet. Or if he is, where he is.'

Again a silence. The Colonel was thinking of the dossier which had arrived in his office that very morning. The dossier that was so urgent that it had arrived on the expensive Fax machine. The dossier with the photo. Again he repeated the single word: 'So?'

'So I might be able to clear up some of the confusion.'

The Colonel looked sceptical. 'You're bluffing, Laker. You're just a petty smuggler trading in petty criminals. You've built up a mirage in your head. We are just having a normal, extended security exercise.'

'Bullshit, and you can't take the personal risk of not dealing with me.'

Laker dropped his cigarette on to the concrete floor and ground his heel on it.

The Colonel looked at the Captain. 'When did he cross into Czechoslovakia?'

The Captain came to attention. 'Two days ago, sir. Eight forty-five a.m. at this crossing.'

'His destination?'

'Brno, sir. A consignment of machine tools for the Skoda factory.'

The Colonel pulled at his nose thoughtfully. Laker helped himself to another cigarette. Finally the Colonel asked, 'You brought someone in on that trip?'

Laker exhaled smoke. 'Colonel, I think it's time you called your boss . . . the big one.'

Four hours later the phone on Colonel Zamiatin's desk rang. It was the KGB station head in Prague – Garik Sholokhov, an old friend. He was very excited. After listening to him for twenty seconds Zamiatin was also excited. Although the call was being recorded he pulled a pad close and started to make notes. Occasionally he glanced at the huge wall map. Finally he grinned and said, 'Excellent, Garik. Now the Australian was certain on identification? . . . Good. Yes, with a moustache. Clever to send the woman along . . . but not clever enough. Now listen. It's obvious that village is their first stop. They might be still there resting up. I want a complete cordon thrown around it and road blocks on every road within fifty kilometres of it. If you have to, use the army. No one is to go in or out until you arrive. Give the instruction now, Garik. I'll wait.'

He laid the phone on his desk and grinned at the three Majors who were watching him intently. Then he stood up and walked over to the map saying, 'Thanks to the good work of Major Gudov, plus a little well-deserved luck, we are closing in on him.' He put his finger on the map. 'He crossed the border here in company with a woman hidden in a secret compartment of a freight truck. He was set down here four kilometres from the village of Blovice. That was two days ago. Pray that he's still there.'

He walked back to his desk and picked up his phone. Thirty seconds later Sholokhov was back on the line. For five minutes Zamiatin issued terse orders, then he hung up and glanced at his watch. It was nine forty-five. He put a call through to his boss, Victor Chebrikov. While waiting for the connection he thought about the dacha in Usovo and General's stars.

Chebrikov briefed Andropov over an early lunch in the First Secretary's private dining room. Andropov was in a pensive mood. He greeted the news without the enthusiasm Chebrikov had expected. The head of the KGB said, 'Yuri, that cordon is going around the village now. There's a good chance that within the hour we'll have caught our fish.'

By coincidence they were lunching on pickled herrings and sour cream. Andropov forked a piece into his mouth, chewed without enthusiasm, swallowed and said, 'Victor,

209

a fish is never caught until it's in the boat . . . and then, unless you kill it quickly, it sometimes jumps out.'

Chebrikov sighed inwardly. His boss was having a bad day. His pale face was haggard. Before the meal he had swallowed three different kinds of pills.

'Anyway,' Andropov said. 'If you don't catch him he will be in Moscow before the tenth of next month.' He looked up. Chebrikov was obviously puzzled. 'Work it out, Victor. That's the date that the Pope flies to the Far East. The Bacon Priest and his cronies in the Vatican will have assumed, correctly, that our attempt on him will be there. They will know from that bastard Yevchenko that I face opposition on it. Even from Chernenko and Gorbachev. They don't see the grand design. If I drop dead tomorrow you would very soon get orders to cancel the operation.'

Chebrikov nodded in agreement. He well understood the power structure and how it worked. If Andropov died he would be fighting for his own job.

'Well, we shall catch him, Yuri, and boat him – and kill him quickly. Meanwhile the arrangements for your personal security are as stringent as I know how to make them.'

For the first time Andropov smiled.

'I can rely on you, Victor. Anyway, from the seventh of next month I go into the Serbsky clinic for a week of rest and treatment. That's probably the most secure place in the world. By the time I come out that damned Pope will be finding out if there really is a heaven.'

It was eleven thirty local time on a cloudless morning as Garik Sholokhov helicoptered into the little village square of Blovice. All the inhabitants, including infants and babies, were waiting, herded into a group in front of the old church. They were very nervous, knowing that their village was ringed by a cordon of soldiers but not knowing why. Within minutes Sholokhov had learned that his quarry had left early that morning.

As his men started to take the little cottage apart he went to an army communications truck and sent out orders to hunt down an old grey Skoda, registration number TN 588 179. In case the plate had been changed all pre-1975 Skodas were to be stopped and thoroughly searched. He knew that this would inconvenience thousands of people but was not concerned a whit. He gave a very detailed description of the two men and two women. He warned that they could be dangerous, especially the younger man.

That done, he phoned Colonel Zamiatin. He could practically feel the disappointment transmitted down the line as he told him the news.

'Don't worry, Oleg. They can't have got far. They won't suspect yet that we are on to them. Their cover was that the Uncle and Aunt were going to give them a two-day tour of the area before they returned to Poland by train. There could be some truth in it.'

Zamiatin started to tell him what to do. Sholokhov cut in.

'Oleg, let me tell you what I've done first. It will save time.'

He quickly ran through the orders he had given and what he personally was going to be doing over the coming hours. When he finished there was a silence while Zamiatin considered everything. Then he said, 'Very good. You appear to have covered everything.' The tone of his voice turned a little plaintive. 'Garik, let me know the moment you have any developments.'

'Of course, Oleg.'

15

The setting was serene and they looked exactly what they purported to be: an elderly couple taking younger relatives out for a treat. Albin and Sylwia sat with their backs to the river, leaving the view for Mirek and Ania. Their table was outside on a wooden platform which jutted out over the river bank. It was enclosed in glass, protecting them from the cold and giving a greenhouse effect in the wintery sun. They had lunched well and drunk a bottle and a half of a Bulgarian Cabernet. The air itself seemed imbued with contentment. Only Sylwia was still not totally relaxed. Her problem was curiosity. It had always been so. She was still wondering about the relationship between the younger couple. Still curious about the events of the night before last. She and Albin had heard, through their bedroom door, the faint sound of argument. They had not heard the words but the awful anguish in Tatania's sobbing voice had penetrated the wood and their minds.

Albin had wanted to go through and intervene but, despite her curiosity, Sylwia had restrained him. However, after the voices had stopped she got up and very quietly went to the bathroom. When she came out she edged along the landing towards their door and listened. She could hear his voice, very faint. She could hear no words but it had a strange tone to it. A sort of pleading tone. It went on for ten minutes and then there was silence.

The next morning Tatania came down first and helped her prepare breakfast. She appeared serene and relaxed in a way that a patient is relaxed after breaking a fever.

During that breakfast it was obvious that whatever had occurred the night before had affected him deeply. He was withdrawn and quiet, but his attitude towards Tatania was strangely protective. His eyes were constantly drawn to her.

It had been that way ever since. On the journey; at the museum in Brno; and now here at the restaurant. He had been attentive towards her, helping her out of the car, helping her off with her coat, holding her chair when she sat down. It was as though he was trying to make up for a lovers' quarrel.

Albin noticed that he kept the small duffle bag with him at all times. Even now it was slung over the back of his chair.

Mirek leaned forward, picked up the bottle and poured more wine into Ania's glass.

She tried to protest but he smiled and said, 'You've only had one glass, Ania. Have a little more.'

Both the older couple noticed the slip but said nothing. Ania said pointedly, 'Thank you, Tadeusz.'

He nodded as if acknowledging his mistake but was not at all put out.

Albin glanced at his watch and signalled for the bill, saying, 'It's thirty kilometres to Cieszyn and your train leaves in just over an hour.'

Albin and Sylwia were in front as they walked out of the restaurant. Albin stopped so suddenly that Mirek bumped into him. Then over his shoulder he saw the reason why the old man had frozen.

Their grey Skoda was forty metres away. A police car was parked broadside in front of it, with both front doors open. One policeman was standing by the windscreen of the Skoda peering at the licence disc. Another was standing by the driver's door of the police car talking urgently into a microphone. They all saw each other at the same time and for a second were a frozen tableau. Then both policemen reached for their holstered guns and the one by the Skoda shouted, 'Halt! Stay where you are!'

213

All four of them ran back through the restaurant, dodging among the tables and startled customers. Albin's hip slammed into one of the tables and sent it over with a crashing of glasses and crockery and yells of shock.

They raced out on to the wooden platform. Near the table where they had been sitting was a flight of steps leading down to a gravel path that paralleled the river. A teenage boy and girl were coming up. Mirek crashed into them, slamming them back and down amid terrified screams. He was holding the duffle bag with his left hand. His right hand was inside it searching frantically. He leapt over the prostrate girl and sprinted down the path. He heard a shout and turned to look. Ania was close behind him. The older couple were trailing. One of the policemen was on the wooden platform raising his gun. He shouted again and then fired. Albin cried out and tumbled on to the path, his hands clutching at his left thigh.

At last Mirek's fingers felt the steel butt of the Makarov and pulled it out in one motion, turning and dropping into a crouch. Ania passed him as he lined up the sights. In his mind he was back in the camp in the desert on the firing range. He squeezed the trigger and heard the wet thwack as the bullet hit the centre of the policeman's chest. He didn't wait to watch him fall. Sylwia had run back to Albin screaming, 'Josef! Josef!' which must have been his real name. Mirek somehow knew that she would not leave him now. He turned and raced after Ania who was about forty metres ahead, approaching some trees and a bend in the path. On the river twenty metres to her left were two old men in a rowing boat watching the scenario with stunned faces. Mirek heard another shout behind him, then the sound of a shot and simultaneously the crack of the bullet over his head. He did not turn. Ania was already passing out of sight around the bend. He dodged to his right, leaping over low bushes, towards the trees. Another shot, again high. Irrationally he heard again the saturnine Portuguese instructor's voice. 'The tendency with pistols is to shoot high.' He hurtled into the little copse as a bullet

214

whacked into a tree next to him. The policeman behind had corrected the tendency, but this time had pulled to the right. He caught up with Ania on the other side of the copse. She had slowed, her head twisted, looking back anxiously. He saw the relief on her face as he sprinted across.

'The others?' she gasped.

'Had it. Come on!'

He grabbed her arm and urged her on. The river twisted back and forth and the path followed. He wondered whether the policeman was coming after them or had gone back to his car to radio a report. He hoped he was following.

He had to slow down to avoid getting ahead of Ania.

'Go on!' she panted. 'Leave me.' He grabbed her arm again, urging her on.

They turned a bend. In front of them the gravel path expanded into an oval parking place. A track from it led away from the river to the right and to the main road. A youth and a girl were just climbing off a motorbike. They wore matching blue crash helmets. They turned as Mirek and Ania ran up. The youth had half raised his helmet. His eyes were startled as they looked at the gun in Mirek's hand. Mirek pointed it at him.

'I'm taking your bike. Where are the keys?'

Fear paralysed the youth. Mirek glanced at the motorbike. The keys were still in the ignition. He thrust the duffle bag at Ania and she grasped it to her chest, panting.

Keeping the gun pointed at the youth, Mirek straddled the motorbike and switched on the ignition. It was a Russian Nerval 650cc. Again he had an irrelevant thought. This kid was obviously the son of someone important. He noted that both he and the terrified girl were wearing faded, genuine Levi jeans and skiing jackets. While these thoughts had been going through his head he had been turning the bike so that his right hand was facing the direction they had come. He listened and heard the thud-

215

ding crunch of someone running. He raised the gun, his arm ramrod straight, and drew a breath.

The policeman came round the bend at full tilt. As he saw Mirek and the gun he started to slow and tried to jink to his left. His foot slipped on the gravel. Mirek waited for him to complete the fall then fired twice. The first bullet stopped his forward motion. The second punched him back to the edge of the river bank. Slowly his body rolled over and into the river.

The girl was screaming hysterically. Mirek kicked the starter and the Nerval shuddered into life. Ania was watching him. He tucked the pistol into his waistband.

'Quick. We have to get to Gottwaldov.' She started to move. 'Hurry, damn it.'

Quickly she climbed on, wedging the duffle bag between them.

'Hold tight.' He felt her hands grip his waist and gunned the motor. Gravel spurted from the back wheel and then they were heading up the track, the girl's screams fading behind them.

The Nerval was well silenced according to the law and as they neared the main road Mirek heard the sound of distant sirens. He pulled off the track into a clump of bushes and waited.

On the road ahead four police cars screamed by in quick succession. He waited as he heard the sirens whimpering into silence at the restaurant and then moved out of the bushes back on to the track. As they slowed at the main road Ania said in his ear, 'You told them we were going to Gottwaldov.'

He turned his head. 'Yes. We're going in the opposite direction. It might give us extra minutes.'

He turned left and opened the throttle and watched the speedometer needle edge up to the statutory speed limit of 100 kph. The traffic was moderate. Again he heard sirens. He was rapidly pulling up to a big container truck. He applied the brakes and slowed and moved close behind it, keeping well to the right. A few seconds later the police car passed in a blur to his left. He pulled out and accelerated past the truck, his mind working like a calculator. Soon the youth and the girl would be at the restaurant. Road blocks would be going up. He could risk staying on this road for no more than two or three minutes. He turned his wrist and looked at his watch. It was almost three o'clock. He superimposed on his mind the map of the area that he had memorised; that Father Heisl had made him memorise.

They had travelled twelve kilometres. There were two fallback safe houses on this part of their route, this side of the Polish border. One was located deliberately near the border itself. A farmhouse on the outskirts of the market town of Opava. The same river alongside which they had lunched, ran past the town and close to the farmhouse which was located on the near side of the town. Opava was about thirty kilometres from the restaurant. In daylight they would never get to the farmhouse unseen. By now the police manning the road blocks would know that they were on a motorbike. He opened up the throttle, deciding to ignore the speed limit. He felt Ania's hands gripping him tighter. The needle climbed until it touched 150 kph. In three minutes they travelled seven kilometres flashing past half a dozen cars and trucks. Far ahead he saw a side road going off to the left, towards the river. His heel came down on the brake pedal. They were still travelling fast as the road approached. He was calculating whether to overshoot and come back when he heard another siren. He clutched at the hand brake and banked over.

He just made the turn, but overshot the tarmac and skidded on the dirt verge. He felt the bike going from under him and pushed backwards and sideways. Ania clung on to him as they hurtled into low bushes and then broke away with a scream as they impacted the first time. He landed hard, bounced twice and then rolled on the icy ground, finally coming to rest about thirty metres from the road. He lay still for a moment, feeling the pain in his side where his gun had dug into his waist. The siren screamed past no more than fifty metres away on the main road.

He shouted, 'Ania!'

Her voice came shakily from a few yards away. 'Here, Mirek.'

'Stay down.'

He realised how lucky they had been. They were lying in low shrub. If they hadn't fallen they would have been easily spotted from the police car.

'Are you all right?'

'I think so. Bruised and scratched and I've hurt my ankle. What about you?'

He moved his limbs. The only pain came from his waist. He pulled out the gun. The ridge of the foresight had gouged his belly on impact, leaving a shallow, bleeding gash. He rolled on to his knees and crawled over to her. She was lying on her side, her knees drawn up, one hand holding her right ankle. Her left arm was scratched and bleeding, but there was no fear or shock in her eyes. He ducked down as a truck passed by, and grinned at her.

'Believe it or not, we were lucky. Without that crash we'd have been spotted. How's the ankle?'

In a matter-of-fact way she said, 'It's not broken but I twisted it badly. It's swelling up.'

'Do you think you can walk on it?'

She sat up, put her heel on the ground and winced. 'Yes, but slowly.'

He made some more calculations. Then he said, 'Ania, we're going for the safe house this side of Opava. It's about twelve kilometres from here. We'll have to hide the bike, and then ourselves, until dark. There'll be helicopters around soon. Then we'll have to go on foot down river.'

He crawled over to the motorbike and quickly inspected it. The front mudguard was twisted and jammed against the tyre, and the handbrake lever had snapped off. Otherwise it looked all right. He pulled the mudguard clear of the tyre and retrieved the duffle bag which was lying a few metres away. Then he called, 'Ania, raise your head until

218

you can see the road. Tell me when there's no traffic.'

Slowly she lifted her head.

'Wait, Mirek.'

He heard a car pass, then a truck going the other way, then she called, 'All clear.'

Quickly he righted the motorbike, climbed on and kicked the starter. After three kicks the engine roared to life. He bent down and scooped up the bag as she hobbled over. Seconds later they had bumped back on to the road and were heading down towards the river, wondering if their luck could hold.

They reached the river unseen. It lay in the bottom of a narrow wooded valley. Mirek managed to get two kilometres along its bank before the trees started to thin out. Twice they had stopped and hidden in thickets while helicopters passed overhead. Mirek decided it was time to hide both the bike and themselves. The river was slow moving and very deep at this point. They climbed off the bike and he inspected the bank. The river curving inwards had eroded the ground beneath it forming a lip. They investigated the motorbike's saddle bags and discovered a plastic container holding cold meats, cheese and bread. There was also a bottle of red wine. After unloading this, Mirek consigned the bike to the riverbed giving it a hefty shove. It landed with a satisfying splash and sank out of sight, leaving a trail of bubbles. He checked his watch. It was just after three thirty. The wood behind them was an obvious hiding place. They would certainly have the army searching it by morning; maybe even within an hour or two. There was still about an hour of daylight left. He could see, about a kilometre downstream, a small copse. That would be less obvious. There were clumps of trees between it and them which would provide cover.

It took them an hour to cover that single kilometre; because twice more they had to hide while helicopters scouted overhead and because Ania's sprained ankle was worse than she had suspected. She had to hop with her arm around Mirek's shoulder. When they finally got there her face was pale from the pain and she sank on to the grass with a sigh of relief. Mirek immediately rummaged in the bag and found her toilet bag and gave her four aspirins. He picked up the wine bottle, pulled off the foil, pushed the cork down inside and handed it to her. She washed down the aspirins and wordlessly handed it back. He took a couple of gulps and then wedged the bottle against a stone outcrop, saying, 'We'll have the rest with our meal later. It's lucky those kids had planned a late lunch. I'll just check the area.' He tossed the bag to her feet. 'Make yourself as comfortable as possible.' He moved away through the trees.

She pulled the bag towards her and felt inside for another sweater. She knew that it was still about ten kilometres to the safe house and she knew that she could never make it. She also knew that he realised it. He would leave her. He had told her that bluntly back in Florence. 'If you can't keep up I'll leave you.'

A sudden thought struck her and as the implications sank in she lowered her head into her hands and she prayed.

He found her like that when he returned and asked, puzzled, 'Ania, what's the matter?'

She lifted her head. Her cheeks were wet. Her eyes blank. She said tonelessly, 'You had better do it now.'

'Do what?'

'Kill me.'

For a moment he was stunned, then he understood her reasoning. He hurried forward and knelt beside her and took her hands in his. She looked at him and he saw the trepidation in her eyes.

Very softly he said, 'Ania, I'm not going to kill you. I know I can't leave you here alive. You know where the safe house is . . . where they all are. They would find you and make you talk. If not by torture then with drugs. I know you can't walk that far . . . I'll carry you, Ania.'

220

The fear left her eyes for a moment and then returned. She said, 'It's ten kilometres . . . over rough country. You could never carry me that far . . . not before daylight.'

He smiled at her. A smile that washed away all her fear. A smile that opened a tiny window to his core.

'Ania, you don't know my strength. I will carry you to the safe house.'

It took seven hours. If they lived a hundred years it was a journey they would never forget. After seven hours she knew his strength. They set out after twilight had faded. There was only a sliver of a moon. He walked with the bag slung around his neck and bouncing against his chest. He carried her on his back. He often stumbled in the darkness and several times fell. He always fell twisting so that his body cushioned hers. He stopped every hour to rest for just a few minutes. She marvelled at his strength. Early in the morning he stopped and lowered her down. They had passed a wide sweep of the river. Ahead of them it curved back the other way. He pointed across the river. 'It should be up the hill there about half a kilometre. I'm going to leave you here and check it out.' He was panting but there was a note of pride in his voice.

Her arms and legs were stiff and aching from clutching on to him and from the cold. She sank to the ground saying, 'Be careful, Mirek.'

He untied the bag and put it beside her, then he took the gun from his waistband, cocked it and moved cautiously down the bank. The river was wider here and shallower. Carefully he waded across holding the gun high. In the middle the water came up to his chest. It was icy cold. She could just make out his dark form as he climbed the opposite bank and disappeared into the trees.

After ten minutes he picked out the loom of a building. Slowly he edged forward, the gun held ready. It was a single storied building, not a light showing. There were

221

two windows. He realised he was at the back of it. He stopped and stood still, listening. The only sound was an owl hooting far away. He felt his skin prickle. There were always dogs on a farm. Why weren't they barking a warning? He moved forward slowly to the corner of the house. He could see the mass of a larger building in front – probably a barn. A twig cracked under his foot. A moment later a voice said from his right, 'Where's the woman?'

He swung around, the gun pointing. He was looking at a clump of low trees. A shadow detached itself and moved forward. There was a smaller shadow on each side of it. As it came closer it solidified into the shape of a man. The smaller shadows materialised into dogs. One of them began growling deep in its throat. The man murmured something to it and it stopped. He said, 'You're supposed to say something to me.'

Mirek's mind was a blank. Then with an effort he scoured his memory and said, 'I'm afraid I'm lost. Can you help me, please?'

The shadowy figure answered carefully, 'Around here it happens all the time.' And then urgently, 'Where's the woman?'

'By the river. She's sprained her ankle. I'll fetch her.'

The relief was evident in the man's voice. 'Good. I'll help you.'

'I'll fetch her.'

The man came closer. A light came on from his side, momentarily blinding Mirek. Then the torch was switched off. The voice said, 'You look all in. Let me help.'

'No,' Mirek said stubbornly. 'I'll fetch her. I'll be back in about half an hour.'

'All right,' the man gestured. 'Bring her to the barn. Everything is ready.'

Mirek carried her across the river holding her above his head, one hand on her back, the other behind her ankles. His exhaustion was forgotten. He had not seen the man's

222

face but he would remember him all his life. Would never forget the timbre and confidence of his voice.

On the other side he lowered Ania to the ground and then hitched her on to his back. Grunting with the exertion, he marched up the hill through the trees.

The man was waiting at the door of the barn, the dogs were nowhere to be seen. At their approach he opened the door and gestured for them to go ahead. As he closed the door behind them he flicked on a switch. A low light came from a bulb hanging from the high ceiling. Carefully Mirek lowered Ania to the ground. She stood on one leg. The man facing them was young. Mirek guessed in his late twenties. Stocky, round-faced, an untidy mop of black hair. He grinned at them.

'At last. I've waited ten years for this.'

'For what?' Mirek asked.

'To be of use. Ten years he's been telling me, "One day Anton and I'll need you"!'

'Who's he?' Ania asked.

The man turned serious. 'I think you know.' He held out his hand. 'Anton at your service.' They shook the hand in turn. He continued, 'Come now. You're exhausted and freezing.' He walked down the barn. Mirek put an arm round Ania's waist and helped her hobble after him. Over his shoulder Anton said, 'I thought you might come tonight. I heard the news. Two policemen murdered by criminals. Descriptions of you. Good descriptions.'

'Where are your dogs?' Mirek asked.

Anton gestured one way, then the other. 'One is half a kilometre down river, the other up. No one will get close without them barking a warning. You can relax, my friends.'

They had reached the back of the barn, which was taken up by a large pig pen. There were three fat pigs in it and a dozen piglets. Anton opened the gate and shooed them out into the barn itself. He pointed to one of the pigs.

'He's a bad tempered old so and so. If I wasn't here he'd charge you.'

The floor of the pen was covered in dirty straw. He scuffed it aside. Under it was a wooden floor. He bent down, put his fingers under a corner and lifted. A whole section came up, revealing a concrete base. Anton smiled at them engagingly.

'Now watch this.'

He reached for a metal ring cemented into the wall and gave it a firm twist. Then he moved forward and pressed down hard with his foot. Silently a whole section of the concrete floor swung; half of it down, half up. They could see that its axle was a thick oiled metal bar embedded on each side of the hole. On the far side a wooden ladder led down into the darkness. With a gesture like a conjuror concluding a successful trick, Anton stepped around the hole and started down the ladder. When his head was level with the floor he reached up. They heard a click and a dim light came on. He said, 'What do you call yourselves?'

Mirek answered, 'Tadeusz and Tatania.'

'All right, you'd better help Tatania down. I'll help from the bottom.'

Ania hobbled round. Mirek held both her wrists. She put her good foot on the top rung. Holding all of her weight Mirek slowly lowered her down. He saw Anton's hands grip her waist and felt the weight transfer.

Anton was very proud of his hide-out, with good reason.

'My grandfather built it during the war. Not for the Resistance – there wasn't much around here – but to hide food from the Germans. They searched a dozen times and they were thorough, those Germans. They never found it.'

It was a spacious room measuring about five metres by six. There were two camp beds already made up with sheets and blankets. Between them was a rough wooden table and two chairs. There were plates, mugs and cutlery on the table. On another wooden table in the corner was a paraffin stove. Shelves had been fixed on the wall alongside and were well stocked with tins and packets of food, milk and coffee. Under the table were two car batteries. A lead from one of them was tacked up the wall to the ceiling and the small bulb. There was a curtain across one end. Anton pointed at it. 'There's a chemical toilet behind there, a washbasin and two big jugs of water. Take your trousers off in there, Tadeusz, and change into dry ones.'

Mirek nodded, opened the bag and took out a dry pair of trousers and went behind the curtain.

Anton pointed to a corner of the ceiling: there was a small wire grille. 'Tatania,' he said, 'the ventilation's good. I put that in myself five years ago and checked it three weeks ago when I heard that the place might be needed.'

Ania hobbled to a chair and sat down. The air was dank and cold. She put her arms round her shoulders.

Anton noticed and hurried to the stove saying, 'In half an hour it will be warm and snug in here.' He lit the stove and turned to her. 'Coffee, Tatania – or hot milk? Fresh from Amethyst – that's my favourite cow.'

'Oh, milk please,' she said, brightening up.

He looked a query at Mirek who was coming out from behind the curtain, zipping up his trousers. Anton gestured at a bottle on the shelf.

'We'll wash it down with a shot of Slivovice. Then you can sleep.' He looked at his watch. 'In three hours I catch the first train to Brno and make my report. You had better brief me now on what happened.'

'Report to whom?'

'My cell leader. He'll send word down the line to you-know-who and give me interim instructions.'

Mirek could see that he was relishing his cloak-and-dagger role.

'Who else lives on the farm?'

'No one. It's very small. It gives a reasonable living to just one man. My father manages a big collective farm in the south. My mother's with him. They visit sometimes. My grandfather left the place to me. An old man comes out from Opava to help me during the week. He knows nothing of this place. Even if he did it wouldn't matter. He hates the authorities.'

He brought three steaming mugs over, then collected the Slivovice and three glasses.

Ania warmed her hands on her mug and sipped at the milk. It was thick and creamy.

She smiled at him. 'Say thank you to Amethyst.'

He sat down and grinned, then said to Mirek seriously, 'Right, what happened?'

As Mirek briefed him his eyes shone with excitement like a young boy hearing an adventure yarn. When he listened to the account of the gun battle with the policemen his eyes drifted to the Makarov lying on the bed where Mirek had tossed it. But he was puzzled when Mirek came to the part where he had ditched the motorbike.

He looked at Ania. 'How did you manage to walk ten kilometres with that ankle?'

'I didn't. He carried me.'

Slowly Anton's gaze shifted back to Mirek. In awe he asked, 'You carried her . . . over that country . . . and at night?'

Mirek nodded curtly and started to go on with the story but Anton held up a hand, lifted his glass and said, 'I drink to you, my friend. I consider myself a strong and fit man but I would never have even attempted it.'

'It was carry her or kill her,' Mirek said shortly.

At first the younger man did not understand. Then as comprehension sank in he nodded soberly. The boyish enthusiasm had left his eyes. He realised that this was more than an adventure.

Quickly Mirek finished the rest of the story. Anton asked one question.

'Tatania, how long do you think it will be before you can walk properly?'

She thought for a moment.

'About two or three days.'

He stood up. 'All right, I'll leave you now. I'll be back this evening. Have a good rest.'

226

Something had been puzzling Mirek. He asked Anton, 'If you're down here, like now, and someone approaches, how would you know? You wouldn't hear your dogs down here, not even with the entrance open.'

Anton smiled and said with pride, 'Tadeusz, I've trained my dogs well. When to bark and when not to. And when they bark where to bark.' He pointed to the grille in the corner of the ceiling. 'That vent comes out in the roots of a big old oak tree behind the barn. If someone were to approach now to within half a kilometre the dogs would go silently and stand beside that tree and bark for about half a minute. You can hear them down here. Then they would go back near to the intruders and keep barking until I call them off.' He grinned. 'Almost certainly the farm will be searched tomorrow. The old man will show them around. The dogs will bark by the tree before they get close. You had better keep quiet then.' He started climbing the ladder and pointed to another ring bolt set into the wall. 'If there's a crisis . . . like I get caught and you have to get out, twist that one hundred and eighty degrees, then push up on either side. It will swing open.'

'What if there's a fat pig on it?' Mirek asked. 'I wouldn't want one of them falling down on me.'

Anton's eyes widened and he grinned down at them.

'Hell! I hadn't thought of that. You'd better bang on it first with a mug or something. That will shift them.'

He climbed out and before closing the slab peered down and said, 'Sleep well. I'll see you in the evening.'

They both called up, 'Thanks.'

As the slab closed they heard his answer.

'You're welcome.'

They knew that he meant it.

Fifteen minutes later they were snug in their beds with the light out. Exhausted as he was, Mirek found sleep difficult. He wondered about Anton. What motivated him to take such a risk? He seemed to welcome it. Surely it was more than just a sense of adventure? Was it religion? He doubted it. Suddenly Ania's soft quiet voice came from out of the darkness.

'Mirek, are you awake?'

'Yes.'

'What . . . what will happen to Albin and Sylwia?'

'Don't ask, Ania . . . and better don't think about it.'

A silence, then she said sadly, 'They were a nice old couple.'

'Yes,' he agreed, 'but they must have made a mistake . . . or someone did. We were lucky this time . . . If there's a next time we might not be.'

Another silence, then her voice again. 'Mirek, do you remember, back in Florence, telling me that if I couldn't keep up you would leave me?'

'Yes.'

'Why didn't you leave me back there?'

'You know why.'

'No. You killed those policemen without a thought. Why didn't you kill me? I was just a burden.'

There was a long silence and she prompted him. 'Mirek?' She heard him sigh. 'I don't know.'

He rolled over and pounded his pillow and tried to settle more comfortably in the narrow bed. It was a question he had asked himself time and again as he stumbled along for all those hours with her on his back. The answer was slowly enfolding him like a warm but frightening embrace. He heard her voice again.

'Don't fall in love with me, Mirek . . . I can never love you . . . never. I'm a nun . . . will always be a nun.'

There was no answer. She heard him pound his pillow again, and then just a pitch black silence.

16

Colonel Oleg Zamiatin took the dressing-down standing stiffly to attention. It was rare for Chebrikov to reprimand one of his senior officers in front of junior officers. But he was in a rage and he did so now. Zamiatin's three Majors sat at their desks with eyes downcast.

'Nearly two hours!' Chebrikov screamed, his red face inches from the Colonel's. 'Two fucking hours before they got that cordon in place. The fucking Czech army couldn't catch a mouse in a bucket!' He turned away in disgust and looked at the wall map. 'You could have had a hundred police in that village from Brno in under an hour. But no, you have to use their army and wait for your bloody friend Sholokhov to arrive from Prague.'

Zamiatin ventured to say, 'The man is highly trained and very dangerous, sir.'

'So what?' Chebrikov exploded. 'You think I care if a few Czech policemen get killed? I don't care if he wipes out a battalion of them as long as he gets killed in the process.' He pointed a finger at him. 'If you had given correct orders the information about that car would have been gained an hour earlier. They would still have been eating in that restaurant.'

Zamiatin said nothing, but keenly felt the injustice of it all. If he had sent less than adequate units rushing into that village and if Scibor had shot his way out and escaped he'd be getting a similar dressing-down now – maybe worse.

Chebrikov turned back to the map. 'Well,' he demanded, 'what are you doing now?'

Zamiatin breathed a little easier. He walked to the map and, with his finger, indicated a circle. 'Every disciplined service in the area, including our own army units, is searching here. Meanwhile the Polish border is virtually sealed off from here,' his finger touched the spot where the Polish, Czech and East German borders met to the north, 'to here.' His finger moved down the Polish border to where it met the Russian border.

'You're a fool,' Chebrikov said disgustedly. 'Or do you think the Bacon Priest is? He'll never try to send him over that border now.' He walked over and ran his hand over a section of the map. 'You can be sure that by now Scibor and the woman will be in a safe place somewhere here. Maybe for two or three days. Not longer, because we suspect he's got a definite timetable.'

'Oh?' Zamiatin said. This was the first he had heard of it.

'Yes. It's not positive but Comrade Andropov himself thinks he has a deadline to be in Moscow before the tenth of next month.'

'Do we know why, sir?'

'Yes, but that's confidential.'

Chebrikov was studying the map. 'No. The Bacon Priest would be more subtle than you think. He will pull his man back from that border and redirect him elsewhere. Somewhere we least expect.' He pointed at the East German border to the north. 'It's my guess that he'll try and cross him into the GDR and from there across the Polish border.' He waved a hand dismissively. 'You can forget the nearby Polish border, Colonel. Concentrate your forces up there . . . and you can forget about looking for a couple. The woman was just cover and now that she's blown he'll pull her off. Now get on with it.'

His face still angry, he strode to the door thinking about his coming confrontation with the First Secretary. Andropov would certainly remind him harshly about fish jumping out of boats.

*

Ania made lamb stew from a tin with new, boiled potatoes.

They had both slept like the dead, and on waking ten hours later were ravenous. Mirek had rolled out of bed with his limbs stiff as boards from his previous night's exertions. As Ania stirred the stew she watched him put his body on the rack with a series of short but punishing exercises. He finished with fifty fast press-ups, then, panting, went behind the curtain. When he emerged five minutes later, drying his hands on a towel, she was putting the stew on the table. As he sat down his nose twitched hungrily.

They ate in a relaxed silence. She served him more stew from the pot and he nodded his thanks.

As he mopped up the last of the gravy with a piece of bread he said seriously, 'Ania, you would make a good, genuine wife.'

She was thinking of an answer when they heard a scraping above them. They looked up to see the heavy concrete slab swing open. Anton's cheerful face peered down.

He called, 'Everything OK?'

'Fine,' Mirek said. 'Welcome to the best restaurant in town.'

Anton grinned and then swung a foot down on to the top rung, saying, 'Give me a hand please, Tadeusz.'

He was wrestling a large, obviously heavy, canvas bag through the opening. Mirek went to the foot of the ladder, climbed the first two rungs and reached up. Slowly Anton transferred the bag to him. Mirek felt the clunk of heavy metal as he lowered it to the floor. He asked, 'What's in it?'

'One thing at a time,' Anton answered, climbing down.

'Have you eaten?' Ania asked.

'I had a sandwich on the train.' He walked over to the table and saw that there was still some stew in the pot. 'But I'll have some of that if you're finished.'

Ania fetched a bowl and spoon while Mirek pulled up a chair, asking with some impatience, 'So what's happening up there?'

Anton rolled his eyes and talked through mouthfuls of stew. 'I've never seen anything like it. Every security unit is out in force. Even the Russian army is out of its cantonments. It's unheard of. My train was searched three times, going and coming, from end to end. They took about a dozen people off it.'

'Were you bothered?' Ania asked.

'No. I have a genuine uncle in Brno, and he's genuinely ill. I visit him regularly.'

Mirek asked, 'What happens now?'

Anton finished his stew, pushed the plate away and went to the bag. He came back with a folded map of the area. Ania cleared the table as he unfolded it. The map was large scale. He pointed to a spot just south of Opava. 'We are here. It seems that the security forces are strangely concentrating their search north-west towards the East German border.' He looked at Mirek and said dramatically, 'We have decided to send you over the border south-east . . . here.' He moved his finger to a spot about one hundred kilometres away. It rested beside a lake. Mirek leaned forward. The lake straddled the border; it was about fifteen kilometres long with perhaps the last five kilometres being in Polish territory. Mirek was looking puzzled.

'We have a unique way of getting you there,' Anton said importantly.

'Who's we?' Mirek asked.

'Our cell . . . well, our cell leader took that decision. Apparently there is a time scale to your journey.'

'What does the Bacon Priest say about it?'

Anton shrugged. 'He doesn't know the circumstances yet. It takes some time to communicate with him. This is a field decision.'

Mirek looked a little sceptical.

Ania asked, 'When do we go?'

Anton turned to her. 'You don't, Tatania. It's been decided that Tadeusz goes alone.'

'Why?' Mirek asked sharply.

232

Anton spread his hands. 'It's obvious. They're looking for a couple. Your faces are well known – in all the papers and on television. A photograph of you, Tadeusz, and an accurate sketch of Tatania. If anyone sees you they are to report to the authorities on pain of severe punishment. My cell leader has decided that it is safer now for Tadeusz to travel alone.'

Mirek was looking at Ania. His lips tightened and he turned to Anton and said belligerently, 'We'll wait for the Bacon Priest's decision.'

The young man abruptly became stubborn and authoritative.

'You will not. You are under our protection and our discipline. The chain of command is clear. My cell leader has the full confidence of the Bacon Priest and is authorised to take field decisions . . .' He paused and said, 'This is a crisis situation. Such decisions must be made on the spot and they have been. At such times it can be unwise to wait. As it happens we have a virtually foolproof way of getting you to that lake and across it to Poland. Such an opportunity might not occur again for some time . . .' He gestured at the bag. 'Besides, there is only equipment for one, and that was very hard to find at short notice.'

He sat back and waited with folded arms. Mirek looked at Ania. She shrugged.

'What about her?' Mirek asked severely.

'She will be fine. She will have to stay here for some time – a week or ten days. She will be safe here. Then when the pressure is off we take her out to Prague and then over the Austrian border. She will be safely back in the West in two or three weeks. By that time the search for you will have moved far to the east of Poland.'

Still Mirek looked unhappy. In sudden understanding Anton softened his voice and said, 'She will be safe, I promise you. Far safer than going with you. The risks for you are very great. You understand them well.'

Ania interjected. 'I don't mind the risks . . .'

233

Anton smiled at her admiringly. 'I know, but you must abide by your orders . . . we all must.'

Mirek made up his mind. 'All right, what's in the bag?'

Anton grinned, jumped up and pulled the bag over. He squatted beside it and pulled out a tightly wrapped bundle of black rubber. It was dusted with talcum powder. Carefully he undid it to reveal a one-piece wet suit. Then, while Mirek and Ania looked on with puzzlement, he hefted out an aqualung tank and laid it carefully on the floor.

'Hell,' Mirek muttered. 'I've got to cross that lake under water?'

Anton grinned and stood up. 'No, my friend. You've got to reach the lake under milk!'

He laughed loudly at their expressions, then explained. Three times a week a co-operative tanker collected milk from all the small farms in the area and took it to the main dairy at Liptovsky. One of those farms was Anton's. On the way to Liptovsky it picked up milk from a farm just outside Namestovo which is on the lake shore. The farmer there was one of them. So was one of the drivers of the milk tanker. He was on duty the next day. Mirek would be hidden inside the milk tanker. By the time it reached Anton's farm it would be half full. By the time it reached the lakeside it would be threequarters full. It would certainly be stopped and searched on the way, maybe several times, but they would hardly think of looking under the milk. It would be cold and very uncomfortable, but he was very fit, as he had demonstrated.

Mirek was looking at the aqualung in consternation.

'But I've never used one of those things.'

Anton smiled disarmingly.

'It's very simple. They showed me. Anyway you're not going anywhere. You only have to go under the milk when the tanker stops. It's foolproof.'

Mirek was still sceptical.

'Have you done this before?'

'No,' Anton admitted. 'We have never transported anybody like that, but we have sent other things. Many times.

The tanker is on a regular scheduled route. It's above suspicion.'

Ania had been listening carefully. She asked, 'What then? When he reaches the lake?'

Anton was glad to change the subject. Enthusiastically he answered, 'The farmer at Namestovo is an old hand at crossing that lake at night. His farm is only three kilometres from the Polish border. He goes by large rowing boat with muffled oars. Quite a few people fish on the lake at night, especially on moonless nights like tomorrow. They use bright lights to attract the fish. It is normal behaviour. Tadeusz will be slipped through, and landed on the Polish side. His contact will be waiting. By dawn he will be in a safe house and ready to go on up the pipeline.'

It was all said with earnest candour.

Mirek asked, 'This farmer at Namestovo is a smuggler? Is he being paid for this?'

Anton hesitated and then nodded. Mirek was relieved. He would rather trust himself to a mercenary professional than an idealistic amateur.

'You leave at three tomorrow,' Anton said, watching him hopefully.

Mirek sat for a minute or two looking down at the wet suit and aqualung. Then he said, 'You had better show me how to use this stuff.'

It was the first time that Father Heisl had openly disagreed with the Bacon Priest; and he disagreed fiercely.

They were holding a council of war in the Vienna safe house, discussing the information that had just arrived from Prague.

Again the Bacon Priest tapped the piece of paper in front of him and repeated, 'But why did he not kill her and go on alone?'

Stubbornly Heisl said, 'Maybe he thought her body would be a pointer to his hunters. A pointer to his direction.'

Van Burgh smiled and shook his head. 'Think, Jan, put

235

yourself in his place. Had he thought that he could have killed her, lashed her to the motorbike and dropped her in the river with it, she would not have been found for days . . . if ever.'

Heisl persisted. 'So maybe he thought the sound of a gun shot, even muffled, would have been heard.'

The Bacon Priest snorted in derision. 'Now you're being deliberately obtuse. He could have killed her ten different ways without a sound – we spent fifteen thousand dollars ensuring that.'

Heisl dropped his eyes, knowing that he was losing the argument. Van Burgh mused, 'He carried her ten kilometres. Swiatek in Prague knows that area well. He describes that feat as incredible. Now why should Scibor do it? You well know what sort of man he is. You remember what he told her. "If you become a burden I'll dump you." Well he carried that burden ten kilometres. Why?'

The Bacon Priest knew why. He also knew that Heisl knew why. He wanted to hear him say it. He pressed. 'Why?'

Father Heisl lifted his head and said dejectedly, 'Because he's fallen in love with her.'

'Precisely.' Van Burgh squeezed his nose between thumb and forefinger and thought deeply. Heisl waited miserably, guessing what was coming.

'And what,' the Bacon Priest asked, 'would you think Ania's reaction would be to having her life saved by a man she would expect to kill her without compunction? Saved at enormous risk to himself.'

Heisl remained determinedly silent. He heard Van Burgh answer his own question.

'It is not unlikely that she in turn fell in love with him. Any analyst in this city of analysts would conclude that such an outcome was likely.'

Frostily Heisl remarked, 'You are forgetting that she is a very devout nun.'

'No, I am not. Neither am I suggesting physical, carnal love. But remember she left on that journey thinking him

236

to be an evil, uncaring human being totally obsessed with his own mission. So did we. It is not possible that she thinks that any more. What he did was not the action of an evil, uncaring man. At least not as it applies to her.' He tapped the paper again. 'I think Swiatek made a mistake. He should have sent them on together. He argues that the Russians would expect us to pull her back now that they know about her. He fails to realise that we must always do the unexpected. The Russians are not subtle. They will now be searching for a man on his own. We shall send word to Prague that they must continue as a couple – disguised, but as a couple.'

'It may be too late. It will take time. He may be gone by then.'

'In that case,' Van Burgh replied firmly, 'she must catch up with him.'

Heisl sighed and stood up to go and arrange the message. The Bacon Priest's voice stopped him. 'We both know, Jan, that two people working as a team . . . a very close team, are always more effective than one person working alone. We have seen over the years many examples. But to work closely there must be a bond – and the strongest bond is love.'

Heisl leaned forward and put both palms on the table and said with great emphasis, 'You are right, of course. But being right in one thing can make you very wrong in another. By sending her on with him you risk destroying her . . . even if she does not get caught.'

The Bacon Priest nodded solemnly. 'Jan, I have to take that risk. I have taken it many times in the past, for the greater good . . . of our Church.'

17

Mirek reached the decision with total certainty.

For the rest of his life he would never again drink milk.

He sat behind bales of hay in a barn right on the edge of Lake Oravska. They had pulled him out of the milk tanker twenty minutes before but his chest still heaved slightly as his heart pumped from the preceding hours of physical effort and near panic. He knew that time was relative; understood the theory very well. But his time in the milk tanker had been a practical demonstration of terrifying proportions.

The journey of just over one hundred kilometres together with five stops to take on milk had lasted just over three hours. Every single minute of the last hour had felt like an hour in itself.

He had climbed into the tank just after three p.m.

The parting from Ania had been painful. They had stood together in the barn. Tactfully Anton had left them alone for this moment. Mirek had felt somewhat ridiculous in his black wet suit. Had he felt no pain at the parting he might have been amused at the incongruity of standing in such a garb in the middle of a continent. As it was, he had watched her eyes carefully, anxiously. He ached to see something in them. Some hint. He did see compassion, even care, but not what he had hoped to see.

His head also ached from the night's drinking and he had cursed himself for his unprofessionalism. Ania had offered aspirin which he had curtly refused, not wanting, in those last moments, to show weakness. His canvas bag was at his feet, tightly wrapped and sealed in a large black plastic bag.

He had put his hands on her shoulders and gently pulled her towards him. She turned her head and offered her cheek to his lips. He pressed his own face against hers. She said, close to his ear, 'Good luck, Mirek. Think only of yourself now. Don't worry about me.'

He felt her body against his, but it was not yielding. With a sigh he released her and bent to pick up his bag. As he straightened he started to say something but then stopped. He nodded briskly and turned towards the door. As he reached it she called his name. He stopped and turned. The light was not good in the barn. He could not make out her expression.

'Yes. What is it?'

She moved towards him. He saw her arms lifting and then he saw that her eyes were wet. He dropped the bag as her arms went around him and her body clung to him.

'I'll . . . I'll pray for you, Mirek.'

He felt the wetness of her cheek against his and then she moved her head and was kissing him on the lips. A chaste, tender kiss, but on the lips. She pulled back and loosened her grip and repeated, 'I'll pray for you.'

He had slowly picked up his bag and said with finality, 'Ania Krol, when this is over, if I get through it, I'll find you.'

Before she could answer he had turned and walked out of the door.

At first the journey had appeared to be simple. Metal rungs were fixed up the bulging side of the tanker. The round hatch on top was open. A metal ladder was fixed to the inside. Anton was sitting on top next to it, holding the aqualung. The driver, an old but burly man in his sixties, took Mirek's bag saying, 'I'll pass it up, son.'

A thought struck Mirek. He looked up at Anton and said, 'If anyone opens that hatch they'll see the bubbles from the aqualung.'

Anton grinned and shook his head.

'Come up and look.'

Mirek climbed up and looked down the hatch. The tanker was about a third full. There was a thick foam on top of the milk.

Anton said, 'That will hide the bubbles. When the tanker is moving you hold on to the steps.' He pointed. 'When it stops you move off to the end there and submerge. It's very unlikely that anyone will even open this hatch. It's only used for cleaning. Just be careful that you don't bang the aqualung against the side when you're moving about.'

Mirek had felt consciously reluctant to climb down; an uncharacteristic touch of fear. The white layer of foam below him looked innocent enough.

'How full will it get?'

'About two-thirds. Don't worry, there'll be plenty of head room. Remember that there's only two hours of air in your tank. Use it sparingly.'

Just then had come the distant sound of a dog barking. Anton looked up sharply.

'I sent the old man into town on an errand. That will be him returning. You'd better get a move on.'

Mirek was grateful for the spur. He lowered himself down the first few rungs, then leaned forward and rumpled Anton's hair.

'Thanks. Look after her.'

Anton nodded reassuringly. 'She'll be safe.'

Mirek descended further, his feet splashing into the milk, then he looked up. Anton was lowering the aqualung slowly through the hatch. Mirek reached up, took the weight and called, 'OK.'

He had practised during the morning and it only took him two minutes to slip into the harness and adjust it comfortably. Anton's voice came down urgently.

'Check it. Quickly, before I close the hatch.'

Mirek fumbled the rubber bit between his teeth. He checked that the air was coming through, then spat out the mouthpiece and called, 'OK.'

Anton passed down his black plastic bag and said, 'Good luck, Tadeusz. Go with God.'

There was a clang and Mirek was in total darkness. He heard the echoing scrape of Anton's footsteps as he climbed down. A minute later the tanker vibrated as the engine started and Mirek was up to his mouth in milk as the load surged backwards with the sudden forward movement. Quickly he moved up a couple of rungs, worried that milk would have got into the mouthpiece. He checked it and decided that he would have to hold it loosely between his teeth the whole way.

During the first hour they had stopped twice to take in milk. By the end of that first hour Mirek knew that he had a major problem. First it was the cold. Gradually it penetrated the wet suit. He wore nothing under the wet suit. Anton had told him that the theory was that it quickly got wet and then insulated the moisture between it and the skin. Body heat then warmed the moisture. It was no longer warm. Then the cold penetrated his skin and his flesh. Finally it seeped into his bones.

Second it was his fingers. Many of the roads the tanker travelled over were nothing but country lanes, winding and bumpy. He had to hang on tight. His fingers began to ache. He tried to put an arm through the ladder to support himself but it was not designed for that. The metal was sharp in places, rough in others. His mind went back to the desert camp and the hours he had used the springed exercisers to strengthen his ten primary weapons. He sent mental thanks to Frank.

Third was the aqualung itself. It was designed to be worn submerged and for a limited period. Above water it was damned heavy and, as the minutes passed, the straps began to bite into his shoulders. Fourth was the milk. It surged back and forth and side to side with a force he had never imagined. It was like being caught in a crazy riptide. The tanker was half full. He knew that by the time it had taken on its final load he would be fighting for survival.

By the end of the second hour that was exactly the situation. His hands were frozen claws, his whole body numb from the cold and the pounding of the milk. They had taken on the last load and he was having to use the aqualung most of the time.

During that last hour survival became a battle of mind over matter. He knew that the human body, and particularly a body as fit as his, could perform beyond normal human tolerances – if the mind willed it. He willed it. He cut off from his mind the pain in his fingers and arms and shoulders. He thought of other things. First of his childhood. His parents and his sister Jolanta. But that memory was also a pain and he quickly moved his mind to other things. His training in the SB, women he had known, songs and tunes he had learned. Twice he vomited into the milk. When he felt himself weakening he dwelt on his target and on his hatred. Finally, towards the end, while each minute passed as an hour, he occupied his mind with Ania. He painted a mental picture of her face, remembered words she had spoken to him, actually heard her voice with its strange husky rasp. He had rubber and milk in his mouth but he could actually taste the touch of her lips and feel their slight pressure. Ania was on his mind, the sight, the feel and the smell of her, as the tanker finally braked to a halt and the milk washed over him for the last time.

It was as though he had been glued to that ladder. They had to prise his fingers from it. The driver was old but strong. The farmer was younger and strong; his son stronger still. It took all three of them to lift him bodily through the hatch and lower him to the ground, then half carry him to the barn.

Now wrapped in three blankets and a quilt, with his feet in sheepskin boots, the circulation slowly returned to his body. Painfully he exercised his fingers. The barn door opened and a moment later the farmer peered over the bales. He had a long pointed nose and thinning brown hair combed straight back. He looked like an avaricious ferret but he smiled pleasantly enough and lifted a metal canteen on to the top bale and a hunk of crusty bread.

'Get that inside you. It's beef broth, home-made. It'll warm you from the inside and put you right. Then try and sleep. We leave at ten o'clock. That's in three and a half hours.'

The head disappeared and, with a muffled groan, Mirek pushed himself to his feet. He prised the top off the canteen and a moment later was drinking what he decided was the best soup in the world. There must have been over a litre of it. He drank it all, washing down chunks of bread. Then he lay down on the straw and tried to sleep.

It was impossible but he did doze a little and when the farmer came back he still ached all over but he felt rested.

The night was dark and cold. Both the farmer and Mirek were dressed in black clothing. Black scarves were adjusted over their faces. The five-metre wooden rowing boat was painted black. Only the white licence numbers showed. The farmer draped a black cloth over them. He was confident and reassuring. He pointed at some distant lights on the lake.

'Polish fishing boats.' He tapped the globe of the light moving from a framework at the stern of his boat. 'If we're stopped the story is that the connection from the gas tank to the light is faulty. We're heading for the other boats to see if anyone has a spare. Your papers are good. Leave all the talking to me.'

He took Mirek's bag and dropped it in the stern, then he sucked his forefinger, held it up high and grunted in satisfaction.

'What wind there is will be astern. We should be there in about two hours. In you get.'

Mirek scrambled in and sat at the stern with his bag at his feet. The farmer cast off from the small jetty, climbed in and pushed off. Quickly he unshipped the oars and set them in the heavily padded rowlocks. The oars were long and heavy.

Mirek whispered, 'I'll take my turn rowing.'

From behind his scarf the farmer said emphatically, 'No, you won't. On a night like this the only way we'll be detected is by the splashing of an oar. Even if you were an Olympic rowing champion I wouldn't let you do it – not in this boat.'

Mirek noted that he was stroking the heavy oars through the water with scarcely a ripple. At the beginning of each stroke the blades turned to a fine angle as they slid into the water.

The farmer explained their route. They would contour the shoreline about four hundred metres out. There was one Polish and one Czech patrol boat. Some nights they were out and some nights they were not. They always kept to the centre of the lake, looking for unlicensed fishing boats. The Polish boat was not much of a problem. The two-man crew usually just drifted and drank vodka.

Finally the farmer said, 'I assume you've got a gun in that bag. If we're challenged you drop it straight over the side, understand?'

'Sure,' Mirek replied. He had no intention of doing so. Nor was he about to tell the farmer that also in the bag was the uniform of an SB Colonel.

'Right,' the farmer said. 'Now no more talking. It's amazing how the sound travels over still water.'

So for two hours they travelled in silence. The farmer stopped rowing several times; not to rest – he appeared to be tireless – but to listen. From far away across the lake Mirek could hear fishermen calling to each other. On the first few occasions the voices were in Czech. Then Mirek began to hear voices talking in his native Polish and was warmed by it. Truly it was amazing how far the sound travelled over the lake. The lights of the boats were very distant but he heard one fisherman laughingly call to another that he couldn't catch a cold at the North Pole.

Several times Mirek saw the sweeping arc of a searchlight away to their right but its beam reached nowhere near them and the farmer rowed on unconcerned. Just after midnight Mirek noticed that they were gradually angling in towards the shore. Now the farmer stopped frequently to peer at the dim dark line. Finally he grunted softly and stroked the left oar a couple of rows and headed straight in.

They bumped softly. The farmer silently shipped the oars, climbed over the bow and pulled the boat further up.

Mirek picked up his bag, climbed forward and with a soft thud jumped on to the mossy shore. The farmer pointed.

'There's a path there. Go up it about a hundred paces. On the left there's a big birch tree, by itself. They'll be waiting for you there . . . Good luck, wherever you're going.'

In one motion he pushed the boat out and jumped into it. Mirek whispered, 'Thanks,' at the departing shadow. Then he opened his bag, took out his gun and slipped off the safety. He located the path and was about to start up it when he remembered he was still wearing the farmer's sheepskin boots. Instinctively he stopped and turned, then smiled to himself. It was too late now. Anyway, the farmer would have been paid well enough.

Cautiously he moved up the path which rose quite steeply from the shore. After counting off eighty paces he saw the loom of the birch tree on his left. As he got closer he saw another darker nucleus beside it. A high-toned woman's voice called softly, 'It's a cold night for a walk.'

He answered, 'It's a cold night for anything.'

The woman giggled. 'Not for anything. Follow me, Mirek Scibor. You're in time for the party.'

She moved up the path. Mirek stood rooted to the spot. She turned. 'Come on then.'

He found his voice. 'How do you know my name? What party? Are you crazy?'

She giggled again. 'Some people think so, but I've never been certified. Who else could you be? I suppose they sent the woman back. Now come on, I'm damned cold.'

She started moving again. Mirek had no choice but to

follow. He put his gun on to safety and started to tuck it into his waistband, but then thought better of it and held it ready.

The path veered to the left and paralleled the lake below. After about five hundred metres they crossed a dirt road. Below them were the lights of a house. In all he followed the woman for about two kilometres. They passed two other lakeshore houses. He assumed they were weekend cottages of senior party officials.

He heard the music before he saw the place. Rock music. Fifty metres later the path turned down towards the lake and he stopped abruptly and looked at the rambling house, all the windows lit up, a bright light over the door. He heard the tinkling of laughter.

'Wait!' he called. 'I'm not going in there among a bunch of people. You really are crazy.'

She turned. Against the light he saw she was tall, wearing an ankle-length fur coat with the hood up covering her head. 'Not a bunch,' she said. 'Just four – and they all know you're coming.'

'Who are they?'

'Friends, good friends. Now do come in. There's hot food and cold vodka and a warm bed.'

He hesitated. She said firmly, 'Don't be concerned. You will be safe here. You are a hero to these people – and to me.'

He sighed and moved forward. He really had no choice.

At the door she paused and pulled the hood back from her face. His immediate impression was of beauty. Mischievous beauty. Blonde curly hair, vivid blue eyes radiating merriment. A mobile mouth with full red lips. About twenty-five years old. She too was studying him. Her lips curved upwards.

'You are indeed handsome. I was worried that you might just be photogenic.'

'Whose house is this?'

'It belongs to the Deputy Commissar of the fair city of Cracow.'

246

'Does he know you're using it?'

Her eyes twinkled. 'Of course. I'm his daughter.'

While he absorbed that she pulled off a fur glove and held out her hand.

'Marian Lydkowska. Very much at your service.' The hand was fine-boned, soft and warm to the touch. It squeezed his intimately. He felt disorientated and she obviously sensed it. She giggled again and then opened the door.

As he followed her through into the opulent hall she asked, 'Do you like Genesis?'

'What's that?'

She laughed. 'This music.'

'Never heard it before.'

'Oh, of course,' she said teasingly. 'It's hardly the sort of stuff the SB would dance to.' She pointed to a chair by the door. 'Leave your bag there. I'll take you up to your room later . . . and you can put that gun away.'

He dropped the bag on to the chair and pushed his gun under his waistband, wondering what on earth the Bacon Priest was up to. As he turned Marian was slipping off the fur coat. Under it she wore a red silk dress with a short flared skirt and a bodice cut to the waist. He could see the outline of her nipples against the thin silk. The skin of her midriff was as pink as a blush. He looked up at her face. She was smiling as if in appreciation of his thoughts. She walked to a door and opened it. The music blared forth. With a sweep of her hand she gestured for him to go in. Feeling bemused and a little irritated, he walked through. It was a vast room with full-length French windows facing the lake. Twin crystal chandeliers cast light over deep plush armchairs and settees, on which the four occupants were sprawled. Two young women in their early twenties, one man of similar age, and one man in his early thirties. Both men wore beards, spectacles and faded denims. One of the women, red-headed and pretty, wore green and white striped overalls over a black blouse; the other, dark, gypsy looking, wore a red shirt dress with blue sequins on

247

the collar. She was the first to jump up, exclaiming, 'It is him! It is Mirek Scibor!'

She rushed over, hugged him and planted a mighty kiss on each cheek. From behind him Mirek heard Marian say, 'Careful, Irena, he's carrying a gun.'

She stood back, saying, 'But of course he is.'

The older man stood up and came over with an outstretched hand. 'Welcome back to Poland. I'm Jerzy Zamojski.' He waved a hand at the younger man and the other woman. 'Antoni Zonn . . . Natalia Banaszek . . . Antoni, please turn that down.'

The young man reached out and turned a knob on the console of a Sony stereo. The music subsided.

'Vodka. Good Polish vodka!' Jerzy announced. He went to a sideboard and pulled a bottle out of a sweating ice bucket.

Harshly Mirek asked, 'Who are you all?'

Jerzy was pouring into a shot glass. The vodka was so cold it seemed to ooze out of the bottle like oil. He held the glass out to Mirek, smiled and said, 'You have just met the editorial board of *Razem*.'

Mirek took the glass, immediately relaxing. *Razem* – 'Together' – was one of the underground newspapers that sprang up after the suppression of Solidarity. It was unique in that apart from being virulently anti-State, it was also anti-Church. Distributed through campuses and schools all over Poland, it was also one of the few underground papers whose origins and editorial whereabouts completely baffled the authorities. Mirek was beginning to understand why.

They had all gathered around him, holding their glasses.

Fervently Jerzy said, 'To Poland . . . and freedom.'

They all repeated the toast and all downed their drinks in one shot. Jerzy turned to Marian and said sternly, 'Now, as hostess it's your duty to make sure our glasses stay filled.' He took Mirek's glass and handed it to her with his own, then he took Mirek's arm and led him to a settee. Jerzy was obviously the leader.

Marian brought their filled glasses and Mirek asked her, 'What if your father walks in?'

'He won't,' she answered. 'He hardly ever comes here. He's far too busy with his work and his two energetic mistresses. They happen to be good friends of mine. They let me know about all his movements.' She caricatured a leer. 'Even the more intimate ones.'

'And your mother?'

She shook her head. 'She died many years ago.'

'And your father knows nothing about *Razem*?'

Jerzy answered for her. 'No, none of our fathers do . . . and they're all big wheels. Mine is Vice Chancellor of the University in Cracow; Antoni's is Secretary General of the Polish Writers' Union.' He gestured. 'Irena's papa is Brigadier General Teador Navkienko of whom doubtless you've heard, and Natalia's sire is the regional director of the State Railways.' Mirek nodded thoughtfully and remarked, 'So a lot of senior jobs will become vacant if you're uncovered.'

'True,' Jerzy answered soberly, 'but they've chosen their paths . . . and we've chosen ours.' He reached forward to the coffee table, opened a silver cigarette box and offered it to Mirek.

'Thanks, I don't smoke.'

'Not even these?'

Mirek looked more closely. The cigarettes were larger than normal, fat at one end, thin at the other. They were bound together by white cotton threads.

'What are they?'

Jerzy grinned through his beard.

'Marijuana. Thai sticks; the best. Just think: a few months ago if SB Major Scibor had caught us with these we'd have been in very hot water!'

Mirek shook his head and, with a trace of bitterness he couldn't help, said, 'I doubt it. One of your daddies would have pulled a string or two and got you off with a slap on the wrist.'

Jerzy lit one of the cigarettes and Mirek watched with

some amazement the ritual of it being passed from one sucking mouth to another.

Antoni said, 'It's clever, don't you think? Everyone takes us for a bunch of spoiled dilettantes. It's a very good cover for our operation.'

Irena laughed loudly. 'We are a bunch of spoiled dilettantes. We're the only underground group whose cover is genuine.' She was sitting on the arm of Antoni's chair, her arm around his neck. They were obviously paired. He wondered whether Jerzy was paired with Marian or Natalia. Or, in this environment, with both? He drank more vodka, savouring the fire of it in his throat. He realised that he was achingly tired. He said to Jerzy, 'Before you all get stoned out of your minds you'd better fill me in. When do you move me on?'

Jerzy's cheeks hollowed in as he drew deep on the joint. He held his breath and then contentedly let the smoke filter out. The last of it puffed as he answered.

'It was supposed to be tomorrow but this afternoon we got a coded message from Warsaw. We're to wait here until further notice. Apparently something's changed.'

'That's all you know?'

'That's all. Your people are not very forthcoming – anyway you'll be comfortable and totally safe. No one's going to think about searching this house.'

Mirek recognised the truth of that. He would sleep easy tonight. He thought for a moment and then asked, 'How did you get involved in this?'

Jerzy replied carefully. 'We're in arm's length contact with other underground groups. Mostly those that distribute our paper. One of them approached us a few weeks ago. Asked us to be on standby. Told us it was unlikely we would be needed.'

'But why did you accept?'

Jerzy grinned. 'Money, dear friend. Well, actually, a thin sheet of metal – very precious metal. It costs a lot of money to run a newspaper. We're really very grateful to you for getting into that mess over the border. Now that we're activated we get another twenty sheets of that shiny metal.'

'I see.' Mirek put his glass down on the coffee table. 'And how did you know it would be me?'

Natalia answered. 'You're famous, Mirek. I doubt if the Pope's face is better known than yours in Poland today. Television, newspaper, police posters. Non-stop for the last three days. We were activated the day you shot those pigs in Ostrava. It didn't take a genius to work out who was coming our way.'

Mirek nodded. 'And where do you pass me on?'

'In Cracow,' Jerzy answered. His eyes were becoming heavy lidded, his voice slurred a little. 'At least that was the original plan . . . I suppose they sent the woman back?'

'Yes.' Mirek stood up grimacing at the ache still in his limbs. 'I'm shattered; I'd like to get some sleep. Thanks for everything.'

Marian jumped up. 'I'll show you your room.'

He shook hands with Jerzy and Antoni. The women gave him a hug and a kiss on the cheek in an adoptive way.

He followed Marian up the stairs. Her dress was backless. Her bottom swayed in front of his eyes. Her legs were smooth. She turned left at the landing and sashayed down the corridor saying, 'I've given you a front room. It has a lovely view over the lake and . . .' she stopped at a door and opened it, '. . . a big and very comfortable bed.'

He looked in. The bed was enormous. She pointed to a door beyond it.

'That's the bathroom. Sunken bath, big enough for two. Don't you love sunken baths?'

He did not answer. He had never seen a sunken bath. He walked in, lifted his bag on to the bed and turned.

'Thanks, Marian.'

She was leaning against the jamb of the door. Her eyes, her posture, threw out an invitation. Her nipples had tightened against her dress in anticipation.

He said, 'I'll see you in the morning then. Thanks again.'

Her lips pouted in disappointment, then she smiled, raised her hand and pointed sideways across her nose.

'My room is next door. If you need anything just let me know . . . Sweet dreams, Mirek.'

Ten minutes later he was lying with very hot water up to his chin in the sunken bath. He figured out it was big enough for four. As the aches were soothed from his bones he wondered at what had happened to him. The Mirek Scibor of only a few days ago would at this moment have been running his hands over the soapy pink body of that blonde temptress. He was amazed that he had been able to counter the physical urge. The last woman he had been with was Leila in the desert; and that seemed a lifetime ago.

He looked around the sumptuous bathroom. Gold-plated taps; heated towel rails; deep pile carpet; gleaming mirrors. He could imagine it in the West. Here it was an obscenity. He felt pleasure at the thought of the Deputy Commissar for Cracow being bamboozled by his sexy renegade daughter. Then he contrasted this luxury with the Spartan conditions that Ania was enduring in her cellar. His thoughts dwelt on her. He felt a lassitude; wondered if she was thinking of him. Tried to imagine her in the bath with him. He closed his eyes to picture it better.

Half an hour later he was coughing and spluttering, with soapy water in his mouth. He had fallen asleep in the bath.

18

Professor Stefan Szafer decided to wait until the coffee was served before making his announcement. It was their usual lunchtime setting of the Wierzynek Restaurant and he thought that Halena had never looked more beautiful. On this occasion she was wearing a roll-neck jet-black pullover and a cream linen skirt. Her hair was pulled back in a tight chignon. He decided that the line of her jaw from chin to ear was nothing less than a work of art. She wore tiny earrings in the shape of a bell.

He was about to impart his news, savouring the moment, when she said, 'You make me unhappy, Stefan.'

The statement alarmed him. He leaned forward with a frown of concern.

'Why, Halena? What have I done?'

She pouted. 'Well, it's almost two weeks now since I told you about my trip to Moscow. You promised to try to visit me there but you've told me nothing since. I assume you don't want to go.'

He smiled with relief, beckoned a waiter and ordered a cognac for himself and a Tia Maria for her. Then he said, 'I was keeping it as a surprise.'

She glared at him in mock anger. 'That's cruel, Stefan. Unfair . . . I'm so anxious.'

He reached forward and took her hand in his. 'You know I would never be cruel to you. The fact is I only found out for sure this morning. I've always known that I could take a few days off, but some time ago a suggestion was advanced which would make my visit official . . . and longer. The Director, Comrade Kurowski, called me to his office this morning. The official aspect of my visit has been confirmed by the Ministry. The Director was very excited and naturally so am I.'

The waiter brought their liqueurs and refilled their coffee cups. Halena took a minuscule sip of Tia Maria and said, 'Then so am I. What will you be doing in this official capacity?'

He shrugged with great nonchalance. 'Giving a couple of lectures.'

'That's all?'

He smiled. 'Halena, my audiences will be the cream of the Soviet medical profession. Also I'm to be interviewed by *Sovetskaya Meditsina*, one of the most respected medical journals in the world . . . It's a great honour.'

She sipped again at her drink, watching him closely.

'And?'

'And what?'

'Oh come on, Stefan! I know you so well. What are you keeping back?'

For a moment he sat watching her, then he glanced quickly around the room and said quietly, 'Halena, naturally while I'm there I'll be consulting with my Russian counterparts about some of their most difficult cases . . . Well, I've been told that one of those cases will concern a very important man.' He held up a hand. 'Don't ask me who, because I cannot tell you. I can tell you that it will be a major step in my career.'

She finished the last of her drink and put the tiny glass on to the table. It clinked against a saucer. He waited eagerly for her reaction, for her plaudits.

She surprised him. Her mouth turned down and she sighed deeply and said in a sombre voice, 'Stefan, I beg you not to do it.'

For a moment he was speechless, then he muttered, 'Why? What do you . . . ?'

Her voice, quiet but incisive, cut him off. 'I'm not a fool. Why do men always think attractive blondes are stupid?

254

Stefan, it's obvious who your important man is. Don't worry, I won't mention his name. There have been rumours – well, there are always rumours in Poland – but these are very strong. Your important man is very ill . . . very. What do you think will happen to your career if you treat him and shortly afterwards he dies? Never mind your career; what about your life? Stefan, never forget that you are a Pole. Never forget how the Russians like to have a scapegoat tied and ready for sacrifice.'

He smiled at her, very touched by her obvious concern. In a reassuring tone he said, 'I am not going to treat him, Halena. I am merely going to be consulted by his very eminent doctors, in particular about my work on dialysis.'

'Oh. Does that mean you won't examine him personally?'

He smiled again. 'Of course I will have to examine him. But I will not personally treat him . . . And another thing: the rumours that you talk about are greatly exaggerated – as usual. I've seen a preliminary report; very confidential. He is not about to die next week, or next month. I will not be a scapegoat for anyone.'

She was mollified and brightened up.

'Well anyway, it's wonderful news that we shall be in Moscow together. Now tell me exactly your itinerary.'

He was pleased at her brighter mood and glad to change the subject. Enthusiastically he said, 'I arrive in Moscow on the afternoon of February 8th.' He grinned. 'Aeroflot, first class, of course. You will be there already. They have booked me a suite at the Kosmos.'

It was her turn to grin. 'Oh, what an important boyfriend I have. I'm sharing a room in the Yunost, which I'm told is little better than a flea pit.'

'Never mind,' he said very offhandedly. 'If you like you can share my suite.'

She smiled archly at him. 'Not the first night I can't. On the 8th our group is going to a mime show in Kaunos. We stay the night there and get back to Moscow early the next morning. I'll come straight to your palace to see you.'

He nodded. 'My first appointment is the important one. They are picking me up at noon. They wanted to take me to lunch afterwards but I delayed it to the next day in anticipation of taking you to lunch at the Lastochka.'

She nodded her head in solemn thanks and asked, 'What then?'

He shrugged. 'Then I have three days of lecturing and visits followed by four days of holiday. Can you take time off from your seminar to go to Leningrad with me?'

She said, 'Well. Of course it will be very difficult. My schedule is very packed and my work so vital to the national interest and humanity as a whole. I must give it very serious thought. I must balance my contribution to the arts and society against the company of a lecherous . . . and, shall we say, poorly qualified, young doctor . . .'

He saw her lips twitching upwards and he smiled with her. Very lightly she said, 'Well, I've always wanted to visit the Hermitage . . . so yes, Stefan. I shall go to Leningrad with you.'

'Good. Let's have a last drink to celebrate that.' He looked around for a waiter and only then noticed that they were the last couple left in the place. With a frown he glanced at his watch and then abruptly stood up.

'Halena, it's almost three. I'm due in the operating theatre in fifteen minutes.' He took out his wallet and extracted twenty hundred-zloty notes and put them on the table.

'Please pay the bill. I'll see you on Friday night. Just before nine.' He bent his head and kissed her quickly and hurried out.

The head waiter approached with the bill on a silver salver. She placed the notes on it, smiled and said, 'Keep the change, but first extract enough to bring me another Tia Maria.'

He smiled and turned away. She called after him. 'Make it a double.'

He half turned and nodded. A couple of paces later her voice stopped him again.

'And waiter. Put a little cream on top.'

In Moscow Victor Chebrikov had also lunched well in a private dining room in the Presidium. He had been invited there by two men senior enough to command his respect. They had been charming and polite but also firmly insistent that he tell them something of what was going on. He could have kept silent or even become angry, invoking the name of his mentor, but he did neither. He was wise in the political maze of the Presidium. He had talked in parallels and fables and they too, being wise, had understood him.

As he walked into Zamiatin's Situation Room he was chewing an antacid pill in opposition to a second portion of chocolate cake.

The Colonel and his three Majors rose rapidly to their feet and saluted crisply.

Amiably Chebrikov asked, 'Anything to report?'

Zamiatin was surprised and relieved by his boss's tone.

He said, 'Very little, sir. Under drugs the Pole calling himself Albin admitted to being a secret priest named Josef Pietkiewicz, legally married to the woman captured with him. We had a strong reaction when we questioned him about the Bacon Priest but the prognosis is that he's never actually met him. Meanwhile the wife suffered a mild heart attack during rigorous interrogation. Before that she had yielded nothing under drugs.'

Chebrikov waved a hand indicating that they should be at ease and sit down.

Major Gudov said musingly, 'It's strange that, but confirms a pattern. Women are more resistant to drugs than men. I don't really understand it.'

Chebrikov replied, 'You would if you'd been married to my wife for thirty years.'

They all laughed, but not too loudly.

Major Jwanow asked, 'Would you like tea, sir?'

Chebrikov nodded and Jwanow went to the samovar which had recently been installed in the corner. His boss was studying the huge wall map when he brought him the glass. There were several minutes of silence while Chebrikov sipped noisily, never taking his gaze from the map.

Then he said to Zamiatin, 'Forget the old couple. The cut-outs will have been complete. We must crack the next pipeline.' He pointed at the map to an area near the East German border.

'Keep concentrating there. That's where you'll find it. That's the weak point. Meanwhile, move the bulk of the Polish SB to the north-west . . . to the border area west of Wroclaw. That's a more likely area than the south-eastern regions. The SB are the only Poles worth using. After all, Scibor was one of them – and they hate renegades.'

Zamiatin seemed about to say something but then closed his mouth. Chebrikov continued studying the map, nodding his head. Then he said, 'I'm ordering our own army units back into their cantonments. They're not doing much good sitting at road blocks and their use goes against general policy.'

Zamiatin was about to protest that such an order would mean taking Polish militia units away from urban searches to man road blocks, but again, at the last moment, held his tongue. He sensed that Chebrikov's amiability would quickly wane if he started arguing.

With a touch of confident finality Chebrikov said, 'He's still in Czechoslovakia. The Bacon Priest is sending him north. It's my guess that he'll try to move him over in the next forty-eight hours. Those hours are crucial.' He turned and gave Zamiatin a considered look. 'Crucial, Colonel. If he gets into Poland his position is stronger. We don't like to admit that but it's true. Now your next report to the Comrade First Secretary is due at noon tomorrow.'

'Yes, sir.'

'Well, let's hope it contains something positive.'

He strode to the door, depositing his empty glass on Gudov's desk.

His departure left a silence. The three Majors could sense Zamiatin's unease.

Finally Gudov said, 'Colonel, should I give the order to concentrate the Polish SB to the border area west of Wroclaw?'

Still thoughtful, Zamiatin nodded, but as Gudov reached for the phone the Colonel said, 'Leave the units in Cracow itself intact.'

Gudov's hand froze on the phone. He and the other two Majors stared at Zamiatin. He shrugged.

'Comrade Chebrikov ordered me to concentrate the SB to the north-west border. He did not order me to denude the south totally. I am following his orders; but Cracow has always been a centre of subversion. Also it is only one hundred and fifty kilometres from the place where Scibor was discovered. If he is across the border already he will be in Cracow . . . or heading there.'

There was another silence, then Major Gudov sucked in air through his teeth and picked up the phone.

Meanwhile Major Jwanow was hesitantly fingering a folder. Finally he made up his mind.

'Comrade Colonel . . . I don't know if this might be important . .'

'What is it?'

Jwanow opened the folder. He said, 'Ever since we knew that the Bacon Priest was involved we have been keeping a close watch on the Collegio Russico in Rome. We photographed people going in and coming out. Well, I was going through those photographs a few days ago. On several occasions a woman was photographed. I noticed a resemblance between her and the drawing of the woman who was with Scibor in Czechoslovakia.' He paused and licked his lips.

Zamiatin said, 'So? Did you follow it up?'

'Yes Comrade Colonel, but I fear it was a dead end. She turned out to be a nun. Polish, but from a convent in Hungary '

Zamiatin snorted. 'A nun!'

'Yes, but the thing is, Comrade Colonel, I had a report yesterday that she has not returned to her convent. No one seems to know where she is. And the likeness is very close.'

'Show me.'

Major Jwanow stood up and carried over the folder. He opened it and pointed to a photograph pinned to the flap. Opposite it was the drawing. Zamiatin studied them for several seconds. Then he nodded and flipped the page.

From the report he intoned: 'Ania Krol. Aged 26. Born Cracow, Poland. Parents killed in car crash October 7th, 1960. Buried Cracow . . .'

He lifted his head and gazed off into space for several minutes.

'I wouldn't put it past the Bacon Priest to use a nun. Gudov, when you get through to Cracow I want to speak to the top man there.'

19

'You must be in love.'

Mirek sighed. 'What makes you think that?'

Marian Lydkowska pointed a red-tipped finger at him. 'You are not gay. You are certainly not a devout Catholic. Yet I offer myself to you and you don't respond.'

Mirek smiled at her frankness. They were alone in the huge sitting room of the lakeshore villa. It was evening. The curtains were open and, from across the lake, pinpoints of light were reflected on the black water. Antoni and Irena had left for Cracow early in the morning. The phone had rung just an hour before and Jerzy had answered it, listening for a few minutes and then replying with a few cryptic words that made no sense to Mirek. Shortly afterwards he and Natalia had wrapped themselves in fur coats and gone out into the night, saying they would be back shortly. Mirek had listened for the sound of a car but had heard nothing. He expected that a courier was arriving and hoped it would mean the recommencement of his journey. This safe house was luxuriously comfortable and certainly safe, but on this second day he was impatient. He looked at Marian sitting beside the crackling log fire, waiting patiently for an answer. She was wearing a short black clinging jersey dress. It was obvious that she was wearing nothing under it.

He said, 'Does every man who is not gay, and not a priest, and not in love, respond to you?'

'Of course.'

'It must get tiresome.'

She smiled. 'I choose only the ones I want. In a way for them it is truly tiresome . . . So who is she?'

He stood and walked to the drinks cabinet and poured himself a Scotch and soda. The bottle was encased in a blue velvet rag. Someone had once told him that such whisky cost over sixteen thousand zlotys in Poland. He poured sparingly, not because of the expense but because he wanted to keep a clear head.

He turned to Marian. 'You want a drink?'

She nodded. 'I'll have the same.'

He poured the drink and carried it over. As he offered it she caught his wrist and said petulantly, 'Tell me. Who is she?'

Irritation washed over him. He pulled his wrist away, spilling some of the whisky on her dress. He put her glass down on the table next to her and moved to the fire, turning and warming his back.

He said harshly, 'You and your friends. You are the *kacyki* – the princesses. As an SB officer I was hated by the people . . . but they hate your type as much or more. Living like royalty. Having everything without work or queuing or contributing a single thing. Look at you – a little red *kacyk* who's miffed because for once in her life she can't have something. I don't need to be in love not to want your body.'

She shook her head, smiling.

'But you do want it. I can tell. I can always tell. I see you looking at it. At my breasts, my legs . . . You want it, Mirek Scibor, but something holds you back. It can only be love for another woman. For a man like you to want, and not to take, she must be special . . . Someone you met in the West?'

He shrugged. 'Forget it, Marian. I'm not here for chit-chat. My mind is on other things. More important things than an over-used, if nubile, body.'

The smile left her face. She said seriously, 'Don't be cruel, Mirek. I am only teasing you. It is only superficial. It passes the time. I am more discerning and less used than you think. Yes, we are *kacyki* but we use that image to be useful. We care about Poland. Don't forget that we use our image to bring truth to the people . . . at great risk . . . and to help people – even you.'

In spite of himself he felt a measure of contrition. He raised his glass to her.

'I know. I don't mean to be cruel. It's just that for many years I had been conditioned to hate people like you. I realise that for your group it's partly an act but, Marian, you don't have to keep up the act for me.'

She smiled winsomely.

'It's just habit. Anyway, my intuition is that you are in love. So be it. We shall just be friends. Now you spilled most of my drink. Can I have another?'

He took her glass across the room. As he poured the drink he heard the slam of the outer door. Marian jumped up and hurried to the living room door. She opened it and went through. After a moment Mirek heard her little-girl voice.

'My God. Is she all right?'

He heard Jerzy's urgent voice. 'Barely. Let's get her close to the fire.'

They came into the room sideways, Jerzy first, enormous in his fur coat. He had his arm around a smaller figure, supporting it. Natalia and Marian followed.

Mirek stood by the cabinet, bemused, a glass in each hand. As they reached the fire Jerzy pulled the fur coat off the smaller figure. It was Natalia's coat. Mirek's view was blocked. He moved forward. It was a woman with her back to him. Marian was rubbing the woman's hands. Natalia pulled a scarf from the woman's head. Her hair was ebony black. Mirek knew that hair. He heard the crash as both glasses dropped to the floor.

'Ania!'

She turned. Her face was white, her black eyes sunken and narrowed. Her lips were quivering. She muttered his name and moved and she was in his arms.

The others stood back silently. Her body was ice cold. He raised her in his embrace and moved her back closer to the fire. Jerzy lifted more logs on to it. Mirek felt her cheeks. They were slabs of ice.

'How did you get here?'

She held on to him and muttered, 'The same way as you.'

It took seconds to penetrate, then anger took over.

'They sent you in that tanker . . . after knowing what I went through? I'll kill the bastards!'

'No, Mirek. It was my decision. They warned me. They helped make it easier.'

'But why?'

'The Bacon Priest. He decided I should continue with you.'

Mirek's mind was in turmoil, but then one thing became clear. The body he was holding was both frozen and exhausted.

He turned his head and said, 'Marian, please fill that sunken bath with hot water. That will warm her quicker than this fire. Jerzy, a brandy please.'

Marian and Natalia left the room. Jerzy brought a glass with an inch of brandy. Mirek held it to her lips. Some went down her throat and some down her leather jacket. She coughed violently. With his hand Mirek wiped her chin, then held the glass up again.

'Try and drink more. It will help.'

He poured some more through her lips and she coughed and spluttered and shook her head. 'Enough, Mirek. I'm all right.'

He reached down and got one hand behind her knees and one under her shoulders and lifted her. 'Come, you're going into the biggest bath you ever saw.'

Jerzy opened the door and then preceded them up the stairs. The bedroom door was open. As they went through they saw steam coming out of the bathroom.

Natalia came out and said, 'All right, we'll take care of her now.'

264

Mirek set her on her feet, gave her a final embrace and said, 'Ania, I'll see you later . . .'

He wanted to say more but couldn't find the words. Natalia put an arm around her and led her into the bathroom and closed the door.

Back downstairs Jerzy put on some muted contemporary jazz and poured two whiskies. Mirek stood with his back to the fire collecting his thoughts and emotions. Finally, as Jerzy passed him a drink, he asked, 'So what happened?'

Jerzy shrugged. 'I had a coded telephone message from Warsaw that someone was arriving at the same delivery spot. They were to be picked up and held here. Further instructions would be delivered tomorrow morning. That's all I know. She's the woman who was travelling with you?'

'Yes.'

Jerzy sniffed and said, 'Well, your people are playing chess. I guess she was a decoy and the authorities would assume that once her cover was gone she would be pulled out. They won't be looking for her now . . . Very clever.'

'Maybe,' Mirek mused. 'But the Russians also play chess and are very good at it. The best.'

'True enough,' Jerzy conceded, 'but they also have a habit of underestimating the intelligence of other people.'

The door opened and Marian came in. She said, 'She'll be fine. Natalia's looking after her. Mirek, I told her to go straight to bed and that I'd bring her some food there but she insists on joining us . . . She tells me that she has been out of Poland since her childhood.'

'Yes.'

'Then I'll make a meal that she will remember.' She walked to the door and turned to look at him. There was a twinkle in her eyes.

'So I was right after all.'

Mirek felt an embarrassing flush.

'She's just a colleague.'

Marian smiled. 'I'm sure.'

She opened the door and went out.

Mirek asked, 'Can that one really cook?'

265

Jerzy grinned. 'Wait and see, my friend. That one has more than just a single obvious talent.'

It was close to midnight when they ate. Ania had slept for two hours. Knowing the ordeal she had come through Mirek was astonished by her composure and her physical state. Only her eyes showed residual exhaustion. She had applied a little make-up and was wearing a long skirt of red and blue stripes cut on the bias, with a white lace blouse. Mirek had never seen the clothes before.

She explained. 'Natalia lent them to me. Mine are all crumpled.'

'They suit you,' he answered. 'They make you look like a gypsy.'

'I'm beginning to feel like one.'

Jerzy had decided that they would not eat in the formal dining room, but in front of the sitting room fire. He and Mirek carried in a small table and five chairs. Natalia lit some candles on the mantelpiece and as she dimmed the lights Marian came in carrying a tray. On it were five gold goblets and a big jug. She put it on the table and said dramatically to Ania, '*Krupnik* to welcome you back to Poland.'

'*Krupnik*?' Ania said uncertainly and Marian and the others looked amazed.

Jerzy said, 'You never had *krupnik*?'

Mirek interjected quickly. 'She left Poland when she was very young, and spent much of her life with people who didn't drink.' To Ania he said, '*Krupnik* is pure spirit mixed with spices and honey. It's a traditional drink of hunters and travellers when they come in from the cold . . . It's served hot.'

Jerzy picked up a goblet and passed it to her. She lowered her nose and sniffed.

'It smells delicious . . . and strong!'

They all had goblets in their hands. Jerzy raised his and said simply, 'Welcome home, both of you.'

Mirek took a sip. He had often drunk it before but as

he savoured the taste he realised that, compared with this, what he had known was pure rotgut.

Marian was wearing a frilly white apron which looked incongruous. The meal she produced was anything but. They started with thinly sliced spiced sausages and smoked meats. Then came *golabki*, a dish of rice and mincemeat with various spices and wrapped in cabbage leaves. They were delicate but firm. Mirek found he could cut it with his fork. Ania knew the dish well but had not eaten it for many years. She exclaimed with pleasure at the first mouthful and complimented Marian on her skills. This was a new Marian, one that Mirek had not seen. Confident, competent, and with no hint of the coquette. He assumed that the *golabki* would be the main course but as Natalia cleared away the dishes Marian came back with another piled up tray. It contained *zrazy nelsonskirz kasza*, a dish made from beaten meat with buckwheat, rolled and skewered and cooked in mushroom sauce.

With it they drank Tokay wine, golden and sweetish. They drank a lot of it, with many toasts. Jerzy asked Ania what music she liked and, when she told him, he searched through a cupboard and found a long playing record of Chopin's mazurkas.

For a Pole the combination of such food and wine and music can have two effects. One is unrestrained gaiety; the other a form of benign introspection. The effect on these Poles was the latter. They sat around the table with the flickering light of the fire and the candles and drank in the wine and the music. There was no conversation, just thoughts.

Finally, when the music ended, Jerzy banged his fist on the table and said, 'Come, on such a night we must not be so thoughtful. It can lead to sadness. Mirek, have you heard some of the latest jokes from our crazy country?'

Mirek shook his head and Jerzy grinned. 'Well, the newest is this. There was a man in Warsaw who had been queuing for hours to buy a loaf of bread. Finally he blew his mind and left the queue shouting, "I've had enough. I'm going to assassinate that incompetent bastard Jaruzelsky." He came back two hours later. Someone asked him, "Did you do it?" He shook his head and replied, "No. The queue was too long."'

Everybody laughed. Natalia poured more Tokay and Marian said, 'I heard one last week. The Mother Superior came running into a militia station in a terrible state. She told the officers that Russian soldiers had invaded her convent and raped all her nuns. She was distraught. She counted them off on her fingers: "There was Sister Jadwiga, Sister Maria, Sister Lidia, Sister Barbara . . . only Sister Honorata was not raped." "Why not?" asked the officer. The Mother Superior replied, "Because she didn't want it."'

She laughed at her own joke as did Natalia. Jerzy guffawed loudly. Slowly the laughter died as they noticed that neither Mirek nor Ania were joining in.

'You don't think it's funny?' Jerzy asked.

'Well . . . sure,' Mirek said.

'So?'

Ania said quietly, 'I was a nun.'

The silence was almost complete. Just the fire crackling. Then Marian said, 'I'm so sorry. I didn't know. I mean, I had no way . . .'

Ania reached out and put a hand on her arm. 'Of course you didn't. Don't be upset . . . I don't mind. Of course, it's a funny joke. It's just that I personally find it hard to laugh at it.'

Mirek sensed that the mood of the night was about to be broken. Lightly he said, 'Jokes are always made about people who take themselves too seriously. Bureaucrats. Policemen . . . and the very religious.'

Looking at Ania, Jerzy asked, 'Are you still devout?'

'Yes, but that doesn't mean to say I don't appreciate a good joke. We even had some in the convent. I'll tell you one. One day the Mother Superior fainted. Can you guess why?'

They all looked puzzled. Ania smiled and said, 'Because she found the toilet seat up.'

It took a few moments for the joke to sink in, then Jerzy was guffawing again and having to explain the joke to Natalia.

The ice was broken and the mood restored. The two girls started to ply Ania with questions about life in the convent. Mirek admired her composure as she answered them in a relaxed and friendly way. When they asked her why she had given up her vows she thought for a few moments and then answered, 'The vows sort of gave me up . . . to something else.'

Neither of the girls, nor Jerzy, understood, but they all nodded their heads at what they took to be something profound.

Mirek noted that Ania was having trouble keeping her eyes open. He said, 'It's late and we may have to move on tomorrow. We had better get some rest.'

They all stood up. For some reason it was an emotional moment, as though they had themselves all passed through a journey together. They embraced each other like brothers and sisters. Marian was modest under the compliments piled over her for the food. She kissed Ania on both cheeks and hugged her tightly, and said, 'Tomorrow we'll go through my clothes and find you lots of warm things to travel with.'

As they left the room Mirek saw Jerzy lighting up a Thai stick. Natalia was rifling through a stack of records looking for some heavy metal.

Going up the stairs he laughed and said, 'These *kacyki* are deeper than they seem.'

Ania looked at him, puzzled.

He explained, 'It's what the ordinary people call them, these layabout kids of rich, powerful families . . . the princesses. But we are lucky. Our bunch are all right.'

It was only when they reached the door of the bedroom that he remembered. 'Ania, this is my room. I'll have to ask Marian for another one. I'll just be a minute and then clear out my stuff.'

She stopped him with a hand on his arm.

'No, Mirek, it's all right. It's a very big bed and I trust you. I'd rather not be alone tonight. I don't know why. I know I'm safe . . . I suppose it was that terrible journey.'

So they went to bed together, separated by a vast expanse of bed. After turning the light out he questioned her about the trip. She explained that orders had come through from the Bacon Priest just after he had left. Her ankle was much better. The only way they knew to get her across was by the same route. When the tanker returned the next day the driver had been graphic in describing Mirek's condition at the end of the journey. He doubted she would survive. Fortunately Mirek had described to the driver some of the problems he had faced. When she had insisted on going they had advised ways to make it easier. First several layers of woollen clothes under the wet suit. Thick leather gloves over woollen ones. A harness to strap her to the ladder and ease the weight. Anton had gone along sitting next to the driver. It was dangerous but he had insisted that if anything happened to her Mirek would come back one day and kill him. They had stopped three times on the journey, in quiet places, and Anton had opened the inspection hatch to check that she was all right. It had been hell, but she had survived.

As she described it he could picture her in that steel cocoon being bashed about by the sloshing mass of milk. The harness and gloves would have helped but he well knew the physical and mental efforts she had made to come through. He wanted to roll across the bed and hold her in his arms, but he remained still. His own eyes were getting heavy.

After a while he heard her voice, rasping but sleepy.

'Mirek, are you awake?'

'Yes.'

'It's . . . It's awful but I was sick twice into that milk.'

In the darkness he smiled to himself.

'Don't worry about it, Ania. So was I.'

Another silence, then she said, 'I did something else into it as well.'

He chuckled and said, 'I bet you didn't lift the seat first.'

20

The word came just after lunch in the shape of Antoni. He arrived in a black BMW. He spoke first to Jerzy in the dining room, then Marian and Natalia were summoned for what was obviously a conference. Ten minutes later they all filed into the sitting room. Mirek and Ania were reading newspapers that Antoni had brought with him.

As they sat down Jerzy said, 'There has been a change of plan by your masters. I don't know what the original plan was, but I guess it involved moving you via Wroclaw and then further north before going east. As it happens the powers that be in Warsaw and presumably Moscow are concentrating the security forces, particularly the SB, in that area. So your people have asked us to funnel you through to Warsaw via Cracow. We have agreed.'

Mirek said, 'That means you're extending your risk.'

Jerzy nodded and smiled. 'True, but for us the risk is easily measured and accepted. Cracow is our patch. We know our way around. We have existed there with our group for more than two years now. What's more, the security forces know us individually – and our family connections. We would be the last people to come under suspicion.'

Ania said, 'We are grateful.'

'No,' answered Jerzy. 'It is we who thank you.' He reached into his shirt pocket and took out a thin strip of shiny metal and passed it to her. 'That is pure gold. We can sell it for fifty thousand zlotys. For this extra assignment we are to be given fifty more. That will finance our newspaper for the next two years. You are obviously very important to someone.'

Ania was fingering the strip of gold. She said, 'Is that the only reason? Money?'

Marian answered. 'No, we don't know what you are doing. We have only been told that your mission is anti-Russian. We would help anyone who is doing something against those bastards.'

'So when do we move?' Mirek asked. 'And to where?'

'This afternoon,' Jerzy answered. 'We drive up to Cracow.'

'Just like that?'

Jerzy grinned. 'Just like that. Your people are astonishingly well prepared. I suspect they are one of the Western Intelligence agencies.' He held up a hand. 'Don't worry, I'm not going to pry. Antoni was given papers for you both. They look genuine to us – and we know what to look for. The only thing missing is the photos to go with them. We have a camera and dark room here and the necessary stamps to emboss them. Antoni was informed that you have the means to disguise yourselves very effectively. I suggest you do that now and then we take your photos, fix them on to your documents, and we can leave for Cracow.'

'Just wait,' Mirek said firmly. 'It's not that I don't trust your strategy or your ability, but I want to know all the details. Where do we stay in Cracow and for how long? How are we to be moved from Cracow to Warsaw?'

Jerzy grinned through his beard. 'In Cracow you stay at the house of Brigadier General Teador Navkienko, Irena's father. She is there now preparing for your arrival. The good General is on official business in Moscow for the next two months. He is a widower and being a mean bastard doesn't like to pay for a housekeeper. Irena looks after the place when he's away. We have some good parties there and drink his best Nalewka vodka and replace it with rotgut. He's never noticed the difference.'

Mirek smiled. 'Do you have a fallback?'

'Of course. Two apartments. They are safe and have

been for two years. But not as safe as the house of a Brigadier General . . .'

'And how long will we be there and how do we get to Warsaw?'

Jerzy flung out a hand towards Natalia. 'You leave just as soon as Natalia here can persuade her dear papa that she needs desperately to go to Warsaw for a shopping trip. You will travel there by train.'

Mirek and Ania exchanged puzzled looks. The others were all grinning. Jerzy said, 'You remember what Natalia's father does?'

Mirek thought and then said, 'Something in the railways?'

'Not something,' Natalia said. 'He's the Regional Director . . . Now how do you think such a man and his family will travel when he goes by train?'

From his past career Mirek did know.

'In decadent luxury. A private carriage with its bedroom, kitchen, dining room and lounge.'

Natalia smiled sweetly. 'Exactly. In daddy's case it's such a waste. He's impatient and hates trains. He flies whenever he can. I use it quite a lot. It's old and lovely. Paderewski used it when he was Prime Minister. It even has a baby grand piano in it.'

Ania had a look of disbelief on her face. Mirek was shaking his head in amazement.

Jerzy grinned at them through his beard and said, 'Natalia is an only child and her father's little darling. The way he indulges her is quite disgusting. He will hold out for a maximum of forty-eight hours.'

Ania asked, 'And what if Natalia's mother decides she wants to go along for the shopping?'

Natalia answered, 'She won't. Mummy hates Warsaw. Both her parents and two brothers were killed in that city by the Germans in the war. She's never been back.'

Jerzy leaned forward. 'It's very safe. On several occasions we have taken shipments of our newspaper to Warsaw and other cities in that carriage. It works this way: the carriage is kept at a special siding. The station authorities are informed when it is to be used. They hitch it on to the end of a regular train. You will have already boarded at the siding. When the train reaches Warsaw the carriage is uncoupled and shunted to another special siding before the train enters the station, so you avoid normal security checks.'

Mirek's shoulders were shaking as he silently laughed. He said, 'No wonder you people haven't been caught. What do you do when you want to fly somewhere? Borrow Jaruzelsky's jet?'

Jerzy raised a finger. 'Not bad. We hadn't thought of that. Now you had better go and change your appearances. Need any help?'

'No thanks. We'll manage.'

Mirek and Ania stood up and left the room.

They were back twenty minutes later. Mirek walked in first. Jerzy was reading the paper. He looked up and for a second there was panic in his eyes, then he started nodding in appreciation. He continued nodding as Ania came in. The others started clapping and crowding around. Jerzy did the same, saying, 'Had I not known, I wouldn't have recognised you.'

Mirek looked fifteen to twenty years older. His moustache and hair were greying in a pepper and salt way. His face was fatter. His brown eyes were now blue. Ania, too, had aged. Her hair was mousy and much longer. Her face was also fatter and her body stouter.

'Hell,' Marian said. 'It's brilliant. The shape of your faces is different.'

'It's the pads we put into our mouths,' Ania explained. 'They take some getting used to . . . and make eating awkward.'

'But not drinking!' Jerzy said. 'A vodka to warm us for the journey while Antoni sets up the camera. Meanwhile, we ought to make you look a little less square. After all, you are travelling with the *kacyki* and should look more

275

the part. Marian, try to find some heavy jewellery for Ania. Bangles, long earrings and so on. Natalia, please fetch a couple of my silk scarves for Mirek, and a handkerchief. We'll make him look a little foppish, like all the would-be poets we have in Cracow.'

They passed through five road blocks on the journey. One each side of Rabka, another before Myslenice, the fourth at the junction of the Bielsko road and finally outside Cracow itself. The pattern became obvious to Mirek at the first one. He and Ania were travelling in the back seat of a Mercedes 380 SE. Marian was driving and Natalia sat next to her. They followed Jerzy and Antoni in the BMW.

At the first road block a young militia Corporal with a sub-machine gun slung over his shoulder approached the car. There were six of them working the waiting queue. Marian pressed the button to wind down the window and, before the militiaman could say a word, asked impatiently, 'Is this going to take long? We're in a hurry.'

The militiaman looked at the stickers on the window and took in the tone of her voice. Nervously he licked his lips.

'No madam, but I have to see your IDs.'

With a sigh Marian turned her head and asked, 'Did you happen to bring along your IDs?'

Mirek reached into his pocket and passed her his and Ania's. Natalia was fumbling about in her handbag muttering 'Bloody nuisance.' Marian rummaged about in the glove compartment and finally found hers. Without looking at him she passed them all to the militiaman. From past experience Mirek could imagine what was going through his head. 'Fucking *kacyki*! It's people like me who keep the masses quiet so spoilt bitches like you in your fancy foreign cars can have a good time.'

Mirek guessed that he was also thinking, 'But I wouldn't mind giving you a good screw . . . and your friend.'

The militiaman asked, 'And the purpose of your journey?'

Marian replied, 'Returning to Cracow from my father's villa on the lake.'

She stressed the words father and villa. The militiaman gave the papers a cursory glance then ducked down to look into the car.

Mirek assumed a bored expression and said to Ania, 'I hope those books have arrived from Paris. I'm just dying to read the new Montague.'

She replied, 'Oh, I think he's become passé.'

Mirek shrugged and said, 'You would, of course.'

The militiaman said, 'You can proceed, madam.'

Marian took the ID cards from his outstretched hand without a word, tossed them into Natalia's lap and pressed the button to raise the window.

As they pulled away she said, 'That's the best way to treat those people.'

Mirek said, 'Would you have talked to an SB officer the same way?'

She smiled at him in the mirror.

'No, I would have been slightly more polite . . . and if he was as handsome as you I might have fluttered my eyelashes at him.'

They entered the outskirts of the city in silence. For both Mirek and Ania it was an emotional time. She had left it as a young orphan. He had left as a fugitive. He was very much conscious of still being a fugitive. She was thinking of her long dead parents. She asked Marian, 'Do you know where the Rakowicki cemetery is?'

Marian nodded. 'Sure. My grandfather is buried there. It's quite near to where we are going. Why?'

'My parents are also buried there. They were killed in a car crash twenty-three years ago.'

Marian asked, 'Do you want to visit their grave?'

Ania looked at Mirek. 'Is it possible?'

Mirek pursed his lips and shrugged.

'It might be dangerous.'

'Nonsense,' Marian exclaimed. 'No one is going to recognise her and her papers are fine. I'll drop you at the house and take her on.'

Ania was looking at Mirek hopefully. He sighed.

'Do you really want to go?'

'Yes, I'd like to put flowers on the grave . . . and say a prayer . . . It won't take long.'

He agreed reluctantly, recognising how much it would mean to her.

They circled the centre of the city. Ania commented on the heavy traffic and the number of expensive foreign cars. Mirek laughed shortly.

'It's always been a mystery where they come from: black marketeers; returned emigrants, people with relatives overseas; and of course spoiled brats like the two sitting in front.'

Marian grinned at him in the rearview mirror and said mockingly, 'I detect a note of jealousy. Wait till you see the house where we're staying . . .'

Ten minutes later she turned down a side road and pulled up in front of a pair of iron gates set in a high stone wall.

Natalia jumped out and pulled a bell handle set into the wall. There were just a few pedestrians about. Mirek reached out a hand to Ania's shoulder and pressed her down a little, at the same time sliding down himself, saying, 'No point in being seen.'

Over the top of the seat in front he saw Irena on the other side of the gates. She waved and called a greeting. A minute later they moved through the open gates. Marian said, 'The men are making a detour to check security in the city. They'll follow in half an hour or so.' She called to Irena, 'Leave the gates open.'

It was an imposing old house at the end of a short gravel drive. Mirek climbed out and looked around with satisfaction. The high wall encircled the entire property and there were no houses that overlooked them.

'You'll be safe here,' Marian said confidently. 'And

don't worry. We'll be back from the cemetery in half an hour.'

She got back into the car and Ania climbed into the front seat. Mirek leaned in the window.

'Be careful, Ania.'

She touched his hand. 'I will. I'm grateful, Mirek. I really do want to see the grave.'

He nodded thoughtfully. 'But please don't be long.'

He stood watching as the car crunched down the drive and then swung out into the road. Irena closed the gates and ran up and kissed him on both cheeks. He picked up his bag and she took his arm and led him into the house.

In the car Marian asked Ania what had happened to her after the death of her parents. Ania gave her a quick, potted autobiography.

'And when did you leave the convent?' Marian asked.

Ania hesitated and then replied, 'Quite recently.'

'So were you ever at this cemetery before?'

'Yes, after the funeral . . . but I was only three. I left Cracow immediately afterwards and have never been back until now.'

'Well, there it is.' Marian pointed ahead with her chin and then quickly swung the car into a parking space that somebody else was trying to back a Skoda into. She laughed at the stream of invective directed at her by the frustrated driver and said, 'The benefits of power steering.' She pointed again through the windscreen. 'That's the office. They will show you on the map where the grave is. Over there are some stalls selling flowers. I'll wait for you there.'

In the office an old woman opened a big register and ran her finger down several columns before muttering, 'Yes, Krol. Husband and wife. Single gravestone. October 14th, 1960 . . . J.14.'

She gave Ania a sheet of paper with a diagram of the cemetery on it. 'Take this path and then turn right here.

It's in this section close to the west wall. The gates close at six. That's in half an hour.'

Ania thanked her and went out and found Marian by the flower stall just paying for two big bunches of assorted flowers. She held one out.

'Here. I'm sure you want to go by yourself.' She held up the other bunch. 'I'll go and put these on my grandfather's grave.' She smiled. 'If he's up there watching that will sure surprise the old bastard . . . I'll be waiting back at the car.'

Ania took the flowers gratefully. She knew that at this time of the year they would be exorbitantly expensive. It was a very cold day and she was glad of the fur coat, gloves and boots that Marian had lent her.

In recent years she had not thought so often of her parents. This had made her feel guilty enough to confess it to the Mother Superior who had been refreshingly blunt, pointing out that it was only natural that as her own life developed, those of others long dead would fade in her memory. She had also remarked that in Ania's case this was even more natural as she had been only an infant at the time of their deaths. But now they were very much on her mind. Her memory did give her just an impression. Her mother, round-faced and cheerful and smelling of bread. Her father, dark and stern-faced but, emotionally, completely at her mercy. She knew that they had been poor but God-fearing people. She was now the same age as her mother had been when she died. She found that a strange thought.

There were very few people about. It was late and those in the cemetery, bundled up against the cold, were moving towards the entrance. They were mostly old. She came to the turn-off on the path and checked her diagram. The grave was on the right hand side, set back a few metres from the path. She had no memory of what the headstone looked like. The graves were tightly packed and it took her several minutes to find the headstone. It looked for-lorn; small and overwhelmed by the granite and marble monoliths surrounding it. But after studying it she decided that it had dignity. The headstone was simple and unpretentious, as was the inscription. The slab of the grave itself was plain but clean. She crossed herself and laid the flowers at the foot of the headstone. With that action she felt a sudden emotional impact. There were tears in her eyes as she knelt and her voice quivered as she started to cry.

A hundred metres away, standing in a group of trees, SB Corporal Bogodar Winid was miserably stamping his feet against the cold, repeatedly glancing at his watch and cursing that he had pulled this particularly useless duty. He had been on it all day except for a one hour relief at lunchtime. No point in complaining. For more than two weeks now everyone on the force had been doing overtime. Besides, the extra money would come in useful. He glanced again at his watch. Only another ten minutes. For the hundredth time he looked across the cemetery towards the grave.

There was a figure kneeling beside it.

In his sudden nervousness his fingers fumbled at the top of his coat and it took him several seconds to pull out the small binoculars. As he tried to focus them his hands shook and he had to take a deep breath and steady himself. The image cleared. Yes the figure was beside the right grave. The one next to the tall black marble obelisk; and it had all the appearance of being female. He dropped the binoculars and they swung at his chest as he reached into his deep coat pocket and brought out the small two-way radio. He quickly put the earplug into his right ear and pressed the transmit button.

'Eight-ten to headquarters. Eight-ten to headquarters.'

Four seconds passed, then he heard the tinny voice.

'Headquarters. Go ahead eight-ten.'

'There's a woman at the Krol grave.'

'Are you sure it's a woman?'

'Almost. She's wrapped up in furs.'

'Young or old?'

'I cannot tell from here.'

'Stand by.'

Fifteen seconds passed, then he recognised the excited voice of Colonel Koczy.

'Corporal, is the man there?'

Winid swept his gaze around the cemetery and took another deep breath. He knew the importance of this moment. Knew its importance to him and his career. In a confident voice he answered, 'I can see no one else in the immediate vicinity. There is an old couple about two hundred metres away walking towards the entrance.'

A few seconds' pause and then Colonel Koczy said, 'All right, keep watch. I'm on my way with a squad.'

Quickly Winid said, 'Colonel, it is five to six. She will know that the cemetery closes at six. She is likely to move at any moment.'

The Colonel made a quick decision and came straight back.

'Right, Corporal. Get close. If she starts to move, arrest her. I doubt she is armed or dangerous but if the man is nearby he will be armed and is certainly dangerous. I'll be there in less than ten minutes. She is to be taken alive. Do you understand?'

'Yes, sir . . . Out.'

Winid put the radio back into his pocket and moved out from the trees. Walking quickly but quietly he approached the grave at an angle, keeping a large monument between it and himself.

Ania finished her prayer and stood up, wiping a glove across her eyes. Then she pulled back a sleeve and looked at her watch. It was almost six o'clock. She would have to hurry. With a last glance at the headstone she crossed herself again and turned.

From behind a marble monument ten metres away a man stepped out across her path. He was wearing a black flat cap and brown leather coat. His face was thin and young. She knew immediately that he represented a danger. She had been warm under the coat. Suddenly her body was cold.

He said, 'What are you doing here?'

She shrugged and gestured. 'Visiting the grave of relatives. Who are you?'

He was approaching her slowly, warily. 'What relatives?'

'An uncle and aunt.' She raised her voice. 'Who are you to ask me questions?'

He was close now. 'Show me your identification.'

She realised what was happening. Realised that this man was SB and had been watching the grave. He was very close now. She sighed deeply and put a hand in her pocket saying, 'Oh well I . . .'

She darted off to her left, vaulting over a low headstone, then dodging to her right to the path.

Two things were against her. First the warm fur boots which were heavy and clumsy. Second, the fact that at school Bogodar Winid had been the one and two hundred metres sprint champion.

He caught her fifty metres down the path in a flying tackle which crushed the breath out of her and sent her fur hat spinning away. The next moment he was sitting on her back, twisting her arms behind her and fumbling handcuffs onto her wrists.

The old couple were at the gate. They turned and watched for a moment and then, as is usual in such situations in Poland, hurried away from the scene.

Marian also watched. She had been approaching the gate from another angled path. She saw the whole thing. At first she thought he might be a robber or even a rapist. She started to run diagonally across towards them. Then she saw the handcuffs and pulled up abruptly. She saw him reach forward and pull off Ania's mousy wig; saw the jet black hair beneath it and his grin of triumph. He was reaching for his radio as she pulled up the hood of her coat and headed for the gate. She did not run but walked very quickly. As she reached the car she heard the distant cacophony of the sirens.

21

'Have a Pilsner and stop worrying.'

Jerzy offered a bottle and a glass. Mirek took the bottle but waved away the glass. As he moodily took a sip Antoni said, 'They'll be back in a few minutes. No one is looking for her. But I wouldn't be happy for you to be wandering around outside . . . even with that disguise.'

They were sitting in the house's ornate lounge. The General had obviously come down from a long line of distinguished soldiers. Large and hideously rendered oil paintings of bewhiskered, bemedalled old men hung on the walls. Again a log fire crackled in a huge fireplace.

A door opened and Natalia came in. She bowed theatrically from the waist and announced, 'Papa has already relented; in record time. I can use his carriage to go to Warsaw on my solemn promise that we don't leave it reeking of what he calls "hasheesh smoke". I promised.'

Jerzy grinned. 'Well done, Natalia. We shall keep your promise. At the very most we'll sniff a little coke . . . When can we go?'

She walked over, took the beer bottle from Antoni's hand, put it to her lips and drained it, then said, 'I let Papa think he was making the decision. He suggested the eleven thirty express tomorrow. He's giving the instructions now. We must be at the siding by ten thirty.' Mirek felt the relief. Try as he would he could never really take this crazy bunch seriously. But here was Natalia calmly informing him that they would be travelling to Warsaw in a private carriage and also supplying the timetable. He was about to thank her when there came the noise of a commotion outside. He heard Irena's voice and then Marian's at high pitch. The door burst open and they rushed in. One look at Marian's face and Mirek knew the worst. It was wet with tears and her eyes radiated fear. The others started talking to her agitatedly. She was choking on her words. Mirek shouted, 'Quiet! All of you!'

They were quiet. He said to Marian, 'Tell us . . . take your time.'

She gulped a few times, then steadied herself and, in a few brief sentences, told the story. At first there was a horrified silence. As the implications sank in, panic took over.

Natalia was sobbing with her face in her hands. Irena was clutching Antoni's shoulders and shouting something incoherent. Jerzy was looking at the floor muttering obscenities.

Mirek was feeling ill. Literally fighting down nausea while his brain refused to come to terms with events.

It was Jerzy who finally stopped the panic by hurling his beer bottle into the fireplace. It smashed with a crack like a rifle shot.

Into the silence he said quietly, 'We must face up to the consequences and take action.' He turned to Mirek. 'We are terribly sorry about Ania . . . But we must think of ourselves now. Obviously the SB have her. They will make her talk . . . or the KGB will . . . Our families will be ruined . . . Well, we accepted that risk. As for ourselves we shall have to go underground immediately and then try to escape the country. Mirek, you will stay with us until we can contact your people and pass you on.'

Mirek still felt like vomiting but now his brain was functioning. He held up a hand.

'Wait, Jerzy. Let me think for a minute.'

It came to him almost immediately. It came like the pattern of a carpet being unrolled at his feet. He mentally examined all parts and corners of the pattern. Finally he examined his own motives. Then he looked at the frightened faces in front of him and said, 'Jerzy is of course right. They will make her talk. You will all be implicated and your families ruined . . . unless we can rescue her.'

Astonishment replaced the fear on their faces. Jerzy was the first to react. He said contemptuously, 'You're crazy. Rescue her from the SB? Within an hour they'll be flying her to Warsaw or even Moscow. How do you get at her?'

Mirek said soberly, 'I have a plan. It involves even more risk to you but it has a chance and if it works both you and your families will be safe and can continue as before.'

Antoni said, 'You are totally mad.'

Mirek drew breath. He knew that to win them over he would have to be brilliantly persuasive. He said, 'You must give me five minutes. Then I will tell you.'

Jerzy answered bitterly, 'Minutes are vital. You know that!'

Quietly Mirek answered, 'Yes they are. And so are those five minutes I need.' He looked Jerzy directly in the eye, knowing that his decision would sway the others. He saw the bearded young man lick his lips nervously and then reluctantly nod.

Mirek said, 'Now this is important. Do you have contacts who can lay their hands quickly on two stolen cars?'

Again Jerzy nodded. Mirek said, 'Within an hour?'

'Yes.'

'Good. Do that now. They should be left in a quiet area not far from here. I'm going to my room and will be down in five minutes. In the meantime try to find a street map of the city.'

The sudden action eased the collective fear. As Mirek left the room Jerzy went to the phone and started dialling. Marian remembered that there was a street map in the Mercedes and went to fetch it. Irena and Natalia, for something to calm their nerves, went to the kitchen to make coffee. Antoni lit a cigarette.

Six minutes later they were standing in a group in front

286

of the fire when the door abruptly opened and Mirek strode in. Instinctively Irena screamed. Marian's coffee cup rattled in its saucer. Antoni moaned in his throat.

As usual, Jerzy was the first to recover, but his voice was strangled as he asked, 'Where the fucking hell did you get that?!'

Mirek was wearing the uniform of a full Colonel of the SB, complete with holstered Makarov, black polished boots, an impressive row of medals and the distinctive peaked cap. He said briskly, 'Someone had the foresight to send it with me. Together with excellent forged papers. Now are you ready to hear my plan?'

They all murmured assent. He had known that the sudden effect of his appearance in that uniform would give his crazy plan a thread of reality. He moved forward, asking, 'Did you have any luck with the cars and the map?'

'Yes.' Jerzy pointed to the map spread out on a table and they all clustered around.

Mirek said, 'I suggest that I detail the plan without interruption. Then you put your points of view. Then we make a decision.' He looked at all their faces. They nodded in agreement. He took a breath.

'All right. There are three things you must understand and keep in mind. First, I was for many years, until recently, a very competent and fast-rising officer in the SB. I am not boasting when I say that had I still been in the force I would soon be wearing this uniform by right. Those years have given me a deep understanding of the workings of the SB and the minds of its senior officers. That brings me to the second point. That knowledge and my membership of the SB already allowed me once to kill two of their most senior officers – and to escape.' Again he looked into all their eyes in turn and saw that he had made his point. They all knew of the famous episode.

He went on. 'Thirdly, since then I have been very highly trained by experts as a terrorist and assassin; training exactly suited for this type of thing. Please keep that in mind . . . I am not an ordinary person.' Again he paused and again felt the response. To Jerzy he said, 'You were right that normally they would quickly fly her to Warsaw. That is the only place where the SB carries out what they call "hard interrogation". But this situation is not normal. They know that time is vital if they are to catch me. It would be several hours before they got her to SB headquarters in Warsaw; but even now she will be at SB headquarters in this city. Instead they will fly the specialists down from Warsaw.' He sighed and stopped for a moment. They knew what was going through his mind, but when he started again his voice was as hard as ever.

'They will instruct the local commander immediately to use any methods to extract information from her. I know where they will do it . . . I think I know who will do it. They will be starting within half an hour. Now,' he pointed at the map, 'one of you will take one of the cars and wait somewhere here. We will fix an exact place. Another of you will drive me to within a few hundred metres of SB headquarters and then wait at this spot quite near to the entrance with the engine running. I shall bluff my way into the headquarters claiming to be from Warsaw down here on a confidential assignment. I will say that I am an expert on "hard interrogation" and was ordered to drop everything and rush there to help them. I bluff my way to the cellars, rescue Ania and then either bluff or shoot my way out. As soon as we appear on the steps the one driving the getaway car accelerates up. We jump in and head for the second car, then to a safe house. That's it.'

The first question surprised Mirek because it presupposed that the plan would go ahead. It came from Jerzy.

'What if she's talked before you get there.'

He answered emphatically. 'She won't have. I know that woman. She will break eventually, everyone does, but it will take them days, even weeks.'

He looked at Marian. She was nodding in agreement.

Amazingly there were no other immediate questions. The others kept looking at Mirek and then at the map. They had never even contemplated such a thing before.

Mirek said, 'You must balance it out. The risks involved against what happens if she talks. In fact the risks won't be increased if I don't come out of that building. You just drive away and disappear underground. If I come out I'll have Ania with me. Then the drivers of the two cars risk their lives in the getaway.'

There was a silence while they contemplated his words. Marian broke it. 'What will you do if we don't agree?'

'I'll try on my own.'

Jerzy said, 'That would be suicide.'

Mirek shrugged. 'There's always a chance . . . But we have to decide . . . now. Do you want to talk it over alone?'

Jerzy shook his head and said, 'Mirek, you need two drivers. I volunteer to be one.'

Immediately Marian said, 'And I the other.'

Antoni was looking at Irena and Natalia. They both nodded in unison. Antoni turned to Mirek and said, 'We are all crazy Poles. We are in.'

Mirek fought down his rising emotions as Jerzy said, 'As it happens, Marian and I are the better drivers. She drives like a lunatic but handles a car well. Irena and Natalia don't drive and Antoni had three crashes last year . . . all his own fault.'

'Now wait,' Antoni said harshly. 'What are we three supposed to do? Sit in a safe house and count our fingers?'

Mirek answered, 'There's nothing more to be done, Antoni.'

'Oh yes there is.' He was leaning over the map. He pointed. 'When you take off from SB headquarters you cross this intersection about two hundred metres away. After a very short time SB cars will be chasing you.' He looked at Jerzy. 'Get back on the phone to Figwer. Tell him we need four more cars or vans, the heavier the better . . . and three drivers. He can use some of those maniacs from Roguska's mob. They'd sell their mothers for money; for gold they'd even deliver.' He turned to Mirek. 'We have those four vehicles parked, two on each side of the intersection. As soon as the first getaway car passes we organise a sweet little pile-up right across the intersection, then the drivers disappear. That will hold the bastards up.'

They quickly discussed it and then agreed. Jerzy went to the phone while the others hammered out minor points. It was agreed that if it succeeded they would return to this house rather than go to one of the safe apartments. If it failed the survivors would fend for themselves. Irena and Natalia would stay in the house by the phone.

It took forty five minutes to set up all the vehicles. Every second ticked away in Mirek's tormented mind. Meanwhile there was a fierce argument between Jerzy and Marian as to who would drive the first and most dangerous getaway car. Curiously Marian won the argument. She did it with logic. The car would be parked close to the SB head-quarters entrance. A passing militia or even SB man might try to move it on. Jerzy was ugly. Even a gay militiaman wouldn't be interested in him. She was beautiful and sexy and with her at the wheel the car stood a much better chance of being there when Mirek and Ania came tearing down those steps. Reluctantly Jerzy agreed. Finally all was ready. Before they left the house they all embraced.

It was a moment to savour and Colonel Oleg Zamiatin savoured it to the full. He made no effort to ease Chebri-kov's discomfort. His report was already on its way to the First Secretary, who would doubtless read between the lines and take note of Zamiatin's brilliance. Once again the vision of his promised dacha loomed in his mind.

Chebrikov tapped the file and looked again at the huge wall map. He muttered, 'Cracow . . . at the cemetery . . .'

Zamiatin glanced at his three Majors. They were all pretending to study paperwork on their desks. He knew that they were as delighted as himself. He said casually, 'Yes, Comrade Director. I reasoned that if the Bacon Priest had double guessed us, he would send the woman on, even though her cover was blown. I also reasoned that if they had passed across the southern part of the border their next staging post would be Cracow . . .'

'I see,' Chebrikov said drily. 'And that's why you ignored my order to move the SB to the north?'

Zamiatin felt no twinge of fear. He exactly understood the strength of his position.

'Certainly not, Comrade Director. You ordered me to concentrate the SB to the north. That I did. However my instincts told me that Cracow should remain a focal point. This was reinforced when we learned the identity of the woman . . . and that she was a nun.'

Chebrikov sniffed. 'I see. And it was an inspired hunch that made you place a watch on her parents' grave?'

Zamiatin spread his hands and said easily, 'Oh, I like to think it was more than a hunch. After all, she is a nun . . . But neither she nor Scibor had any idea that we knew she was a nun. I reasoned,' he stressed the word 'reasoned', 'that if their journey did pass through Cracow such a devout person would take the opportunity to pay her respects to her dead parents . . . and that's exactly what happened.'

Chebrikov would have dearly liked to reach out and swat Zamiatin as though he were a buzzing fly. Instead he said affably, 'It was good work, Colonel. But of course it remains only a lead to Scibor. Until we catch him all good works are meaningless.'

Chebrikov was pleased with the phrase. Particularly with the word 'meaningless'. It would serve to remind Zamiatin that unless he caught Scibor himself he would in no way benefit from this latest bit of sheer luck.

He pressed the point. 'I assume that this time you are not delaying in extracting immediate information.'

Zamiatin was unperturbed. 'Indeed not, Comrade Director.' He looked at a round clock on the wall. 'Ania Krol was arrested forty-eight minutes ago. By now she is at SB headquarters in Cracow. Interrogation will have started by now. Unfortunately they have no experts in Cracow but they will be doing their forceful best.

Meanwhile top experts are on their way from Warsaw and from here. Of course, we have totally sealed off Cracow itself . . .' He paused and said carefully, 'Unfortunately this is taking a little longer than I would have liked because the bulk of the security forces in the area had been moved north.' He would have liked to add 'at your orders' but restrained himself. In any event Chebrikov got the message.

He said curtly, 'I assume you are using our own troops?'

'Of course, Comrade Director. They are moving out of their cantonments now.'

There was not much more for Chebrikov to say but he hated the thought of leaving the room on a down beat. He studied the wall map again and then asked brusquely, 'And you remain certain that Scibor himself is in Cracow?'

Zamiatin nimbly ducked that one. 'Not at all, Comrade Director. He may indeed be further to the north as you yourself hypothesised . . . However, I doubt if the Bacon Priest would have risked sending that nun over the border just to put flowers on her parents' grave.'

Chebrikov grunted. 'Just so, Colonel. We must make sure that this lead is not wasted. I expect to hear very shortly that this woman has given us the necessary information to arrest Scibor . . . and that he does not slip the cordon.'

He gave Zamiatin a stern look, turned on his heel and marched quickly to the door. As it closed behind him the Majors looked up at Zamiatin. He was smiling.

It is an almost universal truth that repressive police or security forces always feel secure in their own headquarters. They believe that it is unthinkable for the oppressed to actually attack them at their base. This is even true during times of unrest and minor uprisings.

At least Mirek hoped that this was true as Marian drove him the last few hundred metres. There was an almost continuous whine of sirens from different parts of the city as the militia and SB roared out to ring the outskirts with road blocks. Ironically, here in the centre there were no road blocks. Indeed the city centre was virtually devoid of uniforms.

He said, 'Pull in here, Marian. I'll walk the rest of the way.'

She pulled in to the kerb and turned to look at him. Her face was pale and tense. He said, 'Put this scarf on now and when you're parked on the other side keep your head down. Pretend to be studying a map or something.'

She nodded and tried to smile. 'I'll be waiting. Good luck, Mirek.'

She leaned across and kissed him lightly on the lips. He said, 'I know you'll be there, but don't forget – if I'm not out in fifteen minutes, drive away. Don't be a heroine. Sound your horn twice at the intersection to warn off Antoni and his drivers and then drive to Jerzy, and finally pick up Irena and Natalia. Do the same thing if you hear a lot of gunshots from inside the building and we don't come out immediately afterwards.'

She nodded, her face sad. 'I understand. If you don't come out . . . well, it's been good knowing you . . . and Ania.'

He smiled bleakly. 'And you . . . and all your crazy bunch. Thanks, Marian.'

He opened the door and climbed out. As he closed it he heard her call again, 'Good luck.'

He stood on the pavement and waved her on and watched the battered blue BMW pass in front of him. It looked a wreck but the engine had sounded fine. He walked briskly. It was a cold, overcast night. Rain threatened. The traffic was quite heavy but pedestrians were sparse. He noted that they averted their eyes as he passed and some even changed direction so as not to pass close to him. In the uniform he felt like a pariah; but he had felt like that for most of his life.

As he crossed the intersection he glanced to his left and saw an old brown furniture van pulling up to the kerb. He could not see the face of the driver. He looked to his right.

Parked across the road was an old grey Skoda in front of an equally aged black Lada saloon. Again he could not see the drivers but he noted that the Skoda had its engine running and guessed that they were part of Antoni's team.

He quickened his step, at the same time rehearsing what he would say and do in the coming minutes, trying to think of questions and how he would answer them. The familiar building loomed up on his left. He felt as if he had only stepped out of it hours ago, instead of months. He had a moment's qualm about his disguise and then brushed it aside. The disguise was good and very much enhanced by the Colonel's uniform. Mirek Scibor was the last person anyone would expect to walk into this building.

He came to the wide flight of slate grey steps and looked up. Relief as he noted that there was only the usual single guard outside the door. But as he rapidly climbed the steps he saw the sub-machine gun slung from his shoulder. That was not normal. The guard wore a long grey overcoat. He came rigidly to attention as Mirek approached and saluted. Mirek returned the salute with barely a glance at him. As he pushed the heavy door open he abruptly realised that at any time in the next few minutes he could most likely be suddenly dead. He vowed at that moment he would not allow himself to be taken alive, and that if he could not get Ania out he would do everything to kill her as well. That thought cleared his mind totally. He felt lightened, as though he was inebriated.

Inside was a large, high-ceilinged vestibule. Corridors angled from it like the spokes on one half of a wheel. There was a long desk to the left. Behind it sat a young, bespectacled Captain writing in a thick ledger. Next to him was an older, mustachioed Sergeant tapping away with two fingers at an old typewriter. They both looked up. He vaguely recognised their faces. They came to their feet with a clatter and saluted. He returned the salutes impatiently, undid the button of his top left tunic pocket and pulled out his ID card, general purpose pass and travel authorisation. He slapped them on the desk and said curtly, 'Colonel Gruzewski. "H" Section, Warsaw. Where is the Krol woman?'

The Captain looked dazed. With uncertainty he reached for the documents. Mirek turned to the Sergeant. 'The Krol woman is here. I've been ordered to take over her interrogation pending the arrival of my colleagues from Warsaw. Time is of the essence. Where are you holding her?'

The Sergeant looked at the Captain, who was nervously fingering the documents. With an impatient sigh Mirek asked harshly, 'Where is Colonel Bartczak?'

The Captain straightened. 'He has gone to the airport, Colonel. To meet the people from Warsaw.' He glanced at his watch. 'They will be landing in ten minutes.'

Inwardly Mirek was elated, outwardly his face showed scorn.

'So he has made himself a messenger boy! No matter. Where is the woman? I suppose the nursery?'

The Captain and the Sergeant exchanged quick glances and Mirek knew that he had guessed right. The Captain said, 'How did you get here so quickly, Colonel?'

'I was in the city, on a confidential assignment linked to this woman and the man. General Kowski telephoned me and ordered me here immediately . . . Now come on, man! Seconds are vital.'

The dropping of the name of the commanding officer of the SB did the trick. The Captain shuffled the papers together and held them out to Mirek.

'Yes, she is in the nursery, sir. With Major Grygorenko. Sergeant Boruc here will show you the way. I will inform Major Janiak of your arrival . . .'

'I know the way, Captain. I've used the nursery when you were still at school . . . and inform whoever you like. If I'm not up in half an hour, send me a mug of very hot coffee . . . black with three heaped spoons of sugar.' He turned away to one of the corridors hearing the Captain behind saying, 'Yes, Colonel.'

*

As he strode down the corridor his brain rapidly reviewed the situation. It was good. He knew Major Grygorenko and had guessed that he would be in charge of the interrogation pending the arrival of the experts. Grygorenko was a known sadist. He hoped he would be alone but doubted it. Meanwhile the Captain would be informing Major Janiak of his arrival. Presumably Janiak was officer-in-charge pending the return of Colonel Bartczak with the brass hats from Warsaw. That too was good. Janiak was a plodder who might well do nothing until his superior returned.

He did not wait for the lift but ran down the two flights of steps. He pushed open the door to the corridor and looked to his left. There was a Corporal sitting on a chair outside the nursery door, cradling a sub-machine gun. Mirek glanced to his right. The corridor was clear all the way down to the cul-de-sac at the end. He walked with an urgent step. The Corporal stood at his approach, holding the gun lightly at his side.

Mirek barked at him, 'Colonel Gruzewski. "H" Section Warsaw. I'm here to take over from Major Grygorenko.'

The Corporal hesitated. Mirek snapped at him, 'Come on, Corporal, I've no time to waste. Colonel Bartczak has been informed.'

His practised authoritarian manner and the mention of the Corporal's superiors were conclusive. The Corporal reached down and turned the handle of the heavy door next to him. As Mirek passed through he said, 'If I want anything I'll call for it. Otherwise I'm not to be disturbed. Is that clear?'

'Yes, Colonel.'

He went through and closed the door behind him. He was in a small space between the door behind him and the one in front. The door in front was heavily padded and soundproofed. This building had been used by a section of the Gestapo during the war and temporarily taken over at the end of the war by the KGB before being passed on to the SB. The whole floor had been known as the nursery since the Germans and the name had stuck.

Mirek paused for a moment and collected himself. He loosened the flap of his holster, then patted the top right-hand pocket of his tunic and felt the reassuring bulge. As he reached for the door handle he heard, even through the padding, the long thin scream. He pressed the handle and pushed the door open.

It took a second for his eyes to adjust to the bright overhead strip lighting. She was lying flat on her back, naked, wrists and ankles strapped to a table. Her scream was dying to a moan. Major Grygorenko was standing beside the table wearing his uniform trousers and an undershirt wet with sweat. Braces dangled alongside his knees. He was holding a metal rod between her legs against her crotch. A cord from it snaked away to a wall socket. Another man was standing at the head of the table, his hands pressing down against her shoulders. He wore the uniform of a Corporal. His wide Slavic face was also sweating. They both looked up, startled. Mirek smiled at them. Grygorenko pulled the rod away from Ania's crotch. Her wet skin quivered.

'Who the hell . . . ?'

Mirek moved forward saying pleasantly, 'Colonel Josef Gruzewski at your service. "H" Section, Warsaw. I'm here to take over the interrogation.'

Grygorenko's face showed his disappointment. Sullenly he said, 'We weren't expecting you for a couple of hours.'

Mirek said, 'I happened to be in Cracow. The others are coming. Have you learned anything?'

He had moved up to the table. He saw Ania's wet face turn towards him and hoped beyond measure that the sound of his voice had forewarned her. It had. She looked at him through listless eyes.

The Major replied, 'Not yet.'

Mirek turned to him. 'What the hell's that you're using?'

The Major shrugged. 'A cattle prod. I was told that your lot are bringing equipment with them. It's all I've got. . .'

He was looking at Mirek closely. 'Haven't we met before?'

Mirek shook his head. 'I doubt it. Anyway I did a two-year course at Blatyn and I can tell you that if that's all you've got you have to use it with skill.'

Grygorenko grinned. 'I was about to ram it up her cunt!'

Mirek smiled again. 'Hardly original. No, Major, it must be used against certain nerve endings which multiply its effect. I will show you.'

He undid the flap of the top right hand pocket of his tunic and took out a thick black marking pen. The brand name 'Denbi' was etched in yellow. He unclipped the top and leaned forward.

'Now watch closely, Major. I will mark the points for you. And you, Corporal. Learn something.'

Slowly he reached out and inked a small cross at a spot on the inside of Ania's knee. Her skin flinched slightly at the soft contact. Then he moved higher and touched the felt to her skin just under her right breast.

'This is a particularly good spot, but it must be under the right breast and it must be in exactly the right spot. Look closely, Major!'

Fascinated, Grygorenko leaned over Ania's body, craning his neck to see the spot. In an instant Mirek turned his wrist, pressed his thumb on the 'D' of Denbi and lunged upwards. Four inches of needle-like steel snaked out, penetrated Grygorenko's left eyeball and pierced through to his brain. He went over backwards, his last living sound an agonised scream.

The Corporal was stunned. He had only just begun to move as Mirek's left hand stabbed at his throat, fingers rigid. He went down with a choking gurgle. Quickly Mirek moved around the table, bent over him and slid the steel needle through his rib cage into his heart.

Both bodies were still twitching convulsively as he started to undo the buckles that bound Ania down.

'Are you all right?'

'Yes, Mirek. You should not have come; it's madness.'

298

He grinned down at her. 'They all say that. Was it very terrible?'

Her arms were released and she sat up rubbing her wrists.

'Not so much the pain . . . only the pleasure they got from it . . . I wanted to die . . . really.'

He unbuckled the last strap and she swung her feet to the ground. He took her in his arms in a brief embrace, then said urgently, 'We're not even half way there. We must be quick.' He saw her clothes on a chair. 'Get dressed, Ania. I'll be back in a moment.'

He went out and she hurried to the chair and started pulling on her clothes. The bodies on the floor were now still. She looked at them and tried to find some compassion . . . even forgiveness. It would not come. She was just putting on her shoes when the door opened. Mirek's head came round it and whispered, 'Come on.'

She hurried over. In the space between the two doors was another body. It was twitching. Mirek was tucking the marker pen back into his pocket. He reached down and picked up a sub-machine gun from beside the body.

He handed it to her, saying, 'You must hold that for me and the spare magazine and do everything I tell you exactly.'

She took the gun. The grip was sticky. She looked at her hand and saw the blood. She avoided looking again at the body. Mirek carefully opened the outer door and looked both ways down the corridor. He turned back and said, 'We are going up two flights of stairs and then along a corridor. I will leave you at a corner there and go on alone. As soon as you hear gunfire you are to follow me as fast as you can and either hand me or throw me that gun. Then stay by me whatever happens.'

At that moment from the room behind them a phone started to ring stridently. To Mirek it sounded like an alarm.

He said, 'Come on, Ania. Whatever happens they won't

299

capture us alive. Either we get out . . . or we die together.'

She followed him out into the corridor.

Two floors up Major Janiak was getting nervous and concurrently irritated.

'How can there be no answer?' he demanded.

With the phone at his ear, the Captain shrugged. 'Major, I shall send Sergeant Boniek down. Maybe the phone is malfunctioning. It sometimes happens.'

The Major snorted. 'Go yourself. You had no right allowing someone to go down there.'

'Major, he was Colonel Gruzewski, from "H" Section . . . orders from General Kowski –'

'So he said. Now get down there!'

The Captain had just begun to move around the desk when Mirek walked into the vestibule. He looked very irritated. His hands were clasped behind his back. To the Major he said starkly, 'Who are you?'

'Major Juliusz Janiak, sir. May I ask . . . ?'

'No, you may not.' Mirek's arms came from behind his back. The Makarov was in his right hand. He shot Major Janiak between the eyes. A second later the barrel had swung and two shots were pumped into the heart of the Captain.

The Sergeant was very quick. His hand was reaching for his holster even as he ducked down behind the heavy desk. There were shouts from nearby offices. Mirek vaulted the desk, turning in the air. The Sergeant had his gun free. It was coming up. He fired at the same time as Mirek. Mirek felt the impact on his left side. He saw the Sergeant smashed back as his gun clattered to the floor. Mirek put a hand to his side. It was completely numb. The shouts were in his ears. He saw Ania running towards him and at the same time saw the door to the main entrance opening. He knew who would be coming through. He screamed at Ania, 'Get down, Ania! Over here!'

She made it by the bat of an eyelid. The outside guard came through the door with his sub-machine gun raised and ready. He paused for a moment to take in the scene, then his finger squeezed the trigger. Ania slid feet first behind the desk as the bullets scythed across the room. Somebody screamed from down the corridor. Mirek grabbed the sub-machine gun from Ania's fingers, flicked off the safety and dived sideways from behind the desk. The guard tried to swing his gun back but was too late. Still in the air Mirek fired a half-second burst. Half a dozen bullets slammed into the guard, spinning him against the doors. Mirek hit the ground and rolled onto his knees. He saw figures down another corridor and fired another burst. More screams. He shouted, 'Ania, come on!'

She ran out from behind the desk in a crouch. The spare magazine was in her left hand. He grabbed it and, discarding the used one, clipped it in. Then he took her hand and they ran through the door.

They paused for a second at the top of the steps. People were running away in both directions. As they started down the steps they heard a car hooting and the blue BMW came screeching to a halt below them. As they reached it the back door opened. He pushed Ania in and then dived after her. The car surged forward and the door slammed with the momentum. As they straightened up Mirek heard the scream of a siren behind. He looked out the back window. A militia Jeep was fifty yards behind. He could see a figure leaning out of the window with a hand gun. He heard and felt the clang as a bullet ricocheted off the side of the Skoda. He felt a rage inside him. They were not going to be stopped now. He wound down his window and leaned out with the sub-machine gun held in front of him, twisted and emptied the magazine at the Jeep. He saw the windscreen disintegrate. The Jeep swerved across the street. He saw a militiaman leap from the back, then the Jeep crashed into and through a shop window.

A moment later they sped across the intersection. Still looking behind, Mirek saw a large van and an old Skoda collide head on. Two more cars crashed into the pile-up, completely blocking the road. He saw figures leaping from the vehicles and running away. He turned, tossed the sub-machine gun out of the window and said, 'Slow down now. Drive normally. Well done, Marian!'

22

Victor Chebrikov had no alternative but to wait out the silence. The last time he had broken it Andropov had simply stated, 'Shut your mouth.'

He could not understand why the First Secretary had summoned him to lunch. Surely the reprimand could have been better delivered in Andropov's office. It had been eighteen hours since the fiasco in Cracow. The First Secretary, of course, had been informed immediately. Chebrikov had spent a sleepless night sitting by the phone waiting for the summons. It had not come until now, the next day.

He had been surprised to see a table for lunch set for two. There was bread and sausages, Molossol caviar, soused herrings and a bowl of fruit.

Andropov had merely grunted at his respectful greeting and gestured at the table. But Chebrikov quickly discovered his boss's mood. As he had spooned himself a generous dollop of caviar, Andropov had said, 'So you haven't lost your appetite.'

It was a famous and chilling phrase within the Kremlin, reportedly first coined by Beria when watching the inmates of a Siberian slave camp fighting over a bucket of thin gruel. Chebrikov had eaten half a spoonful of caviar and then pushed his plate away. Andropov appeared not to notice. Although he appeared increasingly ill, on this day he did have an appetite. He demolished half a bowl of caviar between mouthfuls of coarse bread. As he started on the herring Chebrikov had ventured to speak.

'Comrade First Secretary, I wish to express . . .'

And then Andropov had said, 'Shut your mouth.'

Now the First Secretary had finished the fish and was carefully peeling an apple with a red Swiss army knife that he had taken from his pocket. He seemed oblivious of Chebrikov or the silence. He managed to peel the apple in one continuous curling strip. He sliced the end and laid it on his plate with an air of satisfaction. Then he said, 'I talked before of uncaught fish jumping out of boats. The fish you catch don't jump out. They bite you.'

Chebrikov kept silent, staring down at the grey lumpy mass in front of him. It made him feel nauseous.

Andropov held the knife to his lips and sucked a piece of apple from the blade. He chewed reflectively, then said, 'This Mirek Scibor is like an avalanche. It starts slowly, gathers speed and sweeps everything before it. You try to arrest him and his woman. He kills those who try. You arrest his woman and hold her in what should be the most secure place in Cracow . . . He takes her out as easily as picking an old drunk's pocket . . . and kills people doing it. This avalanche kills people with ease; and this avalanche is gathering speed and coming my way. Tell me, Comrade Director of State Security, what percentage chance does this avalanche have of killing me?'

Chebrikov answered immediately and fervently.

'No chance! None at all!'

Andropov's eyes glittered with anger.

'You are wrong! And you know it. What chance would you have given him to rescue his woman in Cracow? None, of course.'

He sat back breathing deeply. Chebrikov deemed it wise to keep his counsel. He had never seen his boss in this mood before. He supposed that it stemmed from his illness. After a few minutes Andropov spoke again, musingly, as if talking to himself.

'I feel him coming. Like the onset of a bad cold. First a sneeze or two; then a headache. A nose that won't stop running . . . a fever. I feel it coming.' He raised his eyes and looked directly at Chebrikov. His voice hardened. 'Ultimately I don't care. I'm dying anyway. But understand this, Comrade. I care more than anything I have ever cared about that I outlive this Pope. He leaves on his tour in five days. Two days later he will be dead. After that I will face death myself. Now I am moving into the clinic early, in fact tomorrow morning. You will guard that clinic with your life . . . literally. If I die of unnatural causes before that bastard Pope, you will also die . . . within the hour. I have already made the arrangements. They are so tight that neither you nor my successor nor anybody else will be able to countermand them . . . You do believe that, Comrade?'

Slowly and solemnly Chebrikov nodded. He did believe it. Such arrangements were not unheard of in the Soviet Union.

'The arrangements must be changed!'

The Bacon Priest was emphatic. Father Heisl sighed in exasperation and said, 'If you change the plan you increase the risk. We have already deviated too much.'

The Bacon Priest belched and took another sip of lager.

'Father, if we don't change the plan we risk being too late. The margin is too fine. Scibor must be in Moscow at least two days before the event.'

They were facing each other across a table in the Vienna safe house. A report had just arrived detailing the events in Cracow the day before. The Bacon Priest had a sheet of paper with notes on it in front of him. He stabbed a finger at it.

'Scibor is wounded, though not badly. Nevertheless, it will be two days or more before he is fit to travel. So in three days from now they can be in Warsaw. The original plan called for a four to five day transit time between Warsaw and Moscow. That is now too long. Szafer's appointment is for the ninth and of course cannot be changed. So they must be in Moscow by the seventh.'

'But how?'

The Bacon Priest put his empty glass on the table with a loud thump, but his voice was soft.

'It is time for Maxim Saltikov to repay his debt.'

This statement silenced Father Heisl. He sat thinking while his boss waited for a reaction. Then he stood up, went to the fridge in the corner and fetched two more cans of lager. They hissed as he pulled the tabs off. He filled both glasses, sat down and said thoughtfully, 'Well I suppose the event is important enough to justify it. But do you really think he will do so?'

The Bacon Priest nodded solemnly. 'Yes, I do.'

'It's been many years.'

'Yes.'

'And much has happened.'

'It certainly has.'

'But are you sure?'

'I am.'

Father Heisl shrugged. Something was eluding him. He asked, 'When did you last see him?'

Van Burgh's forehead wrinkled in concentration.

'Thirty-eight . . . no, thirty-nine years ago.'

Scepticism showed on Father Heisl's face.

'That was the last time you saw him . . . ? Or even talked to him?'

'Yes.'

'You have not communicated with him since . . . at all?'

'Yes. Brief but cogent messages.'

Another hiatus while Father Heisl thought this through. Then he smiled and shook his head as though in a reprimand. He said with mock sternness, 'Then Father, you have something on him which I don't know about. Something far deeper than the original commitment.'

Now Van Burgh shook his head.

'I do not, Jan. You know the entire story. But you never met Maxim Saltikov. He is not a man to change his mind or his word. Not over thirty-eight years . . . not over a lifetime . . . Now please get me an update on him from the Collegio.'

306

Father Heisl rose and walked to a telephone on a side-board. He dialled a familiar number. It put him through to the duty computer operator at the Collegio Russico in Rome. When the operator answered the priest gave him the current code – a string of numbers and letters. Then he said simply, 'General Maxim Saltikov.'

There was a three-minute wait and then the priest murmured, 'Thank you,' and hung up. He came back to the table, sat down, took a sip of lager and said. 'No change. Just a "B" grade rumour that after this posting he may be assigned to the Far East but without a change of rank. At the moment he's in East Berlin and will stay for a week's consultations.'

Van Burgh smiled. 'I think those "B" grade rumours come from the girls who polish the samovars. The last one concerned Gorbachev and a male dancer from the Kirov Ballet.'

Father Heisl grimaced. 'Yes, but sometimes they pay off. How will you approach him?'

'Personally.'

Father Heisl's face showed his astonishment.

'You will go to East Berlin at such a time?'

The Bacon Priest pushed back his chair, stood up and stretched.

'Yes, Jan. I will leave tomorrow. It must be done personally. Besides, I get uncomfortable sitting here and letting other people take all the risks . . . and also I feel that in some ways this operation is slipping out of my hands. It seems to have acquired a life of its own . . .' He smiled. 'What with *kacyki* and private railway carriages . . .'

Now Father Heisl stood up. Very seriously he said, 'And don't you think it's time that Ania was pulled out once and for all?'

Van Burgh shook his head.

'No, Jan. If the operation has a life of its own it's partly due to her. Together they seem to be unstoppable. A sort of momentum. No. She will go on to Moscow. I will pull her out just before the event.'

He had spoken with such conviction that Father Heisl knew it was pointless to argue. But he did have one other concern.

'I had another call from Father Dziwisz this morning, on behalf of the Holy Father. He wanted to know if we had any information about the events in Cracow yesterday.'

'What did you tell him?'

Father Heisl spread his hands in a helpless gesture.

'I told him that we ourselves were investigating. That I would let him know if, and when, we heard anything.'

'Good.'

'No, Pieter. It is not good. First of all that Dziwisz is very sharp and suspects something. I hate to prevaricate with him. He asked me where you were.'

'And?'

Heisl sighed. 'I told him you were on a mission.'

The Bacon Priest smiled placatingly.

'Well, Jan, from tomorrow I will be . . . Don't worry about Dziwisz; I'll get Versano to talk to him. Explain that in view of the circumstances in Poland right now we are under great pressure. We will be able to be more informative when that pressure is eased.'

Father Heisl sighed again.

'And will the good Archbishop tell him that we are the cause of all the pressure?'

The Bacon Priest grinned.

'No, Jan. But he might say something about fighting pressure with pressure.'

23

The courier with the blonde curly hair moved down the aisle handing back the passports as the huge chrome and gold tourist bus pulled away from Checkpoint Charlie into East Berlin. The courier had a stern, somewhat bored face, but she smiled when she handed the elderly Dutch couple their passports. He was a large, florid-faced man with round twinkling eyes. She was small and plump with a semi-permanent smile on her lips. They seemed so happy together. The courier said, 'Herr and Frau Melkman, I hope you enjoy your day.'

They beamed up at her. He answered, 'I'm sure we will, with the help of such a pretty and intelligent guide.'

She bobbed her head and moved on down the bus, marvelling once again at the ability of the Dutch to master foreign languages.

The bus did the brief but obligatory tour of the massive war memorials and then pulled up outside the Pergamon. The passengers filed off and gathered round the courier. It was a cold but clear day. Quickly she told them that for this, being the high point of the tour, two hours had been allotted. She would guide them round, but if anyone became separated they were to be back at the bus not later than one o'clock.

As she led the way up the steps she noticed the big old Dutchman ambling away down the pavement. She stopped and called out.

'Herr Melkman. Are you not coming with us?'

He turned and, with a smile and a sheepish shrug, said,

'To be honest I'm a Philistine.' He pointed with his chin towards his wife. 'We came on the tour because my dear wife is a culture buff . . . I'll wait down there and get a little refreshment.'

The courier saw beyond him the façade of a bar. She smiled but said sternly, 'Not later than one o'clock. And be careful of touts trying to change money. It's very illegal and the punishment is severe.'

He nodded obediently and, with his gloved hand, blew a kiss to his wife.

The bar was all chrome and plastic. Several people sat at tables drinking. They glanced up incuriously. Twin speakers high on the wall were emitting an old Abba song. The bartender wore a black cap and a bored expression. He was polishing glasses in a desultory manner. The Dutchman moved close to him and said, 'I am Herr Melkman from Rotterdam.'

The bartender nodded without interest and pointed with his chin to a door at the back of the room. The Dutchman shambled over and opened it. Apart from a baize-covered table and two chairs the room was devoid of furniture. A man was sitting hunched over on the far side of the table playing patience with an old deck of cards. He glanced up very briefly and said in a deep, harsh voice, 'Close the door and lock it.' He spoke in Russian.

The Dutchman closed the door and locked it. From behind him the voice said, 'And bolt it.'

He slid home the bolts at the top and bottom of the door, then turned and surveyed the man. He had grey hair, combed straight back from his forehead without a parting. He had a wide face with heavy jowls and a thick-lipped mouth. He looked to be in his early sixties. He wore a dark blue suit and a grey shirt buttoned to the top but without a tie.

The Dutchman decided that he would not have recognised him. Then, briefly, he wondered whether this was in fact the man he had come to meet. He moved forward,

310

looked down at the table and said, 'The red four goes on the black five.'

The Russian sighed. 'I hate people who do that.'

'I always do it.'

'I can imagine so.'

Abruptly the Russian swept the cards into a pile and, with stubby fingers, shuffled the deck together. The backs of his hands were covered with liver marks. He put the deck beside a tray holding two ice buckets. One contained a bottle of vodka, the other schnapps. The Russian pushed himself to his feet and held out his hand. The Dutchman shook it saying, 'I would not have recognised you.'

'Me neither. You do not look like a priest.'

'Nor you a Major General.'

They sat down. The Russian gestured at the tray. 'The schnapps is Dutch.'

'Very thoughtful, but I'll join you with the vodka.'

For the first time the Russian smiled. It lightened the room. As he unscrewed the top he said, 'Father Pieter Van Burgh, come to collect his pound of flesh – or should I say bacon?'

The Bacon Priest smiled and took the proffered glass. He raised it and said, 'To your success, General Saltikov. You came a long way.'

The Russian nodded. 'And you still a priest. I would have expected to be drinking with at least an Archbishop.'

The Bacon Priest downed his drink in a gulp and said, 'Archbishops work too hard . . . I have more fun.'

The General nodded. 'So I hear.'

He too drained his glass and then refilled them both. Then he looked speculatively at the priest and his mind went back thirty-nine winters.

It had been the winter of '44. He had been a young Lieutenant in the Tank Corps. An awful area north-east of Warsaw. Lowlands, near a village called Gasewo. He commanded the lead tank of a line of six following a marked track through swampy ground. The Major com-

311

manding the unit was smart. He was in the rear tank. The Polish partisans must have changed the markers and his tank ended up in a swamp, stuck fast right up to the top treads. Stuck so fast that the other tanks could not pull it out.

The Major should have abandoned the tank but he was looking for medals. Something he would never get for courage. He had ordered Saltikov to stay behind with his crew and wait for a recovery vehicle which he promised would arrive by nightfall.

Of course it never did. The partisans attacked soon after dark. He was knocked senseless by a grenade. His crew was wounded, then, in the nature of things, they had their throats cut. Being an officer they took him back to their headquarters for interrogation, after which he knew he would get the same treatment.

He had a lust for life and managed to string it out for two agonising days. He saw by their faces that his life would end the next morning. That night a priest arrived. A young priest the same age as himself. He sat beside the bound Lieutenant and talked to him; tried to give him solace.

Saltikov hated the bastard; told him he was an atheist. Told him that the Pope was a fornicator and that Jesus Christ had been a sodomist. He did not care; knew that he was going to die anyway. They argued for hours and during those hours something happened; they came to understand each other. Then, as it was getting light, the priest had asked the Russian, 'How would you like to live?'

The Russian replied that he would not be averse to it. The priest carefully noted that a debt would be owed. The Russian replied that he was a Communist and an atheist, and he always paid his debts – always.

The priest took the address of the Russian's parents and other relatives. Two hours later he was released. Back at his unit he was an escaped hero. By the end of the war he was one of the youngest, most highly decorated Majors in the Red Army.

His career had continued on an upward curve ever since. He had often wondered if he had been the only Red Army officer helped in the same way by the same priest. He had often wondered about that.

He had been contacted over the years. The first time was in 1953 just after he had been promoted Colonel. Then again after every subsequent promotion. The message had always been the same: 'Congratulations. Remember Gasewo. Lenin was a transvestite.'

He had always sent back the same message: 'I'm waiting. Get it over with.'

Now Major General Maxim Saltikov, Deputy Commander-in-Chief of Warsaw Pact Forces in Poland, looked into the eyes of the Bacon Priest and gruffly said, 'So get it over with.'

The Bacon Priest sat back in his chair, took a breath and said, 'I want you to transport two people from Warsaw to Moscow.'

'Presumably secretly.'

'Yes.'

The General sighed, reached into the top pocket of his jacket and pulled out a thin black cheroot. He held it out to the Bacon Priest, who shook his head. The General lit the cheroot with a gold Dunhill lighter, inhaled the smoke, lifted his chin and then exhaled over the priest's head. In a cold voice he said, 'I'm sure I know the answer, but tell me – who are they?'

'Mirek Scibor and Ania Krol.'

The General nodded and then there came a screech as, abruptly, he pushed his chair back and stood up. The priest's heart began to pump faster as he noticed that there was a door behind the General. Were there people waiting behind it to arrest him?

But the General did not go to the door. He stretched his bulky frame and then began pacing and talking.

'Over the past days I've deployed hundreds of thousands of my men to catch those two. Only this morning a helicopter crashed while taking a platoon to a remote border area. Fourteen of my men dead . . . good men. In normal circumstances that flight would never have been authorised in such weather conditions . . . fourteen dead. Thanks to those two. I had to cancel important manoeuvres involving a quarter of a million men . . . thanks to those two. Now you sit there and calmly ask me to smuggle them into Moscow.'

He stopped pacing and turned. His face was dark in anger. His jaw jutted belligerently towards the priest.

Seconds passed and then the priest, looking at the table-top, spoke softly. 'Saltikov, you have had a very successful life and a good one. A wonderful wife, two intelligent and loving children who have given you, so far, three wonderful grandchildren.' Slowly he raised his head and his eyes met those of the General. His voice hardened. 'Saltikov, I gave you that life . . . I gave happiness to your wife . . . life to your children and to their children and, in the passage of time, to their children . . . You made a pledge.'

They stared at each other for a long time. Saltikov was the first to move. He walked back to his chair, sat down heavily, leaned forward, put his elbows on the table and asked, 'What will they do in Moscow?'

For half a dozen heartbeats the priest thought. Then he stated, 'He will kill Andropov.'

He expected a shocked reaction but the General merely nodded and murmured, 'That confirms a rumour . . . Why?'

The priest succinctly told him.

Again the General nodded and said, 'It fits. It's known that Andropov has an obsession about this Pope. But why bother? He's dying anyway. It's more or less common knowledge in the Politburo. He can't last more than a few months.'

The priest said, 'I know, but we expect the attack on His Holiness to take place shortly, probably on his forthcoming trip to Asia. Our analysis leads us to believe that Andropov's successor will cancel the operation . . .'

The General mashed out the stub of his cheroot into an ashtray and said, 'Your analysis is correct. Chernenko will probably take over but he's senile. Gorbachev will follow him and anyway, after Andropov's death, he and his pals will be pulling the strings . . . not a bad thing. It's time for new blood. Gorbachev is not an adventurist. He will certainly cancel that operation . . . but . . .' He paused and sighed and poured more vodka.

The priest asked, 'But what?'

The General wagged a finger at him.

'Yes, I can get your assassin to Moscow . . . at minimal risk to myself. But I cannot get him close to Andropov . . . neither can you. The Supreme Leader of the Soviet Union is the most protected human being on earth. Even more so now that he knows about your assassin. Even I could not get close to him without several stringent security checks and a complete body search. Bacon Priest, I know of your organisation and reputation but you will fail.'

The priest took a gulp of vodka and shrugged. 'If that is God's will, so be it . . . But will you get them to Moscow?'

A long silence, then the General said sombrely, 'I will discharge my debt . . . but on conditions.'

'Conditions?'

'Yes. First, your word that this assassin and nun will know nothing of my involvement . . . Nothing!'

'Certainly. Apart from me the only other person to know about it is a priest who works for me . . . I trust him implicitly. But what about your side?'

The General smiled. 'Leave that to me. One or two people owe me debts also. They will take the risks.'

He refilled the glasses and said, 'The second condition is that you write for me now a letter, in your distinctive handwriting, and with a distinctive signature, saying that I, Major General Maxim Saltikov, assisted you in this mission.'

The priest had his glass half raised to his lips. His hand

315

jerked to a stop in astonishment, spilling a little of the vodka.

'But why . . . ? Oh.'

The General was grinning.

'Yes, you are one of the few who would understand. The letter will be kept in a very safe place. If, against all odds, your man succeeds, then at some future date that letter could be very useful to me.'

The Bacon Priest shook his head in awe and said, 'The machinations of Russian politics.'

The Russian smiled. 'Yes. Something similar to Vatican politics . . . Now are they in Warsaw already?'

'No. They will arrive there tomorrow.'

'How?'

'By train from Cracow.'

'Just like that!'

'Yes.'

Now it was the Russian's turn to shake his head in awe. He was about to ask how, when the priest leaned forward and explained about the special train. The General nodded in satisfaction, then asked where they were to be delivered in Moscow.

The priest reached into his pocket and passed over a slip of paper. The Russian read it and again nodded.

'No problem.'

The priest grinned.

'Just like that?'

'Yes.'

'How?'

The General poured more vodka. The bottle was more than half empty. He dropped it back into the ice bucket with a little splash and said, 'The day after tomorrow I will send the bodies of my soldiers who died in the helicopter crash back to Moscow . . . Instead of fourteen coffins there will be sixteen. Your assassin and his nun will see only one disguised face at the beginning. From then on they will know nothing about it until they are in your safe house in Moscow. It's better that way . . . certainly for me.'

316

He reached into an inside pocket and pulled out a wallet and a gold Parker pen. From the wallet he extracted a folded piece of paper. He unfolded it and, together with the pen, pushed it across the table.

'Now write your letter.'

The Bacon Priest uncapped the pen and, with a scrawl, wrote several lines. Then he signed the bottom.

He passed the pen and paper back. The Russian read the words and his thick lips twitched into a grim smile. He waved the paper back and forth a few times then, carefully folding it into his wallet, said, 'I'll make you a wager, Bacon Priest. I bet that your assassin fails.'

'What are the stakes?'

The General grinned. 'A case of good Russian vodka against a side of bacon.'

The priest smiled and reached across the table and they shook hands on it.

The Dutchman was three minutes late getting back to the bus and received a stern look from the courier. He swayed slightly as he moved down the aisle to his seat. A few minutes later the courier forgave him. She could hear his wife ticking him off. She spoke in Dutch but the tone of her words made their content obvious. He was nodding his head in abject repentance. Then he saw the courier watching him. His left eyelid dipped in an elaborate wink.

24

The train rattled through the junction outside Kielce. The *kacyki* played cards. The game was skat and Marian was winning – heavily. Jerzy was the big loser. Antoni and Irena were holding their own. Ania and Natalia were in the little kitchen preparing a meal. Mirek was in the sleeping compartment. He had piled the pillows behind him and was sitting up in bed watching the passing scenery. It had snowed heavily during the night and the countryside was covered with a mantle of white. His side still throbbed painfully. His mind was at peace.

It was the second day after Ania's rescue. Word had come through that the contact in Warsaw would be waiting at the railway siding where the official carriages were parked. Ania had been concerned about moving Mirek so soon. She had wanted to wait several more days but the message had stressed that time was pressing. Also Mirek was impatient himself. After the events of the past three days he wanted only to get the job over and start a new life a great distance away. His mind also was free. Freedom from mental and physical tension. Freedom resulting from a pain that is finally shared; freedom from at last recognising his own identity.

It had happened the night of the rescue. They had returned to the General's house only minutes before road blocks bracketed the road leading to it.

Irena and Natalia wept with relief but then Irena endured a terrible hour before Antoni strolled in grinning broadly. No one had realised that Mirek was wounded until he got out of the car. His left trouser leg was wet with blood. Ania had not spoken a word during the escape or the drive back to the house. She seemed to be in a state of shock. Her face was very pale and she was cold. But when she saw the blood her instincts pulled her out of the shock and she took charge.

Jerzy wanted to call a doctor friend whom he insisted could be trusted. Mirek adamantly refused. He pointed out that the SB would know he was wounded by the blood he had left in the building, on the steps and in the two abandoned cars. He had bled a lot and they would assume that it was more serious than a mere flesh wound. They would also assume that he would need urgent medical attention and their first action would be to monitor the movements of all doctors.

The General was a very organised man and there was an emergency medical kit in the kitchen.

Ania and Marian had taken him upstairs to the General's bedroom, undressed him in the adjoining bathroom and examined the wound. The bullet had angled upwards, ploughing a six-inch furrow from just above his hip to the bottom of his ribcage. From the pain Mirek guessed that the bullet had nicked the bottom rib. He knew what had to be done. He sent Marian down for a bottle of vodka and, when she returned, poured some of it down his throat and a lot more over the wound. He had cried out from the agony, sagging with an arm around both women. Then they dried the wound and bandaged it tightly. To treat it just like a big cut and then hope that it healed was all that could be done. There were broad spectrum antibiotic pills in the medicine box and he took double the normal dose to counteract the vodka. Then he drank some more vodka and fell into bed.

An hour later they had all had a meal; in the bedroom. A celebration was a certainty and they were determined that Mirek should not be left out. Two folding card tables were brought up and a cassette player and bottles, glasses, plates and cutlery. The meal was simple. Thick vegetable soup followed by a beef stew with boiled rice.

The mood had been strange. Not subdued, but not ebullient. There was an air of contentment. After Mirek had briefly told them of the events inside the building the rescue was not mentioned. Marian had been the most relaxed, laughing a lot and teasing everyone. By this time both Mirek and Ania knew that behind her scatterbrained attitude was an intelligent and resilient woman. Mirek was the only one she did not tease. Like the others, she was now treating him with respect bordering on hero worship. For them he had done the virtually impossible and in so doing had saved their families and themselves from ruin, prison and possibly death.

The mood came from shared danger and shared relief. There was now, more than before, a bond between them all. They were a family.

Jerzy was addicted to modern jazz. His favourite was Thelonius Monk. He played his tapes on every possible occasion. One of them had just ended and he got up to change it for another. Marian had objected. She turned to Irena and asked her to sing for them. Irena, normally a little shy, had drunk plenty of vodka. She had raised her head and sung in a clear voice. She sang Polish folksongs: 'Karolinka' and 'Lowiczanka'. Ania knew the words and joined in. An air of nostalgia settled over everybody. Mirek, propped up in bed with pillows, had the feeling that he had finally come home.

The others had left just before midnight. Ania went into the bathroom and ran herself a bath. She came out twenty minutes later wearing her usual ankle-length nightdress and with her hair turbaned up in a towel. The bed was very wide. He was lying in the middle of it. With a wince of pain he moved further over to one side. She pulled back the duvet on the other side and slid in. He turned off the bedside light. The bathroom door was slightly ajar. She had left the light on and it cast a glow through the bedroom. She started to get out of bed to turn it off but he stopped her. He preferred not to sleep in a pitch black room. He had taken strong painkillers but his side was still very painful, especially if he made even the slightest move. He knew that even though he was mentally and physically exhausted he would get little sleep.

He had thought she would fall asleep quickly, but after about half an hour he had heard her low, harsh voice.

'Mirek, in the morning we must talk.'

'What about?'

'About us . . . what has happened . . . what we are doing.'

He had turned his head to look at her. He could just make out the dim profile of her face.

He said, 'All right, Ania. We will talk in the morning.'

For hours he had drifted in and out of sleep. Once he had to inch painfully out of bed and go to the bathroom. While there he took more painkillers. When he climbed back into bed he found that, in her sleep, Ania had rolled over to the centre. He lay next to her on his good side. He could see her face more clearly now. Her sleep was troubled. Considering her ordeal it was to be expected. Occasionally her limbs twitched and she whimpered in her throat. Very slowly he reached out an arm and put it over her and pulled her gently towards him. Her head rolled on the pillow and came to rest in the crook of his shoulder. He softly stroked her hair and felt her breath on his skin. He lowered his hand and ran it slowly up and down her back as though gentling an agitated kitten. Her breathing steadied and he felt her arm come across his waist and her leg came over his and their bodies were close along their entire lengths. Her hand was also moving on his back, up and down. A constant feathery caress. He felt no passion, no sudden sexuality. Just a closeness of body and mind. He could feel the flesh of her legs. The nightdress had ridden up past her knees. She moved against him. He turned his head. Her eyes were closed. He softly kissed one of them; then her cheek close to her mouth; then her

321

lips. They moved against his. The breath from her nostrils mingled with his. He felt her hand on the back of his head, stroking his neck and pulling him closer. He closed his eyes. There was nothing in his mind. All thought was suspended. He only had the sense of her against him. His right leg was clasped between her legs. Very slowly she started to move against it. Involuntarily he pushed his knee higher, hard against the softness of her. The pain in his side was forgotten. His hand slid down to her moving bottom and beyond to the rucked hem of her nightdress. He pulled it higher and his palm was against her bottom, caressing it as she moved against him.

It could have been minutes or hours. Time was in suspension. They lay in half light, one body undulating within itself. Her face was against his neck, her parted lips next to his ear. As the day dawned he felt her breath on his skin quicken. Against his knee the softness of her centre hardened. Her thighs gripped tighter. She moaned and her whole body stiffened and shuddered as it crushed against him.

She was rigid and fused to him and time passed. Then she sighed deeply and her body relaxed and became soft. She murmured something which he could not interpret and moments later her breathing was in the steady rhythm of sleep. He too passed into painless unconsciousness.

His pain had returned with a vengeance the moment he awoke. His whole side felt as though a branding iron was being held against it. He opened his eyes. The bed alongside him was empty. He heard faint words and lifted his head. She was beside the bed, lower down. He could only see the top half of her body. Her head was bowed, her right hand was clutching something at her throat. He realised that she was on her knees praying. He could not understand the words; they were in Latin. With a gasp of pain he sat up. She lifted her head and he saw that her cheeks were wet. She coughed, wiped a sleeve across her

322

face and stood up. He thought how vulnerable she looked, but then she shook her head as though dispelling a mood and said firmly, 'How is your side, Mirek?'

'It hurts like hell. Are you all right, Ania?'

She nodded. 'Yes . . . I will get you some breakfast and then change the dressing.'

She had gone into the bathroom, emerging five minutes later fully dressed and carrying a glass of water. She handed him two pills and the glass.

'Antibiotics. I'll go and get some breakfast and find out what's happening. It's quite late.'

He glanced at his watch and saw to his surprise that it was after ten o'clock. What had happened during the night was at once hazy and very real. She was at the door. He opened his mouth to say something but she held up a hand and said, 'Later.'

Later was half an hour. She had come back carrying a tray laden with a pot of tea, wheatbread, smoked meats, orange juice and a bowl of fruit.

She had sat on the bed and eaten with him. She told him that early in the morning Jerzy and Antoni had taken walks in different directions to see what was happening. The security forces were in massive evidence. Everyone's papers were being carefully checked and even units of the Russian army were in the city. They had also learned that the two safe apartments had been raided by the SB within hours of the rescue. They had been lucky to come back to the General's house.

After this report they ate in silence until she said introspectively, 'I have sinned very deeply.'

He had been waiting for this. He said quickly, 'Look, Ania . . . about last night . . .'

She shook her head.

'I am not talking about last night, Mirek. I have sinned because I took a vow . . . a vow to love only my Lord God. I have broken that vow.'

It took several seconds before the implications sank into

323

Mirek's mind. Then he said very quietly, 'You're saying that you love me?'

She nodded briskly. 'Yes, Mirek. I have been running from it . . . but I can run no more. It is not gratitude for what you have done. Nor is it a reaction to my having been cloistered all my life . . . I don't understand why it happened. I suppose that is one element of love . . . the lack of logic.'

'I love you too, Ania.'

She sighed and nodded. 'I know. Mirek, what is happening to us? What are we doing?'

He reached out and took her hands.

'Ania, when this is over we shall make a life together.'

She shook her head. 'I will not even think of that. Maybe it will never be over. How much longer can we be lucky?'

Fervently he said, 'It will end.'

She pulled her hands from his and then grasped his hands in hers, looking down at them. In her harsh low voice she said, 'I have fallen in love with a killer. I have watched you kill. What is it for, Mirek? What are you going to do in Moscow?'

Automatically he said, 'I cannot tell you that.'

Bluntly she said, 'Then you go on alone. I am involved completely or not at all.'

He raised his head and looked at her face and saw the determination in her eyes. He considered for only a moment, then said, 'My mission is to kill Yuri Andropov.'

Seconds passed and then her fingers tightened around his hands. She shook her head and said, 'That is impossible . . . you . . . they are mad . . . and why . . . why to kill him?'

Succinctly he gave her the background. When he had finished she released his hands and stood up and began to pace up and down the large room.

Finally she stopped and said scathingly, 'I do not believe it. No matter how much danger His Holiness is in, there is no possibility that he would condone such a sin.'

In a tired voice Mirek had said, 'He knows nothing about it.'

At first she had been puzzled, thinking back over the weeks. She said, 'He must know. He gave me his dispensation for what I have been doing.'

Mirek had great difficulty finding the words. In one way he wanted everything out in the open. In another way he was frightened of the effect it would have on her.

Tentatively he said, 'Ania, I promise you that the Pope is totally unaware. It is . . . or was, a group of three. Cardinal Mennini, before he died, Archbishop Versano . . . and the Bacon Priest. They called themselves *Nostra Trinita* and they called me the "*Papa*'s envoy".'

She shook her head. 'No. I saw the dispensation. His Holiness had signed it . . . his seal was on it.'

Mirek just looked at her, not knowing how to tell her. He did not have to. Realisation dawned. She put her hands to her face, drawing in breath.

'A forgery! What have I done . . . What have they done?'

He had pushed back the covers and, in great agony, swung his feet to the ground. He walked to her and put an arm round her shoulders and led her to the bed. They sat side by side while she came to terms with her situation. He thought she would cry, but she did not. He expected that her mind would be numb from the experiences and revelations of the past hours and days. It was not.

She composed herself and said, 'I understand their motives, the *Nostra Trinita*. I think they are terribly wrong but I understand their concern for His Holiness . . . But Mirek, I don't understand yours. It cannot be money.'

He remained silent, considering again, then said, 'No, Ania. It is not money. Nor is it concern for the Pope. It is hatred.'

She turned to him and he explained.

He told her of his early life. Of his conversion to Communism and his absorption by it. He explained that it suited his character. He was ambitious and single minded. Also

325

selfish. The family of his best friend at school had been hard-line Communists for three generations. He was much influenced by them and ended up spending more time in their home than his own. His parents were virulently anti-Communist but he felt that their arguments had no logic; that their minds were only ruled by emotion. The estrangement progressed rapidly. His friend's father arranged for him to get a scholarship to university which would result in recruitment to the SB. It had suited Mirek perfectly. He was a dedicated atheist and considered the Catholic Church to be the most reactionary element in Polish history. He blamed it for the propping up over centuries of a corrupt aristocracy and for being the main cause of Poland's historic ills.

For his parents, his joining the SB was the final straw. His father told him that he no longer had a son and that he would never look on his face again. His mother told him that he no longer had a mother and that she cursed her womb for producing him. He did not care. His vision was straight ahead. The past was finished. His only regret was his sister. She was three years younger, and as children, they had been close. He had deliberately closed his heart to his parents but could never totally close it to her.

His family had lived in Bialystok. He had been posted to Cracow far away. A deliberate move by the SB to keep him at a distance from a residual familial influence. It had been unnecessary. He never contacted them or heard from them again; or from any other relatives or childhood friends. When you joined the SB the regime became your family.

As the years passed he worked hard and intelligently and served his new family well. He explained to Ania that within the SB there is an unofficial inner group. It bears the nickname *Szyszki* – the circle. Many totalitarian security organisations have such groups. They form an elite. They keep themselves secret. They select their candidates with great care and test them well beforehand. Of course everybody in the SB knew about the *Szyszki*. Everybody knew that to be invited to join was the guarantee of success and promotion. The *Szyszki* carried out a lot of dirty work that could never be talked about or put into a report. It was the dark and silent arm of the SB.

As soon as Mirek had been promoted Major he waited with mounting impatience to be asked to join. The invitation came two years later. He was taken to lunch by Colonel Konopka; a very good lunch at Wierzynek. Mirek had been impressed. The Colonel had heaped compliments on his head and then told him that he was being considered for entry into the *Szyszki*. Mirek told him that he was deeply honoured. The Colonel had explained that before entry a candidate had to prove himself and in so doing tie himself for ever to his fellow members. Mirek had assured the Colonel that he would pass any test.

He did. The test was simple and straightforward. There was a subversive group in Warsaw led by a group of three. The group was very clever and had always avoided normal prosecution. They were dangerous and caused both damage and embarrassment. Mirek's initiation test to the brotherhood of the *Szyszki* would be to eliminate them. If he blundered and was exposed the SB would naturally disown him.

Mirek had accepted with alacrity. The Colonel told him that it was simple. The group would be at a certain house on the outskirts of Warsaw at a certain time. Their car would be parked outside in a quiet street. Mirek was to wire up the car to a powerful incendiary bomb. When they turned on the ignition – end of problem.

Mirek was shown how to do the job and he carried it out with total proficiency. Nothing appeared in the newspapers.

Some years later Mirek was sitting on the toilet in the officers' luxurious rest rooms at SB headquarters in Cracow. There were wide gaps above and below the door. He had almost finished when two senior officers came in. One was Colonel Konopka, the other a visiting Colonel from Warsaw. They must have enjoyed a good lunch.

They were jovial and slightly drunk. They talked as they urinated.

The Colonel from Warsaw asked, 'How's young Scibor getting on?'

Konopka answered, 'Brilliantly. He will go far.'

Behind his door Mirek had preened himself. Then the Warsaw Colonel said, 'Yes, but I think we went too far with his initiation.'

Konopka said, 'Well, maybe. But he'll never know. You know, it was Andropov's idea . . . he has a weird mind that one. He was visiting Warsaw at the time and they were comparing our *Szyszki* with the KGB's inner circle. We were talking of the trauma of initiation being equal to the dedication. Someone mentioned that Scibor's parents and sister were becoming a nuisance but were not indictable. Andropov laughed and said, "So have Scibor kill them . . . if he gets caught it will be put down to a family quarrel." Well, old Mieszkowski went along with it . . . you know what an arse-licker he is . . .'

After they had left Mirek had sat on that toilet for an hour. When he stood up he was a different man.

Ania had listened to it all in silence. When he finished she said, 'So I understand your hatred. What he did was despicable, especially as he never intended you to know. He did it for his own obscene pleasure . . . but, Mirek, I cannot understand what kind of man you were. You callously killed people of whom you knew nothing, never mind that they were your parents.'

'That's true,' he admitted. 'Ania, I would probably have gone on doing it. But the experience in that SB rest room was like having a lobotomy. It put me outside of myself and allowed me to see what I was. What I had become. I jumped at the Bacon Priest's offer not just to expiate my own hatred and guilt but to try and redress the evil that I had done and become . . .'

She nodded. 'I believe that. I believe you are a man who would now not be evil.'

He smiled slightly. 'If that's true, Ania, then your

involvement has been a big influence . . . So what happens to us now?'

She shrugged. 'Well now we are both changed. You for the better. Me for the worse. I don't know what I am any more. I take physical pleasure and then rationalise that I have dispensation. Then I find out that I don't. It's confusing. I feel used by your so-called *Nostra Trinita*.'

'It's true,' he agreed. 'They used my hatred and your faith. Ania, we can call it off now. Get out of here. Make a new life far away.'

She had shaken her head. 'No. I cannot even contemplate that, Mirek. Whatever they have done to me I am still a nun . . . And if what you say is true – and I believe it is – then the Holy Father is in terrible danger. We must finish what we have started. Then I will examine myself in God's light and, I hope, His sympathy.'

The train passed through the city of Radom, then into rolling farmlands. Mirek had made this journey many times before but never in such luxury. He was sitting up in a double bed covered by a goose-down duvet. A little chandelier swung overhead. The walls of the carriage were panelled and mirrored. He felt languid. His mind went back again to Ania. Between that momentous night and this journey they had settled into an undemonstrative but very affectionate relationship. They had slept together, in each other's arms, for two more nights but nothing had happened beyond a mutual warmth. She would kiss him in a way that was neither chaste nor salacious. She had, in her mind, put everything into abeyance until this mission was over. It was obvious to the others that they were very close. Presumably lovers. They acted as if they had been together for a very long time.

Now the door opened and Ania stood at the entrance looking at him. She curtsied demurely and said, 'The food is ready. Would Your Honour like his on a tray here

329

or would he deign to join the proletariat in the dining compartment?'

He grinned at her and pulled back the duvet.

'I'm coming. What is it?'

'Nothing very grand,' she answered. 'How's the wound?'

He was putting on one of Natalia's father's silk dressing gowns. He said, 'The wound is improving fast. You have healing fingers.'

In the outer compartment the others were settling up. Jerzy was morosely counting out twenty-zloty notes. Marian was watching him gleefully. She said, 'I keep telling you, Jerzy. You just think I'm a dumb blonde. Well, it takes real intelligence to play skat.' She looked up at Mirek and said triumphantly, 'My mother always said "*In skato veritas*".'

Jerzy counted out the last of the notes, pushed them across to her and said, 'Your mother was an old dypso and that's what you're going to be.'

Marian gathered up the notes. 'Jerzy, you're a lousy loser. I'm also told that you're a lousy lover. Isn't that so, Natalia?'

Jerzy's girlfriend was coming out of the kitchen with a tray. She smiled and nodded.

'I only love him because of his sense of humour.'

They cleared the cards and overflowing ashtrays from the table and all sat down.

The food was bread and cold meats and pickles, pickled fish and cheese together with Bulgarian wine.

For a while they ate in silence, then Antoni looked at his watch and said, 'Warsaw in half an hour. Then we say goodbye.' He smiled at Ania and Mirek. 'It's a contradiction. We'll miss you and at the same time be glad to see the back of you. I'm looking forward to a relatively quiet life.'

Jerzy said, 'You haven't forgotten the password?'

Mirek shook his head and mumbled through a mouthful of pickled fish, 'He says, "You picked a good day to arrive

330

in Warsaw." I reply, "It's always a good day to arrive in Warsaw."'

'I wonder who it will be,' mused Irena.

Mirek sighed and then smiled. 'Whoever it is, I won't get more of a shock than when I found Marian waiting for me by that lake.' To Ania he said, 'She told me I was just in time for the party.'

Marian grinned. 'Yes, and what a disappointment you turned out to be! Ania, I tried to seduce him and he turned me down like an old hag!'

In mock sympathy Ania said, 'I'm sure he was exhausted, Marian. It can be the only explanation.'

The banter went on for the next twenty minutes, partly to hide the impending sadness of parting and partly to cover up the rising tension. They all knew that the hand-over was a dangerous moment. If the other party's security had been breached then a different kind of reception committee would be waiting.

The table was cleared away as they entered the outskirts of Warsaw. Natalia explained that in a couple of minutes the train would stop. Their carriage would be un-coupled and a shunting engine would pull them off to the siding.

'Is it always the same siding?' Mirek asked.

'Always,' she affirmed.

They all got their bags ready. The girls really were going to do some shopping to keep up the cover. They would stay two days in Warsaw with friends and then return the same way to Cracow.

With a series of shudders the train screeched to a stop. Natalia lowered a window and looked out. The others stayed clear of the windows. She gave them a whispered commentary.

'They're uncoupling us now.' She waved to the railway workers. There was the shrill sound of a whistle, then a jolt and then stillness. 'The train is pulling away.' Silence for half a minute, then a chugging noise getting louder. 'The shunting engine is coming.' Half a minute later the carriage was jolted, then again, harder. 'We're coupling up.' She called outside, 'Thanks very much.'

They could hear answering voices, then the carriage moved forward with a jerk. Natalia stayed at the window. There was a clattering as they moved over several rail crossings. The carriage slowed again. Natalia leaned further out of the window. Over her shoulder she said, 'The siding is coming up now.'

The train slowed further. Jerzy called, 'Is there anyone on it?'

'Yes . . .' The carriage slowed to a halt with a hissing of the engine's brakes.

Natalia leaned back from the window and turned. Her face was pale. She stammered, 'It's . . . it's a Red Army Major.'

25

Mirek grabbed Ania's wrist and started to hustle her towards the door of the sleeping compartment. The others stood in petrified stillness. Then, through the open window, in clear but accented Polish, came the words: 'You picked a good day to come to Warsaw.'

Mirek and Ania stopped abruptly. They heard footsteps on the platform, then a head appeared at the window. A man in his late thirties. A dark narrow face, a wide moustache that looked false, dark glasses and a peaked cap. He said again, 'You picked a good day to come to Warsaw.'

Mirek found his voice and said with a croak, 'It's always a good day to come to Warsaw.'

The face smiled and a hand came through the window and turned the door handle. He was tall and very thin. He kept putting a hand up to touch his moustache as if to make sure it was in place. His glance swept around the compartment, lingering a little on Marian and finally coming to rest on Mirek. He bobbed his head in a sort of bow and said, 'I have come to take you and the lady on your way.'

He noticed the rank suspicion on Mirek's face and smiled, then quickly put a hand to his moustache. He said, 'It is not a trap. If the SB or KGB knew you were here this carriage would be surrounded by a battalion of crack troops with heavy weapons. Look for yourself.'

Jerzy went to the window, put his head through it and peered to left and right. Over his shoulder he said, 'No one about except for a couple of railway workers way down the track.'

Mirek asked the Major, 'Who are you?'

The Major spread his hands and glancing at the others said, 'In such circumstances it is better not to advertise one's identity.'

Marian said, 'It could be a trap to bring you in without a fight. He is certainly Russian.'

The Major sighed. 'Relax, Scibor. I come at the Bacon Priest's behest. I gave the correct password. Now hurry. There is no time to waste.'

Still suspicious, Mirek asked belligerently, 'Where will you take us?'

The Major sighed again. 'To someone who will explain everything.' He gestured at the others. 'I'm sure that your friends would not wish to be the recipients of information which could, under certain circumstances, cause you harm.'

Mirek glanced at Ania. She shrugged and said, 'I think we have no choice. There is no one else waiting for us.'

The logic penetrated Mirek's suspicion. He said, 'I'll get the bag.'

The next few minutes were very emotional. The emotion that comes from shared danger. Strangely, Jerzy appeared to be most affected. As he hugged Ania tears poured down his cheeks and into his beard.

The embraces were more eloquent than the muttered words of 'thanks' and 'good luck'. Then they were following the Major on to the platform. There was an icy wind blowing. The Major noticed Ania wrapping her arms around herself. He said, 'It will be warm in the car.'

The car turned out to be a long black Zil with military markings and a red-starred pennant. It was parked behind a store room fifty metres from the platform. As they reached it the Major said, 'Jump in the back. I'll put your bag in the boot.' He held out a hand.

Mirek said, 'I'll keep it with me.'

The Major shook his head. 'It's very unlikely that this

car will be stopped, but if it is then it's better that the bag is out of the way.'

Ania had opened the rear door and slid in. Mirek still hesitated. Irritably the Major said, 'Come on! The schedule is tight. The Bacon Priest has placed you under my orders.'

Perhaps it had been the years of living under military discipline, perhaps a stronger gust of icy wind. Mirek shrugged and handed him the bag and slid into the car next to Ania.

The door clunked shut.

The Major moved around to the boot. It was as he opened it that Mirek noticed there were no inside door handles. Between the back seat and the front was a thick glass partition. Mirek hammered at it with his fist. It barely vibrated.

Ania said, 'Mirek . . . What?'

'It's a trap,' he snarled.

The boot was empty except for a small, green, strapped-down gas cylinder. A black rubber tube snaked from it into a hole in the front bodywork. The Major tossed in the bag, then leaned forward and opened the valve in the cylinder. He closed the boot and moved around and watched through a rear side window.

He watched as Mirek hammered his fists against the partition and the window. Being bullet-proof, the glass was certainly fist-proof.

It took less than a minute. During that minute the Major saw, in brief moments, the hatred emanating from the Pole's eyes. Then his eyelids became heavy. The Major realised that the couple would assume that they were being gassed to death. He watched their reactions with fascination. In the last moments they clutched at each other in a tight embrace. He saw the woman's lips moving against the man's ear.

The Major watched for another minute. The couple in the car were completely still. He had toppled back into the corner, pulling her with him. Her head rested on his chest. The Major went to the back of the car and turned off the valve. Then, holding a handkerchief over his nose, he opened both rear doors, walked a few metres away and waited. Five minutes later he went back to the car, pulled down the roller blinds over the rear windows, closed the doors and climbed into the driver's seat. He took off the dark glasses, turned the mirror, looked at his face and decided that the moustache definitely suited him. As he pulled it off and tucked it into his top pocket he resolved to grow a real one; but perhaps not so large.

He took a circular route around the city. Twice he came to militia road blocks. Both times he simply drove forward at walking pace until one of the militiamen noticed the car and its pennant, came stiffly to attention and saluted. Both times the Major took his right hand off the wheel, returned the salute and accelerated away.

Forty minutes later they arrived at the military airport at Wolomin. Again, as he approached the guardhouse the Major slowed the car to a walking pace. The guards knew the car very well; and the Major. An order was shouted and the barrier raised. As he passed under it the Major returned the salutes.

He drove to a small hangar several hundred metres from the administration block. Its sliding door was open. A Sergeant stood outside and watched as the Zil drove straight into the hangar. Then he pulled the door closed and went inside through a smaller recessed door, locking it behind him.

Inside the hangar sixteen coffins were laid out in a row. Fourteen were closed and draped in Hammer and Sickle flags. Two at the end were open.

As the Major climbed out of the car a figure stood up from a bench against the wall. He was portly and middle-aged and wore the uniform of a Captain. On his epaulettes were the tabs of the medical corps. He carried a black bag. He asked, 'It went all right?'

'I think so,' replied the Major.

He opened the car door. Mirek's head flopped out.

336

Quickly the Sergeant reached forward and cradled it with his hands. The Captain said, 'Let's put them straight into the coffins. I'll check them there.'

The Sergeant shifted his hands under Mirek's armpits and gradually eased him out from under Ania's torso. The Major took his legs and they carried him the few metres to the waiting coffins.

The open coffins were thickly padded. They eased Mirek into one and then went back for Ania.

The Captain opened his black bag and took out a stethoscope. He checked Ania first. He had to pull up her sweater and then undo her blouse. The Major and the Sergeant watched. As the Sergeant saw the swell of her breasts under the white brassière he muttered, 'I wouldn't mind a bit of that.'

The Major gave him a look and the Sergeant swallowed and said, 'Sorry, sir.'

The Captain listened to Ania's heart and then pulled back an eyelid and studied the pupil for a moment. Satisfied, he moved over to the other coffin and examined Mirek. Then he straightened saying, 'No problem.' He looked at his watch. 'They leave in half an hour . . . I'll give them the shots now.'

He reached into his bag and took out a grey box. Inside were syringes and a selection of rubber-topped little bottles. The Major helped him roll the sleeves up, first of Ania, then Mirek. Deftly the Captain gave them both two injections. He grinned and explained to the Major.

'The second one is a large dose of morphine. Should they by chance wake up ahead of schedule they'll think they're in heaven.' He took from his bag another flat plastic box and placed it on Mirek's chest. To the Major he said, 'That's the antidote. Instructions are inside.'

The Major asked, 'Are you sure they'll have enough air?'

'Plenty,' answered the Captain. 'The coffins are well ventilated. Besides, in their unconscious state they use less oxygen than normal . . . like a hibernating animal.'

He straightened up and the three of them stood looking down at the two supine figures. The Sergeant said, 'They look comfortable enough.'

'They do,' agreed the Captain. 'The ultimate resting place . . . Let's close up.'

The coffin lids were on hinges. When lowered they were fastened by wing nuts. The wing nuts were very significant. Military coffins arriving back in Russia fitted with wing nuts invariably contain the contraband of some high officer, especially when accompanied by a Major wearing the red tabs of a staff appointment. Invariably a blind eye is turned. It is unofficially accepted as the perk of a General.

Half an hour later the sixteen coffins were lined up beside an Antonov AN24. A brass band played the national anthem. An honour guard presented arms. The coffins were loaded. The Major went with them.

Three and a half hours later the coffins were unloaded at a military airport outside Moscow. A brass band played the national anthem. An honour guard presented arms. A General on a low dais made a brief speech to assembled, tearful relatives. He pointed out that to die in the uniform of the Red Army was to die a hero, even if the death had been accidental.

A line of military hearses took away the coffins. The General noted that the last two went into a single hearse and were accompanied only by a staff Major. He noted that they were closed by wing nuts. He felt a pang of jealousy.

26

An hour later the hearse pulled up in a street behind the
Lenin Stadium. The buildings had been spared modernis-
ation. On one side they consisted of old four-storey houses
converted into apartments. On the other side was a row
of store rooms and lock-up garages. The street lighting
was sparse and the shadows long. The Major took out his
false moustache and, feeling a bit silly, stuck it into place.
Then he told the driver to wait with the engine running.
He climbed out and crossed the street. He found the
shabby brown door of a garage with the figure eight painted
boldly in black. Beside it was an old-fashioned bell pull.
He pulled it and heard a distant tinkle. A minute passed
and then one of the garage doors opened, a crack of light
filtered out and a voice asked, 'Yes?'

'I wish to speak to Boris Gogol.'

'You are.'

The Major leaned forward and said quietly, 'I have
returned your children.'

The door opened further. The man standing there was
no taller than five feet but one look at his face dispelled
any awareness of lack of stature. It was disproportionately
large with a high, domed forehead and white hair falling
down to narrow, hunched shoulders. But it was the eyes
that dominated. Bright blue, crinkled as though observing
a perpetual joke; luminous with intelligence. The Major
judged him to be in his mid-fifties. He looked round and
saw the hearse and said, 'I have been waiting for them.'

The Major asked, 'Where do you want them?'

'In here.'

The little man pulled up the bolt of the other door and pushed it open. The Major went back to the hearse and told the driver to back it into the garage.

Fortunately the Major and driver were fit and strong. It appeared that Boris Gogol was on his own. He did try to help as they grunted with exertion, sliding the coffins out and lowering them to the oily floor, but his efforts were mostly confined to exhorting them to be careful. The Major told the driver to take the hearse outside and wait. He and Gogol closed the doors behind it. Then the Major said, 'The antidote is in the coffin with the man. Instructions are in the box. You know how to use a syringe?'

The little man bobbed his head. The Major turned to leave and then stopped and said, 'They had a big dose of morphine about six hours ago. If they wake up extra happy, that's the cause.'

'I understand.'

The Major let himself out. As he walked to the hearse he mused that it had been a strange mission and dangerous. No matter. He knew with certainty that within one month he would be a Colonel and within five years a General.

Boris Gogol had trouble opening the first coffin. The Sergeant back in Warsaw had tightened the wing nuts with very strong fingers. Eventually he took a hammer from a workbench and loosened them with a couple of sharp taps. He opened the lid and found himself looking down at the lovely and serene face of Ania. For several seconds he stood there, head cocked to one side, gazing down, then his face suddenly showed alarm. Quickly he bent and picked up her right wrist and felt for the pulse. It was there and steady and he sighed audibly with relief. He dropped the wrist and quickly opened the other coffin. Mirek's face was also serene. Gogol studied it carefully and then nodded with satisfaction. The flat plastic box had slipped down against his left elbow. Gogol retrieved it and opened it. Inside, on top of the syringes and little rubber-capped bottle, was a brief handwritten note. Gogol read it and then read it again. He picked up the bottle and checked the gradations. Then he slid the needle of a syringe through the rubber and extracted the required amount. He injected first Mirek and then Ania. Then he pulled a chair up and sat waiting patiently, taking bets with himself as to who would wake up first.

It was Ania. After ten minutes her eyelids flickered and then opened. It took a while for her eyes to focus. When they did she saw a light bulb hanging on a cord from a dirty ceiling. Then something loomed over her. It was a face. Long white hair, laughing eyes, smiling lips. She smiled back. She felt as though she was floating. The face spoke.

'Do not be alarmed. You are safe. Do you feel all right?'

She realised he was speaking Russian. She answered in the same language and in a slurred voice.

'Yes . . . What . . . where am I?'

'In Moscow.' His smiled widened. 'Actually lying in a coffin . . . but very much alive.'

She lifted her head and looked down. Then to her left and right. She saw the other coffin. Her senses cleared.

'Mirek?'

'He is fine, sleeping in that coffin. He will wake soon.'

She raised herself higher and flexed the muscles of her arms and legs. He said, 'Can you get up? Here, give me your hand.'

With his help she slowly stood up and stepped unsteadily out of the coffin, saying, 'I feel a bit light-headed.'

'Apparently you had a dose of morphine. It will pass soon.'

Just then they heard a moan. Mirek was rubbing a hand over his eyes. Quickly Ania moved and knelt by his head and took his hand in hers. Gogol did not understand Polish but her rapid sentences were obviously an explanation. He heard Mirek ask several questions, some of which she answered briefly, the others she had no answers to. Then she was helping him up. He stepped out of the coffin, ran a hand through his hair and looked at the little Russian with a puzzled expression.

Gogol smiled and said, 'Welcome to Moscow, Mirek Scibor. Apparently you have been unconscious for about six and a half hours. My name is Boris Gogol.'

Mirek shook his head to clear it, then walked forward a little unsteadily and held out his hand. Gogol's grip was very firm.

Mirek asked, 'How did we get here from Warsaw?'

Gogol shrugged. 'I know very little. I was just told that you would be delivered and the approximate time . . . and that the deliverer would use the passwords, "I have returned your children." My answer was, "I have been waiting for them."'

'What did he look like?'

'He was dressed in the uniform of a Red Army Major.'

'Did he have a moustache that looked false?'

Gogol smiled. 'Yes, very . . . He kept touching it to see if it was still there.'

Mirek nodded and ran a hand across his face and then looked around the garage and asked, 'Where are we to stay?'

Gogol gestured at a door set in the rear wall and said apologetically, 'There are modest quarters here, converted from what was a bigger garage. Come, I will get you some tea.'

They followed him through into a tiny, cluttered hallway and then into another room.

The immediate impression was books. They stretched from floor to ceiling and were piled on tables and on the worn carpet. He cleared several from two old armchairs which were in front of a small electric fire and urged them to sit down. Then he went into an alcove kitchen and, after fussing around an ancient samovar, came back with a tray and cups. After pouring the tea he cleared more books from a wicker chair, pulled it over and sat down. Then he said, 'You had an eventful journey.'

Ania answered, 'We are glad that it's over.'

He smiled at her. 'The harder the journey the sweeter the homecoming. Of course, this is not home but I will try to make you comfortable. I'm afraid it's very cramped but you will not be here long.'

Mirek asked, 'Are you alone here?'

With a trace of wistfulness Gogol gestured and answered, 'Yes, apart from my books. They are my friends and family. It is temporary here. I should not have brought them . . . But I need them with me.'

'Have you read them all?' Ania asked.

He nodded. 'Yes. Some many times. Through them I see the world.'

Mirek asked, 'What are the plans?'

The little man took a last sip of tea and laid the cup carefully down. When he looked up his eyes and face were serious and authoritative. He said, 'From this point you come under my direct orders. This is the final phase and I direct it. The planning has been meticulous. The execution and timing of the plan must be equally so if you are to survive.'

Mirek said firmly, 'I place myself in your hands. Is Ania to stay here?'

Gogol dipped his head to her courteously. 'Yes.' He looked at his watch. 'It has now just become February 8th. Professor Szafer's appointment with Andropov at the Serbsky Clinic is for eleven thirty on the morning of the 9th. He will be picked up from his hotel by Academician Yevgeny Chazov at about eleven o'clock. I will go over details of the switch tomorrow. It must be like clockwork. The journey from the hotel to the Clinic, in an official car, takes between fifteen and twenty minutes. After the consultation you will return to the hotel. You will try to dissuade Professor Chazov from accompanying you. It should not be difficult. Szafer is known to be an abrasive personality.'

Mirek said, 'It sounds simple.'

Gogol nodded. 'The best plans are simple. But make no mistake, there are various elements which make it simple. If only one element goes wrong the whole plan collapses.'

Mirek nodded soberly and asked quickly, 'How do I actually kill him?'

Gogol stood up. 'Come, I will show you.'

Mirek rose and looked at Ania. She shook her head and turned it away.

He followed Gogol into another room. It was a bedroom; two narrow single beds, a small table, a chest of drawers and a wooden dumb valet. From it hung a smart dark grey suit. Gogol pointed at it.

'I want you to try that on tonight before you sleep. It should fit you well. If not it can be altered in the morning. Also there is a pair of shoes in the cupboard. They have slightly raised heels. Try those on as well. They should fit.' He gestured at the table. 'There are textbooks there on renal medicine. I thought you might like to refresh your memory over the next twenty-four hours.'

Mirek hardly heard him. He was looking at a series of four photographs pinned to the wall. They were all of the head and shoulders of Stefan Szafer in life size. One in profile, one from the back and two full face. In the full face shots he was gazing fondly at the camera. He studied those two carefully and then moved to a mirror hanging alongside them. The likeness was remarkable. He would have to trim his moustache a little and increase the depth of his eyebrows. His face was a little leaner than Szafer's but that too could be minimised.

Mirek had been nervous, but that was now diminishing. He sensed that the little man had everything under control.

Gogol went to the chest of drawers and pulled open the top drawer. From it he took a small flat leather case. He took it to the table and carefully opened it, saying, 'Even with modern computerised scientific aids, doctors – even specialists – like to listen to their patients' hearts.'

Mirek was looking at an ordinary stethoscope coiled neatly on a bed of velvet. Gingerly Gogol picked it up at the junction of the earpieces. He raised it high. The

chrome-plated head dangled in front of Mirek. Very gently
Gogol lowered the head on to his left palm. He said,
'You will not use the stethoscope until the end of your
examination. In the head of it are two short and very fine
needles. You will, of course, place the head on several
parts of his chest. You will press the head down firmly
with your finger. He will not feel the minute pin-pricks
. . . Believe me, we have tested it. These tiny needles are
impregnated with an extraordinary poison called "*Ricin*".
Interestingly it was developed by KGB researchers and
field-tested for them by the Bulgarian Secret Service
against defectors in Paris and London. They used an um-
brella with a needle tip. Very clumsy but it worked in Paris
and almost did in London. Applied directly over the heart
it will be totally effective.'

Mirek was staring mesmerised at the piece of metal.

Finally he said, 'How long? Before it takes effect?'

Gogol carefully folded the stethoscope back into the
leather box. He said, 'Within twenty minutes he will feel
drowsy and fall asleep. Within an hour he will be in a
coma. Within two hours he will be dead. You have ample
time to return to the hotel and disappear.'

He walked over to the chest of drawers and put the box
away.

Mirek asked, 'Is there no antidote?'

Gogol's silver locks swayed as he shook his head.

Twenty-four hours passed in fitful sleep, snatched meals
and intensive study. At times Mirek despaired. He imagined a thousand questions thrown at him, of which he
had answers for no more than a dozen.

Ania tried to help by taking the role of an inquisitor and
reading him questions from the book, but that exercise
was short-lived. At the first question for which he had no
answer he lost his temper. She understood the tension in
him and went into the other room, where Gogol gave her
a smile of sympathy and a book to read.

At six o'clock on the morning of Friday 9th, Mirek

snapped shut the textbook in anger and frustration. He would rely on wit and aggression.

At seven o'clock he sat on a chair in the bedroom with only a towel round his waist. Ania first trimmed his moustache and then the hair at the nape of his neck, constantly referring to the photographs on the wall. Then with make-up she thickened his eyebrows a little and shaded his cheekbones. She took a long time and very great care over it.

Finally she stood back two paces and studied him, then slowly nodded.

'Take a look.'

He stood up and went to the mirror and gazed at himself, turning his head slowly from side to side. Then he looked at the photographs. He too nodded and said, 'The likeness is near perfect.'

The clothes were laid out on the bed. No alterations had been necessary. He said, 'I'm going to get dressed.'

She sat down on the chair. 'Go ahead.'

For a moment he hesitated, then he dropped the towel. She watched without expression as he dressed. Then she stood up and straightened the knot of his tie. She said, 'You look very smart . . . How do you feel?'

'Very frightened . . . but the hatred is building. It holds down the fear.'

She was very close. They looked at each other. Slowly she reached out a hand and laid the back of it against his cheek. Then she turned away and went to the small window and looked out at the grey morning. For a while he watched her back, then from the dressing table picked up a small device that looked like a hearing aid. He worked it into his left ear.

Gogol inspected him in the book-lined lounge. He held a metal box in his hand the size of a packet of cigarettes. He pressed a button on it twice.

'Do you hear it?'

Mirek nodded. 'Very clearly. You can't hear it from there?'

Ania and Gogol shook their heads.

Gogol took a deep breath and said, 'All right. We go now. Say your goodbyes. I'll wait for you in the hall.'

He left them alone. There was an awkward silence. They both knew that even if Mirek succeeded they would not see each other again in Russia. He would be spirited out through one route and she through another. They had not discussed the future. They had tried not to think about it. They embraced. She was dry-eyed.

He said, 'It will be over in a few hours. I love you, Ania.' He held her tight, then kissed her on the cheek, waiting for her to say something. Her body was rigid.

'Please, Ania. Wish me good fortune.'

She shook her head and said, 'I love you. Just go now.'

He stared at her and finally nodded in understanding and turned away.

She heard the outside door close. Slowly she sank to her knees.

She prayed for his soul, and for hers, and for that of Yuri Andropov.

27

Professor Stefan Szafer shaved with meticulous care. He had suffered from four o'clock shadow since his late teens. It was now ten thirty and he was determined there would be no shadow on this day.

The bathroom of his hotel room was an amalgam of marble and mirror. He felt suitably important. He splashed water over his face and dried it with a fluffy white towel. Then he picked up a pair of long, delicate scissors and carefully trimmed his moustache. He examined himself in the mirror and decided that he was indeed handsome. He shook two Amplex pills out of a bottle and swallowed them. Then he walked out into the bedroom. His white shirt, maroon tie, and dark grey suit were laid out on the double bed. He had just pulled on the trousers and was tucking in the shirt when there came a tap at the door. He zipped up his fly, went over and opened it.

Halena Maresa was standing there with a smile on her face and a half bottle of champagne in her hand. Her smile graduated to a grin when she saw his look of surprise.

'I came to wish you luck, Stefan.'

Bemused, he backed away from the door. She swept in, exclaiming in delight at the luxuriousness of the room, deposited the champagne on a table, shrugged off her fur coat and tossed it on to the bed. Then she threw her arms around his neck and kissed him fiercely on the lips.

He disentangled himself and asked, 'Halena, what are you doing here so early?'

She pouted. 'Our boring session ended early, thank

God. I was just in time to pick up that bottle of champagne and get here before you left. I thought I would wait here and welcome you on your return. Now, where are some glasses?'

He smiled at her fondly. 'Halena, I cannot drink champagne now. I must have a clear head.'

She had opened a cupboard and found glasses. She selected two with long stems and put them on the table saying, 'Pooh! Of course you can have one glass. It will make your head clearer. Are you not happy to see me?'

'Of course.' He moved to the bed, picked up his tie and slipped it under his collar. Over his shoulder he said, 'But no champagne yet, darling. Save it for my return.'

He jumped at the sharp retort. The cork hit the ceiling and bounced into a corner. The champagne foamed into the two glasses. He slipped on his jacket, smiling and shaking his head.

'I cannot drink it, Halena. Save it for my return.'

She looked piqued. 'It will be flat.'

'Never mind. I'll order another bottle.'

'You don't love me.'

He smiled again. 'Of course I do.' He moved to her and enfolded her body in his arms and squeezed tightly. 'They will be picking me up soon. Will you really wait for me here?'

'Yes, Stefan. I will wait for you in that big bed . . . I will wait naked.'

Abruptly she felt his hardness rising against her thigh. In a kittenish voice she said, 'Now don't be a spoilsport. Have a little champagne with me.'

He relented and whispered in her ear. 'All right, but just half a glass.'

He released her and reached for the glass just as the phone rang.

He shrugged and walked to the bedside table and picked it up, saying, 'Szafer here.'

Halena opened her handbag.

Szafer said into the phone, 'Yes, Professor Chazov, I am ready. I will come down immediately.'

He cradled the phone and turned. Halena was facing him. Her legs were straddled, her left hand was holding her right wrist, her right hand was holding a pistol, lengthened by the slug of a silencer. It was pointed at his heart.

Her voice was cold. 'It would have been easier if you had drunk the champagne.'

His mouth opened in astonishment. 'Halena . . . ? What . . . What are you doing?'

She said, 'If you move I will kill you. I know how to use this gun. I'm an expert shot.' Her bag was open on the table beside her. She freed her left hand and reached into it. The aim of the gun never wavered. From the bag she took a small metal box, the size of a cigarette packet. She laid it on the table and, without taking her eyes from Szafer, felt across the front of it for the button and pressed it twice. That action took some of the tension out of her. She breathed more easily and moved closer to Szafer, saying, 'Sit in that chair there. We are going to wait a couple of hours and then I never have to see your face again or smell your stinking breath.'

In a room two floors below, Mirek took the hearing aid from his ear and tossed it to Gogol.

'That's it. I'm going.'

He picked up the black doctor's bag and straightened his tie. Gogol said, 'Good luck. I'll be waiting.'

Mirek swallowed and nodded and walked to the door.

As he got out of the lift he took a deep breath and told himself that this was the culmination of everything. He purged his mind of extraneous thoughts and walked briskly towards the entrance. Gogol had shown him a photograph of Academician Yevgeny Chazov. Mirek recognised his portly figure standing by the concierge's desk. He slowed and angled to pass close to him. Confidently Chazov said, 'Professor Szafer. This is an honour and a pleasure.'

350

Mirek shifted his bag to his left hand and took the proffered hand. It was a limp grasp. Chazov took him by the arm and led him out of the hotel. A long black Zil limousine was waiting with the uniformed driver holding open the rear door. Chazov ushered Mirek into the interior. A glass partition separated them from the front seats.

As they pulled away he said enthusiastically, 'I was intrigued by your recent article in *Sovetskaya Meditsina*, "Metabolic Acidosis after Dialysis". How many patients were in the test sample?'

Mirek felt icy fingers clawing at his guts. He had no knowledge of the article and no knowledge of what would constitute a viable test sample. His mind froze up and then he remembered that Szafer was professionally an egoist and renowned for his abrasiveness. He decided to start as he would continue and said calmly, 'A statistically significant amount.'

Silence. Then Chazov cleared his throat and said apologetically, 'Yes, of course . . . And the conclusion was very positive . . .'

That stifled the conversation for ten minutes as they worked their way out of central Moscow, then Academician Chazov tried again. After another discreet cough he said, 'I had the pleasure of meeting Professor Edward Lenczowski at a symposium in Budapest last October. I understand you've worked with him . . . What's your opinion?'

Mirek glanced at him and said drily, 'I hope I updated his surgical technique.'

This time Chazov smiled bleakly and said, 'Yes. I got the impression that he was somewhat . . . shall we say, overly traditional in his outlook.'

Mirek merely nodded and turned his gaze to look out of the window. A light snow was falling. The few figures on the streets were reduced to anonymous bundles of fur. Mirek had studied the route on a map. He knew they were only minutes away. He felt Chazov stir beside him as he

351

reached into his jacket pocket and produced a plastic wallet of papers. Again his voice was apologetic as he said, 'I have your pass here. I'm afraid that security is extremely strict. You will understand that, of course . . . It does entail a thorough body search . . .'

Mirek glanced at him again and said, 'I fully understand.'

The car turned left into a narrow tree-lined avenue. Mirek noted the soldiers stationed every few metres on each side. He also noted that all carried sub-machine guns.

After two hundred metres they came to a road block. Chazov wound down his window and passed the plastic wallet to a stone-faced Captain. The contents were carefully examined and then, without a smile or a word, the Captain handed back the wallet and waved the driver on. Another hundred metres and they came to a pair of high steel gates set into a concrete wall. Again the papers were scrutinised, and their faces. Again there was no cordiality in the process. Finally the gates were opened and they drove through into a floodlit courtyard.

Mirek counted at least a dozen KGB guards spread around. Some were stamping their feet against the cold. The driver stopped the car, jumped out and opened the rear door. A KGB Major came out and escorted them into the building.

He led them first to a room just inside the entrance. There were several KGB officers waiting including Victor Chebrikov himself. Chazov introduced Mirek with flowery phrases about his professional brilliance. Mirek knew all about Chebrikov. As he shook hands he could feel his heartbeat quickening.

Chebrikov said genially, 'We are grateful for your presence. I regret that you will have to be searched. Please understand that it's routine. Everybody has to go through it.'

Mirek nodded quietly and put his bag on to a table. The search was indeed thorough. He had to take off his jacket and turn out his pockets. Academician Chazov did the same. A young KGB Lieutenant conducted the body search. His careful fingers even probed Mirek's genitals. Mirek tried to look bored and disdainful of the whole thing, while he wondered if he would ever get out of this building alive.

The Lieutenant was finally satisfied. Two other KGB officers had been going through his bag. He saw them open the flat leather case and then close it again upon seeing the familiar shape of the stethoscope. They opened another case, this time of walnut, which contained a set of Solingen scalpels. One of them glanced at Chebrikov who shook his head and said to Mirek, 'Sorry, Professor. Those will have to stay here.' Mirek shrugged disinterestedly.

His bag was carefully repacked and then Chebrikov led the way to the Chief Administrator's office. There was another Russian doctor waiting. Introductions were made. Mirek recognised the name: Academician Leonid Petrov. A man in his late sixties with a bulbous nose and a big reputation. Back in Florence, at what seemed a lifetime ago, Father Gamelli had talked about him. He was Russia's foremost expert in renal medicine and a man often contemptuous of what he liked to call 'Western gimmickry'. He had a cynical, bad-tempered air about him. His attitude made it plain that he considered the Polish professor to be nothing but a young upstart. Mirek, through his nervousness, was grateful that Father Gamelli had given him a few tips on how to handle such a man.

Tea was served and Chazov handed Mirek a file which, he said, contained an in-depth summary of the patient's condition. Mirek placed it on his knees, opened the cover and started to read. It was in Polish. Obviously they were thorough. Obviously they wanted no errors of translation.

Polish or not, most of it was beyond his knowledge. He knew that he had to resort to the cover of Szafer's reputation. It took him fifteen minutes to pretend to study it. There were X-rays, ECGs and the results of biochemical tests of both blood and urine. As he read, the Russians talked quietly among themselves. When he closed the file they stopped talking and looked at him expectantly.

He sniffed and shrugged. Looking at Petrov he asked, 'Is the nephron damage very great?'

Petrov answered, 'Well, it's not good.'

Mirek sighed. 'Naturally. By the way, how current are these tests?'

Chazov said, 'All within forty-eight hours.'

Mirek gave him an enigmatic look which could have meant 'that's good' or 'that's pathetic'. He said, 'Does that include the creatinine test?'

'Yes.'

A look of slight scorn crossed Mirek's face. He said, 'I'd like a very recent urinary sediment test and a current electrolyte profile. I suggest you do one every twelve hours or so.' He was looking at Petrov, who shrugged noncommittally. Mirek took a breath and said, 'Now I am ready to see the patient.'

They all stood up. Chazov picked up Mirek's bag. Chebrikov led the way.

They passed down a long white-walled corridor. They had to go through three sets of swing doors. In front of each was a pair of KGB guards cradling SMGs. There were two more outside the twin ceiling-high doors of the clinic's main VIP suite. They waited outside while Chebrikov went in.

After a couple of minutes of silence Mirek asked, 'How is the patient's mental state?'

Instantly Petrov said harshly, 'That does not concern you. Restrict yourself to his physical condition.'

Mirek knew how Szafer would have reacted to that. He said curtly, 'The mental and physical is intertwined and effective treatment must take both into account. No matter, I will form my own opinion.'

Petrov started to answer but was interrupted by the door opening. Chebrikov beckoned them. They filed through a small anteroom into what could have been the bedroom of a luxurious hotel suite. Floor-to-ceiling windows were draped with damask curtains. A deep pile carpet was underfoot. In one corner was a grouping of easy chairs around a table. The bed was close to the window, its back raised. There were two KGB guards standing in corners, legs apart, sub-machine guns cradled in their arms. Their eyes watched Mirek coldly. Andropov, dressed in a green surgical gown, was sitting up talking on a telephone. He hung up as they came in.

As Mirek set eyes on him all his tension and fear flowed away. His brain cleared. Live or die, he would act this through to perfection.

Professor Chazov led him up to the bed. As Andropov set eyes upon him he suddenly sat up straighter. He stared for a few seconds and then relaxed. As Chazov presented Mirek the First Secretary made no move to shake hands. He merely nodded and said, 'I am indebted to our Polish comrades for sending you.'

Mirek gave a sort of bow and said, 'I am honoured to be of service, Comrade First Secretary . . . Greatly honoured.'

'Proceed,' said Andropov.

Mirek remembered his briefing on Szafer's bedside manner. He said, 'Comrade First Secretary, this will be a brief examination. I have seen the reports of your eminent doctors. I need merely to get a first-hand physical impression.'

Andropov nodded in understanding.

Chazov and Petrov had moved to the other side of the bed. Chebrikov stood at the foot. Mirek noticed the tube attached to Andropov's left arm. He asked Chazov, 'How long has the A/V shunt been in?'

Chazov appeared to be nervous. He answered, 'About thirty hours.'

Mirek pursed his lips. 'Any psychological effects?'

Andropov swivelled his eyes to look at him and said curtly, 'Are you being impertinent?'

Mirek imagined himself to be Szafer. He smiled and shook his head.

'Not at all, Comrade. The purpose of dialysis is to eliminate body waste, particularly urea . . . We know that being wired up to machines for long periods can create subliminal psychological stress which in turn can have a deleterious physical effect. I am in no way impugning your mental state, but I need an opinion from your physicians who have been attending you over a long period.'

Andropov was mollified. Petrov was not. Belligerently he said, 'That's just a hypothesis. There has been no mental change, subliminal or otherwise.'

Mirek said, 'Good.' He decided to use one of Father Gamelli's arrows against Petrov. Looking at him he asked, 'In that report I did not see the results of the ultrasound scan. Where is it?'

Mirek revelled in the stunned silence. He knew that such a procedure had only been in use a few months in only the top Western hospitals. Father Gamelli had guessed that the Russians would not yet be using it. He had guessed right.

In a pained voice Chazov said, 'We have not done one.'

Mirek sighed audibly. 'I suggest you do one . . . and also a Phenolsulphonphthalein excretion test . . . as soon as possible. Perhaps I could see the results tomorrow.'

Andropov was looking at Chazov, who swallowed nervously and said, 'Of course, Professor.'

Petrov kept silent. Mirek sent mental thanks to Father Gamelli. He knew he was now in the driving seat. He leaned over Andropov, pulled up his right eyelid, peered into the eye and said, 'I'm looking for signs of retinal haemorrhages.' He let the eyelid fall back into place saying reassuringly, 'That's fine.' To Petrov he asked, 'Has there been a decrease in the renal concentrating ability?'

Petrov nodded grudgingly. 'A little.'

Airily Mirek said, 'That must be carefully monitored.'

He decided that he had risked his luck and his little knowledge enough. The time had come. His bag was on a table behind him. He turned and opened it and took out the small leather case. As he carefully lifted out the stethoscope Petrov said with a note of scorn, 'I thought all you young wonderboys were only interested in ECGs.'

Mirek gave him a condescending smile.

To Andropov he said, 'Medicine is a combination of science, art and intuition. I would like to listen to your heart, Comrade.'

Andropov was obviously impressed. He gave a benign nod and began to unlace the front of the surgical gown. Now at this moment the hatred riled up in Mirek. He had to choke it down. He fitted the stethoscope into his ears and pulled apart the gown.

The skin of Andropov's chest and upper belly was white and flaccid. He had sparse tufts of white hair on his chest. Most of it had been shaved away for the ECGs. Mirek ran his hand down the rubber tube to the base of the chromium-plated head. He leaned forward. His hand was shaking in anticipation. He took a breath and controlled it. Slowly and carefully he placed the metal on to Andropov's chest just to the right of the heart. As he pressed his finger hard on to it he looked into Andropov's eyes. In his mind he said, 'That is from Bohdan, my father.' He waited for twenty seconds. In his ears he could hear the thump of the heart. He imagined the poison moving, even now, towards it; to strangle it. He moved the head to a point just under the heart. He looked again into those eyes and pressed down hard. His mind said, 'This is from Hanna, my mother.'

Twenty seconds later he moved the head up four inches. It was directly over the heart. With the forefinger of his left hand he tapped it firmly, once, twice, thrice. He could feel himself shuddering from hatred. He almost said it aloud: 'And this is from Jolanta, my sister.'

He was looking again into Andropov's eyes. They were watching his, puzzled. He thought that maybe something had showed on his face. One part of him no longer cared. One part did. It cared that Andropov should not have the satisfaction of taking him to hell as a companion. He straightened up and smiled, saying musingly, 'Remarkable. Under the circumstances remarkably good.'

Andropov's look of puzzlement changed to one of pleasure. He said, 'So what is your prognosis?'

Mirek folded the stethoscope back into its case and slid the case into his bag. He said:

'Comrade First Secretary, I believe that your condition is not as bad as you may have been led to believe. Of course, I would like to study further all the reports and also see the results of the tests I have suggested. I will say, though, that with the correct treatment you may well have many years of a robust life in front of you.'

Neither Chazov nor Petrov could keep traces of scepticism off their faces. But Andropov was beaming at Mirek, who said, 'I may wish to examine you again in two or three days.'

Andropov said, 'I shall insist upon it.' To Chebrikov he said, 'See that Professor Szafer has anything he needs . . . anything.'

At that moment, twenty kilometres away in the Kosmos Hotel, Stefan Szafer's building rage and humiliation finally erupted like a too long constricted volcano. For an hour he had been sitting in the chair looking at her. Thinking about what she had done to him. Thinking of the words he had spoken to her. The feelings he had expressed to her, and to himself. The belief that she had loved him.

He sat looking at her beautiful face over the barrel of the pistol. At her eyes, which gazed back with undisguised contempt. It was the contempt which finally broke him. He had worked out by now what was going on. Worked out that this woman had made him a contemptuous fool. The humiliation welled up. She crossed one elegant leg over the other and sighed from boredom.

Humiliation was blended with rage. With a scream from the bottom of his throat he lunged off the chair and dived towards her, fingers outstretched, seeking her throat.

She had time to fire twice. The first bullet hit him in the centre of the stomach. The second in the lungs. They should have stopped him. But in those moments he was not a normal man. The rage gave him unprecedented strength. He crossed the ten feet of carpet and cannoned into her, sending the gun spinning from her hand. His forearm hammered into her face, stunning her. Then they were lying on the carpet and he had his hands around her throat. Weakly she flailed at him but his hands were a tightening vice, his fingers digging deep into her flesh.

His face was inches from hers. He watched it turn red, then blue. He panted from pain and exertion. He saw her tongue forced out between her lips and her eyes bulge in their sockets.

He was still grunting with rage as she died. He banged her head up and down on the carpet, then flung her away. He scrambled to his feet, feeling the blood pumping from him. He did not care. He staggered over to her body and kicked it, cursing her for a bitch and a whore. Finally he dragged himself to the bed and pulled at the phone, managing to get the mouthpiece close to his dying lips.

28

Mirek turned at the door of the suite and looked one last time at Andropov. The old man stared back at him. Then he lifted his hand and gave a little goodbye wave. Mirek smiled and waved back.

Only Academician Chazov accompanied him to the entrance. As they walked down the long corridor he said, 'I am much looking forward to your lecture at the Institute on Thursday.'

Mirek replied, 'I'm honoured that you'll be there. By the way, Professor, would you mind if I returned to the hotel alone? I have much to consider after this consultation . . . I find it hard to think in company.'

Chazov's face showed his chagrin but then he remembered Andropov's orders to Chebrikov that the Pole was to have anything he wanted. Ingratiatingly he said, 'Of course, Professor. I will arrange another car for myself.'

They shook hands by the car. Chazov gave the driver the pass and told him to take Professor Szafer straight back to his hotel.

Mirek waved goodbye through the rearview mirror as the Zil passed through the main gates.

Back in the clinic Andropov said to Chebrikov, 'Is everything ready for that bastard Pope when he arrives in South Korea?'

Soothingly Chebrikov said, 'Everything is ready. The team is in place. In seventy-two hours he will be no more.'

'Good. Is there any news on the other Pole . . . Scibor?'

'Unfortunately not,' Chebrikov replied ruefully.

'It's strange,' Andropov mused. 'One Pole comes to heal me . . . and the other to kill . . . You know, they even resemble each other.'

Chebrikov would have liked to escape from the room to have a drink and a smoke, but his boss was disposed to talk. Then Andropov yawned.

Quickly Chebrikov said, 'Perhaps you'd like to sleep, Yuri?'

Andropov shook his head in slight irritation. 'No, I just feel a little drowsy . . . You know, something else is strange. In the dossier you showed me it mentioned that this Professor Szafer suffered from chronic bad breath. I had steeled myself against it, but it was not so. His breath was normal.'

Suddenly he lifted his head and looked at Chebrikov. His voice rose in pitch. 'His breath was not bad!'

At that moment the telephone rang stridently.

The Zil had turned off the avenue lined by KGB guards and was cruising at 80 kph towards the city centre. Mirek felt no elation, only a deep sense of relief. He wondered about Ania. Wondered if she was already on her way out. His thoughts turned to the future.

Very faintly he heard, through the glass partition, the crackle of the radio, then abruptly the driver's head swivelled and he was looking into a pair of startled eyes. A second later he was slammed back against the seat as the Zil rapidly accelerated.

He knew instantly. There could be no other explanation. Maybe Andropov had died faster than expected. He grabbed for the door handle but then knew that to dive out at this speed was suicide. The driver would have to slow down somewhere along the road but meanwhile every police and militia car would be heading to intercept them. Within a couple of minutes it would be too late. He cursed that he had no gun; no way to kill himself.

They were speeding down the centre lane, the lane reserved for VIP transport. Up ahead the road curved sharply and in front of them was a car travelling at a more sedate speed. They would have to slow down.

Mirek heard the horn as the driver pounded frantically on it. They were still going too fast but he had no choice. He had to risk it. He reached for the door handle again and steeled himself. Then he heard a siren close alongside. He looked up. It was a white ambulance pulling up on their left side. If he jumped now he would end up under its wheels. He cursed the thing. He could see the driver looking at him.

Suddenly he saw the driver wrench the wheel over.

The front wing of the ambulance slammed into the side of the Zil. Mirek was thrown violently across the back seat. He felt the car swing and heard the scream of its tyres. Then a rending crash as they slid into the central barrier. They had started into the curve. Mirek covered his head with his arms and crouched against the glass partition.

The Zil rolled twice and then came to a screeching stop on its side, across the road. Mirek felt a stabbing pain in his shoulder. He pushed himself to his feet. He was standing on the right-side window. The left door above him had been torn off. Through the glass partition he could see the driver's body crumpled against the splintered windscreen.

He put his left foot on the arm rest in the centre of the seat and, with a gasp of agony, pushed himself up into the space where the door had been. He saw that the ambulance had overshot them and was turning around. He felt light-headed from the shock. Irrationally he thought how convenient it was to get wrecked by an ambulance. Then the instinct for survival took over. He could smell petrol. He pushed himself up and over the side and fell heavily onto the road. People were running towards him. He managed to stagger to his feet.

The ambulance pulled up in front of him. A woman in a red coat had arrived and was asking if he was all right. He was in a daze. Then he heard a deep voice talking to the woman, telling her it was all right, that he would be taken to the hospital in the ambulance. A big hand gripped his arm above the elbow and propelled him forward towards the open front door of the ambulance. He looked up. It was a big old man with a florid face. He was astonishingly strong. He more or less pushed Mirek into the cab, slammed the door and then ran around to the driver's side. A crowd had gathered.

In a haze Mirek heard someone shout, 'What about the driver?'

The ambulance driver shouted back, 'Another ambulance is coming.'

They moved forward, slowly at first, through the parting crowd. Then the driver leaned forward and flicked a switch and the siren started screaming. They accelerated away.

Mirek held his shoulder. He thought it might be dislocated. His brain was telling him that he had to get out, before they reached the hospital.

Abruptly the ambulance swung off the main road and down a narrow street. The driver flicked off the switch and, as the sound of the siren died, said, 'So, apart from your shoulder, how are you, Mirek Scibor?'

Mirek turned his head around to look at him. The big old man glanced at him and smiled. At first Mirek was totally bemused, then realisation dawned. He laughed and said, 'I suppose your best minds worked on this.'

'You could say that,' agreed the Bacon Priest.

Forty-eight hours later the Alitalia DC8 carrying His Holiness Pope John Paul II touched down at Seoul's international airport.

A day earlier three Filipinos had boarded a JAL flight for Tokyo from the same airport.

Two of them were young women. The other a young man.

One of the women was very pretty.

29

Archbishop Versano warmly embraced the Bacon Priest and led him over to a leather chair in the corner of his office, saying, 'Welcome and well done, Pieter. You look tired. Coffee? Or something stronger?'

The priest sat down, shaking his head. 'No thanks, Mario.'

The Archbishop went to his desk and came back carrying a sheet of paper. He sat opposite the priest, grinned at him and said, 'This was issued by the Kremlin three days ago. Quote: Comrade Yuri P. Andropov, President of the USSR and Secretary General of the Communist Party of the USSR, died at sixteen fifty hours on February 9th, 1984. Cause of death: Interstitial nephritis, nephrosclerosis, chronic kidney deficiency, dystrophic changes of internal organs, progressive hypertension and cardiovascular insufficiency.'

He looked up at the Bacon Priest and grinned again. 'Yet another Kremlin lie. They obviously don't want their own people – or anyone else's – to know that their vaunted security was breached.'

Wearily the priest shook his head.

'Not necessarily, Mario.'

'What do you mean?'

'Just that. He could well have died of those causes.'

Puzzled, Versano cocked his head to one side and studied him. Then he said, 'Pieter, what's the matter with you? What about the "*Papa*'s envoy" and "*la cantante*"?'

The Bacon Priest sighed.

'They never existed, Mario. They were figments of imagination.'

The Archbishop stared at him, then an expression of horror crossed his face. 'Oh God . . . you didn't . . . have them eliminated . . . to destroy your evidence?'

Van Burgh sighed again. 'Mario, you cannot eliminate something that never existed.'

Now exasperation was on the Archbishop's face and in his voice. 'Have you gone crazy? Scibor was a real person!'

'Yes, there was a Mirek Scibor. He did kill two of his superiors. Doubtless they caught him and, doubtless, quietly executed him.'

Incredulously Versano barked, 'And the nun – Ania Krol . . . ? Mennini found her in a convent in Hungary.'

Van Burgh spread his hands. 'If you check the records of that convent you will find no mention of a nun called Ania Krol. If you question the Mother Superior she will have no recollection of such a person.'

Versano sneered. 'And of course Mennini is dead.'

'Yes. God rest his soul.'

'And *Nostra Trinita*?'

Van Burgh made a throw-away gesture.

'Three foolish men fantasising after too much wine and brandy.'

'I see, and of course all the well-documented fuss in Eastern Europe, the huge security turn-out, that was just a figment of my imagination, and of millions of others?'

The Bacon Priest shook his head. 'Not at all. My guess is that it resulted from a disinformation campaign, probably the Americans . . . CIA. They would certainly have discovered the extent and mobility of the East's security system.'

'And the killings? At that restaurant? And in Cracow?'

Van Burgh shrugged. 'Dissidents, renegades, such things happen, even in repressed countries.'

Another silence, then Versano remembered something. He leaned forward, angry but triumphant. 'What about the money?'

'What money?'

The Archbishop shouted, 'The dollars! The gold! I sent them! Me! Is that a figment of my imagination?'

The Bacon Priest slowly stood up and stretched. His face was infinitely weary. Very softly he said, 'Mario, the Church spent no money that I know of . . . neither did you personally.' He looked at his watch. 'I have to go.' He gestured at the piece of paper in the Archbishop's hands. 'It is better, for once, that we all believe the Kremlin. Goodbye Mario.'

The Bacon Priest had reached the door and opened it before Versano spoke. He said coldly, 'Whatever you say I know what to believe.'

The Bacon Priest turned and looked at him for a moment, then said, 'As Cardinal Mennini would have said, "Belief is a state of mind." And remember, the Cardinal had a conscience . . . and wore a hair shirt. The knowledge that the "*Papa*'s envoy" never existed is your hair shirt – wear it well.'

He went out, closing the door gently behind him.

Epilogue

The Vumba mountains in the Eastern Highlands of Zimbabwe look out over Mozambique. Or they do when the mists which give the mountains their name dissipate.

In that part of Zimbabwe there are, apart from the indigenous tribes, quite a few Europeans from the Colonial days. These comprise mostly British who have stayed on; a small community of Greeks, and another of Portuguese who crossed the border after Mozambique's independence. There are a few Dutch and a few Germans, mostly farmers. The Poles constitute the smallest community, with barely half a dozen souls.

Early in 1984 their number was increased significantly with the arrival of two more Poles. They came within three weeks of each other. The woman turned up first. She was a nun and joined the convent high in the Vumba which had taken over an old, beautiful but unprofitable hotel. Most of the nuns were Irish, as was the Mother Superior. They looked after orphans and refugees from war-torn Mozambique. The new nun taught English.

The man arrived quietly, stayed at the Impala Arms Hotel for two weeks and then bought three hundred acres of land in the lush Burma Valley. It was rumoured that part of the purchase price had been paid in gold.

There was no house on the land but he pitched a tent and started building one, using the local stone and timber cut from his own trees. He planted coffee and bananas and Protea shrubs for eventual export to Europe.

At first he was looked on as a bit of a joke by his farming

367

neighbours. He was a complete amateur. But he learned fast and he listened. He worked on the house at a leisurely pace, sometimes hiring casual labour but mostly working by himself.

Every evening he would climb into his Land Rover and drive up the Vumba to the convent. He would wait, sitting on an old tree trunk, near the overgrown eighth green of the old golf course. The nun would join him there after evening prayers and they would talk for an hour or so, the nun in her starched white habit, the man in rough work clothes.

On March 9th, 1987, almost three years after he had arrived, the man finished the house. That afternoon a delivery van from a department store in Mutare arrived with furniture, including a large double bed. In the evening the man changed into his best suit and drove up to the convent. This time he parked in front of the main entrance. He climbed out of the Land Rover and waited. After ten minutes the woman came out. She was wearing blue jeans and a white T-shirt. She carried a suitcase.

She was accompanied by the Mother Superior, who kissed her cheek before she climbed into the Land Rover. It was not a goodbye. The woman would be back the next day and the following days to continue her work. But not as a nun. In her suitcase was a Papal dispensation. This time genuine. The date on it was almost three years old. Three years given as penance for a sin she could not explain except to the man she was now joining.

She did not regret the three years.

Neither did he.